GEORGES BORACH

2

consulter …fesseur Vogt, Zurich, Seefeldquai 41, Téléphone: Hottingen 3701. Ecrivez ou téléphonez lui au préalable.

Thrust Syphilis Down to Hell and other Rejoyceana

Studies in the Border-lands of Literature and Medicine.

By the same author

Brief Lives of Irish Doctors
Oliver St. John Gogarty : the Man of Many Talents
The Enigma of Tom Kettle
An Assembly of Irish Surgeons
Scholar and Sceptic
etc.

1. James Joyce by Jacques Emile Blanche.

Thrust Syphilis Down to Hell and other Rejoyceana

Studies in the Border-Lands of Literature and Medicine

J B Lyons

THE GLENDALE PRESS

First published in Ireland by
THE GLENDALE PRESS
18 Sharavogue
Glenageary Road Upper
Dun Laoghaire
Co. Dublin, Ireland

ISBN 0 907606 37 7

Cover by Q Design

Typeset by General Typesetting Ltd., Dublin
Make-up by Paul Bray

Printed in Great Britain by,
Richard Clay Ltd, Bungay, Suffolk

To Simon Lyons,
and the future

Blessed Michael, the ass angel, propel us in the hour of our contact; be our safeguard against the wickedness and snares of the Syph Fiend; May God rebuke him we humbly pray and do Thou, O Prince of the Heavenly Host, thrust Syphilis down to Hell...

James Joyce

The dialogue between medicine and literature is, essentially, a continuing interchange between the flesh and the word; between man's body and his spirit. Both medicine and literature probe, although from radically different perspectives, the same subject: the truths that are revealed — concealed — in man.

Enid Rhodes Peschel

Contents

List of Illustrations

Acknowledgements

The editors of the following periodicals and newspapers permitted the inclusion of essays first published in their pages; *James Joyce Quarterly, Irish Renaissance Annual, Irish Times, Irish Medical Times,* Federated Dublin Hospitals' *Annual Brochure, Dublin Historical Record, British Medical Journal.* Minor alterations have been made to minimise repetition. The title essay is published in *James Joyce: The Centennial Symposium* edited by Morris Beja, Phillip Herring, Maurice Harmon and David Norris; it is republished by agreement with the University of Illinois Press.

Quotation from Joyce's writings was permitted by the Society of Authors, representing the James Joyce Estate, and by the following publishers: Cape *(Stephen Hero);* Cape and Viking Press *(Dubliners* and *A Portrait of the Artist as a Young Man);* Bodley Head and Random House, Inc. *(Ulysses);* Viking Press *(Finnegans Wake);* Faber & Faber and Viking Press *(Letters* and *Critical Writings);* Viking Press *(Giacomo Joyce).*

Material from the following books is used with acknowledgement to their respective authors and publishers: Robert Baldrick, translator, *Pages from the Goncourt Journal,* Oxford University Press; Richard Brown, *James Joyce and Sexuality,* Cambridge University Press; Frank Budgen, *James Joyce and the Making of Ulysses* (Indiana University Press) and *Myselves When Young* (Oxford University Press); Constantine Curran *James Joyce Remembered* (Oxford University Press) and *Under the Receding Wave* (Gill and Macmillan); Richard Ellmann, *James Joyce* (Oxford University Press); John Garvin, *James Joyce's Disunited Kingdom* (Gill and Macmillan); Oliver St. John Gogarty, *Collected Poems* (Constable, Devin-Adair), *As I Was Walking Down Sackville Street* (Rich and Cowan); *Many Lines to Thee* (Dolmen Press); Denis Johnston, *Collected Plays* (Colin Smythe); Stanislaus Joyce, *My Brother's Keeper* (Faber); *The Complete Dublin Diary of Stanislaus Joyce,* ed. George Healey (Cornell University Press); R. Lhombreaud, *Arthur Symons* (Unicorn Press); F. Read, *Pound/Joyce* (New Directions); Arthur Symons, *Confessions: A Study in Pathology;* W.B. Yeats, *Collected Poems* and *Memoirs* (Macmillan). Quotations from articles by K. Beckson and J.M. Munro and by Bozena Delimata are permitted by the editor of *The James Joyce Quarterly.*

The staffs of Dublin's major libraries — NLI, RDS, RIA, TCD, UCD, RCPI and RCSI — are invariably tolerant of my frequent demands on their services. Occasional visits to the Wellcome Institute, London, to the New York Public Library and other transatlantic libraries have been enjoyable and fruitful. Consent to quote from manuscripts have been given by Oliver D. Gogarty, S.C., and by the librarians of University College, Dublin; the Berg Collection, New York Public Library; Houghton Library, Harvard; Morris Library, University of Delaware. Georges Borach's letter to Joyce is adapted as end pages by permission of Lockwood Memorial Library, SUNYAB, Buffalo, NY.

Details are given in the list of illustrations of portraits and illustrations supplied by the National Gallery of Ireland, the National Library of Ireland (Lawrence Collection), the National Portrait Gallery and the Wellcome Institute, London. Photographs from the author's camera were processed in RCSI's department of illustration by Philip Curtis and Barbara Guilfoyle.

It is a pleasure to acknowledge indebtedness to many individuals, and at the risk of causing offence by unintentional omission to record my gratitude to P. Ahern, Seamus Cahalane, Peter Costello, Michael Freyer, Thomas Freysz, K.C. Gay, Andres Giedion, Frances Gillespie, Oliver D. Gogarty, Bob Hogan, the Late Professor W. Löffler, Denis McCarthy, Brenda Maddox, Paddy Matthews, Paddy Meenan, Catherine Moureaux, Eoin O'Brien, Mary O'Doherty, Donal O'Looney, Fritz Senn, David Smyth, Jean C. Sournia.

Finally, I wish to express my thanks to my publisher, Tom Turley, to my secretary, Mrs Brid Kennedy, and to my dear wife, Muriel.

J.B. Lyons, M.D., F.R.C.P.I.

Department of the History of Medicine,
Royal College of Surgeons in Ireland,
St. Stephen's Green, Dublin.

Preface

It is not always possible to say when one fell under the spell of a particular author; in the instance of James Joyce, however, I recall with remarkable clarity reading the poems included in the *Golden Treasury of Irish Verse,* edited by Lennox Robinson, on a bright evening in June 1940. Europe was at war but I was eighteen, lighthearted and had just completed the pre-medical year at University College, Dublin. I had set out on my journey westward in a train which would pass through Mullingar and cross above 'the dark mutinous Shannon waves' at Athlone *en route* for my home in County Mayo.

Before long I had read *Dubliners* and *A Portrait of the Artist as a Young Man* and had glanced disbelievingly at the eccentric pages of *Finnegans Wake. Ulysses,* though never banned in Ireland, was not readily available and I did not become acquainted with it until I borrowed the novel from a public library in 1948, when resident at Mayday Hospital, Croydon. Meanwhile, when walking the wards of the Mater Hospital, I had passed 7 Eccles Street daily, unaware of its association with Mr Leopold Bloom.

My obsessive interest in James Joyce developed later and possibly fortuitously. I have lived in Dalkey (where Joyce taught) for almost thirty years and now as I write I can see from my front window 'the mailboat, vague on the bright skyline, and a sail tacking by the Muglins'. Each morning, driving to the hospital in Dun Laoghaire (the Kingstown of Joyce's day), I pass the Martello Tower and, until 1983, I also practised at Mercer's Hospital — '*The Messiah* was first given for that. Yes Handel...'

Unwittingly, I was drawn into an area (arena?) in which the accustomed objectives of clinical science — the reduction of complex matters to a comprehensible elemental simplicity — are reversed, apparently simple sentences being made to yield up astonishing dividends of meaning. It behoves an interloper from the more sombre of the two cultures to walk warily but, if cautioned that a shoemaker should stick to his last and a neurologist stick to his tendon-hammer, I can plead that medical practice, with its probing case-histories and constant evaluation of symptoms, is an exercise in applied biography. My Joyce studies, therefore, are to be seen as a logical extension of my clinical work and my area of interest one where medicine marches with literature. That they do so march is beyond dispute. Both deal with mankind's despairs and transports and the affinities between literature and medicine explain why many doctors turned to literature and why many authors are physicians manqués. Of the latter, there is no more distinguished example than James Joyce.

My suspicion that some whose métier is the liberal arts would benefit from the disciplines of the laboratory is ventilated in 'Animadversions on paralysis as a symbol'. My belief that the diagnosis of disease should be scrutinized no less impartially in the dead than in the living is expounded in the essay from which the book takes its title. Nor can this courtesy be denied to Father Flynn at a whim or to support a hypothesis. The title, incidentally, derives from Joyce's parody of a prayer formerly recited in Irish churches after the Latin Mass.[1] This I have used as an epigraph; it depicts Satan, unsubtly, as a monster who wanders 'through the world for the ruin of tools'.

To attempt to adjudicate in a private quarrel is often to invite a snub; when the instigator of the row is a generally-acclaimed genius, it may be even a greater folly to intervene but one can at least point out that, while Joyce spurned Oliver St. John Gogarty's outstretched hand, W.B. Yeats grasped it warmly. Some details are added concerning Yeats's illness in the winter of 1929-1930.

Those ill-fated men, Arthur Symons and Tom Kettle, the major reviewers of *Chamber Music,* helped Joyce each in his own way and deserve to be thanked. The biennial International James Joyce Symposium is an important date in the diaries of Joyce scholars. My recollections of meetings in Zurich and Paris,

1. Carens, James F. Joyce and Gogarty. *New Light on Joyce from the Dublin Symposium,* ed. Fritz Senn. Bloomington: Indiana University Press, 1972.

unimportant trivia, are included in the hope that they may evoke pleasant recollections for the friends I met on those vanished occasions.

The doctors in *Ulysses* and its rich content of anatomy were considered in my earlier book, *James Joyce and Medicine,* but the new essays deploy new material and compare the Gilbert-Gorman and Linati schema. 'Clinical Verse', a non-Joycean essay, is a tilly, added for good measure.

The interfaces between medicine and literature are closest in biography. 'Of the literary genres', Stanley Weintraub[2] has written, 'biography has the most to learn from medicine.' The final essay in this collection, 'The Portrait of a Patient', is a limited exercise in clinical pathography.

While it is generally agreed that even Homer nods, many of Joyce's admirers will not have it that he could do so. They are puzzled, too, by the alleged 'coldness' of the Irish towards him, unable to recognise a defensive strategem on the part of those who live in the shadow of their demi-god. A Dublin writer, an admirer of Ezra Pound, sick of being needled on this point, growled at his transatlantic tormentor, 'Well! at least we didn't put him in a cage'.

The Irish idiom is susceptible of misunderstanding. To call Joyce 'illiterate', as Myles na gCopaleen did, was a piece of friendly badinage intended to confuse the serious-minded. For the Irish, Joyce is one of the family; we can laugh with him or even laugh at him — yet love him like a brother. But no Irish person who is fully acquainted with James Joyce's life story can fail to echo Ezra Pound's toast: 'May his spirit meet with Rabelais' ghost at Chinon and may the glasses never be empty'.

2. Weintraub, Stanley. Medicine and the Biographer's Art, in *Medicine and Literature,* ed. Enid Rhodes Peschel. New York: Neale Watson Academic Publications, 1980.

References

Figures in parentheses (except in chapter 3) indicate page numbers in the Penguin edition of *Ulysses* or page and line of *Finnegans Wake* (FW), London: Faber & Faber, 1964.

LETTERS 1, 2, 3 – *Letters of James Joyce,* volume 1 (ed. Stuart Gilbert, 1957) II and III (ed. Richard Ellmann, 1966) London: Faber & Faber.

SL – *Selected Letters of James Joyce,* ed. Richard Ellmann. New York: Viking Press, 1975.

CRITICAL WRITINGS – *The Critical Writings of James Joyce,* ed. Ellsworth Mason and Richard Ellmann. London: Faber, 1959.

SH – *Stephen Hero.* New York: New Directions Paperback, 1963.

GJ – *Giacomo Joyce.* New York: Viking Press, 1968.

PORTRAIT: – *A Portrait of the Artist as a Young Man.* London: Egoist, 1916.

Budgen – *James Joyce and the Making of Ulysses* by F. Budgen. Bloomington: Indiana University Press, 1960.

BECKSON and MUNRO – Letters from Arthur Symons to James Joyce: 1904-1932. Beckson, K. and Munro, J.M. *James Joyce Quarterly,* 4, 91-101, 1967.

CONFESSIONS – *Confessions: A Study in Pathology* by Arthur Symons. New York: The Fountain Press, 1930.

DIARY – *The Complete Dublin Diary of Stanislaus Joyce,* ed. George H. Healey. Ithaca and London: Cornell University Press, 1971.

ELLMANN – *James Joyce* by Richard Ellmann. New York: OUP, 1959.

FRAC – *Syphilis: or a Poetical History of the French Disease Written in Latin by Fracastorius. And now Attempted in English by N. Tate* in J. Dryden's *Miscellany Poems,* Fifth Part. London: Tonson, 1727, 327-373.

GONCOURT – *Pages from the Goncourt Journal,* ed. Robert Baldrick. London: OUP, 1962, 155.

LHOMBREAUD – *Arthur Symons, A Critical Biography* by R. Lhombreaud. London: The Unicorn Press, 1963.

J J Q – *James Joyce Quarterly.*

KETTLE – *The Enigma of Tom Kettle* by J.B. Lyons. Dublin: Glendale Press, 1983.

YEATS – Yeats, W.B. *Memoirs,* ed. Denis Donoghue. London: Macmillan, 1972.

2. *Hieronymus Fracastorius (1493-1553).*

1. Thrust Syphilis Down to Hell*

1

The editor of a widely-distributed study of Joyce in exile[1] recalls Edna O'Brien's question, 'Was he neurotic?', adding that recently the chief question seems to be, 'Was he syphilitic?'. 'Such questions', Mr. Potts writes, 'have their interest but are limiting and in any event have been explored adequately.' If I venture to revive matters which might have been more tactfully avoided on a celebratory occasion it is because I believe that one of these questions still lacks an authoritative answer.

Was he neurotic? The short answer 'yes' is unlikely to be contested and I shall not discuss it further other than to remark how commonly psychoneurosis is creativity's burdensome, albeit fruitful, companion. *Was he syphilitic?* The question, I suspect, is ill-mannered and because those who pose it seem determined to prove that Joyce suffered either from congenital or acquired syphilis, or preferably both, I am glad to say he had neither.

My diffidence in discussing clinical matters before a literary audience is diminished by the fact that syphilis, the unwelcome gift of the last years of the quattrocento, has notable literary associations. The term itself derives from a 16th century poem in Latin hexameters, *Syphilis Sive Morbus Gallicus* by Hieronymus Fracastorius.[2] This work in the manner of Virgil's *Georgics* was

*Presented to the James Joyce Centenary Symposium in Dublin, June 1982.

1. Potts, W. *Portraits of the Artist in Exile.* Dublin: Wolfhound Press, 1979, xiv.
2. Fracastoro, Girolamo. *Syphilis sive Morbus Gallicus.* Verona: S. Nicolini da Sabbio, 1530.

HIERONYMI FRACASTORII
SYPHILIS
SIVE MORBVS GALLICVS

Veronæ, M D X X X, menſe Auguſto.

Non ſine Priuilegio, mulctáq; pecuniaria, & excõmunicationis pœna: pro ut in Priuilegijs continetur.

3. *Title page of Syphilis Sive Morbus Gallicus, Verona, 1530.*

published in Verona in 1530 and is not to be dismissed as a piece of doggerel by a Renaissance physician toying with letters, for it was admired by Scaliger. Fracastorius was a poet, doctor, mathematician and astronomer; his verses were praised by John Addington Symonds and more recently an American critic described his dialogue on poetry *(Naugerius, Sive de Poetica Dialogus)* as a work of consumate art. Nahum Tate, the Dublin-born poet laureate, translated it in 1686 and the following are its opening lines:

Through what Adventures this unknown Disease
So lately did astonish'd *Europe* seize,
Through *Asian Coasts* and *Libyan* Cities ran,
And from what Seeds the Malady began,
Our Song shall tell: To *Naples* first it came
From *France,* and justly took from *France* its Name
Companion of the War —
The Methods next of Cure we shall express,
The wond'rous wit of Mortals in Distress...[3]

In the third book of *Syphilis Sive Morbus Gallicus* the dire punishment of a young shepherd, Syphilus, who has raised an altar to false gods, is described:

A Shepherd once (distrust not ancient Fame)
Possest these Downs, and *Syphilus* his Name.
A thousand Heifers in these Vales he fed.
A thousand Ewes to those fair Rivers led:
For King Alcithoüs he rais'd this Stock,
And shaded in the Covert of the Rock...[4]

Eventually the prejudicial appellation 'French disease' (it was also called 'the Spanish scabies', 'the Neapolitan disease', and by the Turks 'the Christian disease') was replaced by the inoffensive name of Fracastoro's shepherd.

Niccolo Campani, a Sienese poet and playwright who contracted the venereal lues in Rome, composed a *Lamento* first printed in 1511. Shakespeare has catalogued some of its nastiest manifestations in *Timon of Athens:* 'Consumption sow in the

3. Frac, 337.
4. Frac, 369.

hollow bones of man... Crack the lawyer's voice... Down with the nose, down with it flat... Make curl'd pate ruffians bald...' Ibsen's *Ghosts* gives a misleading portrayal of congenital syphilis which may have influenced Joyce.

The roll-call of the victims of syphilis is answered by distinguished voices including those of King Henry VIII of England and King Francis I of France. It destroyed Baudelaire, Guy de Maupassant, and Lord Randolph Churchill with a fury that is relevant, for it commonly claims a heavy debt. The lighter price demanded from Heine and Alphonse Daudet was paid in daily instalments, over many years, the paralysed German poet condemned to 'a mattress grave' in a Paris attic, the gentle author of *Lettres de Mon Moulin* tortured by the lightning pains of tabes dorsalis, an inconceivable and unrelenting agony. Benvenuto Cellini, Robert Schuman, Paul Gaugin, Nietzsche, Hugo Wolf and many other distinguished artists also were infected.

Syphilis is a major theme of the novel, *Doctor Faustus,* by Joyce's contemporary, Thomas Mann. Karen Blixen, who wrote *Out of Africa,* exemplified the Faust legend in her own life. 'I promised the Devil my soul', she told a friend, not altogether in jest, 'and in return he promised me that everything I was going to experience hereafter would be turned into stories'. She was infected with syphilis by her husband, Baron Bror Blixen, the model for the white hunter in Hemingway's 'The Short, Happy Life of Francis Macomber' and subsequently experienced the agonising pains and visceral crises of tabes dorsalis.[5]

It has been suggested that Syphilus is a variant of 'Sipylus', one of the sons of Niobe killed by Apollo and mentioned in Ovid's Metamorphoses. Joyce cannot have known Fracastoro's poem for in a letter to Frank Budgen he derives syphilis from a Greek word which means swinelove[6], erroneous information he may have obtained from Dr Arthur Cooper's article on syphilis in *A Dictionary of Medicine* edited by Sir Richard Quain, a native of County Cork. The first (1882) and third (1902) editions of this work are in the National Library.

5. Thurman, Judith. *Isak Dinesen: the Life of Karen Blixen.* London: Weidenfeld and Nicolson, 1982.
6. *Letters* 1, 147.

2

Do Joyce's traducers believe his hubris deserved chastisement? Do they equate his adolescent desecration of the family's lares and penates with the blasphemy of Fracastor's shepherd, that they so casually attach a demeaning diagnostic label? Dr F.R. Walsh's recollection in the *Irish Medical Times*[7] of how John Stanislaus Joyce told a group of Dublin medical students in 1920 that he had acquired a syphilitic chancre in Cork in 1867, his sole treatment a local application of carbolic acid, prompted Hall and Waisbren,[8] the latter a Milwaukee internist, to say 'that Joyce's father was a profligate who may well have passed on syphilis to his son'.

This, however, is the flimsiest of evidence — the boastful comments of an elderly man whose magnificent constitution and survival to the age of eighty two hardly suggest that he had harboured a major infection. Those who practised medicine when syphilis was common did tests on even the most unlikely patients, knowing that a denial of exposure to risk meant nothing. But if a person actually boasted that he'd been poxed, he, too, was probably to be disbelieved.

When they occur the classic stigmata of congenital syphilis — deafness, interstitial keratitis, and Hutchinson's teeth — are ineradicable but there is no question of James Joyce having had any of them nor was any of his siblings thus affected. Incidentally, the pro-congenital syphilis lobby conveniently exclude Poppie and Stannie and the other children from their accusations.

Those who argue that Joyce acquired syphilis stand on firmer ground. It may well be that he was lucky to escape it, for Oliver St. John Gogarty's letters to Joyce, and to Dr Michael Walsh, indicate that Joyce was treated for a venereal infection in 1904.[9] This appears to have responded to the meagre therapeutic resources then available. Within six months he had left Dublin

7. Walsh, F.R. *Irish Medical Times.* 9 May 1975.
8. Hall, V. and Waisbren, B.A. 'Syphilis as a Major Theme in James Joyce's *Ulysses*'. *Archives of Internal Medicine,* 1980, 140, 963.
9. Lyons, J.B. *James Joyce and Medicine.* Dublin: Dolmen Press, 1973, 215.

with Nora Barnacle in a partnership the least gallant lover would hardly have contracted had he harboured a persisting infection. There has never, to my knowledge, been the slightest hint to suggest that he transmitted an infection to his consort though we have abundant evidence of their erotic fervour.

As a youth, Joyce was healthy and active. His only physical blemish was the myopia for which Dr A.H. Benson prescribed spectacles, the famous glasses broken on the cinder track in Clongowes. Dental decay became bothersome in 1905 — 'My mouth is full of decayed teeth, my soul of decayed ambitions' — and the abdominal symptoms which caused Nora, in Pola, to pray, 'Oh my God, take away Jim's pain', may have been an early manifestation of the duodenal ulcer which killed him in 1941.

His first serious illness (other than the gonorrhoea referred to above) was that for which he was treated in Trieste's Ospitalo Civico in 1907 from mid-July until September. Alarming rumours reached Dublin. 'I heard you were stricken with a grievous distemper', Gogarty wrote, 'and that you were paralysed. You can understand that the sight of your handwriting rejoiced me, as it disproved the statement that your right arm was paralysed.'[10] Joyce's uncle assured Gogarty that the disease was 'altogether ethical' and in his next letter the latter refers to it as rheumatic fever. That explanation is almost certainly incorrect. The combination of acute rheumatic symptoms with iritis suggests to-day either sarcoidosis or Reiter's syndrome, neither of which could have been diagnosed in 1907. Hans Reiter, a German army doctor, described the details of the disease which bears his name in 1916 in the case of a German lieutenant serving on the Balkan front. Acute arthritis as a manifestation of sarcoidosis has been recognised much more recently.

There was a relapse of the iritis in 1908 and in a letter to his sister he wrote: 'I feel a little better of the rheumatism and am now more like a capital S than a capital Z.'[11]

Writing to his wife from Dublin on 1 November 1909, and presumably referring to a genital discharge, Joyce thanks her for enquiring about his nasty disorder. He assured her it was no worse at any rate.* Her silence had worried him in case she was

10. Lyons, J.B. *Ibid.*, 220. 11. *Letters* 2, 226.

*Quotation of Joyce's actual words was forbidden by the Trustees of the James Joyce Estate.

infected. With reiterated apologies and a *mea culpa* he prayed that Nora was all right.[12] Ellmann sees this as 'a minor complaint probably contracted from a prostitute'[13] but one cannot say whether it was a new infection or a relapse of the 'dose' picked up in Nighttown in 1904. Circumstances favour the latter for with the exception of unconsummated affairs with a young pupil in Trieste, with Marthe Fleischman in Zurich and Dr Gertrude Kaempffer in Locarno he does not appear to have been a philanderer.

Joyce's clinical history contains further low-key references to pains in limbs and back but the continuing problem was what he described to Forrest Reid in May 1917 as 'rheumatic iritis complicated with synechia and glaucoma...'[14] Such indeed was his plight that Ezra Pound wrote:

> My dear Job: you will establish an immortal record.
> At what period the shift of terminal sound in your family
> name occurred I am unable to state, but the -yce at the end
> is an obvious error. The arumaic — b is obviously the
> correct spelling.[15]

The features of this chronic eye disorder are unlike syphilitic iritis which occurs in the secondary stage of the disease when other diagnostic signs abound and can be confirmed or excluded by a blood test, the Wasserman Reaction, which became available in 1906 and would have been a routine procedure by the time he had his first eye operation.

Actually Joyce himself, in a letter to Miss Weaver in 1930 provides an assurance that he did not have syphilis:

> Dr. Fontaine is also rather distant with me. I have the highest opinion of her and allowed her to bring me after Borsch's death [1929] to be seen by a young French ophthalmologist, Dr. Hartmann, who said the only possible solution of the case was that my eye trouble proceeded from congenital syphilis which being curable, he said the proper thing for me was to undergo a cure of I have forgotten what... I told this to Dr. Collinson

12. *Letters* 2, 259.
13. *Letters,* 2, footnote 259.
14. *Letters* 2, 395.
15. Read, F. *Pound/Joyce.* New York: New Directions, 1967, 121.

4. James Joyce in 1935 by Sean O'Sullivan.

> and he dissuaded me strongly from undergoing it. He said at the very beginning Dr. Borsch had excluded it categorically on account of the nature of the attacks, the way in which they were cured and the general reactions of the eye.[16]

Lucia Joyce's doctors also excluded syphilis and the final proof that the celebrated novelist did not have a treponemal infection was Dr Zollinger's post-mortem examination[17] which showed no suggestion of syphilis and, indeed, mentions specifically that no plasma calls were seen. Plasma calls are the hall mark of syphilis and their absence is highly significant (p 219).

3

Sexually transmitted diseases inspire fear and remorse in those who contract them, but are a source of rich amusement to others, who ask for nothing better than to hear that an acquaintance has come a cropper on such a banana skin. This comic element has been overlooked by some of *Ulysses's* unsmiling readers and an earlier idiom in which the use of 'poxy' as a general term of derogation or the employment of GPI (general paralysis of the insane) as a synonym for any form of eccentricity has been interpreted literally. Thus Hall and Waisbren are led grievously astray by Buck Mulligan's light-hearted comment 'that fellow I was with in the Ship last night says you have g.p.i....'[18] and because Stephen does not bother to reply they conclude that 'he accepts what Buck says as a fact', whereas Mulligan merely infers that Dedalus is an oddity.

John Garvin supplies another instance of this black humour. An obituary notice credited John S. Joyce as 'late LGB' (Local General Board) but Garvin's friend, Jim Tully, said, 'they should have put him down as "late GPI"'. And Joyce himself could refer to the disease in a spirit of levity. 'Syphilis is for the French', he wrote to Harriet Shaw Weaver, 'what God Save the King is for

16. Ellmann, R. *Selected Letters of James Joyce.* New York: Viking Press, 1975, 348.
17. Lyons, J.B. *James Joyce and Medicine.* Dublin: Dolmen Press, 1973, 221.
18. Garvin, J. *James Joyce's Disunited Kingdom.* Dublin: Gill and Macmillan, 1976, 38.

the English, when it is mentioned tout le monde se decouvre'.[19]

Hall and Waisbren see syphilis as a major theme in *Ulysses* but Shen and Soldo[20] believe they have overstated their case and accuse them of hunting wildly for symbols. That they have 'gone on an unwarranted symbol hunt' is immediately apparent. They regard, for instance, every use of the letter *S* 'as a code symbol' for syphilis and Dr Waisbren seems to have absolved himself of all restraint in attributing every clinical abberation in the book to syphilis.

If one sets out the data in the form of a multiple-choice examination paper —

Stephen fell because of:	a. drink b. multiple sclerosis c. syphilis
Pisser Duffy had:	a. syphilis b. enlarged prostate c. bladder stone
Shakespeare's paralysis results from:	a. arteriosclerosis b. syphilis c. Bell's palsy
Myles Crawford walks jerkily because of:	a. Parkinson's disease b. alcoholism c. syphilis.

— Dr Waisbren scores no marks. I can accept only six items from the seventy-five tabulated by Hall and Waisbren as evidence of syphilis although I do agree that venereal diseases are well represented in *Ulysses* and fifty or so quite convincing references can be readily mustered. I do not, however, see syphilis as a theme but as a reflection of environmental reality.

19. Ellmann, R. *Selected Letters of James Joyce.* New York: Viking Press, 1975, 348.
20. Shen, W.W. and Soldo, J.J. 'Symbol Hunting in James Joyce's "Syphilizations" '. *Archives of Internal Medicine,* 1981, 141, 691-692.

The ambience of *Dubliners,* as I have argued elsewhere, is alcoholism[21] but even a cursory reading of *Ulysses* reveals sufficient Hogarthian depictions of sexual mishap to terrify all but the hardiest of Don Juans. The 'snares of the pox fiend' (423) generally result in 'a hard chancre' (459); its treatment may end in 'a dark mercurialised face' (441). Fortunately Stephen has 'sheltered from the sin of Paris' (31) in the Bibliothèque Sainte Geneviève; back in Dublin he recalls a shawled prostitute soliciting in a dark archway — 'A she fiend's whiteness under her rancid rags' (52). Bloom cautions him on the dangers of nighttown, 'a regular death-trap for young fellows of his age...'. (534)

Syphilis was an occupational risk for servicemen. Bloom remembers how Arthur Griffith's *United Irishman* referred to 'an army rotten with venereal disease' (74); Molly suspects that 'the half of those sailors are rotten again with disease' (699). But its stigma, as the Citizen indicates is not confined to any sect or class: 'There's a bloody sight more pox than pax about that boyo, Edward Guelph-Wettin!' (329).

'God knows what poxy bowsy left them off' (12) is Buck Mulligan's disparaging comment about Stephen's second-hand trousers. Bloom thinks of the 'quack doctor for the clap', Henry Franks, whose advertisements are read by 'some chap with a dose burning in him' (152).

The whores include Bird-in-the-Hand, 'which was within all foul plaques' (393), and the surprisingly well-spoken Biddy the Clap (521). Bloom, in an altercation with Bella, speaks of a 'kip keeper! Pox and gleet vendor!' (502). It is Kitty Ricketts who most clearly describes the appalling consequences of a syphilitic infection (482):

> And Mary Shortall that was in the lock with the pox she got from Jimmy Pidgeon in the blue caps had a child off him that couldn't swallow and was smothered with the convulsions in the mattress and we all subscribed for the funeral.

Joyce's account of the horrors of syphilis carries no moral

21. Lyons, J.B. 'Diseases in *Dubliners:* Tokens of Disaffection', in *Irish Renaissance Annual II,* ed. Zack Bowen. Newark: University of Delaware Press, 1981, 185-194.

implications but could serve well as a warning and deterrent. The reference to 'civilisation' and 'syphilisation' echoes Krafft-Ebing's contention that G.P.I. was commoner in persons of some intellectual attainment than in the unlettered but his own brief enrolment as a medical student did not bring him even to the threshold of clinical instruction, contrary to what Hall and Waisbren imply.

Joyce may have had the 'dose' he acquired in the Kips in mind when Gogarty's articles in *Sinn Féin* made him wish that somebody would publish an account of Ireland's venereal problems. 'It must be rather worse in England, I think. I know very little of the subject but it seems to me to be a disease like any other disease, caused by anti-hygienic conditions. I don't see where the judgement of God comes into it...'[22] He thought any reference to 'excess' inappropriate. Was it not really a matter of 'venereal ill-luck'?

'I don't know much about the "saince" of the subject,' Joyce told Stannie, 'but I presume there are very few mortals in Europe who are not in danger of waking some morning and finding themselves syphilitic.'[23]

Clive Hart's *Concordance to Finnegans Wake* has no entry for 'syphilis' but a synonym, 'lues', is encountered ('or lues the day', 347. 15); also, poxed, ('Cursed that he suppoxed he did' 090. 25), poxy ('Gotopoxy' 386. 31), 'an infamous private ailment (vulgovariovenereal)' (089. 18) and 'he suffered from a vile disease' (033. 18).

There is no direct reference to syphilis in either *A Portrait of the Artist as a Young Man* or *Dubliners* but it is likely that a number of laundresses in 'Clay' had the disease. Others such as Corley, Jack Mooney, Bob Doran and Ignatius Gallagher could fall under suspicion and the amorous couples in the Phoenix Park, whose 'venal and furtive loves' were so disturbing to Mr Duffy ('A Painful Case'), faced the prevailing risk.

Corley ('Two Gallants'), a calculating womanizer, knows that a former girl friend is 'on the turf now', in modern parlance 'on the game'. Jack Mooney 'had the reputation of being a hard case'

22. *Letters* 2, 170.
23. *Letters* 2, 192.

and one of his mother's lodgers ('The Boarding House'), Bob Doran, 'had sown his wild oats'; Ignatius Gallagher ('A Little Cloud') 'summarized the vices of many capitals...' to the astonishment of Little Chandler. The suggestion that Father Flynn's illness ('The Sisters') was general paralysis of the insane is, to my mind, unacceptable and my objections to this attempt to fit the square pegs of a literary theory into clinical medicine's inconveniently round holes are presented in later chapters.

In his essay, 'Ibsen's New Drama', written before he was eighteen, Joyce refers to the harrowing simplicity of *Ghosts*. It seems likely that his knowledge of syphilis is partly based on Oswald Alving's illness, actually unrealistic if intended as a portrayal of congenital syphilis which is a truely baneful inheritance.

When affected infants survive they may, as indicated above, display specific physical depredations — fissured lips, snuffles and saddle nose — and there is a general stunting of growth and failure to thrive. 'A considerable number', according to a leading British neurologist, 'are more or less defective from birth, in the sense that their faculties do not develop normally; but others are children of a promise that is never fulfilled; after a hopeful beginning at school, gradually a cloud creeps over the adolescent mind, obscuring its salient features and finally quenching its fertility'.[24]

Oswald Alving's robust physique and artistic sensitivity would have been unusual endowments and congenital G.P.I., a rare condition, generally occurred between the age of nine and sixteen rather than at the later age that suited the dramatist. This clinical picture of 'juvenile paresis' had not been clearly delineated when Ibsen wrote *Ghosts* in Sorrento in 1881 and his account of Oswald Alving's illness closely follows the features of acquired G.P.I. He may, indeed, have wished to convey that the youngster was infected by a pipe contaminated by his father's saliva.

'Mother, my mind is broken down', Oswald explains during his last evening of sanity, 'ruined — I shall never be able to work again! Never! — never! A living death! Mother, can you imagine anything so horrible?'

24. Wilson, S.A.K. *Neurology*, Vol. 1. London: Butterworth, 1954.

Joyce's 'Epilogue to Ibsen's *Ghosts*' written in 1934, 'Explain, fate if you care and can/ Why one is sound and one is rotten', confirms how imperfect his clinical knowledge was even then.[25] The conundrum is solved when one realises that the lapse of eight years between the conception of the diseased Oswald and the seduction of the servant had rendered the seducer uninfective. Regina's mother, Johanna Engstrang, and her infant, remained healthy.

His inadequate knowledge may have fostered temporarily in Joyce a degree of 'syphilophobia'. This clinical entity, familiar to those who practised medicine before, say, 1950, evoked an obsessional dread of syphilis in a person exposed, however briefly, to the risk of contact and thereafter remaining unable to accept reassurance of freedom from infection. Did Joyce's failure to see the details of *Ghosts* as unlikely fictions cause him to identify with Oswald Alving? Was he misled by Ibsen's portrayal of the promising and apparently healthy artist suddenly stricken by the sins of his father?

> He talks much [Stannie wrote in 1904] of the syphilitic contagion in Europe, is at present writing a series of studies in it in Dublin, tracing practically everything to it. The drift of his talk seems to be that the contagion is congenital and incurable and responsible for all manias, and being so, that it is useless to try to avoid it. Heaven seems to invite you to delight in the manias and to humour each to the top of its bent. In this I do not follow him except to accept his theory of the contagion, which he adduces on medical authority. Even this I do slowly, for I have the idea that the influence of heredity is somewhat overstated. Yet I am rapidly becoming a valetudinarian on the point. I see symptoms in every turn I take.[26]

Little Stephen Dedalus was puzzled by the metaphors in the litany of the Blessed Virgin; his creator, given to what Stanislaus Joyce called 'pseudo-medical phraseology', saw no incongruity in the misappropriation of technical terms to express disparagement. He called Hellenism 'European appendicitis' and on 7 January 1904, in 'A Portrait of the Artist' (the earliest

25. *Critical Writings*, 272.
26. *Diary*, 51.

version of *A Portrait of the Artist as a Young Man)*[27], referred to 'the general paralysis of an insane society', lumping together the innocent and the venal, the ascetic and the concupiscent.

His indulgence in jargon is not unprecedented. A supporter of Mrs. Josephine Butler, founder of the International Abolitionist Federation — its concerns were brothels and white slavery — believed syphilis to be 'the punishment inflicted by nature on vicious men' and stated in 1902 that its eradication would result in the ruin of society and morality through 'a moral syphilization even more than that of the body.'

This misapplication of medical nomenclature is less maladroit than it might at first appear when one understands that in Joyce's youth the cause of syphilis was still arguable. The horror-stricken Neapolitans and the besiegers, the army of Charles VIII of France, accepted that the epidemic of 1495 resulted from a conjunction of Jupiter and Mars in the previous year and Fracastoro, swayed by astrology, accepted that men were 'Slaves to the very Rabble of the Sky'. The principal means of spread cannot have been long in doubt and Fracastoro advised sufferers to avoid noxious winds, to remain active.

Abstain however from the Act of Love,
For nothing can so much destructive prove:
Bright Venus hates polluted Mysteries,
And ev'ry Nymph from foul Embraces flies,
Dire Practice! Poison with Delight to bring,
And with the Lover's Dart, the Serpent's sting.[28]

Paracelsus[29] maintained that the pox took its origin from 'the impure commerce in 1478 of a French leper with a whore who had venereal buboes.' She then infected all who had anything to do with her. 'Thus the pox, proceeding from leprosy and buboes like the mule from the horse and the she-ass, spread throughout the world'. Others blamed cannibalism during the siege of Naples, or wine poisoned with the blood of lepers.

27. Scholes, R. and Kain, R.M. *The Workshop of Daedalus.* Evanston: Northwestern, 1965, 68.
28. *Frac,* 354.
29. Paracelsus. *Chirurgia Magna.* 1536.

Lines prefatory to Nahum Tate's translation are unexpectedly censorious of the female sex:

Whence should that foul infectious Torment flow,
But from the baneful Source of all our Woe?
That wheedling, charming Sex, that draws us in
To ev'ry Punishment, and ev'ry Sin.[30]

Accidental transmission is an occasional occurrence in every century and guilty burgesses have sought refuge hopefully in such a contingency. Thus, Joyce in his 'Epilogue':

Olaf may plod his stony path
And live as chastely as Susanna
Yet pick up in some Turkish bath
His *quantum est* of *Pox Romana.*[31]

The bark of the guaicum tree was held to be curative. Ulrich von Hutten, a humanist whom Helen Waddell mentions in her *Wandering Scholars,* wrote a *Short Account of the Guaic Drug and the French Disease.* Mercury was the other remedy and Fracastoro insists that it be applied liberally, avoiding the head and breast: 'Nor let the foulness of the Course displease, / Obscene indeed, but less than the Disease.' He gives details of how mercurial inunctions are prepared:

And for a Vehicle use lard of Swine;
Larch-gum and Turpentine were added next,
That wrought more safe, and less the Patient vext;
Horse-grease and Bears with them they did compound,
Bdellium and Gum of Cedar useful found;
Then Myrrh and Frankincense were us'd by some,
With living Sulphur and *Arabian* Gum;
But if black Hellebore be added too,
With Rain-bow Flowers, your Method I allow;
Benzoin and Galbanum I next require,
Lint-oil, and Sulphur's e're it feels the Fire.[32]

The next significant therapeutic advance was potassium iodide

30. *Frac,* 336.
31. *Critical Writings,* 272.
32. *Frac,* 360.

introduced by a Dublin doctor, William Wallace of Jervis Street Hospital, in 1835.

Syphilis has been spoken of as 'a fever diluted by time' and Phillipe Ricord of Paris divided it into three stages, primary, secondary and tertiary. A Dublin surgeon, Abraham Colles, formulated a preposition, now known as Colles's law, that though a diseased infant may infect a wet-nurse it never infects its mother. Dr Wallace who had made a similar and earlier observation saw that this indicated that the mother was already infected. 'You may say she was sound... but you have, in my opinion, a proof in her having given birth to an unsound child that she was unsound...' His point is relevant to my argument. Those who favour the idea that James Joyce had congenital syphilis must realise that their contention carries the implication that his mother was infected. There is, however, no evidence to support this unlikely suggestion but Stanislaus Joyce's diary entry may indicate that his brother was misled by a theory current at the turn of the century, and cited by Osler in the fourth edition of his *Principles and Practice of Medicine* (1901), that the disease could be inherited from the father ('sperm inheritance'), the mother being healthy. 'It is, unfortunately,' wrote Osler expressing a now discredited theory, 'an every-day experience to see congenital syphilis in which the infection is clearly paternal.'[33]

The precise cause of syphilis was not established until 1905 when Fritz Schaudinn and Erich Hoffman identified the *Treponema pallidum.* Meanwhile certain disorders, including G.P.I., were considered to be 'not exclusively and necessarily caused by syphilis', an interpretation which increases the scope and lessens the offensiveness of Joyce's metaphor.

As Fracastoro was aware, the disease affects humans exclusively —

The proud Destroyer seeks no common Game,
He scorns the well-finn'd Sporters of the Flood,
He scorns the well-plum'd Singers of the Wood;
Disdains the wanton Browzers of the Rock,
Disdains the lowing Herd and bleating Flock;

33. Osler, W. *The Principles and Practice of Medicine.* London: Appleton, 1901.

With Wolf or Bear despises to engage,
Nor can the generous Horse provoke his Rage:
The Lords of Nature only he annoys,
And Human Frame, Heav'n's Images, destroys[34]

— and Metchnikoff's transmission of syphilis to an experimental animal ('And to such delights has Metchnikoff inoculated anthropoid apes' 482) was duly noted by Joyce in Circe. The organ of this episode is the locomotor apparatus and, as Joyce credibly told Frank Budgen, it has the rhythm of locomotor ataxia, a form of neurosyphilis.[35]

4

I do not find it easy to accept John Garvin's assertion[36] that the 'knowledge' that their father had syphilis in his youth 'was the kinetic factor that drove two of his sons into exile'. Surely Joyce's flight to Pola and Trieste is adequately explained as a lover's retreat from the general squalor of the family home in North Dublin and an evasion of the financial responsibility which an eldest son might have been expected to shoulder. More difficult still to credit, unless as a macabre joke, James Joyce's alleged confidence[37] in 1931 to Tom Kiernan, a member of the Irish diplomatic corps, that 'his father was bedridden in Dublin, near death in the last stages of G.P.I.'. This is impossible to reconcile with his more characteristic statement to Miss Weaver after his father's death: 'I knew he was old, but I thought he would live longer.'[38]

Two years later the 'Epilogue to Ibsen's "Ghosts" included an absolution applicable, I like to think, to John Stanislaus Joyce:

34. *Frac,* 346.
35. Budgen, F. *James Joyce and the Making of 'Ulysses'.* Bloomington: University of Indiana Press, 1960, 228.
36. Garvin, J. *James Joyce's Disunited Kingdom.* Dublin: Gill and Macmillan, 1976, 42.
37. Garvin, J. *Ibid.,* 42.
38. *Letters* 1, 312.

Blame all and none and take to task
The harlot's lure, the swain's desire.
Heal by all means but hardly ask
Did this man sin or did his sire.[39]

By then, as we have seen, Joyce had his doctor's assurance that his eye disorder was not syphilitic and later he learned that he had conveyed no luetic taint to Lucia.

Diagnosis is ordinarily a private matter between doctor and patient and when it becomes a speculative free-for-all, as has happened in James Joyce's case, objectivity must not be obscured or speculation permitted to run rife. In conclusion, therefore, re-echoing Joyce's (424) *Thrust syphilis down to hell,* I submit that there is not a tittle of acceptable evidence that John Stanislaus Joyce had tertiary syphilis, and affirm that there is ample proof that James Joyce escaped this infection.

Fracastoro described a decision to make a placatory sacrifice to 'the offended Sun'.

On *Syphilus* the dreadful Lot did fall,
Who now was plac'd before the Altar bound,
His Head with sacrificial Garlands crown'd,
His Throat laid open to the lifted Knife,
But interceding *Juno* spar'd his Life,
Commands them in his Stead a Heifir slay,
For *Phoebus'* Rage was now remov'd away.[40]

Do we not owe the guiltless Dublin author the duty of a similar liberation from the damaging question 'Did Joyce have syphilis?' by answering it, finally, with a resounding 'No'?

39. *Critical Writings*, 273.
40. *Frac*, 372.

2. Animadversions on Paralysis as a Symbol in 'The Sisters'*

Because of James Joyce's partiality for advertisements, it is not inappropriate that an argumentative advertising jingle — 'It's a biscuit! It's a bar! It's a biscuit! It's a bar!' — should have come to my mind when reading *A Scrupulous Meanness,* Edward Brandabur's psychoanalytic study of Joyce's early work. *It's a biscuit! It's a –!* For to my astonishment a remark from Lenehan in 'Two Gallants' — Well!... that takes the biscuit!' — leads Brandabur to regard *biscuit* as 'a symbol of the female genitals, especially when imagined as an object of oral gratification.'[1]

In the present article, a by-product of participation in a discussion on 'The Sisters' at the Fourth International James Joyce Symposium, I propose to take as a text a comment of Sir Clifford Allbutt, sometime Regius Professor of Physic at Cambridge University: Allbutt insisted that 'the virtue of theories lies not in their ingenuity but in the labour of verification'. Joycean theorists do not lack ingenuity as indicated by the above example, but their explications are spun the more happily in the knowledge that for the most part they can neither be verified nor disproved. That the, at first sight, simple stories in *Dubliners* have been so evocative is a tribute to Joyce's genius and to the perceptiveness of the readers attracted. But Fritz Senn has pointed out that, 'It is tempting to take Joyce's words too far in an unwarranted direction'.[2] Joycean exegesis, in fact, has become

**James Joyce Quarterly,* 11, 3, 257-265, 1974

1. Brandabur, E. *A Scrupulous Meanness: A Study of James Joyce's Early Work*. Urbana: University of Illinois Press, 1971, 89.
2. Senn, F. 'He Was Too Scrupulous Always': Joyce's 'The Sisters'. *JJQ,* 1965, 2, 71.

an academic game played without rules. He who kicks the ball highest and furthest wins the plaudits of the crowd even though the direction is awry and he makes no attempt to retrieve it.

Senn's scholarship is to be respected. He asserts correctly that, 'More than is commonly suspected *Dubliners* is full of echoes, allusions and quotations'.[3] Others lack his common sense: M.W. Murphy of the University of Wisconsin observes the 'pervasive darkness' of *Dubliners* and divides his bets as to causation. Naturalism, poor eyesight, and Yeatsian influence are worth a wager, but he places most of his money on the swift steed symbolism — 'the darkness represents the plight of the Irish people'.[4] And that at a time when his own countrymen were raining napalm on Viet Nam!

His observation that the priests in *Dubliners,* a small atypical sample of the Irish clergy, are 'shabby, untidy, and careless people' leads him to the insupportable conclusion that 'religious darkness covers Ireland'.[5] But sanctity cannot be judged by externals as will be evident to those who have read Canon Sheehan's description of the wretched Benedict Joseph Labré in *Under the Cedars and the Stars,* a book which was published a year before the first version of 'The Sisters', a welcome beam in Mr. Murphy's darkness.

J.W. Corrington is correct in his claim that escape is one of the themes of *Dubliners,* but it really reflects Joyce's personal wish to escape rather than, as Corrington sees it, a universal urge among Dubliners to escape.[6] Joyce's departure with Nora Barnacle was, as I have said elsewhere, not exile but flight.[7]

Asked by AE in July 1904 to write a short story for the *Irish Homestead* for which he would receive a pound in payment, Joyce responded with 'The Sisters' which he rewrote a number of times before publication as the first story of *Dubliners,* a book which James Stephens in a letter to Thomas Bodkin in 1914 described as 'interesting but unpleasant and must be counted as

3. Senn, F. *Ibid.,* 66.
4. Murphy, M.W. Darkness in Dublin. *Modern Fiction Studies,* 1969, 15, 100.
5. Murphy, M.W., *Ibid.*
6. Corrington, J.W. The Sisters in *James Joyce's 'Dubliners',* ed. Clive Hart. London: Faber, 1969, 13.
7. Lyons, J.B. *James Joyce and Medicine.* Dublin: Dolmen Press, 1973.

among his wild oats,' and Edmund Wilson designated 'a straight work of Naturalistic fiction'.[8] Joyce himself informed his friend Constantine Curran (1904) that he would 'call the series *Dubliners* to betray the soul of that hemiplegia or paralysis which many consider a city'[9], a sentiment about which his subsequent interpreters have never disagreed however contradictory their conclusions in other regards.

In 'The Sisters', it will be recalled, a boy-narrator tells how he has waited for the inevitable death from a third stroke of Father James Flynn, and describes his visit with his aunt to the corpse-house where they are greeted by Nannie and Eliza. The latter recalls their brother's earlier days and talks about the misfortunes responsible for his mental breakdown.

I am content to err with Edmund Wilson in admiring this story as naturalistic fiction. By so doing one is entranced by the consummate way in which Joyce handles illness and death. However much Father Flynn's death filled the boy-narrator with fear, it also thrilled him. There is a relevant comment in Oliver St. John Gogarty's *As I Was Going Down Sackville Street:* 'Those who are near to Death fear it not so much as those who are in the fullness of health and the enjoyment of life. These are conscious of what they have to lose, and so the contemplation of the opposite condition becomes frightful.'[10]

And however much the two sisters mourned their dead brother their greater concern was to minimize the stigma of his mental illness. There is masterly understatement in Eliza's final comment.

During a number of the Symposium's seminars the possibility that Americans and others stand at a disadvantage when interpreting nuances of Irish *mores* was contentiously denied. But the ready acceptance of the relationship between Father Flynn and the boy as a homosexual relationship indicates either a return to the inverted Victorian prudery which saw sex in a table leg or ignorance of the pleasant and entirely nonsexual relationship

8. Wilson, E. *Axel's Castle: A Study in Imaginative Literature from 1870-1930.* New York: Scribner's, 1931, 192.
9. *Letters* 1, 55.
10. Gogarty, O. St. J. *As I Was Going Down Sackville Street,* New York: Reynal & Hitchcock, 1937, 50.

between Irish priests and their altar boys. No man who has grown up as a Catholic in Ireland would have thought it necessary to accuse Father Flynn of homosexuality, nor would he seriously consider syphilis as a possible contingency in the late nineteenth century when an infringement of the priestly vow of chastity would have been unthinkable in Dublin. The relevance of the last point will be apparent later.

If the exegesists who have studied 'The Sisters' have not been lacking in ingenuity neither have they lacked industry. The only question which has not, to my knowledge, been asked is whether Mr. Cotter did in fact 'take a pick of the leg of mutton'. But that is not to say that the mutton has escaped attention. Following the carrot of symbolism pertinaciously Corrington has equated that cold leftover with the Lamb of God.

Some have thought the title significant. Peter Spielberg concluded that the old ladies, Eliza and Nannie, in Joyce's tale are meant to symbolize Mary and Martha of Bethany. Eliza = Elizabeth = Bethany, the home of Martha and Mary. Which means that Father Flynn is Lazarus and the boy-narrator Christ. Then an anti-climax: 'But here the parallel ends for there can be no miracles in paralyzed Dublin'.[11]

Margaret Church has a different interpretation. Nannie is the generic for nurse: Elizabeth was the mother of John the Baptist.[12] Other roles in which the Flynns have been cast are enumerated in Florence L. Walzl's comprehensive analysis of 'The Sisters', their multiplicity earning her gentle disapproval.[13] It need hardly be said that all cannot be correct unless symbolism is kaleidoscopic; many could be accepted if Joycean interpreters would indicate that they are writing of their own evocations rather than Joyce's intentions.

But in any case palpable inaccuracies are evidence that imagination is running riot over reason. Where can Margaret Church have got the idea that Father Flynn *sold* his chalice? This is far too realistic an interpretation of the narrator's fascination with the word 'simony' and other words which he hardly understands. John Kuehl makes the extraordinary mistake of

11. Spielberg, P. 'The Sisters': No Christ in Bethany. *JJQ*, 1966, 3, 193.
12. Church, M. *Dubliners* and Vico. *JJQ*, 1968, 5, 151.
13. Walzl, F.L. Joyce's 'The Sisters': A Development. *JJQ*, 1973, 10, 375-421.

identifying the narrator with the boy through whose fault the chalice was broken and compounds it by seeing the chalice as a 'symbol of their great friendship'.[14] Corrington is not familiar with our Irish idiom 'to have a great wish' for a person; it signifies a general warm regard rather than the hope of a particular fulfillment. Julian B. Kaye attributes significance to the fact that Father Flynn's hands *loosely* retains a chalice, as if the passive grip of a corpse could be other than loose.[15]

But to return to the title, so often a story's least important feature, I would suggest that it contains no hidden symbolism and was selected by Joyce almost capriciously. In a letter which he received from Oliver St. John Gogarty in January 1903 his friend mentions 'I go to "the Sisters" on Sunday'. Gogarty also referred to 'the Sisters' when writing to Joyce from Oxford in May 1904. Is it not perfectly credible that when writing his story three months later Joyce echoed Gogarty's 'the Sisters'? They were both fascinated by catchwords. In a similar way Gogarty dedicated his first book of poems, the privately published *Hyperthuleana,* to 'The Companion', an oblique bow to Francis Sheehy Skeffington's designation of Nora Barnacle as Joyce's 'Companion' on their departure to the Continent.

Fritz Senn, referring to Eliza's malapropism, 'them with the rheumatic wheels', thinks it symbolic: 'she is substituting the name of a disease for something spiritual (Gk. *pneuma,* the word also used for the Holy Ghost).[16] He suggests, interestingly, that Joyce's play on rheumatic/pneumatic (which does not appear in the *Homestead* version) was prompted by an advertisement at the foot of a page of the *Irish Homestead* on which the first version was printed advocating Cantrell & Cochrane's Mineral Water for rheumatism. In support of this suggestion I could add that the Lithia water also mentioned in the advertisement was favoured by Joyce who thought it cured his own rheumatic aches, and is cleverly used by Gogarty in a parody of Yeats:

14. Kuehl, J. à la Joyce: The Sisters Fitzgerald's Absolution. *JJQ,* 1964, 2, 5.
15. Kaye, J.B. Simony, the Three Simons, and Joycean Myth. *A James Joyce Miscellany,* ed. Marvin Magalaner. New York: James Joyce Society, 1957, 22.
16. Senn, F. 'He Was Too Scrupulous Always': Joyce's 'The Sisters', *JJQ,* 1965, 2, 71.

I heard the old, old man say:
'Mineral Waters,
The doctor ordered me lithia.'

My difficulty in accepting the genuineness of these rich veins of symbolism which others find in 'The Sisters' makes me turn to a simpler explanation. Collecting malapropisms is an everyday occupation of medical students. 'I had forfets on me first and the last was a sexual' — the remark of a mother in an ante-natal clinic, who had three forceps deliveries and a caesarean section is a classic example. Joyce's receptive ear would have picked up many, one of which the 'medical student's pal' altered to suit Eliza.

It is understandable that the precise import of technical terms may escape those whose *métier* is the Liberal Arts. Should they not, then, use such terms with appropriate care? Senn seems to make a distinction between the synonymous terms palsy and paralysis. Richard Ellmann, with a nonchalance horrifying to anybody who has studied pathology, equates the priest's paralysis with the General Paralysis of the Insane (GPI) which afflicts Ireland.[17]

At a seminar on 'The Sisters' in the 1973 Symposium, the panelists discussed Father Flynn's ill health and to my mind were over-inclined to attribute symbolic significance to insecurely founded interpretations. The clinical details which Joyce has given us, sufficient for his story, are meagre from a viewpoint of diagnosis. They vary from version to version but presumably, as in life, all the evidence is admissable.

There is nothing to indicate that the mental breakdown which unfitted him for his priestly office and the strokes which killed him were in any way related. His oddity dated from his youth. In the *Homestead* version we are told that 'he was always a little queer'. Eliza recalls that, 'Even when we were all growing up together he was queer. One time he didn't speak hardly for a month'. This valuable information is missing in *Dubliners* where, as in reality, the relatives are more reserved concerning details of mental ill health.

17. *Ellmann*, 169.

In the earlier versions Cotter, too, is more outspoken. 'Without a doubt. Upper storey — (he tapped an unnecessary hand at his forehead) — gone.' Cotter says, 'So he was, at times', a comment indicating a considerable time scale. In the story as printed in *Dubliners,* Cotter mainly registers his awareness of the priest's instability by disapproving of his companionship with the boy.

The nature of the mental illness is open to conjecture, probably schizophrenia but possibly a neurotic breakdown in an immature and inadequate personality, or the neurosis of an obsessive personality unable to cope with responsibility. 'But it was his scrupulousness, I think, affected his mind. The duties of the priesthood were too much for him.' This statement in the *Homestead* version is changed ever so slightly in the Yale version where the 'But' is omitted pending the final version. 'He was too scrupulous always,' she said. The changes show increasing literary competence; they have no clinical significance, but may indicate Joyce's increased awareness concerning ill health, personal or otherwise. Another story, 'Eveline', acknowledges the manifestations of psychosomatic disease in the *Homestead* version: 'Her distress awoke a nausea in her body'. An additional detail regarding the ill effects of anxiety was included when the story appeared in *Dubliners:* 'She knew it was that that had given her the palpitations'.

Whatever its cause the final breakdown followed the breaking of a chalice: 'That affected his mind... After that he began to mope by himself, talking to no one and wandering about by himself'. Eliza rationalizes the situation and blames an altar boy even though her acknowledgement of her brother's nervousness — 'But poor James was so nervous, God be merciful to him!' — as a contributory factor confirms that all was not well before the accident. And in *Dubliners* the story ends with Eliza's pathetic euphemism: 'So then, of course, when they saw that, that made them think that there was something gone wrong with him...' *Made them think!* As if the palpable fact of his insanity was not clear and irrefutable! Whatever the symbolists may make of it — and in the Dublin of Joyce's day a mad priest would have been a disproportionately sinister figure — it is a masterly piece of naturalistic fiction. The final perfection is not achieved in the

Homestead or Yale versions which end weakly with the Aunt's pious ejaculation. 'God rest his soul!' Joyce no less than every other writer learned his craft by practice.

The details on which a diagnosis of the physical disease are to be made are equally meagre. In the earlier version, we find the youngster surprised to realize that Father Flynn was only sixty-five; he had thought him much older. His inconsistent comment: 'He seemed like one who could go on living for ever if he only wanted to', has been removed in the second draft. In the final version, Father Flynn has expressed a presentiment of death. *'I am not long for this world'* to the boy who disbelievingly 'had thought his words idle'.

We learn that he sat close to the fire wearing his greatcoat, that his hands were tremulous, and he had a habit of letting his tongue lie on his lower lip. Eliza noticed a change in him: 'Whenever I'd bring his soup to him there I'd find him with his breviary fallen to the floor, lying back in the chair and his mouth open'. At other times he was well enough to plan an outing to Irishtown where he was born.

The general deterioration of health, the partiality for warmth, the lolling tongue might suggest that Father Flynn had an underactive thyroid gland, but in *Dubliners* we are given the explicit information that he has had three strokes and the the outlook is hopeless.

The differential diagnosis of a stroke is extensive: brain tumors, cerebal abscess, trauma, etc. have to be considered, but most commonly it is a complication of hardening of the arteries. Father Flynn's case, indeed, with his gradual loss of faculties, tremulousness, and a succession of strokes is a typical example of a generalized arteriosclerosis.

It is ironic that the word *paralysis* which sounded so strangely in the ears of the boy-narrator has evoked ideas hardly less strange than 'the word *gnomon* in the Euclid and the word *simony* in the Catechism' in the minds of Joycean scholars. For the seminarists' suggestion that Joyce intended to indicate that Father Flynn had GPI, thereby implicating Ireland in this dire pathology, does not withstand objective scrutiny.

It is particularly unsuitable from an epidemiological viewpoint for actually GPI was comparatively rare in Ireland. At the

International Medical Congress in London in 1881, Dr. Isaac Ashe, an Irish alienist (and poet), remarked: 'If one of the medical staff of an English asylum were to visit an asylum in Ireland there is probably no feature which would strike him as being in more marked contrast with those familiar to him in England than the absence of general paralysis among the inmates.' During the course of three years service at an asylum in Derry, Ashe had seen only two cases of GPI. Dr. Eames reported the Cork Asylum free from the disease in 1875. Dublin's Richmond Asylum (the 'Dottyville' of *Ulysses*) admitted more victims of GPI than provincial mental hospitals. These cases averaged 2 or 3 per cent of its male inmates, a much lower figure than in Scotland's asylums where the general average of paretics was 18 per cent of male inmates.[18] Writing at the turn of the century, Dr F.W. Mott of London, arguing correctly that GPI resulted from syphilis, stated: 'in the rural districts of Ireland and Sweden, where alcoholism is common but syphilis rare, general paralysis is either extremely rare or unknown.' He pointed out that 'priests, Quakers and clergymen are extremely seldom affected with general paralysis and syphilis is also correspondingly rare.'[19]

Apart from the fact that at that time a diagnosis of venereal disease would have been extremely unlikely in a Catholic priest in Dublin, GPI, an inexorably progressive type of cerebal syphilis, occurs in a younger age group and presents a different clinical picture. Its victims die within a few years. There is a classic description of GPI in the *Goncourt Journal,* an account far better than will be found in any medical textbook; anyone who reads it will agree that Father Flynn did not suffer from the tragic disease.

Emboldened by Leslie Fiedler's flirtation with literary apostasism at the 1973 Symposium, I venture to take an unorthodox attitude to the symbol of paralysis. This derives from Joyce's letter to Curran which really has been swallowed, hook, line and sinker. An elementary observation has been ignored although there for all to see — it was written on a *wet* Friday, a

18. Ashe, I. *Transactions of the International Medical Congress, London, 1881.* volume 3, ed. Sir William MacCormac. London: Kolckmann, 1881.
19. Mott, F.W. *Archives of Neurology,* 1899, 1, 168.

dismal extenuating circumstance which partly explains Joyce's misanthropy.

It is important to realize that Joyce's objectivity was impaired by a recurring disorder which a colleague of mine of Liffeyside origin who has also experienced it terms 'the Dublins'. When my friend has 'the Dublins' (and it is not unknown to American Joyceans!) the only cure is to cross the Irish Sea and walk the familiar streets. He returns to his medical practice in Manchester, England, healed and with the self-satisfied feeling that Dublin is not the place it used to be.

The ailment, with regional variations, is well known in Irish literature. Oliver Goldsmith mentioned 'this *maladie du Pays*' to his friend Daniel Hodson and the Joyces may be included among its distinguished victims.

Few would dispute that James is the classic case of 'the Dublins', and both Eva Joyce and Mrs Eileen Schaurek (the latter in her viduity) returned from Trieste to live in Ireland. Even Stanislaus Joyce, obstensibly condemnatory of all things Irish, was susceptible. The proof is in the National Library, a letter written by Stanislaus to Katsy Murray from Trieste in 1906: 'Just now the whistle of a steamer blew. It reminds me of the mournful foghorn at the Pigeon House and of how much I would like to be within hearing of that'.

But although Dublin might tug at Stanislaus's heartstrings that complex man nursed a grievance. 'I hate the commonplace', he wrote in his *Diary*. 'I was born amongst it; I belong to it body and blood. Therefore I hate it'.[20] His brother, alienated further from the banal by genius, but more aware of its universality, allowed his rancor to spill over into his letter to Curran and into his stories. Later in repentance for those voluntary tracts on alcoholism he drew a softer picture of the environs of his youth.

> the cornflowers have been staying at Ballymun, the duskrose has choosed out Goatstown's hedges, twolips have pressed togatherthem by sweet Rush, townland of twinedlights, the whitethorn and the redthorn have fairygeyed the mayvalleys of Knockmaroon... (14.36)

20. *Diary*, 110.

That passage, vivid with life, is in itself sufficient to rebuke those who cling to the stultifying idea of paralysis which Curran in 1904 would have treated as an extravagance not to be taken too seriously. But as it has been so solemnly accepted, Joyce's friend later thought it necessary to defend the Irish capital: 'Nothing seemed to me more inept than to qualify the focus of this activity as a hemiplegia or paralysis, however much one might quarrel with its exuberances or fanaticisms'.[21]

Besides, the metaphor of hemiplegia, which may be congenital or acquired, the latter the more disabling, is unsuitable for any swarming city. The City of Hurdles had shaken off congenital weakness when many of the world's cities were unborn; thankfully it continues to flourish. Joyce himself (who celebrated Dublin sacramentally from afar) was as great an argument as any against its moribundity but if another is needed I would remind you that when Joyce's first child was some months old a cradle in Foxrock awaited the birth of Samuel Beckett. So, unless they are prepared to neglect 'the labour of verification' Joyceans would do well, at least for a year and a day, to exclude the word paralysis from their vocabularies.

5. View of a 'paralysed' city.

21. Curran, C. *James Joyce Remembered.* London: OUP, 1968, 55.

3. Diseases in *Dubliners:* Tokens of Disaffection*

In a critique of *Dubliners* Ezra Pound said that James Joyce's 'most engaging merit, is that he carefully avoids telling you a lot that you don't want to know'.[1] Joyce does not, of course, point out that life-expectancy at the turn of the century was short — 48.5 years for males, 52.4 for women (compared to 69.2 and 75.5 respectively in the 1970s) — but few families in this book that begins in a corpse-house and ends in a cemetery have not experienced a bereavement. The narrators of the early stories, all presumably orphans, live with aunts and uncles. In 'Araby' the previous tenant of the house in North Richmond Street was a dead priest. Eveline Hill's mother died leaving her in charge of two schoolchildren; her brother Ernest and a schoolfriend, Tizzie Dunn, have also died. Pat Morkan was dead for thirty years; his sister, Mrs. Ellen Conroy, died after a long illness. Michael Furey, of whom Gretta Conroy says 'I think he died for me', succumbed to tuberculosis at seventeen.

The French critic Edmond Jaloux found that Joyce had brought to *Dubliners* 'the minute and pure application of a botanist or of an entymologist, the seriousness of an Irish Fabré, dedicated to unfortunate human beetles'.[2] Inside the book in a

*Presented to the James Joyce Society of New York, October 1979. Published *Irish Renaissance Annual* II, 185-194. ed. Zack Bowen, Newark: University of Delaware Press, 1981.

Figures in brackets refer to page numbers of *Dubliners,* New York, Viking Press, 1974.

1. Pound, E. in *The Critical Heritage,* Vol 1, ed. Robert H. Deming. New York: Barnes and Noble, 1970, 66.
2. Jaloux, E. *Ibid.,* 220.

double sense, is a study of pathology revealed and unrevealed. Joyce does not mention explicity the sinister galaxy of infections — scarlet fever, diphtheria, typhoid fever, and pneumonia — that took many lives in his boyhood, but he introduces several instances of ill health. His one portrayal of *health* (the slavey in 'Two Gallants') paradoxically is no less ugly, reflecting, I suggest, his own emotional insecurity in the early 1900s: 'Frank rude health glowed in her face, on her fat red cheeks and in her unabashed blue eyes. Her features were blunt. She had broad nostrils, a straggling mouth which lay open in a contented leer, and two projecting front teeth' (55-56).

Through the eyes of Little Chandler ('A Little Cloud') we see Dublin's aged and young, the 'decrepit old men' and the 'grimy children... all that minute verminlike life' (71). Focusing on the senile we see Nannie Flynn ('The Sisters') deaf and bent, toiling upstairs, and the old caretaker ('Ivy Day in the Committee Room') whose face is 'very bony and hairy. The moist blue eyes blinked at the fire and the moist mouth fell open at times, munching once or twice mechanically when it closed' (118). Among the young we find in 'Eveline' 'little Keogh the cripple' (36) (who may yet be as useful a citizen as Hoppy Holohan with the game leg) and the fat boy, Leo Dillon, a not uncommon morphological variant.

Eveline Hill's failure to run away with the sailor cannot surprise us. 'Her eyes gave him no sign of love or farewell or recognition' (41). She is a tired, anxious, irresolute creature who takes no enjoyment in her work at the stores and has never summoned up enough curiosity to ask the name of the priest, her father's friend, whose photograph hangs in the living room. Her mother's death 'in the close dark room at the other side of the hall' (40) reminds us of Mrs. Joyce's death from cancer in 1903 at the age of forty-four.

One of the laundresses in the 'Dublin by Lamplight' refuge in 'Clay' is a deaf-mute. Mr. Duffy of 'A Painful Case' abhorred anything that 'betokened physical or mental disorder' (108). As a matter of fact, he may have been emotionally abnormal, a schizoid personality. 'He had neither companions nor friends, church nor creed' (109). In repose Lenehan's face 'had a ravaged look' (50). He is unhappy, unsettled, and probably undernourished. 'Anxiety and his swift run made him pant' (60).

Current concern with the frequency of parental abuse of children ('the battered baby syndrome', of which there are probably three to four hundred cases in Ireland annually) heightens the interest in *Dubliners*' evidence that the phenomenon is not new. Eveline Hill recalls how her father 'used to go for Harry and Ernest' (38), and little Tom Farrington, savagely beaten, utters a 'squeal of pain as the stick cut his thigh' (98).

The most detailed case history is that of Father James Flynn. Aged sixty-five, he died in his sisters' little house in Great Britain Street on 1 July 1895. No less absorbing than the clinical description is Joyce's portrayal of the effect of his death on relatives and narrator. The latter, a child who has struck up an incongruous friendship with the old priest and brought him snuff from time to time, experiences the vicarious excitement that sickroom dramas convey to uninvolved onlookers. He has waited for this, and it brings him a sense of freedom. 'Every night as I gazed up at the window I said softly to myself the word paralysis... It filled me with fear, and yet I longed to be nearer to it and to look upon its deadly work' (9). Eliza and Nannie Flynn also experience a sense of release, relieved to know, as Eliza says, that 'we done all we could, as poor as we are' (16). Their sorrow is leavened by gratitude; he has brought no disgrace to the cloth.

From the boy we learn of the hopelessness of the situation — 'it was the third stroke' (9). But old Cotter speaks in guarded terms of another matter: 'I have my own theory about it,' he says. 'I think it was one of those... peculiar cases... But it's hard to say' (10). The boy and his aunt go to the 'house of mourning', where Eliza recalls her brother's nervousness. 'It was that chalice he broke...' After that, she explains, he moped, avoided people, and wandered about until the night he was missing when wanted for a call. Eventually they found him 'sitting up by himself in the dark in his confession-box, wide-awake and laughing-like softly to himself'. All of which, Eliza admits, taking pathetic refuge in a euphemism that softens the tragedy, 'made them think that there was something gone wrong with him' (18).

The features of the physical illness are clearly delineated. Father Flynn's hands trembled as he took snuff or beef tea; he dozed in his greatcoat before the fire, 'his breviary fallen to the floor, lying back in the chair and his mouth open' (16). Hardening of the arteries explains the sequence of events. Frank O'Connor admitted once that the point of the story eluded him, but modern critics have invested it with a wealth of symbolism.

The most prevalent disease in *Dubliners* is alcoholism; the book, indeed, could serve as a temperance tract. I do not imply that Joyce intended his work as a preventative to this social problem, but his pages reflect the community's attitudes to alcohol and present a series of object lessons of increasing gravity.

Irish hospitality demands that drinks be served, and group participation is essential. That something suitably 'genteel' is offered to ladies is evident in 'The Sisters'; 'I groped my way towards my usual chair in the corner while Nannie went to the sideboard and brought out a decanter of sherry and some wine-glasses. She set these on the table and invited us to take a little glass of wine' (14-15). 'My aunt fingered the stem of her wine-glass before sipping a little' (15). All very harmless, no doubt and my surprise to find the boy being offered an intoxicant is lessened when I remember being handed a clay pipe filled with tobacco in a country corpse-house in County Mayo when I was hardly ten years old.

Maria in 'Clay' is offered a bottle of stout, but Mrs. Donnelly says there is 'port wine too in the house if she would prefer that' (104). Mr. Bartell D'Arcy in 'The Dead' refuses port and sherry, 'but one of his neighbours nudged him and whispered something to him upon which he allowed his glass to be filled' (201). The seventeen-year-old delivery boy in 'Ivy Day in the Committee Room' is given a bottle of stout even though his seniors are conscious of their folly. The caretaker, whose own son is already a drunken layabout, says, 'That's the way it begins.' Mr. Henchy calls it 'the thin edge of the wedge' (129). Mrs. Kernan's drunken husband has been helped home ('Grace'), but even so she does not wish to neglect the customary civility toward his friend Mr. Power. 'I'm so sorry... that I've nothing in the house to offer you. But if you wait a minute I'll send round to Fogarty's, at the corner' (155).

Attitudes toward drinking include frank disapproval and that peculiar ambivalence which advances extenuating circumstances for what may thus be seen as either a fault or a virtue. In the schoolroom ('An Encounter') Father Butler dismisses the confiscated comic as the work of 'some wretched scribbler who writes these things for a drink' (20). Mr. Browne fills out for himself 'a goodly measure of whisky' at the Morkans' party in 'The Dead'. 'God help me,' he says, smiling, 'it's the doctor's orders'. Encouraged by the young ladies' laughter, he adds, 'Well, you see, I'm like the famous Mrs. Cassidy, who is reported to have said: *Now, Mary Grimes, if I don't take it, make me take it, for I feel I want it*' (183). Mrs. Kearney in 'A Mother' places a decanter before Hoppy Holohan, and when he is helping himself, she urges, 'Don't be afraid! Don't be afraid of it!' (138). It is to King Edward's credit that 'he's fond of his glass of grog!' (132).

The city's ambience is one of inebriation. The narrator of 'Araby' walks with his aunt 'through the flaring streets, jostled by drunken men' (31). Mr. Duffy in 'A Painful Case' recalls 'the hobbling wretches whom he had seen carrying cans and bottles to be filled by the barman' (115). The young men on board *The Belle of Newport* in Kingstown Harbour ('After the Race') drink because it is bohemian. They toast their native lands and drink 'the health of the Queen of Hearts and of the Queen of Diamonds' (48).

The individual inebriates are numerous. The book contains all grades of drinkers, from hesitant sippers to irredeemable soaks. Between booze and 'other things' (76) O'Hara ('A Little Cloud') has 'gone to the dogs' (75), but Mr. Cotter from the distillery, whom the narrator in 'The Sisters' regards as a 'tiresome old red-nosed imbecile' (11), might be misjudged.

Little Chandler, who takes an 'odd half-one or so' (75) when he meets his friends, is unlikely to go far wrong, and Gallaher has the protection of ambition and a good personality. Many of the gregarious young men will sober as they mature, but Jimmy Doyle, who views the dawn over Kingstown Harbour with his throbbing head in his hands ('After the Race'), and the embittered Lenehan ('Two Gallants'), who has spent Sunday afternoon in a Dorset Street tavern, are both men of weak character, and may be less fortunate. Jack Mooney, 'a hard case' (62) with an alcoholic father, also is at risk.

Eveline Hill's father, who 'was usually fairly bad of a Saturday night' (38) may have been a weekend drinker, as is the tardy uncle of the boy impatient to be off to the Araby Bazaar: 'At nine o'clock I heard my uncle's latchkey in the halldoor. I heard him talking to himself and heard the hallstand rocking when it had received the weight of his overcoat. I could interpret these signs' (33). The introverted Mr. Duffy, who 'ordered a hot-punch' (16) in a moment of distress and views the working men with distaste, is safe from all extremes, but Joe Donnelly's geniality may be his downfall. On Halloween in 'Clay' Maria hopes 'that Joe wouldn't come in drunk. He was so different when he took any drink' (100). And yet she does not understand 'why Joe laughed so much over the answer he had made' (104) to the manager. Later Joe is moved by her song 'and his eyes filled up so much with tears that he could not find what he was looking for and in the end he had to ask his wife to tell him where the corkscrew was' (106).

Mrs. Sinico's inebriety ('A Painful Case') solaces the melancholia of reactive depression. A fatal accident cuts short her enslavement to a habit that wreaks havoc with Farrington and others. The youngest of these melancholic types is the caretaker's son ('Ivy Day') who 'goes boosing about' (119). His father complains that 'he takes th'upper hand of me whenever he sees I've a sup taken' (120). Obviously the old man is unaware that the example of that 'sup' may have initiated his son's drinking.

Freddy Malins, a forty-year-old bachelor in 'The Dead', is the only likeable drunk in *Dubliners.* Still socially acceptable, altough his aunts fear that he may 'turn up screwed' (176), Freddy elicits a good deal of amusement. He laughs immoderately but carries his drink well. His applause for Aunt Julia's song is too loud and too long, but decently he repays Gabriel Conroy a sovereign he has borrowed, and having broken the pledge his mother made him take on New Year's Eve, he promises to go to Mount Melleray.

Mr. Mooney of 'The Boarding House' is the extreme case. A butcher's foreman who married the boss's daughter, he went to the devil when his father-in-law died. 'He drank, plundered the till, ran headlong into debt. It was no use making him take the pledge: he was sure to break out a few days after' (61). When he went for his wife with a cleaver she left him, and he degenerated into a 'shabby stooped little drunkard with a white face and a white moustache and white eyebrows, pencilled above his little eyes, which were pink-veined and raw' (61).

Tom Kernan, 'a commercial traveller of the old school' (153), has not reached these depths ('Grace'). His well-intentioned friends may save him, even though we encounter him 'quite helpless' after having fallen downstairs on his way to the public-house lavatory: 'His hat had rolled a few yards away and his clothes were smeared with the filth and ooze of the floor on which he had lain, face downwards' (150). Mrs. Kernan had come to accept 'his frequent intemperance as part of the climate... There were worse husbands' (156). But Mr. Power notes signs of disorder in the children's behaviour and is determined to 'make a new man of him' (155). Even Fogarty the grocer, who is owed money, joins the conspirators for Kernan's good, and Martin Cunningham, whose wife is 'an incurable drunkard' (157), is particularly sympathetic.

Lacking Tom Kernan's good points and good friends, Farrington ('Counterparts') will end up like Mooney. Violent, addicted, and unsettled except in the uncritical surroundings of the tavern, he too is set on a pathway to destruction. 'He had a hanging face, dark wine-coloured, with fair eyebrows and moustache: his eyes bulged forward slightly and the whites of them were dirty' (86). To satisfy his craving, he pawns his watch. 'It was a night for hot punches' (90). The borrowed shillings enabled him to join his cronies in Davy Byrne's. Later they go to the Scotch House and to Mulligan's of Poolbeg Street, but the end of the evening finds Farrington making his way home angrily. 'He felt humiliated and discontented; he did not even feel drunk; and he had only twopence in his pocket' (96-97). In this mood he takes a stick to his son.

Gerald Gould in an early review of *Dubliners* appreciated Joyce's genius but remarked that he seemed to regard 'this objective and dirty and crawling world with the cold detachment of an unamiable god'.[3] A question I find interesting is why a young man should paint his native city in such sombre colours; the current answer, that he regards it as a centre of paralysis, does not satisfy me.

3. Gould, G. *Ibid.*, 63.

Admittedly, the critics' preoccupation with paralysis derives from a hare that Joyce himself set running in 1904 when he informed Constantine Curran that he would call his series of stories *Dubliners* 'to betray the soul of that hemiplegia or paralysis which many consider a city'.[4] He wrote to Grant Richards in a similar vein: 'My intention was to write a chapter of the moral history of my country and I chose Dublin for the scene because that city seemed to me the centre of paralysis'.[5] The Rev. James Flynn's stroke has been seen as an appropriate symbol of this paralysis.

The enthusiasm and ingenuity of those who deal in symbols is difficult to curb, but as I have suggested elsewhere,[6] proponents of symbolism should perhaps consider whether Joyce may not have been motivated consciously or unconsciously by other concerns. The Dublin of his youth was the size of Periclean Athens and in the sphere of literature had some of the virtue of that famous city; it was also a ferment of political and working-class unrest.[7] Denis Johnston* and Samuel Beckett, who gathered their early impressions in Dublin's suburbs in the infant twentieth century, are existing tokens of the city's intellectual vitality. Johnston, for example, in his play *The Old Lady Says 'No!'* scolds Dublin's savage dreamers and isolates a factor inimical to its growth: 'Suckling the bastard brats of Scots, of Englishry, of Huguenot'. Nevertheless, his final affirmation — 'But you, I know will walk the streets of Paradise/Head high, and unashamed' — has the assent of its citizens.[8]

Creativity is an obscure and to some degree involuntary process, susceptible to the vagaries of affect and the subconscious. Aware of his genius but embittered by his poverty, and by the squalor to

*Denis Johnston died in 1984

4. Curran, C. *James Joyce Remembered.* New York: OUP, 1968, 49.
5. *Letters 2,* 134.
6. Lyons, J.B., Animadversions on Paralysis as a Symbol in 'The Sisters'. *JJQ,* 1974, 11, 257-265.
7. Keogh, D. *The Rise of the Irish Working Class.* Belfast: Appletree Press, 1982.
8. Johnston, D. *The Dramatic Works of Denis Johnston,* Vol 2. Gerrards Cross: Colin Smythe, 1977, 74.

which his alcoholic father had reduced the family, Joyce suffered in his early twenties a disaffection that verged on the pathological. Having repudiated the God of his fathers, he invoked in Trieste another deity. 'O Vague Something behind Everything!' while the wind roared about him in the trees:

> For the love of the Lord Christ change my curse-o'-God state of affairs. Give me for Christ' sake a pen and an ink-bottle and some peace of mind and then, by the crucified Jaysus, if I don't sharpen that little pen and dip it into fermented ink and write tiny little sentences about the people who betrayed me send me to hell.[9]

In a different mood he was sufficiently objective to admit harshness and bias. The mature author made amends. Dublin is rehabilitated in *Ulysses,* and praised lovingly in *Finnegans Wake:*

> This seat of our city is of all sides pleasant, comfortable and wholesome. If you would traverse hills, they are not far off. If champain land, it lieth of all parts. If you would be delited with fresh water, the famous river, called of Ptolemy the Libnia Labia, runneth fast by. If you will take the view of the sea, it is at hand. Give heed! (540.3)

9. *Letters 2,* 110.

4. Further Thoughts on the Case of Father Flynn*

Towards the end of his years in America, Oliver St. John Gogarty sent to Horace Reynolds for inclusion in *The Merry Muses of Hibernia*[1] a grotesque piece entitled 'Suppose', which on second thoughts he decided to suppress, as it might give offence. The questionable lines will hardly disturb present-day readers:

Suppose the Pope had G.P.I.
What would you say to that?
To his Infallibility
Would you write, NIL OBSTAT?
And gladlier kiss the Pontifical toes
If the Pontifex hadn't got a bridge to his nose?

But symptoms grow intensified
And the meninges thicker,
Do you think he'd be satisfied
With merely being Vicar,
Nor wake one day with the terrible boast:
I'm Father, Son and the Holy Ghost?[2]

Gogarty's tact is in contrast to the behaviour of Joyce critics, who do not hesitate to traduce the character of Father James Flynn, whose death is the central event of 'The Sisters' in *Dubliners*. The title of that story, incidentally, is an echo from letters which Joyce

*Presented to IXth International James Joyce Symposium, Frankfurt, June 1984.

1. Lyons, J.B. *Oliver St. John Gogarty – the Man of Many Talents*. Dublin: Blackwater Press, 1980, 285
2. Houghton Library, Harvard. b Ms, AM, 1787, 140

received from his friend, Gogarty, in 1903 and 1904.[3]

Sir William Osler, the great physician alluded to in *Finnegans Wake* — 'the ogry Osler will oxmaul us all' (317. 16) — has written: 'To study the phenomena of disease without books is to sail an uncharted sea, while to study books without patients is not to go to sea at all.'[4] I venture to suggest that Joyce scholars who have never sailed the morbid oceans of clinical practice should be more hesitant in making diagnostic pronouncements. If untutored in Latin, for instance, they would hardly expect to appreciate the full beauty of the *Aeneid,* nor would they hazard their reputations in that field of learning if they relied on mere translations. And I sincerely hope that they should wish to avoid, on the basis of so slender an acquaintanceship, the promulgation of theories credulously accepted as facts by their congeners.

It has been suggested by those critics that Joyce intended to convey that Father James Flynn in 'The Sisters' died of GPI, a diagnosis which I find untenable, unless one is to say that the author having set out to describe a rose, succeeded only in describing a thistle. General paralysis of the insane, a tertiary phase of syphilis, occurs 10-20 years after the initial infection, in the prime of life rather than in the elderly. It has a specific pathology, an extensive diffuse sub-acute inflammation of the brain substance, causing destruction and atrophy of the cerebral hemispheres and progresses inexorably, leading in a few years to a fatal outcome. Distinctive tremors of tongue and lips, slurred speech, fits and paralysis accompany a disintegration of personality and intellect which reduces the sufferer to total helplessness. GPI ravages a hitherto active, intelligent and usually successful individual in a manner that has no parallel in medicine.

My 'chart' for the illness would hardly satisfy Osler's demand that the tyro must be shown actual patients. GPI is rare today and many doctors have never seen it. The disease was still prevalent when I commenced practice in 1945 and in the ensuing decade I dealt with a number of cases. This permits me to say with some

3. Lyons, J.B. Animadversions on Paralysis as a Symbol in "The Sisters". *JJQ,* 11, 3, 257-265, 1974.

4. Osler, Sir William, *Aequanimitas with Other Addresses,* 3rd ed. London: H.K. Lewis, 1941, 210.

6. Edmond and Jules de Goncourt. Portrait by Gavarni, 1853.

authority that Joyce either had no intention of describing GPI or did so with an incompetence difficult to credit.

As my affirmation, understandably, may not convince persons committed to another viewpoint, I shall place before you an authentic example of GPI from the pages of the *Goncourt Journal,* where as mentioned in an earlier essay, Edmond de Goncourt recorded characteristic details of the disease as it affected his brother, Jules, who was thirty-nine years old when he died in Paris on 20 June 1870.

The de Goncourts described themselves as 'temperamental, neurotic, unhealthily impressionable creatures'[5] but they collaborated successfully as writers and moved in a *milieu* where artists mixed in easy conviviality with the upper classes and the demi-monde. Jules contracted syphilis at nineteen. It is impossible to say when the subsequent inroads of illness began insidiously to affect him, possibly after 1865. The malaise was at first attributed, in French fashion, to a liver disorder; by the summer of 1869, however, social indiscretions were evident. A gaffe which offended a Bonaparte princess was recorded in the *Journal* on 25 August:

> Yesterday in the course of a discussion about the old Jew Franck, she said something unpleasant to me about my liver complaint. To-day at lunch I was still smarting from her remark, and when she began eulogizing Franck and Jewry in general once more I blurted out, in a moment of sickly irascibility over which I had no control: 'Well then, Princess, why don't you turn Jew?' There was a silence, and every guest turned pale. The remark was impolite, and I regretted it as soon as I had made it, seeing that it had hurt her.[6]

As they rose from the table, Jules apologised to Princess Mathilde, 'and in spite of myself, in my nervous condition, tears dropped from my eyes on her hands as I was kissing them'.

The brothers spent part of October in Trouville, 'the worst twenty days of our lives', during which Jules, aware of his declining powers, worked relentlessly to finish a book on Gavarni, the litographer. His last, sadly perceptive entry in the

5. *Goncourt,* XIX.
6. *Ibid.,* 155.

Journal before the pen fell from his hands was made on 19 January 1870:

> How strange and peculiar nervous diseases are! Vacorbeil, the composer, has a horror of velvet, and suffers absolute agony whenever he is invited somewhere for the first time, wondering whether the dining-room chairs are covered in velvet.[7]

After some months, Edmond resumed the entries:

> We were walking at dusk in the Bois de Boulogne, neither of us speaking. He was sad that evening, sadder than ever. I said to him: 'Look here, old fellow, let's suppose that you need a year, or even two years, to get on your feet again. What of it? You are young: you are not yet forty. Doesn't that leave you plenty of time to turn out books?'
> He looked at me with the astonished stare of a man who sees that his secret thoughts have been divined, and answered, stressing every word: 'I feel that I shall never be able to work again. Never again'.[8]

Jules became tactless and socially inept. His speech was slurred and Edmond realised that he was mortally ill.

> For some time now — and it grows more noticeable every day — there has been certain letters that he pronounces badly, r's that he elides, c's that become t's in his mouth. I remember, when he was a little boy, how sweet and charming it was to hear him stumbling over those two consonants. To hear the same childish pronounciation today, to hear his voice as I used to hear it in the distant and forgotten past, where my memories encounter nothing but things long dead, frightens me.[9]

Affected by the progressive depredations of rapid brain destruction, Jules seemed egotistical and dehumanised. He read Chateaubriand by the hour, his face wearing what his sorrowing brother called 'The haggard mask of imbecility'. He was unable to remember the names of any of his novels.

To witness, day by day, [Edmond wrote] the destruction of

7. *Ibid.*, 157.
8. *Ibid.*, 158.
9. *Ibid.*, *159.*

> everything that once went to mark out this young man — distinguished among all others — to see him emptying the salt-cellar over his fish, holding his fork in both hands, eating like a child, is too much for me to bear.
> So it was not enough that this busy mind should stop producing, should cease creating, should be inhibited by nothingness. The human being had to be stricken in these qualities of grace and elegance which I imagined to be inaccessible to sickness...[10]

In May there was a seizure. Suddenly, throwing back his head, Jules gave a horrifying scream. 'Instantly his handsome face was seized with convulsions which completely transformed it, deforming all his features, while terrible spasms jerked his arms... and his ravaged mouth emitted a trickle of bloody foam.'

From time to time there were less violent fits. There also were panic attacks which Edmond described:

> He would raise his arms above his head, blowing kisses to a vision and appealing to it to come to him. He would throw himself about like a wounded bird trying to take wing, while over his calm face, into his bloodshot eyes, across his livid forehead and on to his half-open, pale violet lips, there spread an expression that was no longer human. More often still, he would be seized with panic, his body would shrink back in terror, and he would cower under the sheets, as if hiding from an apparition stubbornly lodged in the curtains of his bed and against which he would hurl incoherent words, pointing at it with a frightening finger and on one occasion distinctly crying out: 'Go away!'[11]

His hands were 'like moist marble' and Edmond was tortured by his plaintive cries and heart-rending groans. Dr Beni-Barde said on 18 June that a disintegration of the brain had occurred and there was no hope left.

Sometime after dawn on 20 June Edmond de Goncourt made this heart-broken entry as his brother's life ebbed:

> In his eyes an indescribable expression of suffering and

10. *Ibid.*, 159.
11. *Ibid.*, 162.

> misery. To create a being like this, so gifted and intelligent, and then to break it at the age of thirty-nine! Why?[12]

Jules died at twenty minutes to ten, 'after two or three gentle, sighing breaths, like a little child falling asleep'. Father Flynn died like that, too — 'You couldn't tell when the breath went out of him'[13] — but the peaceful and mysterious moment in which all lives end was the only thing they shared.

Let us now look once more at the available details of Father Flynn's ill-health. He had reached a time of life when atherosclerosis ('hardening of the arteries') is increasingly likely to take its toll and when the risk of brain involvement has probably passed for those infected with syphilis — Baudelaire and Lord Randolph Churchill both died from tertiary syphilis at the age of forty-six. From the *Irish Homestead* version of 'The Sisters', we learn of mental instability, arguable in degree; Uncle John thought 'he was sane enough'; Mr. Cotter agreed that 'he was at times'; Miss Flynn admits that her brother 'was always a little queer'.[14] The priest was nervous and over-scrupulous. 'He began to mope by himself, talking to no one and wandering about...'

His physical state is described by the narrator: 'Only sixty-five! He looked older than that. I often saw him sitting at the fire in the close dark room behind the shop, nearly smothered in his great coat. He seemed to have almost stupified himself with heat, and the gesture of his large trembling hand to his nostrils had grown automatic.'[15] The fuller *Dubliners* version is unequivocal — 'there was no hope for him this time: it was the third stroke'.[16]

The clinical history reveals two problems: first, a personality disorder since childhood — 'One time he didn't speak hardly for a month'[17] — culminating in a schizophrenic breakdown; second, the independent physical disorder resulting from hardening of the arteries. There is nothing to suggest GPI. Not only does the priest's age and office make it extremely unlikely but important

12. *Ibid.*, 164.
13. Joyce, James. *Dubliners.* London: Grant Richards, 1914, 17.
14. Daedalus, Stephen. The Sisters. *The Irish Homestead,* 13 August 1904, 676.
15. Daedalus, Stephen, *Ibid,* 676.
16. Joyce, James. *Dubliners.* London: Grant Richards, 1914, 9.
17. Daedalus, Stephen. The Sisters. *The Irish Homestead,* 13 August 1904, 677.

diagnostic criteria are lacking. There were no fits and there is no dementia. A man who talks rationally 'about the catacombs and about Napoleon Bonaparte', who discusses moral philosphy, teaches a youngster Latin, and plans to visit Irishtown with his sisters, is not dying from cerebral syphilis. The diagnosis of GPI must be rejected unless you are prepared to say that Joyce writes fish but means fowl. He did, of course, achieve an intricate coalescence of ideas in *Finnegans Wake,* but that lay years ahead.

By one of those remarkable coincidences that kept recurring in Joyce's career, the *Homestead* version of 'The Sisters' was published on the anniversary of his mother's death, an event that no doubt had lent something to the deathbed scene in Great Britain Street. And may it not be that the boy narrator's nightmare in the re-written story in *Dubliners* foreshadows Stephen Dedalus's appalling vision in 'Circe'?

The *fons et origo* of the syphilis theory is an observation in Stanislaus Joyce's *Dublin Diary,* which informs us that his brother 'talks much of the syphilitic contagion in Europe, is at present writing a series of studies on it in Dublin...'[18] But Stannie was sufficiently objective to recognise 'pseudo-medical phraseology' and to know how James moved from one enthusiasm to another: 'What pleases him for the moment is his god for the moment'. He admitted, too, that James knew 'damn all' about science.[19]

The fervid attention some critics continue to pay to paralysis in a non-specific context also merits correction. Joyce's early references to paralysis occurred in letters to Constantine Curran and Grant Richards. The latter, the son of an Oxford don, the great grandson of a friend of John Keats, has been described as London's best-dressed publisher.[20] He grew to manhood in the *fin-de-siècle* period of which the Bodley Head's *Yellow Book* was the emblem. He would have observed the stir caused by George Moore's *Esther Waters* and seen Mrs Ormiston Chant pursue a puritanical crusade against the promenades at the Empire and the Alhambra. He refused to publish the faintly decadent verses

18. *Diary,* 51.
19. *Ibid.,*53.
20. Waugh, Alec. Preface to *Author Hunting* by Grant Richards, 2nd ed. London: Unicorn Press, 1960.

of *Chamber Music,* which Arthur Symons had recommended, without a subsidy which Joyce could not afford and, having accepted *Dubliners* in 1906, found himself ground between Bowdlerizing printers and his angry client whose arguments included an insistence that he wished to expose Dublin which seemed to him 'the centre of paralysis'.[21]

Richards possessed considerable *savoir faire* and one wonders what he made of Joyce's observation. The publisher's knowledge of Ireland's capital was limited but his Irish acquaintances included John Dillon, W.B. Yeats and George Bernard Shaw. How could he reconcile the springs of GBS's volcanic energy with the torpor of Joyce's invention? He may, indeed, have regarded Joyce, with his determination 'to write a chapter of the moral history' of his country as a reformer of the same ilk as Mrs. Ormiston Chant. Surprisingly, Grant Richards fails to mention Joyce in his autobiography, *Author Hunting.*

Constantine Curran, knowing Dublin intimately, regarded Joyce's comment as so much persiflage.[22] Eighty years later, when 'paralysis' has been incorporated into innumerable PhD. theses and solemnly consecrated in a thousand classrooms, it would require a greater gust of laughter than I can command to dismiss it. But *Dubliners* is an established literary classic and the increasing tendency to see it as a dependable social document demands a re-appraisal of the paralysis theme and a consideration of other viewpoints. Sir Shane Leslie, for instance, has described how, at the time that *Dubliners* was published, it was possible to spend a morning at St. Enda's School and discuss the ideals of Irish education with Pearse and MacDonagh; to catch a vivid minute with George Russell in Plunkett House; in the afternoon to see Yeats and Lady Gregory moving down the quays to a rehearsal at the Abbey Theatre; and in the evening to see a Synge play and pass a late hour with Tom Kettle. In his maiden speech in the House of Commons, Kettle said: 'In spite of many reverses with which we have to deal, Dublin does not stand still but progresses'.[23]

21. *Letters 2,* 13.
22. Curran, C. *James Joyce Remembered.* London: OUP., 1968, 55
23. *Kettle,* 110.

Even Joyce himself admitted to Stannie that he had been biased. 'Sometimes thinking of Ireland it seems to me that I have been unnecessarily harsh*. I have reproduced (in *Dubliners* at least) none of the attraction of the city... its hospitality... its beauty...'.[24] His references in his letters to paralysis are splendid examples of kite-flying; they are the utterances a clever youngster makes, watching his friends to see if he'll get away with it. These statements about paralysis are on a par with H.L. Mencken's assertion[25] that Americans 'have a postive libido for the ugly'. One can, of course, see what he means — but it's not really true.

The validity of the metaphor must, in any case, be questioned. Paralysis is acceptable journalese: 'CHICAGO PARALYSED BY SNOW'; 'ELECTRICAL FAULT PARALYSES STOCK MARKET'. In any deeper sense it is inapplicable to the agony of a struggling people. The famines that literally paralysed and killed a section of the Irish peasantry, caused a diaspora which gave actively to America, among others, the Kennedys, the Reagans, and F. Scott Fitzgerald. The ant-heap of Joyce's own time was being deeply stirred by the birth-pangs of the trades-union movement, the National University,

*A pre-Joycean commentator, Percy Bysshe Shelley, was even harsher He referred to Dubliners of 1812 as 'of scarcely greater elevation in the scale of intellectual being than the oyster: thousands huddled together, one mass of animated filth...'[23a]

It is interesting to note that Shelley and Joyce, both expatriates, had in common debts and afflicted eyes; they shared a prejudice against marriage as an institution and objected to censorship. Shelley's penury was eased with his majority. His 'ophthalmia' caused no permanent damage. Despite his protests against matrimonial bondage he married Harriet Westbrook after the briefest courtship and later married Mary Wollstonecraft Godwin. He wished to express liberal views rather than indulge in freedoms which attracted Joyce and wrote: 'I should consider obscenity to consist in the capability of associating disgusting images with the act of sexual instinct.'[23b]He was more accommodating than Joyce in the matter of censorship — when his publisher, Charles Ollier, felt obliged to withdraw Laoan and Cynthia from circulation Shelley made alterations in sixty-three lines to enable its republication as *The Revolt of Islam* in 1818.

23a. Cited by Richard Holmes in *The Pursuit of Shelley*. London: Quartet Books, 1976, 130.

23b. *Ibid.*, 434.

24. *Letters 2,* 166.

25. Mencken, H.L. *The Vintage Mencken,* ed. Alistair Cooke. New York: Vintage Books, 1955, 180.

the literary renaissance and the Irish Free State.

It is also relevant to say that Joyce's strictures in the opening years of the century did not apply to Dublin alone; he ridiculed France and blasted Austria. If Ireland is paralysed is not Europe similarly afflicted and America beneath his attention?

He wrote to Lady Gregory from Paris on 21 December 1902:

> Paris amuses me very much but I quite understand why there is no poetry in French literature, for to create poetry out of French life is impossible. I have no sympathy with the 'gallant' French. I am glad the Germans beat them and hope they will beat them again...[26]

A letter to his aunt, Mrs. Murray, on New Year's Eve 1904, is far from cheerful:

> I hate this Catholic country with its hundred races and thousand languages... Pola is a back-of-God-speed place... Istria is a long boring place wedged into the Adriatic peopled by ignorant Slavs who wear little red caps and colossal breeches.[27]

His mood is understandable — his publisher 'has smashed', the burden of creativity is unrelieved — explaining to some extent the mood of *Dubliners,* which did not please his Irish acquaintances. Tom Kettle threatened to slate it in the *Freeman's Journal.* James Stephens found it 'anything but representative of Dublin' and Joyce himself in moments of candour agreed that this was so. 'But Ernest [he said to Hemingway in his cups] don't you think what I write is really awfully suburban'.[28]

If I am finally to dispose of the *canard* that Father Flynn had G.P.I., I must refer again to articles in the *Archives* and the *Annals of Internal Medicine* by Dr Burton A. Waisbren. The polarity of our views is, indeed, a confirmation of the taunt that 'doctors differ'. Either he or I is writing nonsense.

Statements which pass muster among literary folk will not be

26. Ms New York Public Library, Berg Collection.
27. *Letters* 1, 57.
28. Hemingway, E. *Selected Letters,* ed. Carlos Baker. New York: Scribner, 1981, 678.

readily accepted by clinicians. Waisbren's claim[29] that every time the letter S occurs in *Ulysses* (from the first upper-case S of *Stately* to the last lower-case s of *Yes*) a symbol for syphilis is intended leaves me aghast and evoked the objections of two New Mexico doctors.[30] Freed from the threat of malpractice suits, which keep American internists on their toes, Waisbren neglects the constraints of differential diagnosis. When Stephen falls in Nighttown, for instance, Waisbren diagnoses syphilis, although any member of the police force could have told him that Dedalus was drunk. He is mistaken, too, in equating a 'steppage gait' with syphilis for actually, as Osler, whose authority he invokes, makes clear, it is a sign of peripheral neuritis.[31] But whether the gaits are jerky, stiff-legged, hobbling or shuffling, Waisbren attributes them all to syphilis.

A foot-note in Florence Walzl's fine essay, 'Joyce's "The Sisters": A Development', records indebtedness to Dr Waisbren[32] but I suspect that his advice has been misleading, for there is insufficient evidence to say that Father Flynn had Parkinson's disease. Waisbren and Walzl designate Father Flynn's tremor as described in the *Homestead* version as an intention tremor[33] but the tremor of Parkinson's disease occurs at rest and is lessened by movement.

Waisbren in his sorties into the field of literary diagnosis has substituted enthusiasm for clinical judgement. His arguments do not hold water.

Moral values have had a bouleversement in our own times and my concern over the diagnosis of a fictional illness may seem disproportionate. Our interpretations, however, should recall values current in the century's opening years. Joyce[34] expected Irish priests to 'denounce "The Sisters"', and said so to Grant

29. Hall, Vernon and Waisbren, Burton, A. Syphilis as a Major Theme of James Joyce's *Ulysses. Archives of Internal Medicine,* 140, 963-965, 1980.
30. Shen, W.W. and Soldo, J.J. *Ibid,* 141, 691-692, 1981.
31. Osler, W. *The Principles and Practice of Medicine.* London: Appleton, 1909, 378.
32. Walzl, F.L. Joyce's 'The Sisters': A Development. *JJQ,* 10, 4, 375-421, 1973.
33. Waisbren, Burton A. and Walzl, Florence L. Paresis and the Priest. *Annals of Internal Medicine,* 80, 758-762, 1974.
34. *Letters* 2, 134.

Richards — madness in a priest is contradictory and sinister. Had an illness acquired through un-chastity been inferred the laity, too, would have been incensed. The idea of a priest dying from G.P.I. would have been unspeakably repugnant to Joyce's Catholic readers at all levels of Irish society. The interpretation, indeed, is not devoid of offence today. It is important, therefore, to confirm that Joyce did not wish so to malign the unfortunate priest and it behoves us to repeat in reparation the closing words of the *Homestead* version of 'The Sisters' — 'God rest his soul!'

5. Did Arthur Symons have GPI?

1

Planning to study at the Catholic University Medical School in Cecilia Street, James Joyce encountered financial difficulties which he hoped to surmount in Paris by giving English lessons. He left Dublin on 1 December 1902 and was met next morning at six a.m. at Euston Station by W.B. Yeats who gave up his day to the indigent student, fed him, introduced him to London editors and took him in the evening to Arthur Symons's elegant flat in Maida Vale.[1] This visit established a lasting link with Symons whose *The Symbolist Movement in Literature* (1899) had kindled Joyce's admiration for the verses of Paul Verlaine.

Joyce and Symons had a good deal in common: they were music lovers; both had experienced a surfeit of religion in boyhood and, as if to compensate, were attracted by the raffish element which Arthur Symons cultivated in London's music halls and the younger man in Dublin's sordid red-light district; their verses were so alike that when George Moore was shown some of Joyce's lines he gave them back to AE (George Russell) with the dismissive comment, 'Symons!' At their first meeting in the Maida Vale flat which Joyce thought 'studiously decadent' Symons sat at the Broadwood piano designed by Burne-Jones and played the Good Friday music from *Parsifal.* 'When I play Wagner,' he said, as he closed the instrument and stood up, 'I am in another world'.

Joyce thought him affected but he held the Irishman's attention with stories of Verlaine, Aubrey Beardsley, Dowson

1. *Ellmann*, 115.

7. W. B. Yeats. Etching by Augustus John.

and Lionel Johnson. He promised to help to find a publisher for Joyce's poems. His goodwill had already been enlisted by Yeats's praise and although he found Joyce 'a curious mixture of sinister genius and uncertain talent' he was determined to do his best for him. He would have been indignant had he heard his departing guests laughing at Yeats's quip: 'Symons has always had a longing to commit great sin, but he has never been able to get beyond ballet girls'.

Failing to establish himself at the Ecole de Médecine Joyce accepted the impossibility of obtaining a medical degree which, as he explained to Lady Gregory, would have enabled him to build up his literary career securely. Obliged to present his work to vacillating editors he was glad to benefit from the advice and influence of Arthur Symons to whom he wrote from Dublin on 14 November 1903. The critic was in Italy and did not reply until the following April. He then wanted to know what had been done with the poems and wished to see them if still unpublished.

Joyce forwarded the verses which form the collection we know as *Chamber Music* and on 4 May Symons wrote to say he thought them 'remarkably good' and merited publication. 'I don't know whether I can do anything, but I will try'[2]

Joyce was to find Symons a punctilious correspondent whom he compared with his brother, Stannie, to the latter's disadvantage: 'Symons... answers my letters by return of post (being an Englishman and a stranger)...'. On 5 May the critic sent the welcome news to Dublin that the editor of the *Saturday Review* had accepted 'Silently she's combing'. Before long he sold two more poems to *The Venture.* When George Duckworth disappointed him he wrote to Grant Richards, a monocled young man whose resources were not equal to his ambitions.

134 Lauderdale Mansions,
Maida Vale W.,
13 July 1904

Dear Grant Richards

I send you Joyce's book of lyrics. Duckworth thinks it too "slight". If you do too will you send it back to the author,

2. *Beckson and Munro,* 91.

whose address is given at the end of his MS. Two of the best poems were cut out by Garnett for the 'Speaker', and two new ones were sent to me on the other day.
We are off to your corner of Cornwall on Friday. I hope we shall see you there.

Yours sincerely,
Arthur Symons.[3]

He wrote to Richards again from Cornwall on 28 July 1904 reaffirming his belief in Joyce — 'I hope you are going to bring out his book: it seems to me so uncommonly good' — but when the critic and the publisher met in the West Country in August the latter said that although he admired the verses he had little hope of selling them. 'Hardly any verse pays', Symons explained to Joyce in a letter written on 23 September 1904.[4] A few days later Joyce wrote to Grant Richards urging him to come to a decision.

In a letter written on the same day[5] to Nora Barnacle, Joyce asked 'do you realise thoroughly what you are about to do' [?]. The couple eloped on 8 October and next day the ungallant lover left Nora alone in a London park and set off for Maida Vale but was disappointed to find that Symons was out. They continued to correspond and after Joyce and Nora had settled in Pola Symons informed him that Richards was bankrupt.

Immediately, Joyce requested the return of his manuscript; he wrote to the firm again on 16 January 1905 demanding a decision by return post and demanding that if the poems were not to be printed they should be sent to him without delay. He was obliged to write to Grant Richards again in May but not until July did the publisher admit that the manuscript had been mislaid, adding that if a copy could be provided the firm, re-constituted under his wife's name, would make an offer for publication.

Grant Richards continued to procrastinate and by October Symons' 'kindly solicitude', as Herbert Gorman called it, for Joyce's career prompted him to recommend *Dubliners* which he had not read.

3. *Ibid*, 93.
4. *Ibid*, 94.
5. *Letters* 2, 56.

> Will you send on approval [he wrote] both your MSS. to Messrs Constable & Co., 16 James Street, Haymarket, W. They have promised to give them attention, but of course it is most uncertain if they will think them likely to make a paying success: that is the difficulty.

Constable turned them down but Grant Richards having finally decided not to publish the verses began to show an interest in *Dubliners* and in February 1906 decided 'to take the risk of its publication'. Authors, like beggars, cannot be choosers; Joyce accepted terms which decreed that no royalty should be paid on the first five hundred copies but was soon engaged in a row with Grant Richards over proposed deletions. When Symons was informed of this unexpected turn of events in the autumn of 1906 he favoured compromise: 'I would be inclined to give in to him [he wrote on 2 October] as far as you can without vitally damaging your work'. He promised to write to Grant Richards urging him not to lose the book.

> Now as to your poems [Symons continued] I feel almost sure that I could get Elkin Matthews to print them in his shilling "Garland" series. You would get little money from him, but I think it would be worth your while to take what he offered — probably a small royalty after expenses are covered. He did for me a little set of translations from Baudelaire's "Petits Poèmes en Prose". The cost was fourteen guineas and it is now nearly covered, when my royalty will begin. Tell me if I may write and advise him to take the book. If it comes out I will give it the best review I can in the "Saturday" or "Athenaeum" and will get one or two other people to give it proper notice.[6]

When Joyce had authorised him to do so, Symons wrote to Matthews:

Island Cottage,
Wittersham,
Kent.
Oct: 9: 06

6. *Beckson and Munro*, 96.

8. Grant Richards in 1893 by William Rothenstein.

My dear Matthews
Would you care to have, for your Vigo Cabinet, a book of verse which is of the most genuine lyric quality of any new work I have read for many years? It is called "A Book of Thirty Songs for Lovers", and the lyrics are almost Elizabethan in their freshness, but quite personal. They are by a young Irishman called J.A. Joyce. He is not in the Celtic Movement, and though Yeats admits his ability he is rather against him because Joyce has attacked the movement. Oddly enough, it is to him that Yeats refers in the prefatory to "The Tables of the Law" in that very series! He is living in Rome now, and will send you the MS if you would care to have it. I have only met him once, and am acting entirely out of admiration of his work. I consider that in offering you this — at my own suggestion, not his — I am offering you a book which cannot fail to attract notice from everyone capable of knowing poetry when he sees it. I should make a point of reviewing it myself in the Athenaeum or Saturday, and would tell others about it.

Yours sincerely,
Arthur Symons.[7]

Joyce sent the manuscript reverting, at Stannie's insistence, to the original title, *Chamber Music,* and on 2 January 1907 Symons posted a letter to him with the news of its acceptance. He returned to Trieste in March and the poems were published early in May. A review of *Chamber Music* by Symons appeared in the *Nation* on 22 June 1907, warmly eulogistic and well-intentioned but couched in a style redolent to-day of preciosity: 'No one who has not tried can realise how difficult it is to do such tiny, evanescent things... for it is to evoke, not only roses in mid-winter, but the very dew on the roses'.

Even the most cynical artist is not averse to praise; whatever Joyce may have thought of the critic's rhapsody — 'they are like a whispered clavichord that someone plays in the evening, when it is getting dark' — he must have come to rely on Symons' encouragement and advice. When *Dubliners* failed to catch a fair wind he asked Symons to recommend a literary agent.

7. *Ibid*, 97.

> The only decent agent I have heard of [the latter replied] is Mr. Watt. I don't know his address but Methuen would know it, and could send on your MS. I wish you could find a publisher. They all seem to object to something or other. Could you not omit it, whatever it might be.[8]

Watt added to Joyce's disappointment by declining to represent him but this was a bagatelle when compared with what lay ahead for Symons. In August 1909, James Joyce's letter from Dublin to his brother[9] contained sinister news: 'Arthur Symons has G.P.I.' Evidently this was no mere rumour. The diagnosis had been confirmed by a London neurologist, Dr. J.S. Risien Russell.[10]

It is impossible to know how this dispiriting development affected Joyce, dependent to some degree on the English literary man who, as Richard Ellmann points out had played 'as central a part in the publication of Joyce's early work as Ezra Pound was to play later'. How horrifying to think that so fine a mind would be destroyed!

Fortunately, the illness did not follow a characteristic course and the diagnosis must be questioned. A diagnosis of G.P.I. cannot, at the time, have surprised Symons' close acquaintances for syphilis would have seemed almost a professional hazard. W.B. Yeats described him as 'a scholar in music-halls as another might be a Greek scholar or an authority on the age of Chaucer... He has gone to travel among them as another might travel in Persia...'. Such excursions entailed the risks inherent in encounters with 'the Juliet of a night' addressed as 'Stella Maris' in *The Yellow Book*:

> Child, I remember, and can tell
> One night we loved each other well;
> And one night's love, at least or most,
> Is not so small a thing to boast.

Symons and Yeats had shared an apartment at Fountain Court in the Middle Temple until the latter, to facilitate an affair with the married lady referred to in his memoirs as Diana Vernon

8. *Ibid*, 98.
9. *Letters* 2, 231.
10. *Lhombreaud*, 247.

(actually Mrs Dorothy Shakespeare) moved to Woburn Buildings.[11] They remained friends and Symons survived his more famous colleague. He was to outlive Joyce, too, and during his last years Arthur Symons was sometimes seen sitting alone in the Café Royal, the sole survivor of his generation. Such longevity is hardly compatible with the diagnosis of G.P.I. and Roger Lhombreaud has argued convincingly that the correct diagnosis was manic-depressive psychosis.[12]

2

Arthur Symons, the second child of Mark Symons and his wife Lydia Pascoe, had Cornish roots but was born on 21 February 1865 in Milford Haven where his father, a Wesleyan preacher, was then stationed. As the Methodist rule obliged its ministers to move to another area every few years, the Symons family lived in many places including Guernsey, St. Ives, Tavistock, Tiverton and Bideford.

The youngster was closer to his mother, a joyous person — 'she felt the sunshine before it came, and knew from what quarter the wind was blowing when she awoke in the morning' — than to his despondent, dyspeptic father, who suffered from migraine. Mark Symons bored his son. 'When he spoke to me of the soul, which he did seriously, sadly, with an undertone of reproach, my whole nature rose up against him. If to be good was to be like this, I did not want to be good.'[13]

He resisted attempts to teach him to read, not learning how to do so until, at the age of nine, he went to school where he failed to understand Euclid, made no more than average showing with maths and algebra, but picked up French and Latin easily. Encouraged by a teacher, Churchill Osborne, he was soon reading omnivorously, delighting in Byron's forbidden pages. Nascent creativity led him, before long, to write his own verses and he became passionately interested in music.

11. *Yeats,* 89.
12. *Lhombreaud,* 250.
13. Symons, A. 'A Prelude to Life' in *Spiritual Adventures.* London: Constable, 1905, 21-22.

His upbringing in the home of a Methodist minister entailed attendance at two Sunday services and family prayers were said regularly. Guilt, evil and hell were spoken of as immediate realities which continued to influence him. After leaving school at seventeen, he remained in correspondence with Osborne, who had engaged increasingly in journalism and was appointed editor of *The Salisbury and Winchester Journal* in 1884.

Symons was not a games player at school. He scorned the values of the crowd, making few friends in the various towns where his family lived, his principal pleasure outside books being long solitary walks:

I have no human love for man, my brother,
My dreams are not his dreams, and I go
A lonely way alone.

At twenty, when the family was living in Nuneaton, Arthur Symons stopped going to church. He read novels and played the piano on Sundays. 'My parents were deeply grieved, but, then as always they respected my liberty.' The rebel continued to live at home, reading and writing, an aspirant man of letters.

Success came slowly and then, as now, budding writers were paid wretchedly. He was a member of the Browning Society through which he met its founder, Frederick Furnivall, who had also founded the New Shakespeare Society and in the 1880s was engaged in publishing a series of Shakespeare Quarto Facsimiles. Furnivall entrusted the introduction to the 12th volume to Symons whose first book, *An Introduction to the Study of Browning* was published in 1886 and favourably reviewed by Walter Pater. His first collection of poems, *Days and Nights,* (1889), was followed by *Silhouettes* (1892), and *London Nights* (1892).

Symons had settled in London by the early 1890s with important studies on Mistral and Villiers de l'Isle Adams to his credit. He visited Paris frequently, becoming friendly with Verlaine and arranging for him to lecture in England in 1893. He joined the regular staff of the *Athenaeum* and was critic of music-hall and ballet for the *Star.* His fellow writers spoke well of him, George Moore, who referred to him as 'a man of somewhat yellowish temperament, whom a wicked fairy had cast for a parson', being a predictable exception. He fell in love with a nineteen year old ballet dancer at the Empire, the 'Bianca' of *London Nights.*

Symons, as Ezra Pound was to point out to Joyce in 1913, was attracted instinctively to the tragic and bizarre. By his fifteenth birthday he had written a monologue called *Mad* and an essay in *The Symbolist Movement in Literature* describes Gerard de Nerval's mental disorder and detention in Dr Emile Blanche's private asylum. This essay contains passages which hint that Symons may already have experienced intimations of how easily sanity is toppled.

> Every artist lives a double life, in which he is for the most part conscious of the illusions of the imagination. He is conscious also of the illusions of the nerves, which he shares with every man of imaginative mind. Nights of insomnia, days of anxious waiting, the sudden shock of an event, any one of these common disturbances may be enough to jangle the tuneless bells of one's nerves. The artist can distinguish these causes of certain of his moods from those other causes which come to him because he is an artist, and are properly concerned with that invention which is his own function. Yet is there not some danger that he may come to confuse one with the other, that he may "lose the thread" which conducts him through the intricacies of the inner world?

A supreme artist, possessing a supreme mind, is immune to this danger and can pass through hell, like Dante, unharmed. It is the vague dreamer, the uncertain mystic, the insecure artist, who are at risk, mastered by the clouded images evoked by their imaginations.

Symons achieved a *succès d'estime* rather than popular acceptance. The press received *London Nights* with 'a singular unanimity of abuse', which he regarded as either ignoble or unintelligent.[14] His delicate verses treated of indelicate matters; instead of the nightingales and Grecian urns beloved of the schoolroom, he highlighted goings-on in sordid corners:

14. Symons, A. Preface to *London Nights*, 2nd ed. London: Smithers, 1897, xiii.

The little bedroom papered red,
The gas's faint malodorous light,
And one beside me in the bed,
Who chatters, chatters, half the night.[15]

He not merely hinted at sexual themes but exalted them in 'Liber Amoris':

What's virtue, Bianca? Have we not
Agreed the word should be forgot,
That ours be every dear device
And all the subtleties of vice,
And in diverse imaginings,
The savour of forbidden things...[16]

In the following decade, now married to Rhoda Bowser, the daughter of a Newcastle ship-builder, he was himself a sufficiently important figure to influence the careers of others. His extensive travels with his wife resulted in *Cities* (1903) and *Cities of Italy* (1907). The purchase of a 12th century property, Island Cottage, at Wittersham, near Rye strained his exiguous financial resources.

Before Arthur and Rhoda Symons left for Italy in September 1908, he outlined his plans in an excited letter to Edward Hutton, the art critic; he proposed to visit Venice, Rome, Naples and Capri and return to Paris in the New Year. In August some of his friends had found Symons 'strange'; the reader of a play on women's suffrage, *The Superwomen,* submitted by him was convinced that it was produced by 'a brain not wholly master of itself.'[17]

The enervating Venetian heat and the suffocating mosquito net disturbed his sleep. He spent his nights writing and an article published by the *Saturday Review* in October contained images of dungeons and the carnality of the Doges that have gained retrospective significance. 'Inexplicable soul of Venice, Satan threw dice with God and won half the game...'.[18]

15. Symons, A. *London Nights,* 2nd ed. London: Smithers, 1897, 46.
16. Symons, A. *Ibid.,* 102.
17. *Lhombreaud,* 239-252.
18. *Confessions,* 10.

To Rhoda's distress her husband left abruptly for Bologna on 26 September. She followed him to the Hotel Brun, where he continued to be oppressed by his surroundings. The enormous courtyard upset him, the massive doors moving on iron hinges jarred his nerves. He felt intensely concerned by the recollection of sins committed and uncommitted. He recalled later in *Confessions* how he visited a circus and talked to the performers — 'one was a queer little girl, who sat on my knees and wickedly caressed me.'[19] He spent another sleepless night in a miserable hotel which reminded him of those frequented by Baudelaire 'when the exasperation of the nerves of Jeanne Duval reacted on him and hurled him on to the pavements of Paris'.

Rhoda was relieved when he rejoined her at the Hotel Brun but he refused to accompany her to London. He decided to go to Perugia but went instead to Ferrara, where he wandered alone in the streets and saw appalling shapes and shadows. He wrote an almost illegible letter ('two scribbled lines') to a friend, the Comtesse de la Tour, from the Hotel Europa, asking for 20 Francs, a useless amount. She sent 100 Francs to pay his bill, inviting him to Frascati as her guest but instead of going there he drifted through the outskirts of the city, losing his direction. He fell into a ditch and slept in a haystack. Finally he was given food in a farmhouse, allowed to sleep in a barn, and directed back to Ferrara where he was apprehended by the police who put him in irons in the cells of the Castello Vecchio. When he attacked the gaolers, they stamped on his bare feet with their hob-nailed boots.

Meanwhile Rhoda had sought the aid of the Italian ambassador in London. A search was mounted and when located he was taken to a neighbouring *Stabilmento di bagni* where his wounds were dressed. He was transferred in due course to an asylum near Bologna and soon taken to England by two male nurses.

Details of the homeward rail journey have not survived but in his *Confessions* Symons recorded his relief to reach England.[20] 'When I saw the white impregnable cliffs of Dover loom up

19. *Ibid.*, 15.
20. *Ibid.*, 29.

before me — yet with I knew not what menace — my heart leapt with joy: that gate of England is always open, and there are always wardens awake at the gate.' At the station he was met by his wife's brother-in-law and a solicitor friend, E.S.P. Haynes. They took him home but in the night, tormented by fears and troubled by delirious hallucinations, he became intensely excited and ran into the street.

A doctor gave him a hypnotic and called in Dr. J.S. Risien Russell, physician to out-patients at the National Hospital, who diagnosed general paralysis of the insane and arranged for his admission to Beacon Court, a private mental home kept by Dr. Albert W. Griffin, at Crowborough, Sussex. Griffin in his report to Rhoda agreed with the diagnosis — 'there is no doubt, or at any rate but very little that Mr. Symons is suffering from the initial stages of General Paralysis...'.[21]

Symons was amused by the medical superintendent's name, Griffin — 'he was the very image of one', he observed, 'but I must say he was most kind to me'. Two warders, an Irishman whom Symons liked and another to whom he did not warm, were placed in charge of him. One evening he escaped and went to a local hotel where he ordered the best food and a bottle of champagne. When given the bill he said, 'Dr. Griffin will pay'. He asked for a car to take him to London but to his chagrin the warders arrived instead, the Irishman treating the matter as a great joke, and took him back to Beacon Court where he resumed his scribbling and read Byron and Burns with exalted pleasure.

When visited by his wife and a woman friend, he said to the latter, 'You and I will people the world with men children.' And he told his wife that he was planning a map of the world.[22] 'I shall divide it into small divisions; each shall have a King and Queen; I have not yet decided as to what these shall be.' He also claimed that he was the Pope.

Beacon Court was expensive so he was moved to Brooke House, Upper Clapton Road, London, and certified insane. W.B. Yeats visited him and told Lady Gregory, 'He is sane when you speak of books, but in a moment wanders away into his

21. *Lhombreaud,* 245.
22. *Confessions,* 33.

madness'. Risien Russell[23] re-examined him, charged two guineas for the consultation and told Mrs. Symons that had there been any doubts in his mind about the diagnosis, these were now dispelled by the delusions which were 'of a kind highly characteristic of General Paralysis'. Symons believed he was a millionaire, promised gifts to those who helped him, accepted an invitation to dine with the king and assumed the title of Duke of Cornwall. He told a friend that he had forty pianos upstairs which Pachman played on. He would break off a conversation by rushing out of the room and stripped himself naked in the garden. He imagined that he was in heaven where the great poets of other times had gathered. The angels stood in groups of three as Symons prepared to receive Swinburne.[24]

Symons' *Confessions: A Study in Pathology,* inspired by de Nerval's *Le Rêve et la Vie,* was written after his recovery and must be treated with a certain reserve as an example of the incoherence of madness rendered coherent and embellished by literary skill. He was enchanted by colours which he believed he had invented and spent much time daubing with a box of paints, copying the whirling masses of serpents that drifted in his mind like incense. 'I prided myself on my prodigious serpents coloured with all the colours I could contrive to accumulate upon them, hugely coiled and convulsed, and cruel...'

Another delusion was that he could compose music which he wrote down and played. 'I really heard every note in my head, and used to play these compositions on an awful piano in the smoking-room which was crammed with people who drank and played cards and smoked their pipes...'[25] He also completed imaginary books: 'These wonderful volumes of mine — so I supposed them to be — were duly written and severely revised and remained heaped up on tables and chairs, awaiting the publication which they never had. There were mystical numbers and all kinds of jargons...'[26] His attempt to translate Balzac's *Une Succube* 'went into its proper limbo'.

These parodies of creative fulfillment did not fully occupy his easily-distracted mind which was obsessed, too, with thoughts of

23. *Lhombreaud,* 247.
24. *Yeats,* 214.
25. *Confessions,* 56.
26. *Ibid.,* 83.

sex and its perversities. 'Even when the body has lost most of its vitality... one's brain and one's imagination are in a state of continual ferment. So, one's sex, when it does not function naturally, functions unnaturally'.[27]

At other times resentment dominated. Inadequate sanitary arrangements were irksome and he hated having to sit at meals at a long table where 'an odious lot of hideous patients were assembled', a doctor at each end. He felt like a caged beast pacing relentlessly, 'all on fire with a life that tingles in every vein and dilates the nostrils'. At night his day clothes were removed and his door double locked with a finality that made him shudder.

He exercised in a garden enclosed by high walls and studied his fellow inmates. 'There was one who seemed raving mad who always walked and cursed and laughed like a hyena.' There was a great Greek scholar who was confined to a padded room 'where he used to exhaust himself with wild leaps in the air, stamping his feet in a regular rhythm (he always said it was the rhythm of the angels)...'

His plight reminded him of the Spanish Inquisition and he believed his keepers to be cruel, inflexible and implacable. They did what they did in cold blood, remorselessly and with abnormal self-confidence. There were other things branded on his memory which Symons preferred not to recall — 'things of the fruitless imagination, of the senseless senses, of the absent instinct, of the deadened impulses, of the checked desires' — remnants from a world of torture and annihilation.[28]

Dr. Risien Russell re-affirmed the diagnosis of G.P.I. on 17 February 1909. He expressed the opinion that the patient's life expectancy was less than two years and waived his fee.[29] His prognosis was almost justified through the agency of pneumonia, which, in the spring of 1909, reduced Symons for weeks to the status of a gibbering, grimacing lunatic. He survived the physical illness, however, and almost imperceptibly his mental condition slowly improved, though for many months he remained suspicious and disturbed, excitable and credulous.

27. *Ibid.*, 84.
28. *Ibid.*, 80.
29. *Lhombreaud*, 248.

Gradually the fiends who were the keepers and the mad people they watched over became more human in Symons' eyes. 'I always loathed being there...', he insisted and, when taken across London for periodic examinations, he envied all in sight, men and women, whores and priests, criminals and rakes. They were free while he, a travelled man of letters, came from a prison to which he would be returned.

Some of the neurologists were encouraging, others not. Their repetitive examinations were resented:

> Always the same, to my mind absurd but inevitable examination: how one's knees dance, how one's pulse beats, one's temperature, sometimes one's blood pressure; mostly one's eyes, in the depths of which are centred one's nerves, with flash lights. Then the questions: one's memory, one's former occupations, one's sense of oneself and of others: and all this, of course, and every examination, had one meaning only — the testing of one's nerves; then the chance of one's recovery. All tried to detect my errors, which varied a good deal: errors, naturally enough in the state I was in just then, which are always supposed to be the proof of an unstable mind.[30]

When his improvement permitted, his friends were occasionally allowed to take him out to museums, galleries or restaurants. Agnes Tobin, an American poet and translator of Petrarch whom, according to Symons, she treated 'without any respect, though with a good deal of affection', was particularly thoughtful in arranging lunches and dinners at the Carlton, Claridges, the Cafe Royal and Treviglio's in Soho. They were generally joined by Augustus John. Had it not been for John's psychological support, Symons averred, he could not have survived the tortures he endured at Brooke House.

One of these outings was to Chelsea to lunch with Stella Conder, the widow of Charles Conder, 'the painter of disillusion', who in February 1909 died insane at Virginia Water Asylum, possibly the victim of GPI. After a meal at which a lot of wine was drunk, he accompanied his hostess upstairs to see

30. *Confessions,* 59.

Conder's paintings and when they were alone she propositioned him.[31]

Augustus John re-introduced him to John Quinn whom, some years previously, Symons had met with W.B. Yeats at Woburn Buildings. Quinn, an American lawyer, collector and patron of the arts, assisted Symons generously by buying whatever manuscripts he cared to send him. Ludwig Mond and many of Arthur Symons' friends also assisted him financially and he received a grant from the Royal Literary Fund.

On 7 April 1910, Arthur Symons was allowed to leave Brooke House, crossing 'that narrow bridge of one step which lies between the Heaven I hoped for and the Hell I had left'.[32] The Board of Control finally discharged him on 6 November 1910.

He lived at Island Cottage, occasionally visiting London and going now and then to France. Roger Lhombreaud divides the years after his illness into three periods: between 1910 and 1919 he slowly recovered his faculties and his publications were mainly based on manuscripts written before his breakdown; between 1919 and 1931, he regained some measure of his previous fecundity and published original material; between 1931 and his death on 22 January 1945, age lessened his vigour and energy. His wife, a victim of leukaemia, predeceased him, dying on 3 November 1936.

It might be argued that Risien Russell was correct and that Symons did have G.P.I., which was influenced beneficially by pneumococcal infection in the same way that the malarial therapy introduced by Wagner von Jauregg in 1917 was effective. This is difficult to accept, however, and the remarkable recovery accords better with the diagnosis of manic-depressive psychosis, suggested by Lhombreaud after discussion with Dr. J.S.I. Skottowe, then at Warneford Hospital, Oxford.

Dr. Griffin of Beacon Court agreed with Risien Russell but, with a note of caution, added, 'there are however just one or two signs that at present do not exist. I only fear they will before long'. He admitted that there have been cases in which experts have been proved wrong.[33]

31. *Ibid.*, 88.
32. *Ibid.*, 88.
33. *Lhombreaud*, 246.

Lhombreaud is incorrect in claiming that the doctors omitted to look for the Argyll Robertson sign commonly seen in neurosyphilis, as Symons' account of the neurological examinations shows that they did so repeatedly. Gerald Cumberland's description of Symons' remarkable eyes dilating with wonder suggests that he did not have abnormal pupils.[34] Frank Harris,[35] on the other hand, recalled in *Contemporary Portraits* Augustus John's unflattering portrait of Symons in 1917 and mentions how 'the lid hangs across the left eyeball like a broken curtain.' Does the detail indicate ptosis and point to an organic component?

Symons did not have the convulsive or paralytic seizures characteristic of G.P.I., but the most telling argument against Risien Russell's diagnosis is the absence of dementia. However grotesque and grandiose his delusions, however unrestrained his behaviour, Symons retained his command of the literature of several languages and after his recovery published important critical studies. Padraic Colum in 1919 acclaimed him as the most influential critic since Walter Pater.

Promiscuity in gas-lit London carried risks already referred to but the wantonness of Symons' verses reflects an urban mood rather than personal predilections. One reviewer of *London Nights* suggested that he was a *poseur* trying to appear a more abandoned sensualist than he really was. 'He does his best to paint exceptional depravity, as if he drew upon his own experience; but to the credit of his morals be it said, the result is unconvincing and unreal.' His ardent romance with Bianca, who was a 'tease', seems to have been unconsummated, or at any rate until they met again after her unhappy marriage. The early lines of 'Liber Amoris', quoted above, are blatantly erotic but lead to the revelation of their agreement that the natural embrace of love shall be,

Too obvious for you and me,
And the one vulgar final act
Remain an unadmitted fact.[36]

34. Cumberland, G. Cited in *Lhombreaud,* 297.
35. Harris, F. Cited in *Lhombreaud,* 268.
36. Symons, A. *London Nights.* 2nd ed. London: Smithers, 1897, 102.

He never forgot her but finally realised that, 'Her most fatal and deadly vice was that she was virtuous; virtuous in the sense in which the world uses it'. By refusing her favours, she had held him helplessly in thrall.

The author[37] of an article published in the *Journal of Medical Psychology* in Symons' lifetime misjudged his character. His indifference to his neighbours in youth was not due to schizoid coldness but to preoccupation with literary matters. As soon as possible he established communication with those in his chosen métier and before long had a host of friends in London and abroad.

It is unlikely that Symons would have disagreed with his biographer's interpretation of his breakdown. He believed that he had inherited madness from certain ancestors. His mother, who died in 1896, was not fully in her right mind for some years before her death. John Pascoe, his uncle, had been in a mental hospital.

And besides, Arthur Symons was aware of his ironic resemblance to his own creation, Christian Trevalga, a character in *Spiritual Adventures* (1905) who loses his reason. He felt that it was as impossible to say how madness begins as to divine why one is sane but knew that 'Great wits are sure to madness near allied'. As Symons saw it, insanity is sometimes a necessary evil; for Gerard de Nerval's genius, for instance, madness had been 'the liberating spirit, disengaging its finer essence'.[38] He saw de Nerval's derangement[39] as 'a fortunate accident' but could hardly have felt equally detached towards his personal experience of insanity which did nothing to enhance his creativity.

3

Joyce used excerpts from reviews of *Chamber Music* in *The Nation* and elsewhere which he had printed in Trieste for advertising purposes. He also sent Symons's review in 1913 to Guido

37. Bragman, L.J. 'The Case of Arthur Symons — the Psychopathology of a Man of Letters'. *Brit. J. Med. Psychol.* 1932, 12, 346-362.
38. *Confessions*, 2.
39. Symons, A. *The Symbolist Movement in Literature*, 2nd ed. London: Archibald Constable, 1908, 34.

Mazzoni who was supporting his application for authorization to teach English in Italian schools. He resumed occasional correspondence with Symons after the latter's recovery. A presentation copy of *Dubliners* which Grant Richards eventually published was gracefully acknowledged:

Island Cottage
June 29, 1914

Dear Mr. Joyce,
No, I have not forgotten you. I still have your verses here. I find a great deal to like in *Dubliners* — unequal as the short stories are, but original, Irish, a kind of French realism, of minute detail, sordid, single sentences tell: I like the kind of abrupt style in the book. "Counterparts" is quite fine — grim humour — a sense of Dublin as I saw it — a lurid glare over it. It gave me a sensation of Fountain Court and the pubs. But the best is the last: the end imaginative.
I have been wandering for the last 3 years as usual. Last November Heinemann printed my *Knave of Hearts* — verse & translations.
By the way not long ago an American magazine printed a MS of mine called "Notes on the Sensations of a Lady of the Ballet" — which I wrote in Fountain Court. So in return I send you a copy.

Yours sincerely,
Arthur Symons.[40]

Grant Richards and Martin Secker rejected *A Portrait* in 1915. Joyce then sent it to Duckworth and explained to his agent, James B. Pinker, that he had invoked Symons' aid, authorizing him to let the critic see the manuscript if he wished to do so. Symons, no longer a force in the publishing world was unable to help and to Joyce's disappointment he did nothing to push the book when it came out in 1917. A presentation copy was not acknowledged.

Despite the vicissitudes which had engulfed Symons he

40. *Beckson and Munro*, 98.

retained for Joyce an enviable aura of success. He urged Robert McAlmon unsuccessfully to get the Englishman to write a short preface for the *Contact Collection of Contemporary Writers* which contained the first version of the 'Earwicker episode' in *Finnegans Wake.*[41]

Symons lived in semi-retirement in Kent but he met Joyce in the summer of 1924 when with Havelock Ellis he visited Paris. They met again in the following year, possibly in Shakespeare & Co, and when Symons expressed a wish to meet Valery Larbaud, Joyce invited the latter to dinner at the Hotel Castile, 37 Rue de Cambon.

Joyce's letters written at this period fail to describe Symons but the latter did record his impression of the middle-aged Irish author. 'Refined, reserved, not without a touch of humour, speaking with a slight Irish accent, he has a fascination which is purely his own: at times, I must confess, diabolical.'

When Rhoda Symons was in Paris in 1926 she lunched with Joyce. She found him charming and hoped to meet him again at Syliva Beach's for, as she explained in a letter to her husband, 'he wants me to bring back his verse, written recently — for you to read and advise upon — said he hadn't the courage to show it to you — I think he's *awfully nice* looking — très croyant evidently...'[42] Arthur and Rhoda Symons restored Joyce's shattered faith in verses which Ezra Pound disparaged. They were published as *Pomes Penyeach* (1927) by Shakespeare & Co.

Symons was one of a hundred and sixty-two signators of a letter of protest against the pirating of *Ulysses* in 1927. He contributed an Epilogue to the *Joyce Book* (1933) which contains the poems of *Pomes Penyeach* set to music. Beckson and Munro suggest that there was delay in its publication for he enquired from Joyce about the book in October 1932: 'Did your book of Poems about which you wrote me in 1930 ever come out? I had the proofs of my *Epilogue* ever so long ago... Last year I brought out my *Wanderings* and *Jezebel Mort and Other Poems...*' In what was probably his last letter to Joyce he expressed delight to have learned that Augustus John was doing Joyce's portrait and

41. *Letters* 3, 118.
42. *Beckson and Munro,* 99.

assured him of his own well-being: 'I am certainly not lacking in spirits'. It would surely have interested him, too, had he known that Joyce's portrait was also painted by Jacques-Emile Blanche a son of Dr Antoine-Emile Blanche in whose *maison de santé* at Passy Gerard de Nerval had sheltered.

The Epilogue to *The Joyce Book* reprints Symons' review of *Chamber Music* and quotes from Joyce's letter to him in 1927: 'As for *Pomes Penyeach* I don't think they would have been published but for Mrs Symons's suggestion when she was with me.'

Comparing Joyce's exile with Byron's, Symons observed that 'Byron suffered, as Pater and Joyce and myself have suffered, from that too vivid sense of humanity which is like a disease, that obsession to which every face is a challenge and every look an acceptance or a rebuff.' Writers were magnets which attracted or repelled all living things, a property which does not make for a man's happiness. 'It leaves him at the crowd's mercy, as he ceaselessly feels the shock of every disturbance which he causes them.'

Joyce's large vocabulary impressed him. He sensed the mediaeval element in Father Arnall's sermon and compared it with his own translation of St. John of the Cross. *Ulysses* was such an outstanding achievement that Joyce 'has been and... will be considered the most complex literary problem of this generation', a *tour de force* which made Symons 'turn to the greatest satire ever written, the *Gargantua* of Rabelais'.

Joyce and Symons never met again. The one, engaged on *Work in Progress,* was attracting increasing notoriety, the other had experienced a diminished authority. Joyce, in his own household, knew the sorrows of mental derangement that Symons had known in person while by a quirk of fate they were both threatened with blindness. On the advice of an eye specialist, Symons submitted to an operation for cataract. Less patient than Joyce, he complained when it was unsuccessful, saying, 'the man didn't know what he was talking about'.

The German occupation of Paris caused the Joyces to join the exodus from the outraged city. Later they obtained sanctuary in Zurich where James Joyce died unexpectedly on 13 January 1941. Symons, for many years a widower, left Kent, a threatened area and sat out the blitz in St. John's Wood, London, old, elegant and still a fascinating conversationalist. When the danger to Kent abated he returned to Island Cottage where he died, possibly from pneumonia, on 22 January 1945.

9. Arthur W. Symons, 1935, by R.H. Sauter.

6. James Joyce and Tom Kettle*

1

As John Stanislaus Joyce was out, Andy Kettle asked the girls to say he'd called. 'You wont't forget now — Mr. Kettle — what you boil water in'. Little Mabel re-told it as a joke but Eva Joyce said: 'It's just as well he didn't know it's Mr. Teapot we boil the water in'. They had no kettle.

The incident is mentioned in Stanislaus Joyce's *Dublin Diary*[1] but Stannie doesn't say what business Mr. Kettle, a prosperous farmer, can have had with his improvident father. They had little in common other than being Parnellites and the fathers of brilliant sons.

Tom Kettle was two years older than James Joyce. Their paths first crossed in 1893 when James and Stanislaus Joyce attended CBS North Richmond Street before moving to Belvedere where in 1897 James Joyce's prizes in the Middle grade of the Intermediate Examinations included £3 for the best English composition, the Senior grade for composition being taken that year by Tom Kettle, then in Clongowes.[2]

They became acquainted in 1898 when Joyce joined the Literary & Historical Society in University College and as the years passed what might be best described as a sort of friendship developed between them, its warmth or lack of it depending on Joyce's state of mind. Herbert Gorman's biography[3] presents Joyce as 'evasive, slightly withdrawn and coldly polite with Tom Kettle who had been magnified by university students into a second Parnell', but according to Stanislaus Joyce his brother

*Presented in abbreviated version to the second Provincetown conference, June 1983.

1. *Diary*, 25.
2. *Results of Examinations and Exhibitions*. Dublin: Intermediate Board.
3. Gorman, H. *James Joyce*. London: John Lane, 1941, 64.

10. Thomas M. Kettle.

valued Kettle's opinion 'because his Catholicism was an intellectual conviction, not just a phase of nationalism', and Constantine Curran recalled Joyce's limerick, an amusing intimation of cordiality:

A holy Hegelian Kettle
Has faith which we cannot unsettle;
If no one abused it,
He might have reduced it,
But now he is quite on his mettle.[4]

They met frequently in the 'L & H' and served on its committee. Both spoke on 28 January 1899 against the motion 'That in the last decade of the nineteenth century English literature has reached a very low ebb.' When Joyce read a paper, 'Drama and Life', on 20 January 1900, Kettle proposed and Skeffington seconded the vote of thanks which, according to Curran, was passed unanimously but with a notable lack of enthusiasm. Joyce and Hugh Kennedy, proposed by Skeffington and Kettle respectively, contested the auditorship for the opening session of the new century. Richard and Eugene Sheehy canvassed for Joyce but Kennedy was elected by fifteen votes to nine.[5]

Joyce presented a paper on Mangan on 1 February 1902 which contained much that was above the heads of his audience, not all of whom were literary, and omitted a lot of what they expected. John E. Kennedy demanded to know whether, behind Joyce's pretentious statements, Mangan was really a drunkard and an opium eater. He pressed the question offensively in a way that distressed Kettle who in a complimentary speech restored the debate to a more courteous line.

Joyce's and Kettle's careers and personalities display interesting parallels and divergences reflecting a shared environment, similar tastes and rather different beliefs and ambitions. They were, for instance, equally superstitious. When preparing the first issue of the *Nationist,* Kettle noticed that his editorial office was lit by three candles and blew out one of them. Ellmann[6] points

4. Curran, C. *James Joyce Remembered.* London: OUP, 1968, 76.
5. Ms/University College, Dublin. Minutes of L & H.
6. Ellmann, 64.

11. *86 St. Stephen's Green, formerly University College.*

12. Kettle cartoon.

out that Kettle was the only student with whom Joyce bothered to discuss Thomistic philosophy and that he pleased Joyce with the comment, 'The difficulty about Aquinas is that what he says is so like what the man in the street says.'

They were both victims of censorship. Father Delany objected to Joyce's *The Day of the Rabblement* and during Kettle's editorship of *St. Stephen's* the Rector ruled out his notice of *Dana*, a new literary periodical edited by John Eglinton (to which Joyce contributed a lyric.) Kettle resigned[7] saying he could no longer work in harmony with an Order that had expelled an eminent thinker [Father Tyrrell] from its ranks. But later Kettle said, 'Tyrrell was never really a Catholic. They let him in without examining his ticket.'

Unlike Joyce, who did not sign the protest against the *Countess Cathleen*, Kettle was one of those who objected to Yeats's play. He probably wrote the letter to the *Freeman's Journal* which Ellmann has described as 'narrow-minded' but his argument was subsequently defended by Curran in *Under the Receding Wave*. Curran claims that the promoters had not fulfilled their promise to provide plays that were exemplifications of Irish life. He adds that Yeats eventually removed as 'encumbrances' the objectionable scenes and points out that the protesters remained among the theatre's most appreciative supporters.[8]

Joyce and Kettle went regularly to the Sheehys' 'at home' at 2 Belvedere Place. Further along the street at number 43 a Cork widow, Mrs O'Brien, kept a boarding house; her teenage son, William, a future trades union leader was called 'hoofie' on account of a club-foot[9]. Have we here the prototype of 'Hoppy' Holohan or a seed for 'The Boarding House', a story in *Dubliners*?

It has recently been suggested that Mary Cleary, who married Professor James N. Meenan, MD, is the model[9a] for Emma

7. Ms/UCD/ CUR L 123.
8. Curran, C. *Under the Receding Wave*. Dublin: Gill and Macmillan, 1970, 104.
9. Keogh, D. *The Rise of the Irish Working Class*. Belfast: Appletree Press, 1982, 53.
9a. Newman House Centenary Exhibition, 1982. To be presented in fuller detail later by Peter Costello.

Clery in *Stephen Hero,* but Mary Sheehy is generally accepted as the original Emma and it is tempting to identify Kettle with Hughes who arouses pangs of jealously in Joyce's surrogate, Stephen Daedalus. 'She spoke to him very little during the evening and seemed to be deep in conversation with Hughes... Stephen glanced from her eyes to Hughes's face and sat down again at the piano.'[10] Hughes is an inferior poet, a contributor to *St. Stephen's* and other periodicals. 'One of these days he will be a barrister...' On these points the identification with Kettle is acceptable but as Hughes is a teacher — 'attendance in Mr. Hughes's class was no longer possible' — and speaks in a northern accent he may be a composite of Kettle and others.

Stanislaus Joyce was also a guest of the Sheehys. He liked Mary's voice and her engaging laugh. 'She seems to be happy and lazy and is often amused. She is very handsome and wears an immense plait of soft black hair.'[11] Emma Clery 'was dressed in cream colour and the great mass of her hair lay heavily upon her cream-coloured neck.'[12]

Eugene Sheehy recalled an outing to the Dublin hills with Joyce, Skeffington and the Sheehy girls.[13] Joyce swaggered along wearing a yachting cap and canvas shoes. He spent his time covertly admiring Mary Sheehy. He capped her comment that the rising moon looked 'tearful' by saying it resembled the chubby hooded face of some jolly fat Capuchin. 'I think you're very wicked', Mary said. 'No', Joyce said, 'but I do my best.' The incident inspired stanzas beginning 'What counsel has the hooded moon/ Put in thy heart, my shyly sweet' included in *Chamber Music.* Mary Sheehy also inspired poem xxv in this collection.

Hanna Sheehy-Skeffington, in an undated interview with Dr Charles Dickson, remembered Joyce as 'gay and boyish, flinging himself into topical charades. He loved to "dress up" and produce plays and parodies, and to sing old folk ballads in his sweet tenor.'[14]

10. SH, 155.
11. *Diary,* 13.
12. SH, 155.
13. Sheehy, E. *May it Please the Court.* Dublin 1951.
14. Sheehy-Skeffington, H. Ms/National Library of Ireland.

Joyce was especially friendly with Richard Sheehy, a good-humoured youth who, making play with his middle name, called him James Disgustin' Joyce. Kathleen Sheehy's conversation after a visit to the Aran Islands was given in 'The Dead' to Miss Ivors who calls Gabriel Conroy a West Briton because he has travelled abroad but does not know his own country. Mrs. Sheehy earned a prominent place in *Ulysses* but she was not immune to disrespect and in 1905 Vincent Cosgrave found it amusing to tell Joyce that her antero-posterior diameter was unaltered.[15]

For Mary Sheehy, the 'sweet sentimentalist' of *Chamber Music* Joyce secretly entertained romantic feelings which he could not express and which embarrassed him in her company. Dancing with Mary he held her in a limp way that made it difficult to follow him. 'Hold my thumb', he suggested when he noticed her difficulty. 'How can I?' she asked with surprise. 'My thumb', Joyce repeated. 'Oh, I thought you said your tongue!' The girl's reply made Joyce whoop with laughter but he remained stiff in her presence.

Like any would-be lover of his years his feelings were both lyrical ('A glory kindles in those eyes, / Trembles to starlight, Mine, O Mine!) and lustful, the latter demanding an immediate expression that most convent-educated girls of that time would have instinctively rejected.

Stephen Daedalus's directness to Emma was calculated to arouse her. 'Do you know, Emma, even from my window I could see your hips moving inside your waterproof?'[16] But his proposition — 'Just to live one night together' — spoke for rampant needs rather than for commonsense; needs vainly augmented by the belief that the girl's virginal rectitude concealed smouldering passion. 'It is very unfair of her to tantalise me. I must go to where I am sure of my ground.'[17]

Joyce was to feel more self-confident with nineteen-year-old Nora Barnacle, a direct and more experienced girl, who rewarded his ardour and accompanied him to a field beside the Dodder where they could lie together. 'You say I am mad', Stephen

15. *Letters* 2, 125.
16. SH, 197.
17. SH, 191.

rebukes Emma, 'because I do not bargain with you or say I love you or swear to you.' Nora accepted Joyce's unconventional terms and won his life-long loyalty.

David Sheehy, MP, was a member of the Nationalist Party; both he and his wife felt that Tom Kettle had a promising political future. They were delighted when he became Mary's suitor but the engagement was protracted for Kettle, unlike Joyce, was not impelled to precipitate consummation. The few existing love letters are lugubrious rather than passionate.[18]

2

In their youth, Kettle was more popular than Joyce and with wider interests. 'He spoke to you', Oliver Gogarty[19] recalled, 'as from some Elysium where everyone was merry, unmalicious and full of gay wisdom'. Kettle would have been voted the more likely to succeed but to-day a comparison of his scattered remnant with Joyce's books is not sustainable. I merely place them side by side so that this Joycean occasion affords an opportunity to re-introduce Kettle, not so much as a tragic 'might-have-been', but in his rightful place on the lower steps of Ireland's literary Pantheon. To borrow Bonnie Scott's words in the *Irish Literary Journal:* 'He merits not just tolerance but appreciation.'[20]

The Day's Burden, a collection of Kettle's essays, does not include his essay on Eoghan Roe O'Neill, a prize-winning item of juvenilia published in the *Clongownian,* or his study of Lionel Johnson in *St. Stephen's* which proclaims an adherence to the faith Joyce had the misfortune to lose. Johnson's work, Kettle tells us, 'is most valuable as the history of a deep Catholic mind gradually coming to terms with modern life and art, thoroughly Pagan as these are in many respects.'[21]

The outstanding literary pieces in *The Day's Burden* are 'Body v. Soul', a review of Francis Thompson's *Health and Holiness,*

18. *Kettle,* 147-149.
19. Gogarty, O. St J. *Start From Somewhere Else,* 76. New York: Doubleday, 1955.
20. Scott, B.K. 'Appraisals: Thomas Kettle: 1880-1916.' *Journal of Irish Literature,* 3, 2, 75-91, 1974.
21. Kettle, T.M., 'Lionel Johnson.' *St. Stephen's,* 1903, 1, 10, 210-213.

and 'The Fatigue of Anatole France', but even Kettle's journalism was endowed with striking images. Describing a socialist meeting, he asks: 'in which of all the Utopias, smouldering in certain fierce eyes that met yours today in Stuttgart will there be no stain of the burden and sorrow of women?'

The influence of Chesterton is evident in the essay on Francis Thompson or perhaps it is only an affinity; GKC was Kettle's senior by six years.

> When a man's eyes [Kettle wrote] have been once opened the common day flames and vibrates with bladed chariots. The most insignificant object or experience stands vested with endless relations, or rather there is nothing that can any longer be called insignificant. The lightest caprice of love has its metaphysical implications and to salute a primrose is to proclaim a philosphy.[22]

Counterbalancing the enhanced perception is an awareness of miseries derived, presumably, from Kettle's ill-health, a cognisance 'of lives that have become a dread Rosary in which there are only sorrowful mysteries.'

Kettle's graceful essay on Anatole France is appreciative of 'the great French master of irony, tenderness, and despair', but he is prepared to chide him in a certain respect: 'Anatole France is a scandal and a stumbling block to many serious minds. Of the deep waters of religion he has never tasted; he is a sense short, or, as the psychologists say, he has a blind spot on his soul.' Towards the conclusion of this essay there is a passage which could serve as an analysis of Kettle's own philosophy:

> A pessimism stabbed and gashed with the radiance of epigrams, as a thundercloud is stabbed by lightning, is a type of spiritual life far from contemptible. A reasonable sadness, chastened by the music of consummate prose, is an attitude and achievement that will help many men to bear with more resignation the burden of our century.[23]

Joyce praying in Trieste for a change of fortune promised if it

22. *New Ireland Review*, 1905. 23, 237-243.
23. 'The Fatigue of Anatole France.' *Fortnightly Review*, 1909. 352-358.

were granted to go to Paris 'where, I believe, there is a person by the name of Anatole France much admired by a Celtic philologist by the name of Goodbetterbest [Richard Best] and I'll say to him 'Respected master, is this pen pointed enough?[23a] He was indebted to France for the inspiration of two stories in *Dubliners,* 'Ivy Day in the Committee Room' and 'The Dead'[23b]

Kettle defined an epigram, in his introduction to *Irish Orators and Oratory,* as 'the image that closes up in a little room the infinite riches of an argument.'[24] On another occasion he twisted Marlowe's lovely phrase to dismiss the Arts Club as 'infinite bitches in a little room'. His most polished essay praises Nietzsche: 'He was abundantly dowered with the insight of malice, and malice always writes briefly and well. It has not the time to be obscure.'[25]

Neither Joyce's nor Kettle's verses are highly regarded but they both wrote at least one perfect poem, Joyce's exquisite 'Ecce Puer' and Kettle's passionate anti-war sonnet 'To my daughter Betty'. They both indulged, too, in an efflorescence of temperament — Joyce's 'Gas from a Burner' and Kettle's 'Ballade Autumnal', which Katharine Tynan thought worthy of François Villon. The editor of the *Clongownian* had been promised something but Kettle procrastinated until a friend told him that the priests were disappointed and they were talking about his drinking. There and then, in the bar of the Wicklow Hotel, Kettle wrote down the Ballade with its confessional refrain, *We have not lived as wisely as the rest.*

Kettle's unwisdom lay in his heavy drinking but when one recalls that Stanislaus Joyce blamed Gogarty for his brother's abuse of alcohol it is amusing to read Mrs. Gogarty's letter to Kettle blaming James Joyce for leading her son astray.

> You can do him an inestimable service, [she wrote] by your companionship and advice to counteract the bad effects of others, one, especially a bad Catholic who spent a great deal of time with Oliver last winter before I discovered he was, or

23a. *Letters* 2, 110.
23b. *Ellmann,* 262.
24. Kettle, T.M. *Irish Orators and Oratory,* 1915, XVI. Dublin: Talbot Press.
25. Kettle, T.M. Introduction to *The Life of Friedrich Nietzsche* by Daniel Halevy, translated by J M Hone. London, 1911.

> pretended to be an Agnostic, so I forbade him to call here any more.[26]

Reviewing *Poems and Parodies,* Katharine Tynan[27] accepted frankly and fairly that Kettle 'had not made a business nor a profession of poetry... Much of the contents of this book are verses *à servir.* One is tolerably certain that he himself would not have included them.' She appreciated his gifts, regretting that they remained — apart from two perfect sonnets — largely latent. 'He had when he chose an extraordinary deftness in poetry... his imitations or adaptations of Kipling are so good that one grudges them.'

William Dawson found Kettle 'national in his soul and cosmopolitan in his outlook'; he has found 'an Elsinore in Earlsfort Terrace and an 'Arden' in Artane'. But Dawson's stylistic enthusiasms ruled, however correct his analysis: 'The aid of apt alliteration he availed of amply... He combined the wit of Wilde with the cheeriness of Chesterton.'[28]

It would be unrealistic to compare Joyce's and Kettle's writings but now and then one is struck by these word-masters' use of an unusual adjective such as *circumambient* in Oxen of the Sun (420) and in Kettle's 'November First: the Day of All the Dead'[29] or by the resemblance, however vague, between an unpublished fragment in Kettle's papers —

> I admit to the dreams we have betrayed. How they sweep by in a trampling tumult with waving hair and all the anguish of all the world's fallen women in their eyes[30]

— and Joyce's more decorated passage in *Ulysses:* 'And on the highway of the clouds they come, muttering thunder of rebellion... trooping to the sunken sea...' (411).

Lynch issued a warning against Nighttown in *Stephen Hero:* 'You may get a dose that will last you your life. I wonder you have not got it before this.'[31] Kettle's admonition was more formal:

26. *Kettle,* 54.
27. Tynan, K. *Studies,* 1917, 206-207.
28. Dawson, W. *Ibid,* 1931, 598-610.
29. Kettle, T.M. *The Day's Burden.* Dublin: Browne and Nolan, 1937, 197.
30. Ms/UCD, Curran papers.
31. SH, 192.

> After all, the richest and most reckless voluptuary soon comes to the frontier of pleasure; he may disregard the prescriptions of morality, but the outraged divinities of hygiene will lay him by the heel.[32]

In his maiden speech in the House of Commons on 2 May 1907, Kettle said: 'It spite of the many reverses with which we have to deal Dublin doesn't stand still but progresses.'[33] What could be more clearly opposed to the concept of 'paralysis' expounded by *Dubliners*? On another occasion Kettle said:

> It would be absurd to call this capital a poor city. There is no luxury so recondite that Dublin is not able to afford it. I have often found words choking in my throat as I took French, American or German journalists along that glorious coast-line jewelled everywhere with rich and beautiful villas which runs from about Lansdowne Road to Greystones. Confronted with it, how could I call Ireland the poorest country in Europe?[34]

He knew the other side of the coin, too, and when a tenement house collapsed in Church Street in 1913, he said, referring to Dublin's housing: 'As a citizen of Dublin I rend my garments and cry for forgiveness at the word. The mansion-slums of Dublin go as close as any national fact can go to a denial of the ways of God.'[35]

Perhaps we should ask ourselves whether Kettle's unequivocal statement or Joyce's vague innuendos have the greater force. I am sure that the utterances of men like Martin Luther King and Jesse Jackson have done more to redress a deplorable situation than the books of any contemporary American novelist.

3

The important student activities in University College in the early years of the century included the Library Conferences at which a member of the Sodality read a paper on a theme related to

32. Kettle, T.M. Ms/UCD, Curran papers.
33. *Hansard*, 2 May 1907.
34. Kettle, T.M. *Freeman's Journal*, 24 September 1913, 8.
35. Kettle, T.M. *Ibid*, 24 September 1913, 8.

13. Padraic Colum. Medallion by G. Spicer-Simpson.

Catholic beliefs on literature. Joyce attended at least two of these and joined in the discussion. He was present on 16 June 1901 when Father Henry Browne, SJ, spoke on *My New Curate* and on 2 February 1902 when J.F. Byrne read a paper on *The Imitation of Christ* — these dates, the future 'Bloomsday' and Joyce's birthday form an interesting coincidence for which prophetic significance can hardly be claimed.

Kettle's name does not appear in the Library Conference Minute Book for the years 1901-1903 but he presented a paper, 'Art for art's sake', on 7 December 1904 and was among those who discussed (29 January 1905) Felix Hackett's paper, 'The old riddle and the newest answer', dealing with Father John Gerard's criticism of Haeckel, and William Dawson's paper (12 March 1905), 'The place of the layman in the Church.'[36]

Kettle lived at Tritonville Cottage, Cranford Place, in 1903 and on summer evenings he walked with his friends on nearby Sandymount Strand. Padraic Colum recalled an evening when he and Kettle were joined by Joyce and Gogarty. Joyce's mother's death had left him despondent and introspective.

> His was the talk of one for whom all thought was in a few pages of Aristotle or Aquinas, all poetry in a few lyrics of Shakespeare's or Ben Johnson's, or in that lyric of Shelley's which he would repeat so beautifully, 'False friend, wilt thou smile or weep when my life is laid asleep?' All drama in Ibsen's 'Hedda Gebler'. Gogarty, of course, was the wit of Dublin. But when he repeated a passage of Swinburne's or some Greek poet's it was with joy. Kettle had taken to Schopenhauer — the greatest Christian apologist, he declared, because he had made the doctine of redemption necessary. And he spoke of the Danish philosopher Kirkegaard, who has now become fashionable — he was the first I had heard speak of him — he had read Kirkegaard, I suppose, in a German translation.[37]

Aware that Joyce's venture in the Ecole de Médecine had come to nothing, Kettle suggested sympathetically that he should stay at home and start in Trinity College. This was not to be; instead on 12 October 1904, accompanied by a companion more resolute than the Eveline of *Dubliners,* Joyce set off for Europe.

A few weeks after his arrival in Pola there were student demonstrations, the indirect outcome of riots in Innsbruck where Kettle had happened to spend most of that summer. Italian-speaking law students demanded their own university in Trieste while the Germans insisted that their traditions must not be changed. Kettle watched the Italians retreat into the Café Flunger and bar the doors against their adversaries who to his amusement stood in the street shouting 'Boycottieran Flunger!' It was so like the unresolved 'university question' at home.

Joyce and Kettle both appreciated the value of the boycott, a revolutionary Irish invention. They were in broad agreement,

36. Ms/UCD. Minutes of the Library Conference.
37. Colum, P. 'Tom Kettle: A Memory'. *Dublin Magazine,* XXIV, 28-35, 1949.

too, in their support for the movement for national independence. Kettle saw Ireland separated from England by 'the Irish Sea, the Act of Union and the perorations of the Tory party'; Joyce said 'St George's channel makes an abyss deeper than the ocean between Ireland and her proud dominator.'[38] They differed fundamentally, however, as to how Irish independence might be secured.

With almost mystical fervour, Kettle regarded parliament not as 'a mere gabble and squabble of selfish interests' but as the State in action. 'And the state is the name by which we call the great human conspiracy against hunger and cold, against loneliness and ignorance; the State is the foster-mother and warden of the arts, of love, of comradeship, of all that redeems from despair that strange adventure which we call human life.'[39] For him Fenianism was the fountain from which all subsequent Irish movements had sprung. 'But for the movement for which Allen, Larkin and O'Brien had gone to the scaffold the revolution under Parnell would have been impossible.' He managed to see the Irish parliamentary party as the orthodox spearhead of the separatist movement and refused to accept Sinn Féin's proposal to withdraw from Westminster. 'My answer is that what was good enough for Parnell is good enough for me.'

Joyce, more prosaically, believed the parliamentary party to be a discredited group which had talked fruitlessly for almost thirty years and had 'sold their leader, Parnell, to the pharisaical conscience of the English Dissenters without exacting the thirty pieces of silver.'[40] He regarded Sinn Féin as 'the new Fenians'.

From Trieste Joyce kept in touch with Dublin and wrote anxiously to Stannie in 1905 to enquire about the manuscript of *Stephen Hero* which, according to Charlie Joyce, Curran had passed on to Kettle. 'You must get it from Kettle at once and send it to me safely registered. Kettle, of course, is a decent kind of fellow but some of those imposters might wheedle it from him. He is too polite to suspect treachery.'[41]

As soon as Stannie heard of the manuscript's casual handling

38. *Critical Writings*, 199.
39. Kettle, T.M. *The Day's Burden*. Dublin: Browne & Nolan, 1937, 16.
40. *Critical Writings*, 196.
41. *Letters* 2, 114.

14. Bust of Kettle in St. Stephen's Green.

15. Bust of Joyce by Marjorie Fitzgibbon in St. Stephen's Green.

he dressed and went to Kettle's office. He called four times and went once to Curran's house. He had retrieved the precious pages by the following morning but Kettle said it was safe in his hands and Curran thought Stannie was being unduly fussy.

> When I went [Stannie wrote] to get back your Ms. from Kettle he told me — you know the way he talks, as if he was afraid someone in the next room might hear him and breathing out a weak laugh at every second word — that his *soul* wasn't in his work. I said I thought the idea of the *Nationist* was his. He wouldn't be sorry if he were out of it; he didn't take much interest in what boots people wore (saving your presence, in glancing over the pages of advertisements, the price lists for "ladies knickers" was the first thing that caught my eye).'[42]

Curran, perhaps to make up for his indiscretion with the manuscript, reminded Stannie that Kettle was now editor of the *Nationist* which might provide a market for Joyce's poems and stories. Stannie proposed to offer him 'Bid Adieu'.

When Stannie decided to join his brother in Trieste, the latter empowered him to tell Kettle. 'You can tell Kettle you are going, if you like, and you can sell him any of the songs you like provided he pays you the money for them.'[43] In the following year he complained from Rome that he had not been told of Kettle's election as M.P. for East Tyrone. 'I suppose it is by merest chance I learn this. Who knows what else has taken place in Dublin?'[44]

In another mood he intimated that Kettle's election did not interest him. When Stannie objected Joyce disavowed interest in parliamentarianism and described himself as unsuited to male friendship. Nevertheless, he asked Aunt Josephine to send a copy of the *Nationist.*

Joyce's indifference toward Kettle changed when the latter praised *Chamber Music* on 1 June 1907 in the *Freeman's Journal.* Kettle's review actually gave more space to *The Town Tenants Act, 1905* by his contemporaries, Arthur Clery, Hugh Kennedy and Michael Ponsonby, and a slight sting was intended in the reference to a lack of national feeling.

42. *Ibid,* 117.
43. *Ibid,* 122.
44. *Ibid,* 147.

> The title of the book [Kettle wrote] evokes that atmosphere of remoteness, restraint, accomplished execution characteristic of its whole contents. There is but one theme behind the music, a love, gracious — and, in its way, strangely intense, but fashioned by temperamental and literary moulds, too strict to permit it to pass ever into the great tumult of passion. The inspiration of the book is almost entirely literate. There is no trace of the folk-lore, the folk-dialect, or even the National feeling that have coloured the work of practically every writer in contemporary Ireland. Neither is there any sense of that modern point of view which consumes all life in the languages of 'problems'. It is clear, delicate, distinguished playing, of the same kindred with harps, with wood-birds, and with Paul Verlaine.

The acceptance of his verses as 'different' and the comparison with Paul Verlaine would have pleased Joyce. He sent the reviewer a note of thanks which has not survived and was determined to look him up when he visited Dublin aware that Kettle, by then a public figure, was in a position to pull strings.

When Joyce came to Dublin in 1909 he must have missed Kettle narrowly at Dr Robert Kenny's funeral which they both attended on 3 August, an act of piety on Joyce's part towards his mother's doctor and on Kettle's towards a political associate. They eventually met on August 10. Kettle seemed friendly and willing to help. He suggested that Joyce should apply for a chair in Italian at the new university but when this turned out to be a lectureship in commercial Italian Joyce aspired instead to an examinership.

He was disappointed to receive no invitation to 2 Belvedere Place but fascinated to learn that Kettle was to marry Mary Sheehy, whose beauty had once disturbed him, on September 8th. With surprising tact he decided not to show Kettle the manuscript of *A Portrait.* He was not invited to the wedding but attended a pre-wedding celebration in the Gresham Hotel on September 5th. He sent a presentation copy of *Chamber Music* and invited the Kettles to visit him in Trieste during the honeymoon. Joyce urged Nora to prepare for their arrival, to have a piano there and to see that her dresses were right. He said Kettle was his best friend in Ireland, adding a characteristic 'I think'. He told her how helpful he had been. 'He is a good-hearted fellow and I am sure you will like his wife.'[45] He did not mention his own erstwhile passion for Mary Sheehy.

The newly-weds spent the first days of their honeymoon in Geneva where Tom wished to attend the Jeunesse Egyptienne Congress at which he delivered a fiery speech demanding liberty for Egypt. They proceeded to Austria but did not take up Joyce's invitation.

When Joyce returned to Dublin in 1909 to open a cinema he was alarmed by the plight of his indigent brother, Charlie, who was on his uppers in Boston, Massachussetts. 'You see Charlie is in a bad way [he wrote to Stannie]. I wish I could do something for him with T.M.K. but cannot in face of later developments.'[46] What were these developments? It is unlikely that the Kettles' failure to turn up in Trieste still rankled. Was Joyce at odds with the Sheehys who had snubbed him?

Towards the end of 1911 George Roberts, the managing-director of Maunsel & Co the firm which agreed to publish *Dubliners*, sent Kettle's *Home Rule Finance* to Joyce who disapproved of the binding and lettering and hoped for something better for his own book. Roberts, on the other hand, was uneasy about Joyce's stories and continued to postpone publication.

When Joyce visited Dublin again in 1912 he sought Kettle's aid. Roberts was under an obligation[46a] to Kettle who had recommended him as printer and publisher to the National University of Ireland, where he held the chair of economics, and might have been an acceptable arbitrator. But Kettle disliked what he had read of *Dubliners* and attacked it.[47] 'Oh, I'll slate that book when it comes out,' he promised. 'I'll slate it!' He objected particularly to 'An Encounter', the story based on the events of a day when James and Stanislaus Joyce 'mitched' and encountered a middle-aged pederast. 'For us', Stannie recalled, 'he was just a "juggins".' They sensed something odd and unhealthy about him, not fully understanding the nature of his menace. Joyce

45. *Ibid*, 247.
46. *Ibid*, 262.
46a. Harvard, bMs Thr 24 (144).
47. Joyce, S. *My Brother's Keeper*, 1958, London: Faber, 79.

pointed out to Kettle that the story was factually based. Kettle waved away the explanation. 'I know', he said, 'we've all met him.' He also believed that the publishers risked libel suits.

When eventually *Dubliners* was published by Grant Richards on 15 June 1914 Kettle was embroiled in the affairs of the Irish Volunteers and had no opportunity to review it. We lack an extended account of his objections but Kettle's review of William Barry's *Heralds of Revolt* (1904) provides insights into his views on a critic's duties. 'The first and most indispensable quality of a critic is to have himself struck out a philosphy, a theory of experience; his next is the capacity to project himself into the thought-fabrics of other men; and the finished outcome of his activity is a valuation of ideas and achievements in the light of what he considers the true laws of existence.'

Kettle accepted that the criticism of imaginative works required 'quick artistic sympathy and the power to penetrate the shell of image and fable' revealing the underlying philosophy determining their creation. And most important of all the critic should ask is the book true to the actual laws of life?

> For literature [Kettle wrote] is no abstraction, no neutral arena in which hostile philosophies can forget their hostility; on the contrary, it is the highest and most perfect enunciation of these hostilities, which are external and not to be reconciled. Flaubert dreamed of an impersonal novel — a story from which the author would eliminate himself. But the thing is impossible. 'A novel', and it is Zola who says it, 'is a corner of reality viewed through a temperament'; it is experience coloured by a system of ideas; and if these ideas are radically false, the novel, however powerfully written, is bad art.[48]

Kettle was staunch to the Catholicism Joyce had rejected and believed that it should 'be kept in the forefront of all movements literary and social, contributing to them beneficial forces, standing out through the medium of criticism against those which it perceives to be maleficient.'[49] *Dubliners* makes no attack on Catholic doctrines and if Kettle adhered to the rules laid down in his review he may have felt that the 'corner of reality' (Dublin)

48. Kettle, T.M. *New Ireland Review*, 22, 248-251, 1904.
49. Kettle, T.M. *Ibid*, 251.

was distorted by the vagaries of Joyce's temperament. His reasons for disliking *Dubliners,* however, were probably more personal: like James Stephens and others he would have reacted to the representation of Ireland's capital as a graceless city.

4

At the outbreak of war Kettle was in Belgium buying arms for the Irish Volunteers. Temporarily he acted as a correspondent for the *Daily News.* 'There is no calculus of suffering [he wrote] that can sum up the agonies endured since the sentence of blood was daubed on the lintel of every cottage in Europe.'[50] On his return to Ireland he volunteered for service and was commissioned in the Dublin Fusiliers. Because of his poor health and oratorical powers he was posted to duties as a recruiting agent in Ireland and the north of England but after the rebellion at Easter 1916, to which he was opposed, he demanded to be sent to France on active service. He perished in the Battle of the Somme on 9 September 1916 and from Zurich, a neutral city, Joyce sent a letter of condolence to his widow.[51]

Kettle had lent something to the creation of Robert Hand[52] and had influenced *Exiles* in other ways. Hand's epigram, 'If Ireland is to become a new Ireland, she must first become European', echoes Kettle's, 'My only counsel to Ireland is, that to become deeply Irish, she must become European', and Hand's claim to be 'a descendant of the dark foreigners' recalls Kettle's pride in his Norse ancestry: 'We came up out of the sea along the Black Beach. We won all before us. We won it with our battle-axes. We have been in the neighbourhood ever since.'[53]

Joyce used an extract from Kettle's review of *Chamber Music* — 'A rare and exquisite accent... lyrics which, although at first reading so slight and frail, still hold one curiously by their integrity of form' — in a notice printed for him in Trieste and sent to Grant Richards to be inserted in press copies of *Dubliners.* In January 1927 he asked Stannie, who had stayed in Trieste, to

50. Kettle, T.M. *The Ways of War,* London: Constable, 1917, 63.
51. *Letters* 1, 96.
52. Ellmann, 300.
53. *Kettle,* 17.

send him 'Lecky and Kettle's two books'.[54] He was then working on *Finnegans Wake* where Kettle is securely memorialised the most unequivocal reference being 'the high priest's hieroglyph of kettletom and odd bones.'[55]

Kettle is therefore entitled to an astral place, however remote, in the crowded literary skies under which Joyce's art was nurtured. He merits his own place, too, in our consideration because of his endearing personality and on account of books and articles which deserve wider reading.

54. *Letters* 3, 149.
55. FW, 122. 7.

7. Anatomy in *Ulysses**

A first visit to Chartres, or Rheims, or any great European cathedral city is an exciting event. The immense structure dwarfs the viewer; the shadows in the nave, the highlights of the stained glass stun the imagination; only on subsequent visits does the detachment of familiarity permit an examination of details, the intricacy of the vaulting or the grimacing gargoyles. Similarly with *Ulysses:* on first reading James Joyce's novel one is hypnotised by word music and captivated by Buck Mulligan, the Blooms, Dedalus *père et fils* and a host of minor characters. Re-reading allows consideration of Homeric parallels, symbolism and the rest which have been discussed — dare one say *ad nauseam?* — in innumerable books and articles. Surprisingly, relatively little has been written about its anatomical content.[1]

Joyce told his friend Frank Budgen, 'Among other things my book is the epic of the human body. The only man I know who has attempted the same thing in Phineas Fletcher. But then his Purple Island is purely descriptive, a kind of coloured anatomical chart of the human body. In my book the body lives in and moves through space and is the home of a full human personality'.[2] Writing to Carlo Linati, his Italian translator, on 21 September 1920, he described *Ulysses,* then nearer to completion, as 'an epic of two races (Israelite-Irish) and at the same time the cycle of the human body as well as a little story of a day'.[3] Tokens of sleep and

*Presented to the University of New Mexico's James Joyce Symposium, Albuquerque, New Mexico, 14th June 1981.

1. Lyons, J.B. *The Practitioner.* 1972, 209, 374-379.
2. *Budgen.* 21.
3. *Letters* 1, 146.

awakening, birth and death, ingestion, defecation, menstruation and copulation, those events which form the physical cycle of our lives, are supplied by the Blooms, Mrs Purefoy, Paddy Dignam, Blazes Boylan, Molly and others.

Joyce also sent Linati what he called 'a sort of summary-key-skeleton-schema' for *Ulysses.* In the following year he gave Valery Larbaud a slightly different schema which was eventually used by Herbert Gorman and published in Stuart Gilbert's *James Joyce's 'Ulysses'*[4]. It tabulates (Table 1) the titles of the episodes with the appropriate hour, organ, art, colour, symbol and technic for each.

Table 1. Organs in Gilbert-Gorman schema.

	Episodes	**Organs**
1.	Telemachus	—
2.	Nestor	—
3.	Proteus	—
4.	Calypso	Kidney
5.	Lotus-eaters	Genitals
6.	Hades	Heart
7.	Aeolus	Lungs
8.	Lestrygonians	Esophagus
9.	Scylla & Charybdis	Brain
10.	Wandering rocks	Blood
11.	Sirens	Ear
12.	Cyclops	Muscle
13.	Nausicaa	Eye Nose
14.	Oxen of the Sun	Womb
15.	Circe	Locomotor apparatus
16.	Eumaeus	Nerves
17.	Ithaca	Skeleton
18.	Penelope	Flesh

4. Gilbert, S. *James Joyce's Ulysses: A Study.* Harmondsworth: Penguin Books, 1963, 38.

Confining ourselves to the organs mentioned by Joyce, it is difficult on first consideration to credit a meaningful representation of anatomical structure in his pages but careful examination entailing, indeed, a dissection or teasing out of the text, does confirm a surprising number of correspondences either with the nominated organ, or a variant, or a manifestation of its functions. There is no organ for the first three episodes, for Telemachus does not yet possess a body. The kidney is the organ of the Calypso episode in which we first meet Leopold Bloom. 'Most of all he liked grilled mutton kidneys which gave to his palate a fine tang of faintly scented urine...'. In the pork-butcher's, 'His hand accepted the moist tender gland...' The word kidney occurs eleven times in this episode and excretion is featured in a variety of ways: the chamber-pot, Mrs. Bloom's soiled drawers, her husband's easful evacuation in the outside lavatory, the 'flop and fall of dung' in the cattle market, the hen's droppings in a neighbouring garden. A watering cart, rain, thirst, the steaming kettle and the teapot may be indirectly relevant.

Rather than attempt to discuss the episodes seriatim I shall refer to some of the more unequivocal correspondences. The heart, the organ of 'Hades' is mentioned at least forty-one times: 'He took it to heart', 'Wear the heart out of a stone', 'good-heartedness', 'the Sacred Heart', 'Heart on his sleeve', etc. Bloom's attitude is just as detached as a modern cardiologist's: 'Seat of affections. Broken heart. A pump after all, pumping thousands of gallons of blood every day. One fine day it gets bunged up and there you are. Lots of them lying around here: lungs, hearts, livers. Old rusty pumps: damn the thing else'.

The lung is the well-chosen organ of the 'Aeolus' episode but structure is less evident than the subsidiary functions: 'flatulence', 'wind off my chest', 'inflated windbag', 'blowing out', 'loud cough', 'puffing', 'panting', 'grunting'. We encounter 'breathless', 'breath of life', and 'you take my breath away', but there is no indication of the interchange of gases which is the essence of pulmonary function. Richard Ellmann[5] has indicated additional devices — paired phrases and words, e.g. 'Scissors and

5. Ellmann, R. *Ulysses on the Liffey*. London: Faber, 1972, 72.

paste', 'Way in. Way out'; opposed actions, doors opening and closing, trains stopping and starting, people coming and going; inflated newspaper headlines — which represent respiratory inspirations and expirations.

'Sirens', the most melodious episode in the book, features in addition to songs a variety of sounds, 'hoofirons, steelyringing', and the creaking of shoes. Its overture presents barmaids listening to a vice-regal procession passing the Ormond Hotel; at the finale 'an unseeing stripling' stands in the doorway his blindness making hearing more vital than ever. The ear is the episode's organ occurring at least seventeen times in its own right and present, too, in other words (n*ear*, an*ear*, an*ear*by, h*ear*d), synonyms ('red lugs', 'Lugugugubrious', 'peeping lobe', 'purply lobes') and by implication in the imperative 'Listen!' as well as negatively in 'deaf Pat' and 'Pat doesn't hear.'

I am uncertain whether additional conjunctions and dispositions of the letters 'e', 'a', 'r', are to be included — c*rea*m, b*rea*th, p*aper*, *sea*ho*r*n, ho*arse*ly — possibly straining credulity, but the terms tympanum, drum, and shell are certainly relevant. The following passage illustrates Joyce's method:

> Ah, now he heard, she holding it to his ear. Hear! He heard. Wonderful. She held it to her own and through the sifted light pale gold in contrast glided. To hear.
> Tap.
> Bloom through the bardoor saw a shell held at their ears. He heard more faintly that that they heard, each for herself alone, then each for other, hearing the plash of waves, loudly, a silent roar.
> Bronze by a weary gold, anear, afar, they listened.
> Her ear too is a shell, the peeping lobe there (280).

In Gilbert's schema the genitals are the organs of the Lotus-eaters' episode but the correspondences in the book are vague ('Venereal diseases'; 'Women all for caste until you touch the spot.' 'Gelded too; a stump of black guttapercha wagging limp between their haunches'. 'Angry tulips', 'Eunuch') until we see Bloom in his bath: 'the dark tangled curls of his bush floating, floating hair of the stream around the limp father of thousands, a languid floating flower.' (88)

The organ given for this episode in the Linati schema is skin and while experts in amatory titillation will protest that skin can be subsumed under a sexual rubric this is a surprising divergence. Correspondences for skin are, however, easily found and Denis McCarthy, MD, has reminded me that formerly dermatologists also practised venereology:

> By Brady's cottages a boy for the skins lolled... A smaller girl with scars of eczema on her forehead eyed him... (72)

The word skin occurs five times in the short episode; we also encounter 'skinfood', '*Peau d'Espagne*', 'scalp' and 'armpit'. The beauty of a female complexion is mentioned — 'It certainly did make her skin so delicate like white wax' — substances pertaining to its nurture are prominent — soap, lotions, ointments and perfumes.

Blemishes are additional inverse tokens of Joyce's intention; smallpox, warts, bunions and pimples, dandruff and Barber's itch.

Animal hides have gone to make the leather hatband and the 'bright fawn skin' of a lady's gloves, but the broadest expanse of skin is Leopold Bloom's: 'He foresaw his pale body reclined in it at full, naked, in a womb of warmth...' (88)

As skin seems more credible than genitals it is worth looking at the Gorman-Gilbert and the Linati Schemata for other possibly significant variants (Table 2.).

Table 2. Organ variations.

Gilbert-Gorman	**Linati**
Genitals	Skin
Muscle	Muscles, bones
Womb	Matrix, uterus
Skeleton	Juices
Flesh	Fat

Ideally suited as an organ for 'Cyclops' the eye is referred to ingeniously and repeatedly in this episode, but the stated organ is muscle. Overt correspondences are relatively few — 'broad-shouldered, deep-chested, strong-limbed' and 'brawny forearm', 'meat', 'muscular bosom', 'corpora cavernosa' — but following the Linati schema, which offers bone as a second organ, we find 'ribs', 'sacral', 'skull', 'skulls', 'cervical vertebrae' and 'bones'.

The variant of the Oxen of the Sun episode is one of terminology; the organ is the womb (Gorman-Gilbert), matrix or uterus (Linati). The symbolism is complex. Nurse Callan represents the ovum, Bloom the sperm, Stephen the embryo and the hospital the womb.

The skeleton, the Gorman-Gilbert schema's organ for Ithaca, may be represented by a recapitulation providing an outline or skeleton of the day's happenings and by an occasional osseous token, 'nasal and frontal formation', 'cranium', 'osteopathic surgery'. Admittedly, this is not altogether convincing besides being difficult to reconcile with the Linati schema where the so-called organ for Ithaca is 'juices'.

Unequivocal tokens for this interpretation also are comparatively few and principally taken from crude aspects of physiology — spitting, 'the monotonous menstruation of simian and (particularly) human females extending from the age of puberty to the menopause', 'gastric inanition', micturition, 'intestinal congestion and premeditative defecation', 'ejaculation of semen within the natural female organ' — Leopold Bloom's microscopic meditation on blood being a highly imaginative exception,

> ... the universe of human serum constellated with other bodies, themselves universes of void space constellated with other bodies, each, in continuity, its universe of divisible component bodies... (620)

If a more general representation of juices is acceptable it may be found in Ithaca's liquid language and the episode's general fluidity. There are frequent references to water ('constituting 90% of the human body') and to the 'steady flow of heat', thought ('cerebration') and 'electrical discharge'.

Water is a vital juice for the city. We follow its piped flow from Roundwood reservoir to Eccles Street. Bloom is a 'waterlover, drawer of water, water carrier' (592), Stephen a 'hydrophobe hating partial contact by immersion or total submersion in cold water...' (593) but in the form of a beverage it is acceptable to both — 'water plus sugar plus cream plus cocoa' (611).

One further lunar example of Joyce's frequent references to water in Ithaca — 'the lake of dreams, the sea of rains, the gulf of dews, the ocean of fecundity' (622) — must suffice as evidence for the acceptibility of 'juices' as the organ of this episode.

If a literal representation of the organ of 'Penelope' is desired it is again better to accept the Linati variant, 'fat'. The term occurs three times in Molly Bloom's soliloquy; also 'fattish', 'fatten' and 'antifat'. Lard, swollen, swollen out, swelling, and swelled out may also be relevant.

The words 'flesh' and 'incarnation' occur only once but flesh and fat are disposed so closely in nature that this may not be a valid variant. The flesh of fish ('plaice', and 'eelscod') and of animals ('butchers meat from Buckleys, loin chops and leg beef and rib steak and scrag of mutton and calfs pluck', 'veal and ham') as well as human flesh are celebrated in the Penelope episode. The symbols for human flesh (and fat) are venal and include 'bottom', 'bare bum', 'breasts all perfume', and 'round and white'.

From the viewpoint of anatomy the Linati schema is the more convincing but there is nothing in *Ulysses* quite so remarkable as a passage from *Finnegans Wake* where we encounter the pinna or external ear, the auricle, the tympanum or ear drum, the Eustachian tube, the ossicles and other relevant terms:

> (to) pinnatrate inthro an auricular forfickle (known as the Vakingfar sleeper, monofractured by Piaras Ua Rhuamhaighaudhlug, tympan founder, Eustache Straight, Bauliaughacleeagh) a meatus conch culpable of conduncing Naul and Santry... up his corpular fruent and down his reuctionary buckling, hummer, enville and cstorrap (the man of Iren, thore's Curlymane for you!), lill the lubberendth of his otological life (310. 9).

This may derive from the *Purple Island* in which Phineas Fletcher (1582-1650) describes the stapes or stirrup discovered by Ingrassias in 1548. J.S. Atherton[6] in *Books at the Wake*

6. Atherton, J.S. *The Books at the Wake.* London: Faber, 1959, 249.

identified a number of references to Fletcher and R.M. Adams showed that a phrase in the 'Sirens' episode of *Ulysses* — 'Well it's a sea Corpuscle islands' — was 'Blood is a sea, sea with purple islands' in an early manuscript version now in the University of Buffalo.[7]

Phineas Fletcher whom Izaak Walton referred to as 'an excellent divine and an excellent angler' was born on 18 April 1582 in Cranbrook, Kent, the eldest son of Giles Fletcher and a cousin of John Fletcher, the dramatist. *The Purple Island or the Isle of Man* was published in 1633. The second volume of an edition of the collected poems of Giles and Phineas Fletcher containing the *Purple Island* was published in 1909, the year in which Joyce made two visits to Ireland. It is surprising that he dismissed it as 'a kind of coloured anatomical chart' for it is a great deal more than that, as well as being the inspiration of his more subtle inclusion of anatomy in *Ulysses.*

7. Adams, R.M. *Surface and Symbol.* New York: OUP, 1962, 150.

8. The Doctors in *Ulysses**

Forty or fifty doctors are mentioned in *Ulysses;* precise enumeration is not feasible for many students receive courtesy titles as the novel evolves, and in the phantasmagoric Nighttown episode Leopold Bloom includes himself when speaking of 'we medical men' (442).

The doctors might be considered under the rubrics *fact* and *fiction* but one soon learns how hazardous it is to designate characters in *Ulysses* as fictional. Bloom's reflections of the popularity of Dr. Tibbles' Vi-cocoa suggests an advertiser's creation or a quack and *Ulysses* was published before Joyce consulted Mr. Sydney Granville Tibbles, a London ophthalmologist, thus contriving to confirm that his writings possessed a prophetic quality. By a similar coincidence he consulted Drs Henry and James, during a visit to London in 1922, pleased to remember his inclusion in the novel of the Dublin drapers, Henry and James.

Some years ago I was chided for expressing the opinion that Dr Finucane who pronounced Paddy Dignam's life extinct (452) was fictional.[1] I had known that there was a Dr Thomas Dawson Finucane in Blackrock but thought it unlikely that a family living in Sandymount and not on the direct tram route would have selected him as their doctor rather than one of the practitioners in nearby Trintonville Road. My critic evidently thought otherwise and made the interesting but highly speculative suggestion that

*Presented to a special meeting to celebrate the 75th anniversary of Bloomsday in the National Maternity Hospital, Holles Street 23rd June 1979

1. Staples, H. 'Finucane Lives!' *A Wake Newslitter.* 1973, X, 15.

Finucane attended Mrs John Stanislaus Joyce in Leoville, Blackrock, when Florence Elizabeth was born in November 1892. But as this was her tenth delivery a doctor may have seemed to be a dispensable luxury and besides, Dr Finucane who qualified in 1855 at the Apothecaries' Hall (where at a later date Stanislaus Joyce was a clerk) must have reached an age at which doctors no longer favour obstetrics.[2]

It is really not known what doctor, if any, attended Mrs Joyce's confinements. A male infant born in 1881 did not survive. She gave birth again on 2 February 1882 and on 16 June 1904 the sight of an old midwife prompts Stephen Dedalus to think, 'One of her sisterhood lugged me squealing into life' (43). And we learn from Ellmann that Margaret Joyce was delivered on 18 January 1884 by a midwife, Mrs Thornton of 19A Denzille Street, who was also present at the births of Charles, Eileen and Florence.[3]

The impecunious Joyces found their way to the Eye and Ear Hospital's out-patients department and Dr A.H. Benson prescribed glasses for James who may have consulted Dr Michael Walsh for urethritis in 1904. Dr Robert Kenny, FRCSI, was called in during Mrs Joyce's terminal illness and is the only one of this trio of personal doctors referred to in *Ulysses*. 'Dr Bob Kenny is attending her' (207). In her confusion the poor woman called him Sir Peter Teazle a cultured expression of disorientation. Dr Kenny lived at 30 Rutland Square and was Superintendent of the North Dublin Union. His brother, the late Dr Joseph E. Kenny, sometime City Coroner and MP for the St Stephen's Green Division was a close friend of Charles Stewart Parnell.

The medicals in *Ulysses* could also be considered under the headings *historical* and *contemporary* for Joyce included worthies such as Averroës, Maimonides and Paracelsus as well as local celebrities, Surgeon McArdle, Dr Louis Byrne the coroner, and Sir Charles Cameron. The shadowy figures of Gerard the herbalist, Lopez, leech to Queen Elizabeth, the O'Shiels and other Irish mediaeval hereditary physicians are encountered, and on the first Bloomsday Metchnikoff, Sir Arthur Conan Doyle, and Wilhelm Rontgen were enjoying international fame. Such

2. Lyons, J.B. 'Finucane Lives! Or Does He?' *Ibid.*, 1973, X, 42.
3. *Ellmann*, 760.

16. Sir Charles Cameron.

17. Sir William Wilde's former residence, 1 Merrion Square.

18. Plaque on 1 Merrion Square.

quasi-academic groupings, however, are artificial and unprofitable and I propose, instead, to follow gynaecological and allied themes. But first it may be of interest to examine attitudes expressed in *Ulysses* towards doctors and the function of the latter in the novel.

Since Dickens created Bob Sawyer, medical students are expected to be wild but what puzzles Bloom is how does the acquisition of medical degrees transform 'these votaries of levity into exemplary practitioners of an art which most men anywise eminent have esteemed the noblest' (406). The Bawd in Nighttown reserves her venom for their present status: 'Trinity medicals. Fallopian tube. All prick and no pence' (427). Young Gerty MacDowell views them romantically, knowing that Reggie Wylie 'was going to Trinity College to study for a doctor when he left the high school..." (347). Stephen Dedalus resents the deference shown by an old woman towards Buck Mulligan: 'she bows her old head to a voice that speaks to her loudly, her bonesetter, her medicineman; me she slights' (20).

Mrs Bloom observes the air of opulence in her doctor's house but the students, when she ogles them, are slow on the uptake: 'where does their great intelligence come in I'd like to know grey matter they have it all in their tail if you ask me' (679). Her husband, with 'snuffy Dr Murren' in mind ponders the practitioner's lot: 'People knocking him up at all hours. For God's sake doctor. Wife in her throes. Then keep them waiting months for their fee. To attendance of your wife. No gratitude in people. Human doctors, most of them' (161).

The profession's affectations are not overlooked. 'The bedside manner it is that they use in the Mater-hospice. Demme does not Doctor O'Gargle chuck the nuns there under the chin?' (401).

For the most part individual doctors contribute little to the narrative's momentum. Very often, indeed, they are mere landmarks — Wilde's corner and 'Mr Lewis Werner's cheerful windows' mark opposite ends of Merrion Square, North — but the fact that Mrs Bellingham can say, without further explanation 'he closed my carriage door outside Sir Thornley Stoker's one sleety day during the cold snap of February ninety three' (448) suggests that the leaders of the profession were better known to the general public in 1904 than in the present day. Sir Thornley Stoker, I should add, was honorary surgeon to the Richmond Hospital and a brother of Bram Stoker creator of 'Dracula'. Sir William Wilde, father of Oscar, was a pioneer otologist and the author of books on many subjects.

The Medical Superintendent of the Richmond Asylum (the present St Brendan's Hospital) is the first doctor mentioned in *Ulysses.* He is referred to by Buck Mulligan who is speaking to Stephen Dedalus.

> — That fellow I was with in the Ship, said Buck Mulligan, says you have g.p.i. He's up in Dottyville with Connolly Norman. General paralysis of the insane (12).

Connolly Norman was a prolific author. An article of his on Dementia Praecox (nowadays called schizophrenia) refers to cases 'in which the brightest hopes and anticipations of parents [are] blasted and crushed; for the majority of such cases never recover at all.' Lucia Joyce had the misfortune to fulfil this gloomy prognosis, benefitting symptomatically from modern therapy. Through the *British Medical Journal's* correspondence columns in 1904 Dr Norman objected to the proposed erection of a memorial of Sir Thomas Browne in Norwich because Sir Thomas had been a prosecution witness in 1664 when two old women were tried for witchcraft at Bury St. Edmunds Assizes and found guilty.

> Browne was great [Connolly Norman protested] merely as a writer of stately prose. His *Religio Medici, Vulgar Facts* etc. are a sufficient monument to his literary fame. Science and humanity are the watchwords of our profession. The author of *Religio Medici* was neither scientific nor humane. His record is stained with innocent blood, the blood of innocent blood, the blood of poor and defenceless people shed with his connivance, almost, one might say at his instigation.[4]

The last doctor in the book — 'that dry old stick Dr Collins for women's diseases on Pembroke Road' (691) — appears in the final episode of Molly Bloom's ruminations but the greatest

4. Norman, C. *British Medical Journal,* 1904, 2, 474.

19. Dr. Connolly Norman, from a portrait in the Royal College of Physicians of Ireland.

aggregation of doctors, as one might expect, is encountered in the 'Oxen of the Sun' episode in which the art is medicine, the colour white and the location the National Maternity Hospital, Holles Street. The presiding genius is Dr (later Sir Andrew) Horne, a suitable phallic symbol as Master of a maternity hospital.

> Of that house A. Horne is lord. Seventy beds keeps he there teeming mothers are wont that they lie for to thole and bring forth bairns hale so God's angel to Mary quoth. Watchers they there walk, white sisters in ward sleepless (382).

Earlier in the book, with the terminal 'e' elided, Sir Andrew's amatory function is plainly stated — 'Horn. Have you the?' (268) — to the accompaniment of the jingling of an outside car, a prelude to bedsprings soon to jingle in Eccles Street. The obverse side of the coin, so to say, is presented in the Circe episode where Realdus Columbus, who succeeded Vesalius in the chair of anatomy in Padua, is credited with being the first to recognise the clitoris as an anatomical entity. The advice 'Tumble her. Columble her' (476) is therefore highly meaningful and the suggestion that the dorsal nerve of the clitoris is four times larger than the corresponding nerve in the male stirred Joyce's imagination.[5]

Dr Horne is also a symbol of fecundity during a discussion on birth control in the Oxen of the Sun episode — 'in Cape Horn, they have a rain that will wet through any, even the strongest cloak' (402).

We do not actually meet Dr Horne but he '...is reported by eye-witnesses as having stated that once a woman has let the cat into the bag... she must let it out again to give it life...to save her own' (417).

By the evening of Bloomsday Mrs Mina Purefoy was three days in labour. I presume that Joyce borrowed her unusual name from that of Richard Dancer Purefoy, ex-Master of the Rotunda Hospital who, incidentally, had a fine voice and was a son of Dr Purefoy of Lucan, presumably well known in the Chapelizod area where John Stanislaus Joyce was once a director of a distillery.

5. Adams, R.M. *Surface and Symbol.* New York: OUP, 1967, 140.

20. Holles Street Hospital in 1904.

I have always taken it that Mrs Purefoy's infant was eventually delivered vaginally but the statement 'All that surgical skill could do was done' (417) might suggest a Caesarean section an operation Horne was certainly competent to perform. His publication on Caesarean section in the *Medical Press and Circular* in 1902 stressed the operation's value. 'No longer shall we be confronted with the words or sayin: "Spare the mother, no matter about the child.' His comments may have some relevance to the demand from the students: 'nay, by our Virgin Mother, the wife should live and the babe to die' (386).

The fictional Purefoys, mother and son, are unofficial shadows but according to Dr Seamus Cahalane[6] the records of Holles Street Hospital for 16 June 1904 indicate that five mothers were delivered in the National Maternity Hospital between the hours of 2.30 am and 6 pm at which time a complicated delivery was attended by the joint Masters, P.J. Barry and Andrew Horne, and their assistants. Cahalane's confirmation of an obstructed labour adds an element of verisimilitude to Bloomsday and to the cognate occasion described in Gogarty's *Tumbling in the Hay* which credits Joyce with the comment 'there are three things that should be small in a woman, the ankles are included'.

Dr Jack O'Hare, the Assistant Master in 1904, was a popular young man and 'into everything' as one would say nowadays; he played soccer for Bohemians and was the first vice-president of the Young Ireland Branch of the United Irish League. Bloom recalls that Nurse Callan had a soft spot for him 'that young doctor O'Hare I noticed her brushing his coat' (370) — but when he enquires about him he is told 'that O'Hare Doctor in heaven was... he died in Mona island through bellycrab three years agone come Childermas' (383). Actually Dr O'Hare was twenty-nine when he died of typhus on 3 May 1907 while temporary Dispensary Medical Officer in his native Newry.

Philip Herring[7] has painstakingly identified in Joyce's scarcely legible note-sheets in the British Library the names of Hippocrates, Galen, Harvey, John Hunter and others, some of

6. Cahalane, S. 'Joygarty in Holles'. Presented to VII International James Joyce Symposium, Zurich, 1979.
7. Herring, P. *Joyce's Ulysses Notesheets in the British Museum.* Charlottesville: University Press of Virginia, 1972.

21. Sir Andrew Horne.

22. Richard Dancer Purefoy, F.R.C.S.I.

whom were fitted into the mosaic of *Ulysses.* The note-sheets contain embryological data which Joyce used in the 'Oxen' episode.

> Must we accept the view of Empedocles of Trinacria that the right ovary (the post menstrual period, assert others) is responsible for the birth of males or are the too long neglected spermatozoa or nemasperms the differentiating factors or is it, as most embryologists incline to opine, such as Culpepper, Spallanzani, Blumenbach, Lusk, Hertwig, Leopold and Valenti, a mixture of both? (415)

Had he wished to tell us more about those embryologists and biologists the career of Lazaro Spallanzani, an 18th century Italian, could have afforded rich comic opportunities. Spallanzani studied mating in frogs, a process during which eggs extruded from the female cloaca are fertilized by a shower of semen from the tightly clasping male. He demonstrated that when a male frog's hindquarters were covered with a waxed green taffeta breeches the amatory clasp was not weakened but fertilization did not occur.

The fact that her period comes early makes Molly Bloom ask, 'have I something growing in me' (691). Should she go to the doctor? Yes, but it might be like the time before her marriage when she consulted Dr Collins for leucorrhoea: 'your vagina he called it I suppose thats how he got all the gilt mirrors and carpets getting round those rich ones off Stephens green running up to him for every little fiddle faddle her vagina and her cochin china theyve money of course so theyre all right' (691).

She recalls the doctor asking 'if what I did' had an offensive odour and could she pass it easily — 'pass what I thought he was talking about the rock of Gibraltar...' (692). The indignity of the proceedings and the idea of having to pay Dr Collins a guinea rankle equally with Mrs Bloom whose earthy distaste is not so expressive as that of a character in Edna O'Brien's *Girls in their Married Bliss* who feels helpless and outraged in a gynaecologist's chair by 'all that poking and probing and hurt.'

Niall Montgomery described *Ulysses* pithily as 'more a public labyrinth than a celtic toilet.' Molly occupies the centre of that labyrinth perched on a chamber pot. Some see her as an earth-mother others as a slut, but her faults can be forgiven her for an inspired comment on feminine physiology which could serve as an epigraph for a textbook of gynaecology: 'you wouldnt know which to laugh or cry were such a mixture of plum and apple' (702).

The model for Dr Collins remains uncertain. He has been identified with Dr Joseph Collins a New York neurologist whom Joyce met in Paris in 1921 but R.M. Adams pointed out that there was an actual Dr J.R. Collins at 65 Pembroke Road.[8] The householder, however, was the Rev. T.R.S. Collins whose son, Jonathan Rupert Collins, did not graduate from Trinity until 1901 whereas Molly Tweedy sought advice thirteen years earlier.

Collins and O'Hare are further examples of Joyce's habit of using a novelist's licence to gain augmented verisimilitude by deploying contemporary names, events, and locations to suit his purpose. The 'Mirus' Bazaar in aid of Mercer's Hospital, for instance, commenced on 31 May and not on 'Bloomsday' and Countess Dudley, who is featured in the Sirens episode, was pregnant and did not attend. Incidentally, Dr Purefoy, the Master of the Rotunda who gave his name to the parturient Mina, established the hospital's first pathology laboratory by organizing the 'Lucina' Bazaar.

Bloom gave his name as 'Dr Bloom, Leopold, dental surgeon' (441) an oblique reference, perhaps, to Marcus Joseph Bloom of Clare Street whose name was removed from the *Dental Register* in 1905 at his own request. Ellmann identified a Triestine, Ettore Schmitz, as a model for Leopold Bloom (John Stanislaus Joyce 'also enters into Bloom'[9]) and has mentioned the Blooms who lived in Joyce's Dublin, one of whom resided at 38 Lombard Street West.[10] *Ulysses* refers to conversations between Julius Mastiansky and Leopold Bloom in the latter's house in Lombard Street West in 1892 and 1893. Molly remembers the wallpaper in the Lombard Street house and that frosty-faced Professor Goodwin called there inopportunely. The residents of Lombard Street in 1890s were largely but not exclusively Jewish. Mr T. Bloom succeeded Luke Kavanagh of the Dublin Metropolitan

8. Adam, R.M. *Surface and Symbol.* New York: OUP, 1967, 223.
9. *Ellmann,* 21.
10. *Ibid.,* 386.

23. *Programme of Mirus Bazaar.*

Police as the householder at 38 Lombard Street West in 1892. His neighbours on either side were Isaac Freedman and L. Newman. He was succeeded as a householder in 1895 by John Bloom an illiterate Russian-born Jewish pedlar.[11]

The Dental Act (1878) regularised dental practice and imposed rules for professional behaviour. The *Dental Register,* first issued in 1879, contains the names of Mark Joseph Bloom and his son, Joseph, whose full name was Marcus Joseph Bloom. According to Ellmann, Mark Bloom had changed his religion in order to marry a Catholic. He was one of the founders of the Dental Hospital and served on its staff.[12] Father and son both practised at 23 Westland Row moving to 18 Westland Row in 1883. They were dental surgeons to Maynooth College and held other prestigious appointments.

Marcus Joseph Bloom moved to 2 Clare Street in 1893. His house was close to Finn's Hotel and sandwiched between a firm of wine merchants, W. and A. Gilbey, whose white invalid port was favoured by the Blooms of Eccles Street (595), and the residence of Dr George Sigerson whose rooms were said to resemble a Balzac interior.

Joyce knew that Dr Sigerson lived at 3 Clare Street. 'Go out and see old Sigerson and get him to prescribe for you', he advised Nora Barnacle on 1 September 1904.[13] He must have become well-acquainted with Clare Street during their courtship. His eye was attracted, too, by 'Mr. Bloom's dental windows' (249). If there was something additionally unusual about the dentist's career this would have fixed his name in the writer's mind. Consequently it is thought provoking to find that Bloom's name does not appear in the *Dental Register* between 1897 and 1899 inclusive.

Erasure from the register may follow failure to notify a change of address but it generally results from more serious infraction of rules or even infamous conduct in a professional respect. Charity would ordinarily dictate that the simpler possibility should be accepted but when one learns that in 1905 Marcus Joseph Bloom

11. *Thom's Directory,* 1890-1904; Census of Ireland, 1911.
12. Cohen, R.A. A General History of Dentistry from the 18th Century with Special Reference to Irish Practitioners. *Irish Journal of Medical Science,* 1952, 133.
13. *Letters 2,* 51.

actually requested[14] that his name should be removed from the *Dental Register* an entirely innocent motivation is no longer credible.

He was then approaching an age which diminished the danger of acting like the dentist in the limerick who 'in a fit of depravity /... filled the wrong cavity'. The more likely professional crime for which retribution may have threatened was advertising. This would have set Bloom at odds with his colleagues earning their opprobrium. It would soon have been whispered abroad making him a suitable model for Leopold Bloom, a canvasser of advertisements.*

Dr Brady prescribed Belladonna for Molly's profuse lactation (675); the helter skelter of 'Circe' includes 'old doctor Brady with stethoscope' (519); Leopold Bloom, a *mari complaisant,* lists Dr Francis Brady among the less credible of his wife's lovers (652). There are several Dr Bradys in the *Medical Registers* of the period but clear-cut identification is not possible.

Joyce's return to Dublin in the summer of 1909 coincided with the death of Dr Robert Kenny. His name, James A. Joyce, B.A., appears in the *Freeman's Journal* report of Dr Kenny's funeral which John Stanislaus Joyce also dutifully attended. The relevance of this biographical detail to *Ulysses* is arguable. The impressive cortege left Rutland Square for Golden Bridge, Inchicore, rather than for Glasnevin yet it may have lent something to the creation of Paddy Dignam's funeral. We have seen, when seeking models for O'Hare and Collins, that Joyce anchored his novel to a bedrock of actuality gaining freedom of manoeuvre by doing so.

*Since going to press I have learned from the General Dental Council that notification of *Mark* Bloom's death resulted in the inadvertent removal of his son's name from the *Register.* This was restored in 1900 when the error was noticed. When Marcus asked the Council to remove his name in 1905 he gave retirement from practice as the unconvincing reason for the request. His age was forty-four and Thom's Directory continued to carry his name and dental qualifications until 1917.

14. Ms. R.C.S.I. Minutes of the Council, 4 May 1905.

9. Joyce's Doctor*

Stuart Gilbert, author and translator of Simenon, Camus and others, lived in Paris with his charming French wife in an apartment in a tall old-world house with a balcony overlooking the Seine at 7 Rue Jean de Bellay on the Ile de St. Louis. I visited them there in 1967 when writing a book on James Joyce. He seemed extraordinarily active for his years. As his study of *Ulysses* had been published in 1930 I calculated that if he had retired early from the Burma Civil Service he might still be in his late seventies but when I met Frank Budgen in Dublin a week later at the first International James Joyce Symposium he assured me that Stuart Gilbert had passed his 90th birthday.**

My proposed title was 'Joyce and Medicine' and Gilbert thought it unlikely that he had any relevant information. He said Joyce wasn't a man to allow his illnesses to be a bore to others but as the novelist and Mrs Gilbert both suffered from 'stomach pains' they often compared symptoms and treatments. Mrs Gilbert was known to have a duodenal ulcer. They naturally wondered if Joyce, too, had an ulcer but the 'official' diagnosis was 'nervous dyspepsia'.

When I asked him if he thought Joyce was dependent on others Gilbert said that he 'used' others. He referred, in an amused way, to 'Joyce's fetch-and-carry boys'.

Gilbert's 'Letters of James Joyce' was published in 1957. He

**Irish Medical Times,* June 1982

**This was incorrect. Stuart Arthur Gilbert (d. January 1969) was born on 25 October 1883, the son of Major Gilbert of 8 Montpellier Villas, Cheltenham. After an education at Dean Close School, Cheltenham, and Hertford College, Oxford, he joined the Indian Civil Service. He settled in Paris in 1927.

mentioned to me that Stephen Joyce forbade the inclusion of his grandfather's four letters to Fraulein Marthe Fleischmann, believing them to be forgeries. They were genuine, Gilbert insisted, and in due course these letters were published in the collection edited by Richard Ellmann, a token of a love affair which Ellmann assures us was 'a matter mostly of looking and letter-writing, at once naughty and operatic.'[1]

Marthe Fleischmann reminded Joyce of a girl he had described in *A Portrait.* 'She seemed like one whom magic had changed into the likeness of a strange and beautiful seabird.'[2] She was born in Basle in 1885 and was thirty-three when he saw her in a street in Zurich. Marthe has been described as poised and lovely but according to Frank Budgen an old shipmate of his would have said 'she was as high up in the fo'c'sle and fairly broad in the beam'.[3] In his first letter, Joyce, registered immediate impressions: 'You were dressed in black, wearing a big hat with waving feathers. The colour suited you very well. And I thought: a pretty animal'.[4]

Susan Mitchell complained that George Moore 'Didn't kiss, but told'. Joyce also outraged the romantic conventions. Writing to his brother, Stannie, during his honeymoon in 1904 he confided: 'Finalement, elle n'est pas encore vierge; elle est touchée'.[5] And after an hour alone with Marthe Fleischmann in Budgen's studio he told the latter that he had 'explored that evening the coldest and hottest parts of a woman's body'.[6]

Joyce imbibed white wine in generous measure. The Gilberts bought an extra bottle or two when the Joyces were coming to dinner and the bottles were always finished. The wine went to his legs rather than his head. And as it never affected him next day he could go on and drink more whereas Gilbert would feel ill.

Mrs Gilbert stressed Joyce's politeness, his formality — the Joyces preferred to go on holidays with others and were sometimes accompanied by the Gilberts but he continued to

1. *Letters* 2, 347.
2. Joyce, J. *A Portrait of the Artist as a Young Man.* London: Egoist, 1916, 199.
3. Budgen, F. *Myselves When Young.* London: OUP, 1970. 194.
4. *Letters* 2, 433.
5. *Letters* 2, 66.
6. Budgen, F. *Myselves When Young.* London: OUP, 1970, 194.

address them as Mr and Mrs Gilbert — and the absence of any vulgarity in his speech. He thought women should wear long skirts, lace and numerous petticoats.

Gilbert said Joyce regarded the man of letters as a man apart, somebody to whom the world owed a living. He once told Gilbert who when filling forms put down his occupation as 'rentier' to call himself 'homme de lettres' and he would gain increased respect.

'Joyce had a special affection for the Jews', Stuart Gilbert said. 'Their "loyalty" — as if he were a king! — was something he valued'. He thought Joyce enjoyed writing *Finnegans Wake* and was, in his own mind, a Christ-like figure.

I also interviewed Dr Thérèse Bertrand Fontaine (b 1895) who had a medical practice on the Left Bank. Mrs Joyce was one of her first private patients, recommended by Sylvia Beach. She had cancer of the womb. Dr Fontaine was dismayed, as any young doctor would be if called upon to deal with a celebrity's wife suffering from such an unpromising complaint.[6a] Fortunately the operation she advised was 'miraculously' successful and there was no recurrence.*

As a result Joyce became her patient. She looked after him for several years but apart from the eye disorder found no evidence

*Thérèse Bertrand was born into what a colleague called *'une famille d'universitaires remarquablement douée.'* She was a pupil of Boidin and of Menetrier the director of the Hartmann Laboratory at the Hôtel Dieu. Thus she gained a useful grounding in pathology but influenced by Abrami was to retain a dominating attachment to general internal medicine with a particular interest in infectious diseases and renal disorders.

The medical school was conveniently close to the rue Dupuytren and Sylvia Beach's Shakespeare and Company. 'With all her work [Miss Beach recalled], Thérèse Bertrand found time to read all the new American books in my library, and was a member of it to the day it closed.'[6a] Despite this distraction she was the first woman to be appointed (1930) Médecin des Hôpitaux de Paris.

Dr Bertrand Fontaine published observations on liver abscess and cerebral filariasis and in 1949 reported the first case of Q fever in Paris. She was president of the Société de Nephrologie, secretary and later president of the Société Médicale des Hôpitaux de Paris and in recognition of her work in the Resistance was awarded the *grand-croix de la légion d'Honneur.*

6a. Beach, S. *Shakespeare and Company.* New York: Harcourt, Brace of World, 1959, 22.

of organic disease. There were occasional gastric symptoms, their pattern never that of ulceration, and the stomach x-rays were normal. He had arthritis at an earlier period but the heart was unaffected.

Dr Fontaine found Joyce a charming, interesting patient but unco-operative, believing that he knew more than his doctors. He had a good sense of humour. Mrs Joyce, on the other hand, seemed a person of narrow mind and small intellect — but an excellent wife for Joyce. Their son, Giorgio, developed Basedow's disease (in Ireland we call it Graves' disease), hyperthyroidism, and Dr Fontaine recommended an operation. Lucia, whom she discussed with a psychiatrist, was schizophrenic but her father never accepted the diagnosis.

The doctor appeared to disapprove of the frequent eye operations which Joyce endured and to disagree with Dr Borsch's management. To my surprise she also disapproved of Vogt who treated Joyce (and Eamon de Valera) in Zurich. She believed that the Swiss were over-confident. Most ailments were attributed to tuberculosis in Switzerland and to syphilis in France: nothing in Joyce's case pointed to either — it was what we now call allergic or auto-immune.

She thought Joyce immature. He had no religion substituting, instead, superstition. He never mentioned to her his reasons for becoming a medical student or expressed disappointment for his inability to pursue a medical career. He had some medical knowledge of an unscientific type. He once explained to her a short sentence of about six words from 'Work in Progress' and showed her how it was derived from Turkish, Dutch, Spanish, Latin and Italian.

Now and then Joyce referred to his doctor in his correspondence. He was impressed by her 'rivery name Fontaine', reassured when she reported favourably on his physical state to Dr Arthur Collinson (who was in dispute with an oculist in Salzburg over Joyce's case), and responded to her arsenic and phosphorous tonics with a ravenous appetite.[7]

When Sylvia Beach urged Joyce to leave Borsch and seek advice in Munich, Dr Fontaine recommended 'a younger specialist' but because of what he called 'my sluggish, slimy,

7. *Letters* 1, 271.

slithy, sliddery, stick -in-the-mud disposition' he was reluctant to do so. 'However, we shall see and then perhaps I shall see.'[8] From time to time Dr Fontaine consulted with Collinson, Borsch's assistant, over Joyce's eyes but he was obliged to conclude that they were 'as much in the dark as I am.'[9]

Joyce urged Stuart Gilbert and other friends to consult Dr Fontaine. She treated Padraic Colum for fatigue and his wife for a sprained ankle and also was Hemingway's and Samuel Beckett's doctor. When Beckett was stabbed in the early hours of 7 January 1938 he was taken to Hôpital Broussais where Verlaine had sheltered.[10] Dr Fontaine called on him and urged him to remain there until the blood had cleared from the pleural cavity.[11]

Writing to Mrs Victor A. Sax in August 1939 Joyce reassured her about her sister whom he had arranged to have seen by Dr Fontaine: 'My wife saw your sister twice this week. She, your sister, said the tonic Dr Fontaine gave her did her great good. By the way our doctor is a woman and a very clever one too.'[12]

During the war she was active in the Resistance. Her twenty-year-old son died in Mauthausen prison camp but she survived and was elected to the French Academy of Medicine on 20 May 1969, an unusual honour for a woman doctor. Time and experience had left their traces on this grey-haired lady's countenance which was handsome and authoritative rather than showing a faded prettiness. She was cordial when I called on her in Paris in 1967 but to my disappointment would not allow me to take her photograph. Now she still lives in Paris at an advanced age, no longer prepared to engage in correspondence because of poor eyesight. But my enquiries evoked an unsolicited compliment from an archiviste who wrote: 'Je connais mal Joyce, mais il s'etait choisi une grande femme médecin pour le soigner.'[13] And when Mary Colum said that 'doctors are the nearest approach to saints on earth' — a statement many would vigorously contest — she had Dr Fontaine specifically in mind.[14]

8. *Letters 1,* 277.
9. *Letters 1,* 288.
10. Bair, D. *Samuel Beckett.* London: Cape, 1978, 278.
11. *Letters 3,* 412.
12. *Letters 3,* 451.
13. Catherine Moureaux / J.B.L.
14. Colum, Mary. *Life and the Dream. London: Macmillan, 1947, 399.*

10. A Miscellany

1 Publishing Day*

The events which make headlines are not necessarily the most far-reaching. On 2 February 1922 censorship of films had just come into operation in Dublin by order of the Public Health Committee; Sir James Craig and Michael Collins met at the City Hall; foot-and-mouth disease was spreading rapidly in Great Britain; there were riots and civil commotion in India, and in Rome the conclave met to elect a Pope. Beside these stirring happenings the errand of an American lady in Paris who met an express train from Dijon would have seemed trivial indeed. She collected two books dispatched by Maurice Darantière, the publisher, delivered one to its author and put the other on display in her bookshop in the rue de l'Odéon.[1]

The lady was, of course, Sylvia Beach, the bookshop Shakespeare & Co., the author James Joyce, the book *Ulysses.* That it came out on its author's fortieth birthday was a carefully contrived coincidence. Some months previously Joyce had mentioned to Harriet Shaw Weaver that *A Portrait of the Artist as a Young Man* had first appeared serially in the *Egoist* on his birthday, that he had started *Ulysses* on Frank Budgen's birthday and had finished it on Ezra Pound's. He bombarded the printer with corrections and additions and at Sylvia Beach's urging Darantière agreed to complete the job on time. He promised to post three copies to Paris on 1 February. But the least chance could not be taken as the matter had come to assume disproportionate importance in Joyce's mind; Darantière was

**Irish Times,* 2 February 1972

1. Ellmann, 538 and *passim.*

prevailed upon to send the books by the Paris-Dijon express hence Miss Beach's early morning journey to the Gare de Lyon.

That evening the double-event was celebrated by dinner at an Italian restaurant, Ferrari's. Joyce wore a new ring as a token of his achievement. He deposited the parcelled book beneath his chair at the head of the table and sat rather glumly, sighing a little and eating practically nothing. He seemed reluctant to gratify his guests' curiosity by showing them his book and not until after the dessert was the parcel untied. *Ulysses* was revealed bound in the Greek colours, white letters on a blue field. It was duly toasted. The waiters came to admire it and bore it off for the proprietor to see. The party went on to the Café Weber. By then Joyce was in celebratory mood but Nora kept him on a tight rein.

There was a short delay before further copies became available — the edition consisted of 100 de luxe copies on Holland hand-made paper, signed by the author, 150 copies on *vergé d'Arches,* and 750 on slightly less expensive linen paper — but writing to his brother Stanislaus on 20 March Joyce reported that only a small number of the dearer books remained unsold.

George Rehm's review in the European edition of the *Chicago Tribune* was on the whole favourable. He thought *Ulysses* could do great good or great harm and defended Joyce from a 'Comstockery that reigned with iron hand by an imposition of censorship.' Many critics, however, were struck by a visual resemblance between *Ulysses* and the London *Telephone Directory* and mollified by its price which would restrict its readership. But 'Man-About-Town' in the *Evening News* saw it as a good investment. How right he was! The copy which a former registrar of the Royal College of Physicians of Ireland, Dr T.P.C. Kirkpatrick a bibliophile and medical historian, left to the College on his death with his other books was sold for something over a hundred pounds; later Mr George Leinwall paid £450 at Sotheby's for an uncut, unopened copy, and in February 1970 a copy of the signed de luxe issue was auctioned for 4,000 dollars in the Parke-Bernet Galleries, New York City.

'Amaris' in the *Sporting Times,* whose readers, presumably, were not scared of bar-maids, was disturbed by Miss Douce's little trick with her elastic, 'which she only displays to her favourite swains — one is inclined to say swines'; but the racism inherent in his famous comment that the contents of *Ulysses* would 'make a Hottentot sick' today seems more reprehensible than mere references to ordure.[2]

Shane Leslie's critique[3] was wounding — 'we say not only for the *Dublin Review* but for Dublin *écrasez l'infâme!*' — but Edmund Wilson supplied balm for the hurt by stating that the importance of *Ulysses* lay in 'once more setting the standard of the novel so high that it need not be ashamed to take its place beside poetry and drama'.[4]

As early as April 1921 when Sylvia Beach was arranging to publish his book Joyce was envisaging its rapid acclaim. Pointing to the Concierge's son he said, 'One day that boy will be a reader of *Ulysses*'.

How he misjudged it! Judge Woolsey's verdict eventually enabled Random House to publish the first American edition in February 1934. The first English edition appeared two years later. In Ireland, although never officially interdicted, it was not until comparatively recently favoured by the booksellers and librarians who so often constitute an unofficial censorship. Furthermore it remained a rather expensive book. But in April 1969 the popularly-priced Penguin edition appeared.

Now that it is freely available it may be gradually accepted as caviare to the general. Excerpts are already included in schoolbooks, a sure way to create an unread classic. The man-in-the-street, with the splendid independence which enables him to pronounce judgement on sport, politics, theology, and the arts with equal authority, will deem it (read or unread) over-rated. And the few who return to it obsessively year after year will continue to marvel as fresh layers of meaning are uncovered in this quite extraordinary book.

2. 'Aramis' in *James Joyce the Critical Heritage* Vol. 1, ed. Robert H. Deming. London: Routledge and Kegan Paul, 1970, 192.
3. Leslie, S. *Ibid.,* 200.
4. Wilson, E. *Ibid.,* 227.

2 Symposia

The International James Joyce Symposia, the inspiration of Thomas F. Staley and Fritz Senn, are seen as esoteric occasions by outsiders while participants, especially 'old-timers' who have attended most with profit, recall them with affection. The publication[1] of Murray Beja's 'Informal History' of the symposia may indicate the existence of an interest in collecting information about individual reactions to those Bloomsday gatherings and prompts the re-printing in this collection of essays of my reports to the *Irish Medical Times,* an unexpected source, perhaps, of Joyceana. Giorgio Joyce attended the first symposium. The registration fee was $15 which included luncheon on June 15 and breakfast and dinner on Bloomsday.

Paris, France*

It is true, in many respects, that they order things better in France, but in my limited experience this generalisation does not extend to conferences. Some years ago when I attended a meeting at the Hôpital de la Salpêtrière the foreign delegates received neither a welcoming smile nor a cup of coffee, although at the last hour our hosts redeemed themselves with a veritable fountain of champagne. The Joyce enthusiasts who trooped into Paris on Sunday, 15 June 1975 to register for the fifth International James Joyce Symposium hardly fared better.

In the great amphitheatre of the Sorbonne on Bloomsday, welcoming smiles were not lacking but interpreters were notable absentees, badly missed by those (the majority) whose French was less than *couramment.* Odd, isn't it, how different the French voice sounds compared to the clarity of those admirable speakers on the Linguaphone tapes? And the Minister for Education sent a last-minute substitute.

The next item for our delectation was a visit to the site of the future Centre Beaubourg, a gargantuan building project. A thrilling spectacle for architects, no doubt, but for literary types

**Irish Medical Times,* 11 July 1975

1. Beja, M. 'An Informal History of the International James Joyce Symposia'. JJQ, 1985, 22, 113-129.

24. Programme of first James Joyce Symposium.

25. At the first symposium. Rt. to l., Giorgio Joyce, Francis Warner, J.B. Lyons.

I am glad to hear of the first International James Joyce symposium and that it is being held in Dublin. I send my best wishes for the success, and to all those attending it

Saluti cordiali and lots of love

Lucia Joyce

14 June 1967

26. *Message from Lucia Joyce.*

a non-event.

Then later on Monday afternoon, in an improvised exhibition hall lacking the common amenities and with walls of burlap that made the acoustics a mock of what should have been, the *exposition of James Joyce et Paris* was unceremoniously inaugurated. It is a rich and interesting exhibition though at first sight an Irish visitor might have thought it designed to prove to any American who might wish to have it otherwise that Monsieur Joyce was a *vrai Parisien,* and included some interesting fragments such as these lines written in July 1935:

Le bon repos
Des Espagneux
Et les roseaux d'Annecy
Leurrent notre âme
Et nous nous pâmes
Pour une Paname
Loin d'ici.

After two more indecipherable stanzas it breaks off: 'Too hot to go on — J.J.'

The verbal onslaught started on Tuesday when the speakers included such stalwarts as Richard Ellmann, Zack Bowen and James F. Carens. Ellmann said that Joyce who wanted his work to shine with truth rather than art treated his literary mission as a social obligation. In a *Portrait* Joyce wishes to catch the conscience of his people. His method was urbanity in warfare, *Ulysses* his Trojan Horse containing armed men to undermine civil and religious authority, personified by the Viceroy and Father Conmee.

Ellmann sees the pun as Joyce's stock-in-trade, a key to his work, and not merely verbal for persons and actions double and separate in conformity with the essence of a pun which establishes not complete but incomplete identity. Joyce uses the pun to make all the quarky particles of life adhere and unity is achieved.

The text for Wednesday's major theme "Political Perspectives on Joyce's Work" was Joyce's own comment that he had no interest in politics, only in style, and Seamus Deane claimed that Joyce's achievement was to have transmuted history into art and

Irish politics into style. Joyce's was a classical colonial type of mind; he was determined to reconquer by a style. This suggestion prompted somebody to ask if Joyce had hoped to defeat England by taking her language away from her in *Finnegans Wake.*

Philip Sollers, a left-wing French writer, said that *Finnegans Wake* dismantles, analyses and transcends nationalism; it is a manifestation of internationalism and the most important antifascist book written between the two world wars. This extravagant claim was challenged by Leslie Fiedler who pointed out that *Finnegans Wake* is itself written in a dead language, the private language of a private cult; it does not speak to masses of people but to scholars and exegesists.

Maria Jolas, one of the few people present who had known Joyce personally, said that he was a regionalist rather than a nationalist. As a young man he had had the ear of internationalism and, echoing Lytton Strachey, she said that he had found it a very dirty ear. She recalled his surprise by adverse communist criticism. 'I don't see why they dislike me', he said. 'No one in my books has any money'.

The theme of Joyce's politics was argued vigorously, the more imaginative speakers countered by the question 'Why the present wish to push Joyce to the left?' and the contention that his politics were esoteric politics useless to his time and to ours.

During the 'political' session a piece of folded paper was passed from the body of the house to the Chairman who read 'Up the IRA' and then expressed uncertainty as to whether this was intended as an affirmative slogan or in a more vulgar colloquial sense.

The text of *Ulysses* is known to contain a host of printer's errors and Jack Dalton, an expert textual critic who seems to have every word in the book and manuscript imprinted in his mind, has a contract to produce a definitive text for Random House by 1979.[2]

Other highlights were Fiedler's 'Shakespeare and Joyce', Madame Kathleen Bernard's readings, and Basil Payne's Dublin

2. This project failed to prosper but the three-volume cricital edition of *Ulysses,* sponsored by Garland Publishing and edited by Hans Walter Gabler and his colleagues, was published at the Frankfurt Symposium, 1984.

collage. But the appalling ventilation, the unbelievable acoustics, and the frequent changes of programme took their toll. It was agreed that conferences are ordered better in Dublin and other attractions of Paris prevailed.

Belatedly, on the last evening, someone took his finger out, so to say, and a few cases of Power's whiskey materialised. The revival of interest was remarkable and I suspect that for some of the more convivial Joyceans the Circe episode was re-enacted in Paris.

By the Zurichsee*

Zurich's Universitätstrasse slopes down towards the centre of the city. A I walked along it on a Sunday in June 1979 I noticed an elderly couple approaching on the pavement. He had a hat, stooped a little, and carried a white cane; she was plainly dressed, almost dowdy. Could it be Joyce and Nora? They had once lived in this street...

The thought, of course, was fanciful for their mortal remains now rest in the Fluntern Cemetry higher up the Zurichberg and it was to honour him (and to resume their discussion of his works) that the Joyceans, with the unerring instincts of homing pigeons, had gathered in Switzerland for the Seventh International James Joyce Symposium.

The programme catered for a variety of interests with papers on 'The Joyce of sex', 'Joyce and Faulkner', 'Shem and the language of exile', 'Joyce and the occult', and 'The chap who wrote like Pynchon' to cite some examples. In order to fit in all the talks two lecture rooms were kept going concurrently. Unfortunately, because of this duplication, I missed Riana O'Dwyer's contribution on *Finnegans Wake.* Another Irish girl, Margaret Chesnutt, gave an extremely sensible and sensitive talk on *Dubliners* which remains a battle-ground where readers who favour naturalistic interpretations meet the highly imaginative and endlessly industrious miners of rich veins of symbolism. It could be summed up, I suppose, as good fun, but hardly as good clean fun.

**Irish Medical Times,* 11 July 1975

A panel which discussed 'Joyce and the gnosis of modern science' included a professor of physics from Berkeley, California who described contemporary developments in physics at the time that *Ulysses* was written.

One of the more unusual events was a visit to the Thomas Mann Archive. The great German novelist lived in Zurich from 1933 to 1938. He returned in 1953 and when he died in 1955 his literary effects were bequeathed to Switzerland. The archive is now housed in a mansion once the property of H. Jacob Bodner who was visited there by Goethe in 1775. It contains about 600 manuscripts and typescripts and many thousands of letters.

By Thursday an element of truancy affected the less-committed scholars who took time off to visit Basle, or Lucerne, or the mountains and in the evening Zurich's James Joyce Pub was an attractive gathering place. Saturday, Bloomsday, brought a resurgence of interest. Dr Seamus Cahalane's paper 'Joygarty in Holles' presented factual obstetrical information about 16 June 1904 (P 137) as well as some interesting interpretative suggestions regarding the Oxen of the Sun episode.

Joyce's letters provided material for another profitable discussion; they aren't 'literary letters', written for posterity but those to Stanislaus Joyce and Frank Budgen are informative about his intentions when writing *Dubliners* and the *Portrait* respectively, while the letters to Harriet Shaw Weaver add glosses to the *Wake.* It was interesting to learn from Mary T. Reynolds of Yale, who has examined the Weaver papers in the British Library, that Miss Weaver edited her letters from Joyce before releasing them for publication, cutting out all references to her own generosity and to his requests for additional money. In one letter Joyce declared that he had obeyed Dr Borsch's advice and Miss Weaver's to such an extent that he was doing no work and the Dublin newspapers were accumulating. 'Sean is asleep at his post.' Most interesting still the information that because Miss Weaver's handwriting resembled Joyce's closely some of her fair copies of his letters have been taken for originals.

An exhibition in the Zentralbibliothek included manuscripts and memorabilia. Paul Ruggiero's description of Joyce's last days contained pathetic details of those sad hours. Ruggiero, a bank official, had helped the Joyces to obtain entry permits from the Swiss authorities in 1940.

The Ruggieros and the Joyces dined in the Kronenhalle Restaurant on 9 January 1941, a wet and dismal evening. Joyce was in poor form — *'il buvait seulement et fumait son long Virginia'* — but thanked Ruggiero for what he had done to facilitate his departure from France, saying that he should have been a diplomat. As they left the restaurant Nora Joyce slipped but Ruggiero prevented her from falling. When they reached the Joyce's *pension* Ruggiero suggested, as they bade them goodnight a hot grog as a night-cap. Joyce said to Nora, 'Did you hear that? Ruggiero recommends a grog'.

During the small hours the duodenal ulcer perforated but his transfer to hospital was delayed until the evening. When Ruggiero visited him next morning Joyce looked so ill that it occurred to the banker that his friend might not survive the operation. If so, neither Nora nor Giorgio Joyce could draw on their funds in the bank. He went down to the office and having drawn up an authorisation in Giorgio's name took it back for Joyce's signature explaining the document's purpose. 'Ruggiero, do everything that is best for us,' said Joyce, signing the paper without reading it. And those were his last words to Paul Ruggiero.

3 The *Wake* for Beginners*

Unless you have a command of eight languages and can approach *Finnegans Wake* rationally with notebook and knitted brow it is best to read aloud and to skim. Build up your own anthology, collect the things that appeal, classify them if you wish. And don't forget it's fun! 'Hip it and trip it and chirrub and sing. Lord Chuffy's sky sheraph and Glugg's got to swing' (p. 226, line 19).

'Treely and rurally' (90, 31) at its simplest is an amusing spoonerism; 'Jeg suis, vos wore a gentleman, thou arr, I am a quean' (269.20) brings you back to the schoolroom. And from there to history: 'As Rhombulus and Rhebus went building rhomes one day' (286.32).

**Irish Medical Times,* 28 January 1983

'Nonsery reams' (619.19) are plentiful: 'Sing: Old Fincoole, he's a mellow old saoul when he swills with his fuddlers free! (590.23). 'That's handsel and gertles!' (618.2). And the fairy stories merge into other things. 'Back we were by the jerk of the beamstark, backed in paladays last, on the brinks of the wobblish' (615.25).

'Daunty, Gouty and Shopkeeper' (539.6) are easily penetrated disguises for three great writers. Snatches of Gaelic are spotted with equal ease: 'O thaw bron orm. A'Cothraige, thinkin thou gaily?' (54.14); 'deah smorregos' (407.2); 'Sdrats ye, Gus Paudheen! Kenny's thought ye, Dinny Oozle!' (332.22). A host of other references are available in Brendan O'Hehir's *A Gaelic Lexicon for Finnegans Wake.*

'Is that the Poolbeg flasher beyant, pharphar, or a fireboat coasting nyar the Kishtna?' (215.1) yields up at least some of its meaning to those who live on Dublin Bay, who also are at home 'where G.P.O. is zentrum and D.U.T.C. are radiants write down by the frequency of the scores and crones of your refractions and valuations in the price of dingyings on N.C.R. and S.C.R.' (256.29).

They too can enjoy 'his groundould diablen liondubh the flay the flegm, the floody fleshener' (73.34) without worrying about the juxtaposition of the devil (diable) and the blackbird (londubh).

There are familiar prayers for the 'romance catholeens' (239.21) 'so help me symethew, samarc, selluc and singin' (533.11). 'In the name of the former and of the latter and of their holocaust. Allmen' (419.19). 'Oura vatars that arred in Himmel, harraud bathar namas' (509.5), 'Hail many fell of greats! Horey morey smother of fog!' (502.2); and there are biblical echoes: 'The gist is the gist of Shaum but the hand is the hand of Sameas' (483.3). 'Let her peel to thee as the hoyden and the impudent!' (167.34).

A line of Goldsmith's verse and one of his plays are linked in 'when lovely woman stoops to conk him' (170.14) and there are many other literary allusions: 'the batblack night o'er flown then' (405.36); 'With the sounds and the scents in the morning' (319.1); 'Sink deep and touch not the Cartesian spring!' (301.24); 'Glamors had moidered lieb and herefore Coldours must leap no more' (250.16). 'Lack breath must leap no more' (250.16).

And there are songs 'Wells she'd woo and wills she'd win but now the deer knowed where she'd marry' (79.23); 'Lilt a belero, bulling a law' (206.4); 'Let Elvin bemember for Gates of Gold for their fadeless sons berayed her' (493.27); 'Lay off for Fellagulphia in the farming' (320.50).

And there are lovers, 'She and myself, the redheaded girl, firstnighting down Sycomore Lane. Fine feelplay we had of it mid the kissabetts frisking in the kool kurkle dusk of the lushiness' (95.20). And advice for lovers: 'The pleasures of love lasts but a fleeting but the pledges of life outlusts a lifetime' (444.24).

'Yawn in a semiswoon lay awailing' (474.11) is like a photographic double exposure. Parnell had something to say to 'no mouth had the might to set a mearbound to the march of a landsmaul' (292.26).

'Ulcer, Moonster, Leanstare and Cannought' (389.5) makes you look anew and questionly at the four green fields but the days of the week can hardly pass so sadly: 'moanday, tearsday, wailsday, thumpsday, frightday, shatterday' (301.20) 'all one with Tournay, Yestoslay and Temorah' (87.8).

This approach to Joyce's masterpiece is, of course, only for amateurs but once across the threshold of the *Wake* they may remain. In due course the general reader finds himself taking out a subscription to the *James Joyce Quarterly* and *A Wake Newslitter* where there are high jinks indeed.

4 Joygarty and The Federated Hospitals*

A useful term, 'the Chesterbelloc' described a prolific literary quadruped which frequented London's Fleet Street. A similar term 'Joygarty', was coined by Dr Seamus Cahalane to designate a contemporaneous Dublin relationship in the early 1900s. Elsewhere[1] I have discussed the sundered friendship of James Joyce and Oliver St. John Gogarty and confine myself here to

*Federated Dublin Voluntary Hospitals, *Annual Brochure* 1981

1. Lyons, J.B. *Oliver St. John Gogarty, the Man of Many Talents.* Dublin: Blackwater Press, 1980, 211-223.

Joygartian associations with the Federated Hospitals.

Unlike Brendan Behan who patronised the casualty departments of many Dublin hospitals (he favoured Baggot Street but died in the Meath) James Joyce had no personal acquaintance with these institutions though a number of them are featured in his books. The Mater — 'Big place. Ward for incurables there. Very encouraging' — and Holles Street Hospitals, important focal points in *Ulysses,* are outside my terms of reference. There is an explicit reference to Sir Patrick Dun's Hospital; Doctor Steevens' Hospital is not included but the founder's sister, Madame Grissel Steevens (according to an ill-informed legend she had a face like a pig's snout) is recalled in a discourse on monstrous births.

Walking through Molesworth Street, Leopold Bloom, the hero of *Ulysses,* notices a placard advertising the Mirus Bazaar, 'in aid of funds for Mercer's hospital. The Messiah was first given for that...' Later in the evening a fireworks display reminds Bloom of Mercer's. 'A long lost candle wandering up the sky in search of funds for Mercer's Hospital ...'

Madame Steevens and a number of hospitals are mentioned in *Finnegans Wake:* 'he after having been trying all he knew with the lady's help of Madame Gristle for upwards of eighteen calendars to get out of Sir Patrick Dun's, through Sir Humphrey Jervis's and into the St. Kevin's bed in the Adelaide's hosspittles...'

A story in *Dubliners* features Baggot Street Hospital where the inquest on the body of Mrs. Sinicio, an alcoholic, was held. 'Dr. Halpin, assistant house-surgeon of the City of Dublin Hospital, stated that the deceased had two lower ribs fractured and had sustained severe contusions of the right shoulder... Death, in his opinion, had been probably due to shock and sudden failure of the heart's action.'

Ulysses is a multitudinous book in which Joyce includes many doctors but our group of hospitals has only two representatives. Richard Dancer Purefoy whose surname is given to a woman in labour in Holles Street Hospital was gynaecologist to the Adelaide and a sometime Master of the Rotunda. Sir Philip Crampton's memorial fountain attracts Bloom's interest prompting him to ask, 'Who was he?' He was, of course, surgeon to the Meath throughout the first half of the 19th century.

27. Grissel Steevens.

28. *Mercer's Hospital.*

Pondering on communal kitchens Bloom again thinks of Crampton. 'After you with our incorporated drinking' cup. Like Sir Philip Crampton's fountain. Rub off the microbes with your handkerchief. Next chap rubs on a new batch with his.'

Crampton ('so inseuladed as Crampton's pear tree') reappears in *Finnegans Wake,* where 'Gougerotty' may be Gogarty towards whom, in middle-age, Joyce's animosity may have lessened. He spoke of *I Follow Saint Patrick* to Jacques Mercanton.[2] 'It is a title of an erudite book by my friend Gogarty, the Buck Mulligan of Ulysses.' During his colourful career Senator Oliver St. John Gogarty, an ear-nose-and-throat surgeon who joined the staff of the Meath Hospital in 1911, made as many enemies as friends. He was said to have the kindest heart in Dublin and the dirtiest tongue. A house-surgeon told the ENT surgeon that his patients had overflowed into Sir Lambert Ormsby's beds and Ormsby, the senior surgeon, needed them. 'Beds!' Gogarty said 'He needs slabs.'

Robert Collis[3] mentioned in his autobiography, *To Be A Pilgrim,* Dr. Lennon's coffee-time anecdote in the Meath's Boardroom centred on Boss Croker in bed with three girls. 'Boss what are you doing?' Lennon asked. "Trying to keep warm —' Collis never heard the end of the story for just then Gogarty entered and they all turned towards him. 'He made some Wildean kind of brilliant quip and everybody laughed.'

The paediatrician's senior colleagues thought him a bumptious young man and let him know it but Gogarty was exceptionally kind. 'Don't mind the bastards', he said. 'We all suffer from old cods.' And when the parents of a child with an earache paid him five guineas he insisted that young Collis should keep the whole fee. 'You look hungry', Gogarty said.

'If Niagara were a voice with an Irish accent,' an American journalist wrote, 'it would be called Oliver St. John Gogarty. I doubt that there is anything that can approach the conversational powers of the man.' This liveliness was not apparent in his portrait. 'You look so stern in your picture', Florence Dickinson Stearns, President of the Poetry Society of Virginia complained.

2. Potts, W, *Portraits of the Artist in Exile.* Dublin: Wolfhound Press, 1979, 219.
3. Collis, R. *To Be a Pilgrim.* London: Secker & Warburg, 1975, 72.

'I feel as though you were going to amputate something. However it takes a stern man to carry the burden of 'Wit, Poet, Surgeon, Statesman and Raconteur".'

Gogarty retired from practice in 1939. Eight years later he received a letter from a Dun Laoghaire woman, the wife of a former patient:

Dear Dr. Gogarty: As long ago as June 1913 you operated on Mr. P.J. Moran, Windsor Terrace and there was a balance of £3.3.0 due – he has had a lot of illness since, and is at present in St. Michael's Hospital here and is still unable to pay...

She asked him to drop a line foregoing the matter and when he did so she wrote again to thank him: 'As soon as I read your letter to my husband he exclaimed "that is just typical of the man" always a gentleman.'

In case the *Annual Brochure's* more serious-minded readers should object to the irrelevancy of these Joygartian glosses a moral may be drawn from the canon. Joyce viewed his native city with a critical eye and referred sardonically to a fire in the Irish Sweepstake Office in 1935:

'... it seems to me that lady Anna Livia did not do her duty even if the firemen did theirs. Much smoke and little water. But they will find another edifice in which to continue their noble work for the benefit of the Dublin hospitals and the poor doctors, the poor sisters, the poor sick people and the poor priests, consolers of these latter. Let me weep. And cheers for the racehorse.' Had he known that the Government mulcted the funds by way of stamp-duty he might have thought the enterprise more haphazard than he had imagined.

Gogarty's *As I was Going Down Sackville Street* diagnosed the basic fault of our hospital system. 'There are eighteen hospitals in Dublin and all of them unmergeable into one... There is a greater vested interest in disease than in Guinness's Brewery.'

When that passage was written in the early 1930s a plan was already afoot to merge Baggot Street, Dun's and Mercer's[4]. The plan was succeeded by the more ambitious scheme which, consecrated by an Act of the Oireachtas, created a warmly-welcomed Federation.

4. Lyons, J.B. 'Mercer's Hospital 1734-1972'. *Journal of the Irish Medical Association,* 1972, 65, 299-306.

Unfortunately, the consummation envisaged by generations of planners is still awaited. Platitudes paper-over the unconscionable delays. Joygarty, thou shouldst be living at this hour!

29. Sir Patrick Dun's Hospital.

30. Portrait of Sir Philip Crampton.

11. Kinch and the Buck: Friends or Foes?*

Joyce studies may be compared to a super-saturated solution which has deposited crystals of reality and the amorphous dross of sophistry. The latter includes the eagerly-accepted axiom that Oliver Gogarty was a cad who got his come uppance in *Ulysses*. Yet, as we know, Gogarty's *I Follow Saint Patrick* which he had praised lay on James Joyce's desk as the tide of his life ebbed in January 1941 while Oliver through his last years kept a portrait of Professor Robert Yelverton Tyrrell in a prominent place in his New York apartment. To gaze at either would in an instant have substituted the Liffey for the Limmat or the East River and in the silence of their rooms those exiles — for there is balm in nostalgia — may have experienced kinder sentiments and entertained more moderate judgements than we can tell from the utterances wrested from them on public occasions.

How inordinately susceptible they were to invective as an intoxicant! Their deliriums may not have always been correctly diagnosed by critics whose predetermined conclusions commonly derive from biased contributions of other participants in a notorious quarrel. Once, they were close friends... that much is certain. And irreconcilable enemies? I beg leave to wonder.

Unfortunately, it had become de rigeur to quote Gogarty's nastier remarks, forgetting his tribute in a review of *Finnegans Wake* in 1939 to Joyce's 'indomitable spirit' and 'immense erudition' and the revealing comment in the same review, 'Mr. Yeats confessed to me that his kind of prose made any other

*Presented to IX International James Joyce Symposium, Frankfurt, June 1984.

colourless.'[1] And if in one mood Gogarty resented the picture Joyce drew of him as Buck Mulligan in another he could treat it with humour. 'Now Yeats like Joyce has placed me with the Bucks', he wrote to Horace Reynolds[2] referring to his prominence in the *Oxford Book of Modern Verse.*

The first words spoken in *Ulysses* are the first words of the Latin Mass *Introibo ad altare Dei.* The response, which Joyce does not immediately include, is *Ad Deum qui laetificat juventutem meum,* to God who has given joy to my youth. Buck Mulligan personifies that joy, a contrast to the 'displeased and sleepy' (9) Dedalus. Malachi's friendly words have had for Stephen the warmth of 'running sunlight' (17) and Joyce expresses the perfection his wayward friend's unbounded capacity for delight when Mulligan exclaims, 'We'll have a glorious drunk to astonish the druidy druids' (17).

Stephen conceals resentment and malice as a milkwoman addresses the medical student deferentially. He is already determined not to return to the Tower. As the morning evolves there are discreditable tokens of envy. 'He saved men from drowning and you shake at a cur's yelping' (51). Others, too, augment the swelling wave of disaffection that breaks in the avowal, 'Hast thou found me, O mine enemy?' (197). Simon Dedalus speaks of 'that Mulligan cad' (89) and in the late hours, Bloom, hinting that Stephen's drink was doctored, says, 'I wouldn't personally repose much trust in that boon companion of yours...' (540).

While the fallacy of equating Gogarty and Joyce with their fictional surrogates in an absolute sense is to be avoided it has been pointed out by James F. Carens[3] that the former would have been entitled to take solace in the fact that Joyce's 'image of him as Mulligan... [was] far more human and attractive than the image of Stephen'. Gogarty's open-heartedness attracted many friends among those robust enough to withstand his quips. He

1. Gogarty, O. *The Observer,* 7 May 1939, 4.
2. O.G./Horace Reynolds, Harvard, b. Ms. AM, 1787.
3. Carens, J.F. 'Joyce and Gogarty' in *New Light on Joyce from the Dublin Symposium,* ed. Fritz Senn. Bloomington: Indiana University Press, 1972, 43.

had a fund of good will for Joyce, the more intractable of the pair.

One of Joyce's epiphanies was inspired by the confidence with which Gogarty placed an order with Hamilton Long, the pharmacist, and by the respectful way the assistant repeated the family address, 5 Rutland Square.[4] Joyce envied his good fortune and Gogarty attributed their quarrel to the fact that he had given his friend a suit of clothes. Stephen Dedalus's debts to Buck Mulligan are mentioned in *Ulysses,* 'nine pounds, three pairs of socks, one pair brogues, ties'.

At about the same time that this envious epiphany was recorded, Gogarty was telling G.K.A. Bell of a plan to help Joyce by renting a Martello Tower: 'He must have a year in which to finish his novel'.[5] His good intention is an instance of Gogarty's soft heart, a quality which his wit has hidden but is also illustrated by his concern for Samuel Chenevix Trench, the Haines of *Ulysses,* his guest in the Sandycove Tower.

'Trench is delightful'; Gogarty wrote in a letter to their mutual friend, Bell, 'erratic and neurotic but this latter is getting better with the sea air'.[6] The improvement was temporary and in 1905 Gogarty hoped for an opportunity to meet Trench and restore his spirits. 'His nerves are ailing and I am afraid he may shoot himself in a fit of despondency at the futility of his labours...'.[7] He expressed anxiety, too, to Dermot Freyer: 'Poor dear old Trench: it would be dreadful and for me irreparable calamity if anything happened to him'.[8] Trench did kill himself in 1909.

Gogarty's fundamental kindness is also evident in his depiction in *Tumbling in the Hay* of John Elwood the 'Temple' of *A Portrait* of whom Cranly says, 'Sure, you might as well be talking... to a flaming chamber pot as talking to Temple'. Gogarty regards Elwood affectionately and speaks of his dancing eyes and beautiful mouth, and of 'his exaltations and exclamations at the wonder of the world and his adventures in it'.

4. Scholes, R. and Kain, R.M. *The Workshop of Daedalus.* Evanston: Northwestern University Press, 1965, 50.
5. Gogarty, O. *Many Lines to Thee,* ed. James F. Carens. Dublin: Dolmen Press, 1971, 16.
6. Gogarty, O. *Ibid,* 39.
7. Gogarty, O. *Ibid,* 103.
8. O.G./Dermot Freyer, 5 May 1905. Ulick O'Connor papers, Morris Library, University of Delaware.

Tumbling in the Hay also contains an account of the evening in Holles Street Hospital on which Joyce based the 'Oxen in the Hay' episode of *Ulysses.*

'The Bard Joyce is to do the house keeping', Gogarty informed Bell optimistically on 22 July 1904 but in the event Joyce did not stay in the Tower until September. Meanwhile he had annoyed Gogarty by publishing 'The Holy Office' so disrespectful to AE, Yeats and others who had helped him but it may actually have been his courtship of Nora Barnacle which delayed him from taking up residence at such a distance from Finn's Hotel where she worked. The knowledge that Nora's father, a journeyman baker, had been an employee of John Oliver, Gogarty's grandfather, would surely have rankled with Joyce. It is now known that when Nora and Joyce eloped her distressed mother wrote to Mrs. Gogarty (whom Mrs. Barnacle presumably had known when they were growing up in Galway) to enquire about their possible whereabouts.[9]

'Break my spirit, will he?' (510) Dedalus in *Ulysses* re-echoes an allegation circulated by Stanislaus Joyce that Oliver Gogarty tried to gain ascendency over his brother by making him drink. This rumour which has done Gogarty incalculable harm would not be credited for an instant by those familiar with Dublin's taverns.

'That Mulligan is a contaminated bloody doubledyed ruffian', snarled Mr Dedalus (90) who threatened to write a letter to his mother or his aunt. It is unlikely that John Stanislaus Joyce was so lacking in a sense of reality as to have penned that letter but the Curran papers in UCD contain Mrs Gogarty's appeal to Tom Kettle quoted in an earlier chapter.

Richard Ellmann mentions composite characters, Ignatius Gallagher and Robert Hand, to which Gogarty lent something. To these Jimmy Byrne in 'After the Race' should be added; there are obvious parallels — 'educated in a big Catholic college' in England and afterwards at Dublin University where he 'did not study very earnestly and took to bad courses for a while'. Called

9. I am indebted to Nora's biographer, Brenda Maddox, for information about Mrs Barnacle's letter.

Goggins in *Stephen Hero,* Gogarty 'fades into Boylan' in *Ulysses* and is charged with snobbery in 'Thy Holy Office'.

Gogarty could hardly have been expected to respond sympathetically to Joyce's genius which GBS, Virginia Woolf and the majority of his contemporaries discounted. Predictably, instead of hedging his bets, he burst into abuse. 'Why', Gogarty asked, 'except for the sake of erudition compare him to Swift? He has no *Saeva Indignatio.* He lies down with the abandoned and howls Holy Murder — He is not a mocking Dante but a mockery of him: all Dublin is his *Inferno.* It is, as he sees it, damnable enough without demonstration other than its existence.'[10] His own account of Dublin, *As I was Going Down Sackville Street,* is a Dantesque tour leading from the political Inferno of the 'thirties to the distant Paradise of his youth. His title derives from a Dublin ballad which, he informed Horace Reynolds, 'Joyce found and rescued from oblivion and obloquy in Faithful Place'[11]

As I was going down Sackville Street
  Hey, Ho me Randy O!
Three bloody fine whores did I chance to meet
  With me gallopin' rearin' Randy O!

The Dublin of *Sackville Street* is closer to the Dublin of Yeats's 'Easter, 1916' than to Joyce's city and closer still to the Dublin of George Moore. Terence de Vere White has said it is Moore again with less malice and less art. Unfortunately its malice led to a damaging libel suit which I have described elsewhere.[12]

James F. Carens' detailed consideration[13] at an earlier symposium of Gogarty's literary influence on Joyce leaves me few additional glosses to offer but Gogarty's reference in his correspondence with Bell to Professor Tyrrell's 'inimitable iambic walk' reappears in *Ulysses* where 'Puck Mulligan, panama

10. Gogarty, O. 'The Veritable James Joyce According to Stuart Gilbert and Oliver St. John Gogarty', by a Fellow Dubliner. *Transition,* 1932, 21, 281.
11. O.G./Horace Reynolds, Harvard, b. Ms. AM, 1787.
12. Lyons, J.B. *Oliver St. John Gogarty: the Man of Many Talents.* Dublin: Blackwater Press, 1980, 182-194.
13. Carens, J.F., 'Joyce and Gogarty', in *Newlight on Joyce from the Dublin Symposium,* ed Fritz Senn. Bloomington: Indiana University Press, 1972, 28-45.

helmeted, went step by step, iambling, trolling' (215). And may it not be that Bloom's memory of his lovely day (176) which Molly, too, recalls — 'the day we were lying among the rhododendrons on Howth head' (703) — was Gogarty's inspiration? We know from Joyce's letters that he took Nora for privacy to a field in Ringsend near the Dodder, a less lyrical setting for courtship than the bower in Howth which in 1904 Gogarty described to Bell and possibly to Joyce: 'I lay under a rhododendron and watched the midges dance like a fountain for joy of the sunlight. I mixed light purple rhododendron leaves in a girl's red brown hair — hair that's golden in the sunlight'.[14] A pretty picture, even though the auburn-haired maiden who may or may not have said 'Yes' remains unidentified.

31. Oliver St. John Gogarty.

14. Gogarty, O. *Many Lines to Thee,* ed. James F. Carens. Dublin: Dolmen Press, 1971, 8.

absurdities. His mind observed the lovely and the inane with equal facility. 'The Old Goose' pleased AE; Vivian Mercier selected 'Leda and the Swan' as a tour de force; 'To a Cock', a poem of fourteen stanzas from which three are quoted below, is a third example.

Why do you strut and crow,
And thus, all gaudy go,
Through squalor with a show
That tempts derision?
Do you a livery use,
Or dress you up in hues
Which you were free to choose
Of your own vision?

Colours of dawn and joy
That with delight destroy:
Your body all a Troy
To house Desire;
Your mien is proud and brave
As his who fought to save
The fatal Queen who gave
But gifts of fire.

Strange, that a small brown hen
...Should charm you thus! For men
Great Beauty shines, as when
The Argive valleys
Bore her limbs, for whom Greece
For ten years knew no peace:
Or our own Western seas
Bore Grace O'Malley's.[10]

Norman Jeffares devoted the Chatterton Lecture to Gogarty in 1960, but the only extended study of the poet in recent years is James F. Carens' *Surpassing Wit.* Jeffares discussed Gogarty's verses under three headings: the descriptive poems to which all Irish poets are given; poems of attitudes; and the classico-romantic poems which were his forte. He sees him as a minor

10. Gogarty, O. *Collected* Poems. New York: Devin-Adair, 1954, 16.

32. *Oliver St. John Gogarty by Sir William Orpen.*

poet, but 'a very memorable minor poet indeed'.[11] Carens, following a lengthy analysis, conceded that Gogarty does not appeal to the avant-garde, but affirmed that 'In the whole body of Gogarty's poetry, published and unpublished, there are perhaps a hundred poems by which he will live. Of these, at the very least, some two dozen shorter lyrics, and a dozen longer poems are exceptional enough to hold their own in the diverse body of modern poetry. Uneven at times, and sometimes careless... Gogarty could also carry off whole poems flawlessly and achieve effects of unequalled lightness, delicacy and wit'.[12] Their judgements are a rebuke to the condescensions shown of late to Gogarty by Ireland's literary establishment and to the cliques which denigrate him.

At every phase of a varied career, Oliver St. John Gogarty was, in H.L. Mencken's phrase, 'a salient individual' — a conspicuous athlete in his youth, an antic medical student, a leading ENT surgeon, an outspoken Senator, a controversial poet and author. At all stages of his life too, whether in the Hay Hotel, the boardroom of the Meath Hospital, an English country house, or a Third Avenue bar, he was gregarious and good-humoured. Joyce scholars have cast him as the villain of the piece in their versions of a sundered friendship with James Joyce, but the record of unbroken friendships with Major Freyer, AE, Dunsany, W.B. Yeats and others can be read in his correspondence.

Gogarty attributed Joyce's malice to the fact that 'he never forgave me for giving him a suit of clothes' — Joyce was not to know that when Ibsen was a poorly-paid apothecary's apprentice he gratefully accepted the gift of a discarded trousers. Stanislaus Joyce blamed Gogarty for his brother's drinking, but Mrs Gogarty's letters to Tom Kettle[13] make it clear that she believed that Joyce was leading her son astray. Following his characterisation as 'Malachy Mulligan' in *Ulysses,* the surgeon-poet over-reacted. His comments about Joyce became as overdone as his incessant jibes at de Valera — he has paid a heavy price for them.

His informal advice to John Millington Synge was given with

11. Jeffares, A.N. *The Circus Animals.* London: Macmillan, 1970, 174.
12. Carens, J.F. *Surpassing Wit.* Dublin: Gill and Macmillan, 1979, 237.
13. *Kettle,* 54.

encouraging optimism. 'I met Dr Gogarty the other day,' the dramatist reported to Marie O'Neill, 'and he says I ought to get the glands out as soon as ever I can and that I will be all right then'.[13a]

His friendship with Dermot Freyer had kindled in 1904 when the latter, a Cambridge medical student, visited Trench (the 'Haines' of *Ulysses*) at the Martello Tower in Sandycove. They shared a common interest in poetry and had incidentally cavalier attitudes towards university studies. Freyer amused Gogarty with stories of Yeats, who had lectured at Cambridge, and then he photographed the Tower and the group gathered there, including AE who had done an oil painting of the seascape. They arranged to meet again either in Cambridge or in London where the Freyers lived at 40 Harley Street. Dermot's father, Connemara-born Sir Peter Freyer, had settled in London on his retirement from the Indian Medical Service and was a pioneer in the surgery of the prostate gland.[13b]

Gogarty and Freyer corresponded over a number of years. Gogarty thanked him in 1905 for the gift of Oscar Wilde's 'De Profundis' and at Christmas sent him *Sixteen Poems* by William Allingham: 'They are perhaps the first to give the "sentiment" of Irish scenery in English verse. It deals with your ancestral West'.

On 19 September 1907 Gogarty reported that since his last letter he had visited America, married, qualified at Trinity 'and I have an only begotten son in whom I am well pleased.'

He planned to visit Freyer in London on his way to Vienna. 'I am going strong at the Throat, Nose and Ear branch of the profession. I intend doing ½ or ¾ of a year in Vienna, and then looking in at some of the London hospitals. If you know any nose-men or if you have a rhinologist at your own hospital take me around to that rhinoceros.'

When he received Freyer's *Rhymes and Vanities* he replied with an amusing villanelle:

13a. Synge, J.M. *Letters to Molly,* ed. A. Saddlemeyer, Cambridge (Mass):- Belknap Press, 1971.

13b. Copies of Gogarty's letters to Dermot Freyer are deposited in Morris Library, University of Delaware.

33. Dermot Freyer.

I got a book of verse
In lighter vein from Freyer
(It wasn't very dear,
I didn't disimburse):
A friend can oft amerce
The price of papi-er
I got a book of verse
In lighter vein from Freyer.

They met in the Langham Hotel and were joined by another young poet, F.W. Tancred, who knew Herrick's every line. Some days later Gogarty wrote from Nürnberg the lovely town of Durer, Fischer, and Hans Sachs the greatest of the Meistersingers. After some amusing moralising he demanded that Freyer shall,

Write me anon a line of grace
From that your proud prostatic place
A word about yourself and Tancred
Who sang for sons of fathers chancred.
Write to Vienna, be not lax:
This leaves the city of Hans Sachs.

Back in Dublin Gogarty wrote to Freyer in Edinburgh in April 1908. 'What wrath what ire drove thee forth to the cold Causasian confines of the North??!! What prostatic pressure forced thee up?' Gogarty surmised that parental displeasure had led to Dermot's exile. It was Gogarty's guess that Sir Peter Freyer was blind to Dermot's virtues and having failed university examinations himself, he was on the side of the underdog.

Leave him the bladder filled with brine
And prostates yielding to his finger,
This 'slight impasse' will pass as mine
And, as you know, I once did linger!
Then screw your courage to be bold
Not to the 'sticking place' but pass it
And be not cast down in the cold
Like Albumin with Nitric Acid.

34. Medallion of Lord Dunsany by T. Spicer-Simpson.

When writing to Freyer in December 1908 he made light of a recent misfortune. 'That I did not at once reply blame not me but my Appendix which narrowly escaped Chirurgery! I lay abed 8 days what time fair maids thrust ivory bobbins in behind and "threw up" turpentine! O Alfred Douglas! I am better now.' It was a temporary reprieve for a few months later he wrote again from the Elpis Private Hospital: 'My dear Freyer: they have carried me kicking from my own house, muzzled me with alien airs [ether] and cut the appendix out of me!'

Gogarty's letter to Freyer in 1911 was brief and unremarkable and when he wrote again in October 1913 Dermot was married. He invited the Freyers to Ireland offering to put them up. 'How goes the Muse, demurely, eh? Ah, we marry the Muse: but what of the Muse when we marry?' A good question! It remains unanswered.*

AE was convinced of Gogarty's poetic talents. 'I think you have a couple of masterpieces tucked away inside your skull somewhere', he wrote, thanking his young friend for *Blight,* 'and I would like the humble office of midwife to the creatures of your mind... All you want to do is to take yourself seriously. You've got the genius necessary, and the only doubt in my mind is whether the genius has got hold of you".[14]

Gogarty's sonnet 'To AE Going to America' credits Russell with 'the wisest heart and gentlest', AE wrote to the surgeon from Chicago on 1 April 1928, enthralled by the architecture: 'Skyscraper rises beside skyscraper, the later ones were beautiful shapes. They look the most ancient things, these last pyramids. I

*Dermot J. Freyer did not complete his medical studies. He served in the London-Irish Rifles and later lived for many years at Captain Boycott's former residence, Corrymore House, on Achill Island. His publications include *Rhymes and Vanities: verses in lighter vein* (1907); *Sunlit Leaves: a second book of verse, including some translations* (1909); *In Lavender Covers; verses, a third trespass* (1912); *For Christmas and for Easter: little poems of Christian tradition* (1915); *Night on the River: a queer story,* together with *Two stories of childhood and The Cloud etc.* (1923) and *Not All Joy* [short stories] 1932. His son, the late Grattan Freyer, owned Terrybawn Pottery in County Mayo; an editor and literary critic, he wrote *Peadar O'Donnell* (1975) and *W.B. Yeats and the Anti-democratic Tradition* (1982).

14. Harvard, b Ms, AM, 1787, 550; 2.

35. Bust of A.E. in Merrion Square.

expect a Chaldean wizard at the topmost pinnacle calculating horoscopes for King Nebuchadnezzer. It is truly a marvellous country; the people kind, eager, simple and forceful, with an amazing generosity and hospitality. They seem to be impelled from within by some force beyond themselves to build and then to get tired, finding it not equal to the unrevealed archetype and they tear down and build again, higher and more haughty and more beautiful.'[15]

AE realised that he could earn six times more in America than at home, but he longed for the quiet of Ireland. '[I] would not for millions live or work here. There is not time for reverie. All life is hurried and instinctive, pushed from within by some yet unrevealed demiurge, and I prefer to be out of it.'

Gogarty sent a poem (unidentified) to AE in 1932 when the editor of the *Irish Statesman* was embroiled in a libel action. 'The poem is one of your most beautiful', he wrote. 'I could not read it when there was a crowd here. This morning I read it and it made me forget the courts and Geoghegan K.C., and that I was like a butterfly transfixed by a pin in the witness box. Is it for the IS?'

AE's letter from London on 20 October 1934 referred to an attack by Sean O'Casey:

'I don't mind O'Casey devouring me. As I grow old and insensitive somebody shouting at me helps me to feel alive. I feel so much of the elderly, on the shelf, poet, that it gives me a thrill to think anyone thinks it worthwhile denouncing me. Is my position on the shelf too permanent? I don't mind in what dusty corner I am put. It may be a feeling carried over from a past life in India, where after being a householder and citizen the yogi retired to the jungle. I have retired to my jungle.'[16]

Pamela Travers' letter describes AE's peaceful death: 'You were the last person he spoke of. You will always proudly remember that and I shall always proudly remember how you came to him. I never felt more your friend than then. Though I have often silently praised you for your steady love of him that I recognised and for letting me perceive, under the gallimaufry, the true man in you.'[17]

15. Harvard, b Ms, AM, 1787, 550, 4.
16. Harvard, b Ms, AM, 1787, 550, 6.
17. Harvard, b Ms, AM, 1787, 550, 7.

When Lord Dunsany's gamekeeper, Toomey, was locked up by Free State troops during the Civil War, Dunsany asked Senator Gogarty to intervene. 'Think, Gogarty, how many publishers are at large while Toomey lies in prison.'

With the Tailteann games literary prizes in mind, Gogarty urged Dunsany to compete 'for the gold nose-ring of the ancient kings of Tara'. Dunsany was reluctant to compromise his status by filling the entry form. 'And by the way', he asked, 'what does an amateur mean? For instance is Yeats an amateur?' Replying to a further communication from Gogarty, he added a postscript: 'I'd like to be clear about the word "amateur", for according to its modern and now accepted meaning to receive a prize as an amateur would be to put me in a class never even visited by Yeats's jealousy'. He invited him to dinner to discuss the matter.[18]

James Montgomery, the film censor, recalled a dinner given in 1934 for the new editor of the *Irish Times,* R.M. Smyllie, which most of the Dublin writers attended. The Minister for Finance, the late Sean MacEntee, proposed the toast for 'Peace and Unity in Ireland'. Gogarty replied: 'God forbid! Peace would mean national constipation, as movement is as essential in a nation as it is in a bowel, and God has instituted Ulster as a perpetual purge for the health of our dear land'.[19]

That was the year in which Yeats's 'rejuvenation' operation was performed, possibly by Norman Haire, an Australian sexologist, who practised at 127 Harley Street, London.[20] The event was widely discussed; Harold Nicholson noted in his diary[21] how Virginia Woolf imitated Yeats telling a story about the occult, the punch-line of which was '— enough to say, I finally recovered my potency'. Gogarty referred to the operation in a letter to Horace Reynolds.[22] [Yeats] has undergone Steinach's operation, and is now trapped and enmeshed in sex. When I parodied his poem into, "I heard the old, old men say

18. Harvard, b Ms, AM, 1787, 517.
19. Harvard, b Ms, AM, 1684.
20. Lock, S. 'Yeats and the Steinach Operation'. *British Medical Journal*, 1983, 287, 1965.
21. Nicholson, H. *Diaries and Letters* 1930-1939. London: Fontana, 184.
22. Harvard, b Ms, AM, 1787, 140.

Everything's phallic', little did I think he would become so obsessed before the end. He cannot explode it by pornography (as Joyce) or jocularity as I try to do.' Later, Gogarty wrote: 'Yeats submitted to that humbug, Steinach... he never consulted me... Ethel Mannin told me that she 'did my best for him' after the operation;but of course without effect!'[23]

Gogarty admired his American friend, Horace Reynolds, as 'a stylist to whom all things are subordinated and melted in his zest for life. Harmonised, I should say'. He endeavoured to get a chair of Anglo-Irish Literature founded for him in Harvard. Gogarty's letters to Reynolds, over a 30-year period (1927-1957), provide an interesting testimony of enduring amity. They contain many gossipy comments about Gogarty's contemporaries, praise and detraction accorded in about equal measure. He urges Reynolds to read Tyrrell's *Lectures on the Latin Poets* and mentions Macran. 'His wife had a hard time with him, though he was the gentlest of human beings.' Colonel Maurice Moore is described as 'the most persistently upright mischief maker in Ireland in our time... One wonders what would George have been, had he been able to pass into Sandhurst'. He returns to the novelist in another letter: 'I don't know whether Moore was great or not. I don't think he was simply for the fact that he imagined that "style" was something separate or separable from subject. He imitated W.S. Landor, a stylist because he was a scholar. Moore was no scholar — he paid a fellow called Atkinson (now a reader to Harrap & Co.), to keep his grammar according to usage! Yeats is greatly concerned of late — "Was Moore potent?" Yeats has just undergone Steinach's operation for rejuvenation, and it has been quite a success so far as his interest in other people's Cryprian exercises goes'.[24]

Tom Kettle is judged by Gogarty to be 'one of the best prose writers of his day', F.R. Higgins, 'one of the best'; Frank O'Connor, 'the best short-story writer alive'; Gerald Brockhurst, 'the best etcher living — possibly the best who has ever lived'. Padraic Colum is 'a good little man, but his wife is rancid'. Austin Clarke is probably sick with self-love. James

23. Harvard b Ms, AM, 1787, 140, 234.
24. Harvard, b Ms, AM, 1787, 140.

36. Padraic Colum by Robert Gregory.

Stephens's death gave Gogarty a jolt — 'He was the greatest lyrist of them when it comes to lightness and airiness'. Aldous Huxley, whom Gogarty had heard speaking, was 'clever, competent and overdone'.

Gogarty said that Shane Leslie was 'a bad friend to himself and turned many good fellows against him by his reserve of friendship, not reticence or propriety. He cannot put his gun on the table like so many men who have gone native in London and distrust mankind'.

Judge Joseph O'Connor made a minor contribution to *Blight;* he was the author of *Studies in Blue* and wrote under the pseudonym 'Heblon' in the *Evening Mail.* Gogarty described him 'as one of the wittiest men and the best of story-tellers'.

James A. Healy, a book collector, was deemed to be a good fellow but 'best when unseen and unheard like the still small voice of conscience. He buys first editions... (It saves him from reading) and he may be useful during the next spell of hard-uppishness'.

When the poet-editor of the *Dublin Magazine,* Seumas O'Sullivan, married an artist, Estella Solomons, Gogarty spoke of him as Seumas O'Solomons. He said that since his marriage, Seumas 'had been very usurious with his poems, rubbing them together like gold pieces. Some of them are pure gold, but they are being worn thin by too much trituration. Usurious, if not uxorious. It would take Joyce to blend these words. His Wasp is very good. "The sunlight sought the sun again". When the wasp flew out of the bus which was filled with gloomy faces'.

Eamon de Valera '... took courage and risked a joy-ride with the world's most trustworthy pilot Charles Lindberg... It was his first flight, though he has looped in more disastrous regions than Lindberg'.[25]

When *As I Was Going Down Sackville Street* reached the printers, Gogarty became apprehensive about its reception: '"As I was going" is getting into galley stage. I hope I don't adorn an oar in some such compartment after it is published'. The wrapper for the English edition was by Jack B. Yeats and Leo Whelan.

The *Oxford Book of Modern Verse* evoked the expected storm of protest. Gogarty explained to Reynolds that 'the English

25. Harvard, b Ms, AM, 1787, 140, 49.

critics, who have never forgiven Yeats for taking the Nobel Prize from their despairing poets, or, rather, poets of despair, are hard on his heels over this Anthology'. *The Times* was an exception; it has trodden warily, 'careful not to exclude Yeats and his Parisian Judgement from their Mount Ida'.

A letter from Renvyle in the spring of 1937 shows us Gogarty, the host: 'Here we are at Easter in lovely bright weather but with a chill in the air. That keeps it all the clearer. I am off 58 miles to meet a friend in Galway who comes from London this morning. Then to collect three dozen of lager for the Editor of the *Irish Times* whom we expect on Saturday'.[26]

Possibly still smarting from the libel action, Gogarty read a personal reference in Patrick Kavanagh's *The Green Fool,* which he considered to be defamatory, and decided to sue the publishers Michael Joseph & Co. 'I want a few thousand damages, and I mean to get them because they have brought my wife and my reputation as a medical man into it...'[27] He won the case, but today the action is seen by Patrick Kavanagh's admirers in the same way as Joyce scholars received his 'They Think They Know Joyce'.

Meanwhile he has completed his next novel *(Tumbling in the Hay):* 'I am putting the Hay into a Cock now. I am glad it is finished'.

Deirdre Bair, in her 'life'[28] of Samuel Beckett, says that after many years had elapsed, Harry Sinclair, the plaintiff in the *Sackville Street* libel action, had not received a penny of the damages awarded to him. If this is correct, it can only mean that the solicitors and client bill swallowed it up.

When Gogarty's one-act play, 'Incurables', was rejected by Ernest Blythe, a director of the Abbey Theatre, he sent him a postcard inscribed, 'Bird thou never wert'.[29]

Throughout his mature years, Gogarty was on terms of affectionate friendship with W.B. Yeats; he helped the older man in many ways, sat with him in the Senate, rejoiced over the Nobel Prize, and wrote a poem urging him to build a fountain to commemorate the occasion —

26. Harvard, b Ms, AM, 1787, 140, 25.
27. Harvard, b Ms, AM, 1787, 140, 56.
28. Bair, D. *Samuel Beckett.* London: Cape, 1978, 268.
29. Harvard, b Ms, 1787, 509.

37. *Renyvle House.*

Now that a town of the North
In which a discerning band
Has caused your name to go forth,
And lifted on high your hand
Before all men on the Earth
As a sign of a contest won;
What should you do with your wealth
But spill it in water and stone;
With a Dolphin to scatter the spilth,[30]

but he could write of Yeats with almost clinical detachment or even poke fun at him, in his correspondence with Reynolds. 'At present [he wrote in March 1930] he is recovering at Rapallo from Malta Fever (undulating or Mediterranean Fever) and, if I can help him, with Ezra Pound — who has suppressed many of Yeats's lyrics — as if anything that Yeats pours in now does not take a beautiful shape from the very mould of his style and mannerism!'[31]

Charts giving details of Yeats's fever were passed on to Gogarty. They confirm the gravity of the illness. A diagnosis of Malta fever (brucellosis) was made by a consultant. Dr Pende of Genoa, who visited the poet on 22 January. Serum injections and arsenic were prescribed and a half bottle of champagne daily recommended. The infection could have been acquired from contaminated milk in Galway but with hindsight Pende's diagnosis must be viewed sceptically. Yeats coughed blood in London in November 1929 and may have developed a low-grade suppurative pneumonia.

Six years later Gogarty reported a more ominous illness affecting heart and kidneys: 'I fear that he will write no more. The last news from La Palma in Mallorca is that his feet are swelling. Seumas O'Sullivan who doesn't love either Yeats or F.R. Higgins complained that one poet had swollen feet, the other a swollen head'. Fortunately the poet recovered, and Gogarty sent the dramatic news of Margot Ruddock's extraordinary behaviour: 'Old man Yeats had gone one further in the London Mercury in overpraising the girl who had played in his Player Queen, and

30. Gogarty, O. *Collected Poems.* New York: Devin-Adair, 1954, 30.
31. Harvard, b Ms, AM, 1787, 6.

38. Senators Yeats and Gogarty at Punchestown Races.

later leaped out of a window in Barcelona after an interview with him in his retreat in Mallorca... But as I wrote already, it's not every man of 70 who can make a woman die of love or try the Sapphic leap'.[32]

Yeats's *Oxford Book of Modern Verse* elicited the quip from Gogarty, 'Now like Joyce, Yeats has put me with the Bucks!' Yeats's play, *Purgatory,* evoked protests from an American priest, Father Connolly, at the Abbey Theatre Festival and, at the conclusion of a lecture by F.R. Higgins, the priest caused a sensation by demanding interpretation. Gogarty[33] described for Reynolds how Higgins had protested that it was not for him to interpret a work of art; the chairman, Lennox Robinson, said Dr Yeats was the only person who could answer the question; Shelagh Richards thought the questioner should be answered but F.R. Higgins said that the play was surely more in the province of Father Connolly than his. When Yeats spoke to the press he said: 'Father Connolly found my plot perfectly clear but does not understand my meaning. My plot is my meaning. I think the dead suffer remorse, and re-create their old lives just as I have described'.

Gogarty was convinced that Yeats hated Edward Martyn for his Catholicism. 'There was in Yeats, derived doubtless from his parson grandfather, a bigotry that probably could not have been discovered in the grandparent, but which brooded in Yeats'.

When Jack B. Yeats, the artist, revived his 'Broadsides', a collection of illustrated ballads, Gogarty was surprised when W.B. Yeats called to his house in Ely Place one evening with the suggestion that 'The Hay Hotel' should be included. 'It is supposed now to be traditional', Gogarty wrote. 'That is fame indeed'.

Shortly before Yeats's *Words upon a Window-pane* was due for production in the Abbey Theatre, Gogarty referred to it: 'It is a seance: Swift's spirit speaks through a control. So do three other spirits. Hard on the control. But as a seance on the stage will get much attention, the control may make a success of it, even if it is hardly a play'. The inspiration for the play, incidentally, was

32. Harvard, b Ms, AM, 1787, 32.
33. Harvard, b Ms, AM, 1787, 57.

the chance finding by Yeats in 1910 of words inscribed on a window pane in a bedroom at Fairfield, Glasnevin, a Gogarty property; 'Mary Kilpatrick — very young/Ugly face and pleasant tongue'.

Observing Yeats's growing attraction for upper-class hostesses, Gogarty said, 'He has raised himself to the position of a Tacitus in whose hands lay the immortality of his contemporaries'. When the poems of Yeats's later phase gained increasing acceptance, Gogarty, like others, had a pang of nostalgia for the 'early Yeats'. 'It must be awful to have become so good a writer that all one's youth is ipso facto repudiated'. Himself gifted in the depiction of landscape, Gogarty took exception to Lady Dorothy Wellesley's comment that Yeats had no eye for natural beauty and cited *I stood by the edge/Of the drear Hart Lake.* 'Why with a word he can conjure a climate.'

Occasionally, having read one of Gogarty's poems, Yeats pointed out to him how it might be improved, making suggestions which were generally, but not invariably, accepted. When the surgeon showed him lines inspired by a patient's fatalism —

I told him he would soon be dead.
'I have seen all the pictures', said
My patient, 'And I do not care'.
What could a doctor do but stare
In admiration —[34]

Yeats hummed for a moment before offering an alternative: 'I told him he would soon be dead./'I've seen the pictures all', he said;/'and not a thrawneen do I care'. But Gogarty objected, not to the Kiltartanese, but because his patient, in the natural order of speech, had said 'all the pictures'.[35]

He eased Yeats's anxiety about raised blood pressure. 'One of our medical bugbears,' Gogarty said. 'What man is worth his salt whose blood pressure is not high?' But when Yeats, in indifferent health was invited to Florida by an American millionaire he expressed reservations. 'Clearly an alarm bell is sounding above my head. (Gogarty is probably pulling the

34. Gogarty, O. *Collected Poems.* New York: Devin-Adair, 1954, 189.
35. Harvard, b Ms, AM, 1787, 56.

string.) I have cabled my refusal and my gratitude'.[35b]

A scene almost of high comedy was recreated by Gogarty after a visit to Yeats's Rathfarnham house in November 1938. 'Yesterday I called on Yeats to find him sitting in his curule chair with his silver locks blue-washed like Carmel Snow's of Harper Bazaar! "Yeats, you have put blue-wash in your hair!" He nodded assent as if it were an act of God or of Apollo himself at the request of the Muses. But the allure of more mundane ladies may have accounted for it because he changed the subject but not as much as he thought he was changing it. "Gogarty, I have come to the conclusion that the best life consists of six weeks in England and six weeks in Ireland alternately. The best conversation is to be found in English country houses". This is true but Yeats has first to be there to make it'.[36]

None of Gogarty's comments should be misinterpreted. Irreverence came naturally to him; it was a part of his make-up. Towards the end of 1939, being then in America, he wrote: 'I have not yet recovered from the loss of the Archpoet and I never shall. I hear that he died in his sleep'.[37]

'I am attempting an elegy', he reported in the following year, 'but this is no country for poems on death'.[38] The elegy was published in 1941: 'A spray cut from that fine/And rare plant, Gratitude'. Gogarty paid his debt to Yeats with that poem and with his luminous description of the elderly poet in *Going Native:* 'He stood tall and very stately as if his magnificent countenance was transfigured in the light. He raised his right arm in greeting and bowed his head in a way suggestive of a strange resignation to my presence or the interruption by the mundane of his communion with his kin in faeryland...'[39]

Did Yeats recognise, too, that he had a debt to pay when he featured[40] Oliver St. John Gogarty as Malachi Stilt Jack in 'High Talk'?

35b. *Letters on Poetry, from W.B. Yeats to Dorothy Wellesley.* London: OUP, 1940, 140.
36. Harvard, b Ms, AM, 1787, 60.
37. Harvard, b Ms, AM, 1787, 67.
38. Harvard, b Ms, AM, 1787, 83.
39. Gogarty, O. *Going Native.* New York: Duell, Sloan & Pearce, 1940, 4.
40. Carens, J.F. *Surpassing Wit.* Dublin: Gill and MacMillan, 1979, 7.

Malachi Stilt-Jack am I, whatever I learned has run wild,
From collar to collar, from stilt to stilt, from father to child.
All metaphor, Malachi, stilts and all.[41]

Yeats certainly owed something to Gogarty, who had urged his appointment, albeit unsuccessfully, as Dowden's successor in Trinity College; secured his nomination as a Senator of the Irish Free State; removed his tonsils with an 'exuberant gaity' that concealed the stress of operating on a friend; acted as welcoming host in Dublin and Renvyle; and amused and sustained him in his declining years.[42] 'Gogarty has come and gone', Yeats wrote to Dorothy Wellesley in 1936, 'shedding behind him an admirable "limerick".[43] And to Margot Ruddock: 'My wife saw my gloom without knowing its cause and made an appointment for me for last evening with Ireland's chief wit Gogarty'.[44]

This record of uncalculated good fellowship cannot be reconciled with the opinions of those who blame Gogarty for the quarrel with Joyce and warrants a reversal of their judgements.

41. Yeats, W.B. *Collected Poems.* 2nd ed. London: MacMillan, 1973, 386.
42. Lyons, J.B. *Oliver St. John Gogarty – The Man of Many Talents.* Dublin: Blackwater Press, 1980.
43. Yeats, W.B. *Letters on Poetry to Dorothy Wellesley.* London: O.U.P., 1940, 110.
44. McHugh, R. *Ah, Sweet Dancer.* London: MacMillan, 1970.

39. *Gravestone, Ballinakill Cemetery.*

13. Clinical Verse*

Although aware that daffodils and young Lochinvar are no longer favoured subjects for poetry I was surprised to find that the *Oxford Book of Twentieth-Century Verse,* edited by Philip Larkin,[1] contains so much clinical verse. The term 'clinical' is sometimes used in a pejorative sense to indicate an aseptic or non-sentimental approach to a subject, but here I apply it to verses relating to hospitals, illness, or suffering. The genre, if it can be so designated, is by no means new; an outstanding nineteenth-century example is W E Henley's "In Hospital," which presents portraits of patients and staff in the old Edinburgh Royal Infirmary — including a special tribute to Mr Joseph (later Lord) Lister, who treated Henley for a chronic tuberculous infection.[2] Paul Verlaine addressed a similar paean to Professor Chauffard in 1890 from the shelter of *l'hôpital Broussais.*[3]

Larkin's anthology is arranged in chronological order and opens with an impeccable Victorian love sonnet by Wilfrid Scawen Blunt — a poet recently shown to be, among other things, a tireless satyr.[4] This is followed by poems of Thomas Hardy, whose second wife, Florence Dugdale, had been employed for some years by Sir Thornley Stoker (surgeon to the Richmond Hospital, Dublin) as a companion (a euphemism for wardress)

**British Medical Journal,* 2, 1658-1660, 1979.

1. Larkin, P. *The Oxford Book of Twentieth-Century Verse.* Oxford: Clarendon Press, 1974.
2. Henley, W E, *Poems.* London, Macmillan: 1926.
3. Vallery-Radot, *Verlaine à Broussais.* Paris: Guillemot et De Lamothe, 1956.
4. Longford, E. *A Pilgrimage of Passion – The Life of Wilfrid Scawen Blunt.* London: Weidenfeld and Nicholson, 1979.

40. John Millington Synge.

for the demented Lady Stoker. The first clinical verse encountered is John Millington Synge's 'A Question', which he sent to his fiancée, the Abbey Theatre actress Máire O'Neill, on 2 October 1908. 'I asked if I got sick and died, would you/With my black funeral go walking too...' Synge, who was a patient of Dr Alfred Parsons and Sir Charles Ball, was a victim of Hodgkin's disease. The course of his malady is outlined in *Letters to Molly*[5] — a correspondence dominated by an invincible expectation of recovery, despite which he died in Dublin in the Elpis Nursing Home in 1909 at the age of 38.

The most unequivocal examples of the clinical genre in the anthology are from a later period — J B S Haldane's 'Cancer's a Funny Thing' and James Kirkup's 'A Correct Compassion'. The editor refers to the former's poem as 'a rare example of the truly public poem' written with the express purpose of urging cancer patients to submit early and cheerfully to operation. Having held a number of important academic appointments in England, John Burdon Sanderson Haldane, FRS (a son of Haldane, the respiratory physiologist, and, in his given names, commemorating another great physiologist) took a post with the Indian Statistical Institute, Calcutta, and later became head of the Genetics and Biometry Laboratory at Orissa, India. In 1964 Haldane noticed that he was passing blood ('only a few drops, not a flood') rectally:

So pausing on my homeward way
From Tallahassee to Bombay
I asked a doctor, now my friend,
To peer into my hinder end
To prove or to disprove the rumour
That I had a malignant tumour.
They pumped in Ba So_4
Till I could really stand no more,
And, when sufficient had been pressed in,
They photographed my large intestine.

A biopsy gave the answer, 'That I have certainly got cancer.' An abdominoperineal resection left him like a kipper:

5. Synge, J.M. *Letters to Molly,* ed. A Saddlemeyer. Cambridge (Mass): Belknap Press, 1971.

Through this incision, I don't doubt,
The neoplasm was taken out,
Along with colon, and lymph nodes
Where cancer cells might find abodes.
A third much smaller hole is meant
To function as a ventral vent:
So now I am like two-faced Janus
The only god who sees his anus.

Haldane thought of it as 'a snappy bit of surgery', and advised others not to wait for aches and pains before having a surgeon mend their drains.

My final word, before I'm done,
Is "Cancer can be rather fun."
Thanks to the nurses and Nye Bevan
The NHS is quite like heaven
Provided one confronts the tumour
With a sufficient sense of humour.
I know that cancer often kills,
But so do cars and sleeping pills.

After recovering from the operation J B S Haldane sent his unusual poem to the *New Statesman,* where it was published on 21 February 1964. Despite his optimism, he died on 1 December 1964.

James Kirkup was Gregory fellow in poetry in Leeds University when he watched the late Mr Philip Allison perform a mitral valvotomy in Leeds General Infirmary:

Cleanly, sir, you went to the core of the matter,
Using the purest kind of wit, a balance of belief and art,
You with a curious nervous elegance laid bare
The root of life, and put your finger on its beating heart.

Sterile instruments shine against a dull background of green draped tables; the bodily appurtenances of the masked and gowned participators are reduced to hands and eyes. A woman, 'who does not know she is a patient', lies sleeping without a sound 'withing a tent of green' beneath lamps capable of illuminating the deepest wound.

A calligraphic master, improvising, you invent
The first incision, and no poet's hesitation
Below his snow-blank page mars your intent:
The flowing stroke is drawn like an uncalculated inspiration.

Across the painted flesh 'a garland of flowers unfurls'. Pressure forceps click and ligatures are knotted. 'Transfused, the blood preserves its rose, though it is sick'. A scalpel 'bears a creamy rib', beneath it, 'the pink, black-mottled lung like a revolted creature heaves.'

Finally, the heart — 'love's poignant image' — is revealed. Asking for more light, the surgeon slits the pericardium and makes a purse-string suture:

'How's she breathing Doug? Do you feel quite happy?' — 'Yes, fairly Happy.' — 'Now, I am putting my finger in the opening of the valve.
I can only get the tip of my finger in. — It's gradually
Giving way. — I'm inside. — No clots. — I can feel the valve
Breathing freely now around my finger, and the heart working.
Not too much blood. It opened very nicely.
This is a perfect case. — Anatomically.
For of course anatomy is not physiology.'

The tension eases. Street noises are again audible. Mr Allison does not find it necessary to stitch up the pericardium, a detail that fascinates the ruminating poet:

For this is imagination's other place
Where only necessary things are done, with the supreme and grave
Dexterity that ignores technique; with proper grace
Informing a correct compassion, that performs its love, and makes it live.

Mary Lou McDonough's *Poet Physicians,*[6] an anthology of verses written by doctors, shows that a great many clinicians have written poems, reflective or didactic, on professional matters. Chereau's *Le Parnasse Médical Français*[7] affords additional Continental examples of this amiable 'eccentricity,' and gives us

6. McDonough, M.L. *Poet Physicians.* Springfield: Charles C. Thomas, 1945.
7. Chereau, A. *Le Parnasse Médical Français.* Paris: Adrien Delahaye, 1874.

such notabilities as Prosper Menière and Paul Broca in poetic guise. The latter used a pseudonym 'Bap Lacour' as an anagrammatic cloak.

At least four of Larkin's poets — Robert Bridges, MB, FRCP, Oliver St John Gogarty, MD, FRCSI, Francis Brett Young, MB, BCh, and Alex Comfort, MB, BChir, DSc — had clinical experience, but it is not they who talk shop in this anthology. Brett Young does describe a burial at sea, but one feels that the deceased, a drunken Portuguese official from Mozambique who 'Took to his bunk, and drank and drank and died,' is no more than a lay figure included to justify the "Seascape."

Instinctively, and perhaps the better for being untrammelled by nosological data, the average poetic sensibility effectively ponders human agony, vicarious or personal. The narrowed world of the alcoholic is captured vividly in 'Delirium in Vera Cruz' and 'He Liked the Dead' by Malcolm Lowry, himself a denizen of that subworld and a martyr to its abhorred joys.

He seemed to have known no love, or have valued dread
above all human feelings. He liked the dead.
The grass was not green nor even grass to him;
nor was sun, sun; rose, rose; smoke, smoke; limb, limb.

Dylan Thomas, on the other hand, sublimated similar personal problems by recalling days when he was 'happy as the grass was green,' and, in a poem worthy of a biologist, acknowledges not some vague pantheism but a plainly stated kinship to all things natural.

The force that drives the water through the rocks
Drives my red blood; that dries the mouthing streams
Turns mine to wax.
And I am dumb to mouth unto my veins
How at the mountain spring that same mouth sucks.

Unlike some of the more worldly poets — who proclaim the gracious or play cynical games with the banal — in Larkin's pages D J Enright faces a starker reality: 'This vale of teargas/ More a hospital than an inn.'

A hospital in the tropics is the background to Susan Mile's 'Microscosmos.' A brown-faced nurse is distressed because her patient has not eaten her dinner, a heavy plate of liver and rice. Then sister brings in for inspection a tiny newborn infant whose child mother died in parturition. From across the compound creeps a naked child to squat on the verendah. There are yellow marigolds about her neck and sores on her skin.

And while I listen to her unintelligible babble,
As she displays now her marigolds,
Now her sores,
Her little voice becomes for me the voice
Of the unintelligible universe,
Beautiful and appalling.

Perhaps the riddle of nature's inescapable cruelty has been answered in evolutionary terms and is an acceptable part of the challenge of existence, but Thomas Blackburn's torment is to reconcile the plight of the mentally retarded with the designs of a beneficent Providence.

Lord of the Images, whose love,
The eyelid and the rose,
Takes for a metaphor, today
Beneath the warder's blows,
The unleavened man did not cry out
Or turn his face away;
Through such men in a turnip field
What is it that you say?

Blackburn also describes an attempted suicide, unfairly overstating the practitioner's lack of concern:

'Thirty,' the doctor said, 'three grains, each one,
That's quite a lot of sodium amytal!
Five, ten more minutes, and the job was done,
Just why do you think she wished to end it all?
Ah, well, that's not my business. You've her things?
Damn lucky that I had the stomach pump —
Take them up to her if the sister rings.'

There are several poems of geriatric import. Joseph Campbell, an Irish poet, presents an ideal picture of contented old age, an exceptional consummation of time and fulfilment — 'As a white candle/In a holy place/So is the beauty/Of an aged face.' Do we not seem more frequently to see Siegfried Sassoon's 'Miss Clara, deaf and old, alert and queer'? Or Colin Ellis's old ladies: 'And one was rather mad/ And all were rather trying/ So little life they had./ So long they spent a-dying.' The old tend to be pushed away from the warm centre of affairs, and it is a pleasure to read Hugh MacDiarmid's 'Old Wife in High Spirits' who is given a dram in an Edinburgh pub:

The rod that struck water frae the rocks in the desert
Was naething to the life that sprang oot o'her;
The dowie auld soul as twinklin' and fizzin' wi' fire;
You never saw ocht sae souple and kir.

Laurence Lerner — who presents an often overlooked truism, 'Only ill-health, recurring, inevitable,/Can teach the taste of what it is to be well' — measures the distance between fathers of the race (and male obstetricians?) and a true experience of the birth pangs:

No man has been a protagonist in the story,
Lying back bleeding, exhausted and in pain,
Waiting for stitches and sleep and to be alone,
And listened with tender breasts to the hesitant croak
At the bedside growing continuous as you wake.

Roy Fuller expresses astonishment that a girl in trousers wheeling an infant:

Has gathered herself together from
The chaos of parturition and
Appears now with a lacquered bouffant
Top-know and her old wiles unimpaired.
Why should one trouble to disguise the
Origin of the terrifying
Earth-mother, that lies in wait for men
With her odours and bergamot and
Plasma, and her soft rind filled with tripes?

His lines lend emphasis to the prodigal mysteries of reproductive physiology and add depth to an observation of Rosemary Tonks on coitus, highly relevant to the context of human reproduction:

— If the act is clean, authentic, sumptuous
The concurring deep love of the heart
Follows the naked work, profoundly moved by it.

We, in the medical profession, grow increasingly aware that the contributions of technology are extending the scope of diagnosis immeasurably — an augmentation not always paralleled by treatment, and carrying a risk of dehumanising medicine. It has been found necessary to form ethical committees to discipline our enthusiasms and curb our aspirations, but the perusal of verses written by such poets as have looked over our shoulders, or have, perhaps, perceived more acutely than case-hardened doctors can, the agonies we seek to relieve, may be equally valuable.

Poetry, however indefinable, can say more in a line than a chapter of prose, more in a stanza than a monograph, and acts as a vehicle for life's most tenuous stuffs, gossamer and irreplaceable. It supplies, too, as in W E Henley's 'Invictus,' sustaining messages of courage and adversity, with balm to neutralise commonplace irritations. Sir William Osler's prescription for *aequanimitas* — 'consume your own smoke' — is elegantly rewritten in this anthology by K W Gransden: 'Try and grow used to the place of every star/ And forget your own dark house.'

14. The Portrait of a Patient

Who the hell is this Joyce who demands so many waking hours of the few thousands I have still to live for a proper appreciation of his quirks and fancies and flashes of rendering?

H.G. Wells
Letters of James Joyce, Volume 1

1

Joyce's wasted appearance shocked his Swiss friends when he arrived in Zurich on 17 December 1940. Had he sought medical advice, which he refused to do, the case-notes (assuming that the doctor had all the information now available) could have resembled the following:-

Name:	Joyce, James A.	age: 58
Address:	Hotel Pension Delphin, Zurich.	occupation: writer

c/o Abdominal pain

Previous illnesses:
Myopia, dental sepsis, urethritis 1904, 1909
'rheumatic fever' with iritis 1907

relapsing iritis; iridectomies — 1917-30
Headache ?meningitis; irritable, lachrymose, 'colitis' — 1933

Family history:
grandfather d. typhoid fever
F. d. 1931 aet 82. Had typhoid, rheumatic fever, ?sy, alcoholic
M. 'a naked nerve' d. 1903, 42 ca of liver

Sibs: 6♂ ♀6
Elder brother d. perinatal
George d. ? TB
Frederick d. infancy
— d. perinatal
Charlie, slight squint, pleurisy
Eileen, tonsillectomy
May, eyes 'small ulcers'
Mabel, d. typhoid 1911
W. a. & w. but subject to 'nerves'; 1 miscarriage op. for uterine ca

C. ♂1 goitre op 1936
♀1 slight squint
schizophrenia

Habits: cigarette smoker
drinks wine ++? alcoholic

H.P.C.
? onset of abdominal pain Pola 1904
Trieste 1905: 'severe gastrical derrangement'.
Rome 1907 remarked: 'All this trouble and bustle always finds its way to the bosom of my stomach.'
Paris 1920s compared notes with Mrs Stuart Gilbert who had peptic ulcer — struck by

similarity of symptoms.
1939 stomach cramps and indigestion, despondent. '*Finnegans Wake* will be my last book. There is nothing left for me but to die.'

O/E Looks older than stated years; underweight, pale and unwell. Chronic iritis, glaucoma and cataracts; no further physical data available

Opinion: ? peptic ulcer ?? affective disorder
Requires rest, diet, antacids; eschew alcohol and cigarettes.

Instead of an orderly and leisurely consultation, however, fate ordained that Joyce sent for a doctor only when at about four a.m. on Friday 10 January 1941, several hours after Paul Ruggiero's birthday party, he was taken acutely ill with 'sudden very intense pain in the abdomen, marked flatulence and vomiting.' He told Dr Wehrlii who came to his bedside at that dark hour that for years he had been subject almost annually to acute attacks 'with spasmodic contractions, spasms in the abdomen lasting for approximately 24 hours.' He explained that he had been examined recently in Paris and was assured that no organic changes were detected.

Joyce's insistence that he had experienced this agony previously may have swayed the doctor's judgement, persuading him that he could safely accede to the patient's demand for an anodyne. Morphia was given thus delaying the sick man's admission to hospital where an immediate operation would then have had a high expectancy of success.

The grim events of Friday and Saturday are summarised by Professor Wilhelm Löffler who describes how Dr Wehrilii, concerned by Joyce's condition, called in an experienced surgeon, Heinrich Freysz, a former pupil of Kocher and Sauerbruch.

41. Heinrich Freysz.

He finds the patient in a very nervous condition. Abdomen with moderate meteorism, slight tension and tenderness all over, no reflectory contractions, no pain in sudden relaxation of pressure. Pulse rate 106. Patient says he feels better than in the morning. An accurate diagnosis is not possible for the moment. So the patient is transferred to the Red Cross Hospital the same evening. (Patient knew this hospital for having been treated there by Prof. Vogt.)
Saturday 11th, morning, general condition worse. Washing out of the stomach, contents brown. Benzidin-reaction [test for blood] positive. Upper abdomen rather flat, lower abdomen ballooned. Fluoroscopic examination and x-ray-photo shows a water level in the right upper half of the abdomen with an air-bubble about it. So the diagnosis of a perforation of stomach or duodenum was made sure.[1]

The laparotomy (exploratory operation) was performed at midday on Saturday under a local anaesthetic. A 3 mm perforation in the plyoric region was sutured and covered by omentum. By Sunday morning Joyce seemed 'rather to improve'. But in the afternoon (after an attempt to move the bowels) 'collapse'. At this juncture when the situation was aggravated by internal bleeding Dr Löffler was called to give a blood transfusion using a Bécquart syringe. The procedure was accomplished without any hitch and Löffler expressed the belief that 'the treatment of the patient was as good as possible in that time.' Regrettably, perhaps because of Joyce's undernourished condition and probably on account of the initial delay in diagnosis, it was unsuccessful. Joyce died at 2 a.m. on 13 January 1941 and at 4.30 p.m. on that day Löffler and Freysez attended the post-mortem examination carried out by Professor Zollinger. An abbreviated protocol (because of war-time mobilization) recorded at the time and signed by Zollinger was made available to me in 1968 by Professor Löffler.[2]

1. Medical report from W. Löffler to J.B.L., 31 May 1968.
2. Translated by B.G. Marlow and E. Poeschl, Viennese medical students doing a summer elective in Mercer's Hospital in 1968.

Postmortem number 55/12 F. Obd.: Dr. Zollinger. Clinic: Red Cross
Name: Joyce, James
Age: 58 years Occupation: Writer, Poet
Died: January 13, 1941, 2 a.m. Postmortem: 13th Jan., 1941, 4.30 p.m.
Clinical diagnosis: perforated ulcer, generalized peritonitis.
Findings at laparotomy, Paralytic Ileus.
Pathological-anatomical findings:
Condition after closure of perforated duodenal ulcer near pylorus. Fibrous peritonitis.
Paralytic ileus. Extensive bleeding from a second duodenal ulcer, marked oedema of lungs and hypostasis. Mesaortitis en plaques.

Extract
Section of head was not permitted.
External inspection revealed an upper midline laparotomy incision, otherwise nothing remarkable.
Chest and Abdomen.
On opening the abdomen there were enormously dilated loops of small bowel as large as a thigh, coloured purple exhibiting easily removed fibrous deposits.
No appreciable collection of pus was observed.
Spleen and liver normal. Th anterior wall of the duodenum shows recent suturing. The chest and heart normal. In contrast the lungs very large, blue red and the pleura taut. The cut surface is dark, blue red with a marked blood-stain and aerated ooze.
No marked increase in fragility.
Regional lymph nodes and thyroid gland normal.
The lung arteries contain fluid but very little.
The thoracic aorta measures 7½ cms. and exhibits some coinlike yellow intimal plaques in size between a threepenny and sixpenny piece.
In the abdominal aorta intima is extensively destroyed or calcified, sparse thrombotic deposits.
Spleen and liver normal.
Bile ducts clear.
Pancreas has a raglike consistency.

The stomach and oesophagus are filled with a thin dark brown fluid, the same is found in the upper part of the small intestine. The mucous membrane of the stomach is fragile. In the duodenum just distal to the pylorus which is difficult to recognize there are two shallow ulcers the size of a threepenny piece of which one is sutured while recognizable in the base of the other are a few blood clots. The ulcers were not adherent to neighbouring structures. Kidneys and genito-urinary tract normal. Mesentery without fat.

Histology:
Aorta: Broad lipoid deposits present in the intima which are partly calcified. The media exhibits occasional infiltrations by lymphocytes which generally surround the vaso vasorum. No plasma cells present. In the adventitia there is similar gross infiltration to which however there are added many large pale centred histiocytes. All other organs normal.
Signed: Professor Zollinger.

42. Red Cross Hospital, Zurich.

2

The chilling revelations of the autopsy-table, the rapacious court of final diagnostic appeal, and the dehumanizing bleakness of clinical phraseology both appear somewhat removed from medicine's ultimate goal, the restoration of vitality and well-being. The physician, accustomed to move among the ailing and etiolated, hearing the incessant demands of desperate suppliants, should have in his mind's eye an ideal of physical health, a comely reminder of the desired commonplace of all utopias, a vision of the kind evoked by Baudelaire's 'À Celle qui est trop gaie':

> Your health is radiant, infinite,
> Superb: When you go down the street
> Each mournful passer-by you meet
> Is dazzled by the blaze of it![3]

One cannot be sure that Joyce enjoyed for long in his own person the superplus of energy which is the endowment of a *mens sana in corpore sano.* A graphic portrait of ill-health is drawn with difficulty: the resignment of the middle-aged Joyce known to Dr Vogt, the Swiss ophthalmologist who attended the funeral in the Fluntern Cemetery on the bitter morning of January 15, contrasted greatly with the impatience of the young English-teacher in Trieste who complained in 1905, 'My glasses annoy me... It is a bloody nuisance to have to carry bits of glass in your eye'[4]; different still the little lad who went with his mother to consult Dr Arthur Benson who prescribed that first pair of spectacles broken on the cinder track.

A problem, too, the evaluation of evidence from so many sources, much of it over-eulogistic — 'Jim has a face like a scientist,' Stannie wrote in his diary. 'Not an old fumbler like Huxley or Tyndall, but like one of those young foreigners, like Finsen or Marconi!'[5] — some of it contradictory (Louis Gillet would have it that Joyce rarely drank but Robert McAlmon[6] gives chapter and verse), and a little of it hardly credible. The statement that in his fourteenth year he had sexual intercourse

3. Dillon, G. and Vincent, E. St V. *Flowers of Evil from the French of Charles Baudelaire.* London: Hamish Hamilton, *ND,* 142.
4. *Letters* 2, 81.
5. *Diary,* 57.
6. McAlmon, R. and Boyle, K. *Being Geniuses Together.* London: Michael Joseph, 1970.

with a whore on the canal bank really rests on doubtful evidence, the assertion of a boastful 'show-off' to a younger brother. Is it not far more likely that his sexual gratification at that age, and in the Dublin of that time, was solely masturbatory and that the undeniable commerce he had with prostitutes came a few years later? But Richard Ellmann, having accepted the veracity of Stanislaus's dubious evidence, cites the 'experiment' as having helped 'to fix his image of the sexual act as shameful'.[7] That this was his image of coitus is additionally conjectural. His letters to Nora suggest that he believed that no expression of desire or sexual curiosity between reciprocating lovers need be shameful. Comic or brutal, yes — the latter indubitably so in a literal sense — but shameful only because Western culture decrees with commendable delicacy that certain bodily acts associated with abandonment of personal dignity deserve privacy in varying degrees.

James Joyce was the eldest surviving child of John Stanislaus Joyce and his wife, Mary Jane Murray, whose first-born son died in infancy in 1881 at Northumberland Road, Kingstown (now Dun Laoghaire). He was born on Candlemas Day, 2 February 1882 at 41 Brighton Square, Rathgar, a middle-class residential Dublin suburb but his early memories would have been of Bray where the Joyces moved to in 1887. The family lived at 1 Martello Terrace a comfortable and roomy house close to the sea and facing Bray Head.

The innocent, healthy youngster displayed the euphoria of childhood to a degree that won him the pet-name 'Sunny Jim', his happiness and material circumstances not yet invaded by the knowledge of his father's improvidence. But by taking out the first of a succession of mortgages John Stanislaus Joyce had already embarked on a Hogarthian decline. He steps from his son's pages as Simon Dedalus who in middle life was to be a signal example of a not uncommon hybrid, street-angel and home devil. 'Our father who art not in heaven', his daughter said but now and then Simon Dedalus's comicality steals our affection.

One of Hilaire Belloc's verses speaks of 'men that lose their fairy lands' and I suspect that John Stanislaus Joyce was such a

7. *Ellmann*, 48.

43. 1, Martello Terrace, Bray.

man. Through sheer gregariousness he lost a fairyland which had its high noon in Cork when he walked along the Mardyke with Mick Lacy, Harry Peard, Jack Mountain and others and cut his name on a desk in the anatomy theatre in the medical school where from 1865 to 1870 he was a student. Whatever academic flair he possessed could not compete with his enthusiasm and talent for athletics and dramatics. He was registered in 1865-66 as First Year Faculty of Medicine and subsequently as 'First year from other years'. This indicates that he did not get beyond first year and suggests that he either failed examinations or did not sit them.[8] His disappointment must have been considerably mollified, when he came of age on July 4th, 1870 by his grandfather's gift of a thousand pounds and by the inheritance of property bringing him a comfortable income. This inheritance was diminished by mortgages and gradually frittered away.

The first of the inevitable traumas of a youngster's life, other than insidious Freudian conflicts and enuresis, is to be thrust into the alien atmosphere of a school. That James Joyce was no exception is confirmed by *A Portrait* which contains the first record of illness (probably influenza) in his surrogate's life. 'He was not foxing. And he felt the prefect's hand on his forehead; and he felt his forehead warm and damp against the prefect's cold damp hand.'[9]

His younger brother's mortal illness in 1902 inspired the account of the ailing Isabel in *Stephen Hero.* George Alfred Joyce may have succumbed to typhoid fever, a common infection at the turn of the century, but the development of what appears to have been a discharging abdominal sinus — 'There's some matter coming away from the hole in Isabel's stomach'[10] — suggests that he was actually suffering from tuberculous peritonitis, an equally common disease. Mabel, the youngest child, certainly did die from typhoid fever in Cork Street Fever Hospital in 1911.

The Joyce's tenancy in 1892 of Leoville, a comfortable house in Blackrock, was followed by a move to a 'bare cheerless house' on the city's North Side. By then Sunny Jim's equanimity had been

8. Information supplied by P. Ahern from archives of Queen's College, Cork.
9. *Portrait,* 19.
10. *SH,* 163.

44. *Leoville, Blackrock.*

disturbed in a way 'which had sickened his heart and made his legs sag suddenly'; he sensed that 'these changes in what he had deemed unchangeable' indicated that his father was in trouble and before long the least reference to his father by a teacher or a schoolmate 'put his calm to rout in a moment.'

As Joyce grew up his relationship with his father was an uneasy one though the latter never quite destroyed his son's strong affection for him or his admiration for his parent's Cork gift of the gab. Their visit to Cork in 1894 was a trial for the boy who did not fail to notice that his father's stories were punctuated by 'sighs or draughts from his pocket flask.'[11]

They walked through Cork — 'Along the Mardyke the trees were in bloom' — and entered the Queen's College making their way to the anatomy theatre where on a desk Stephen Dedalus read 'the word *Foetus* cut several times in the dark stained wood.' It affected him in the way the narrator in 'The Sisters' was moved by the terms simony, paralysis and gnomon. It reflected the arcane knowledge acquired by medical students and may have been a motivating factor when in 1902 Joyce decided to study medicine.

His relationship with his mother was deep and loving. She sometimes went with him to the Sheehys' 'At Homes' and played his accompaniment when he sang. Eugene Sheehy remembered her as 'a frail, sad-faced, and gentle lady whose skill at music suggested a sensitive, artistic temperament. She was very fond of James and he worshipped her. I can still see him linking her towards the piano with a grave old world courtesy.'

Sheehy also supplies a pen-picture of his contemporary at University College:

> As I remember him then, he was a tall slight stripling, with flashing teeth — white as a hound's — pale blue eyes that sometimes had an icy look, and a mobile sensitive mouth. He was fond of throwing back his head as he walked, and his mood alternated between cold, slightly haughty, aloofness and sudden boisterous merriment.[12]

Meanwhile at Belvedere College he had experienced, like many adolescents, the stresses of post-pubertal sexuality so impossible

11. *Portrait,* 97.
12. Sheehy, E. *May It Please the Court.* Dublin: Fallon, 1951.

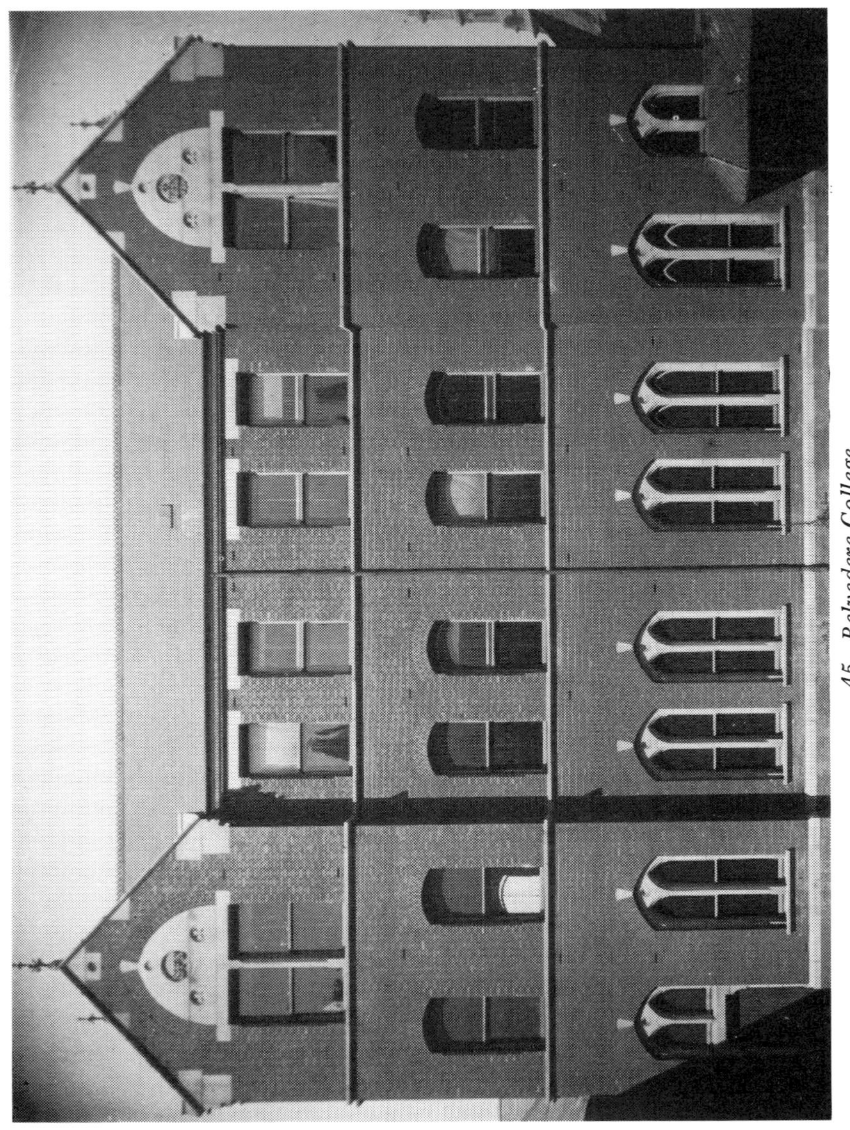

45. Belvedere College

to reconcile with the then rigorously imposed chastity of Irish Catholicism, and an increasing disintegration of religious faith. One must add to these the nascent stirrings of a creativity which was likely to have been both a torment and a joy.

The detumescent self-loathing that may accompany the almost universal habit of masturbation in young males was described from personal experience by W.B. Yeats.[13] For Joyce the act's 'sinfulness' magnified his guilt feelings, adequately accounting for Stephen Dedalus's horror as he listens to Father Arnall's sermon. The burden of guilt is increased by obligatory confession of sins to a priest, a liberating catharsis, perhaps, but a cause of mental torment for boys and girls. Was Nora Barnacle the source of Molly Bloom's candid reflections on this unwelcome sacrament? 'I hate that confession when I used to go to Father Corrigan he touched me father and what harm if he did where and I said on the canal bank like a fool but whereabouts on your person my child...' (662).

Had Joyce's natural piety persisted his goal might have been Holy Orders; instead the adventures of ideas instinctive to the maturing mind left him adrift on an ocean of disbelief. His loss of faith will be regarded as a grave misfortune by co-religionists while others will judge it to have been pure gain. Be this as it may, its inarguable consequence was to create a gulf between the now impious son and his deeply orthodox mother whose adherence to Catholicism was probably mystic rather than rational. When her son had given up religion she rarely reproached him 'except for one bitter and painful altercation' but according to Stannie a scar remained on his brother's mind affected by 'the idea of conflict between the mother who lives in fear of God and the outcast son, wandering cursed upon the hostile earth.'[14]

The legend that he refused his dying mother's request to kneel and pray for her is untrue. The command to do so was given peremptorily by an uncle when she was already comatose. After her death from cancer on 13 August 1903 the household became increasingly chaotic; Joyce, his brother Charlie and their father were frequently drunk.

13. *Yeats,* 72.
14. Joyce, Stanislaus. *My Brother's Keeper.* London: Faber, 1958.

Spiritual tribulations are less tangible than bodily ills. From Fresh Nelly or one or other of the street-walkers with whom he consorted Joyce acquired gonorrhea in 1904 or earlier and Gogarty sent him for treatment to Dr Michael Walsh. Apparently this was symptomatically successful but the infection may have been the remote cause of an acute illness that lay ahead. This was the so-called rheumatic fever.

John Stanislaus Joyce is said to have had rheumatic fever in his youth but the illness to which James fell victim in 1907, evidently polyarthritis with ocular complications, seems more likely to have been attack of what is nowadays called Reiter's syndrome. The acute arthritis subsided but there were recurring rheumatic symptoms; the iritis flared from time to time and there appears to have been a recrudescence of urethritis to which he alluded in a letter to Nora from Dublin on 1 November 1909: 'It is very good of you to enquire about that damned dirty affair of mine. It is no worse anyhow...'[15]

The concept of a disordered immune response explains how a focal infection (e.g. urethral) can subsequently lead to involvement of distant organs but malnutrition and alcohol abuse are important contributory factors. The large Joyce household was regularly on short commons and when the would-be-author fled to Europe he and Nora were obliged to lead a hand-to-mouth existence. Stannie added an element of stability when he joined them in Trieste but to control his brother's drinking was beyond him. Sack was an affectation replaced for economic reaons in Dublin by porter and in Europe Joyce's favourite tipple was white wine. Material circumstances improved as he attained success and patronage and although he spoke of himself as 'a man of little virtue inclined to alcoholism' this weakness was controlled as he grew older.

Stannie's *Dublin Diary* presents a picture of his brother in his rôle of dissipated genius which caused him to run after 'every chit with a petticoat on it in the street':

> He has come home drunk three or four times within the last month (on one occasion he came home sick and dirty-looking on Sunday morning having been out all night) and he is

15. *Letters 2*, 259.

engaged at present in sampling wines and liquers and at procuring for himself the means of living. He has or seems to have taken a liking to conviviality, even with those whose jealousy and ill-will towards himself he well knows...[16]

Charlie Joyce, a former seminarist, had a flair for writing but the surviving fragments of his verses are execrable. Stannie dismissed him unsympathetically as 'an absurd creature' and deplored his emulation of their elder brother. 'Charlie has been in gaol for drunkeness. The fine was paid after four days, and he was released. He is in with Jim's medical friends...'[17]

Joyce's boon companion, Oliver St. John Gogarty, was blamed by Stannie for his brother's lapses but when time sundered the antic pair James Joyce's waywardness was undiminished. The fantasy that had recreated the Mermaid Tavern in Dublin rebuilt it in Trieste where with his father's fecklessness he wasted on drink money that should have been spent on his family.

The last of his raffish drinking companions was probably Robert McAlmon a young American without means whose brief marriage to Bryher, the daughter of a British shipping magnate, had given him access to funds which he used to the advantage of impecunious writers in Paris. When Joyce was completing *Ulysses* he developed a habit of meeting McAlmon for aperitifs. Even when working steadily he was prepared to spend at least one night a week drinking with the American until the small hours in the Gypsy Bar off the Boul' Mich' where foul-spoken Jeanette and Alys, her sweet delicate companion, must have reminded him of the bawds of Nighttown, Fresh Nelly and Piano Mary. And sooner or later he would recite Dante to the *filles de joie* in a way that reminded McAlmon of a priest saying mass.[18]

At an earlier phase of the genesis of *Ulysses* Frank Budgen, a British artist whom he met in 1918 was his closest friend. Budgen's account of Joyce in Zurich reveals his many attractive qualities:

16. *Diary*, 1.
17. *Ibid.*, 34.
18. McAlmon, R. and Boyle, K. *Being Geniuses Together*. London: Michael Joseph, 1970, 28.

> Joyce's sense of humour was of a tonic and refreshing kind that delighted in strange words, puns, incongruities, odd situations, exaggerations and impish angles of vision. There was no sniggering defeatism in it; it was not a bitter sardonic humour, nor did one ever feel that it was an armour for vulnerable sensibility... His humour was altogether unforced and boyish.[19]

His prodigious memory had enabled him to store his mind with whole pages of many classic authors. One evening when Budgen mentioned Milton's 'Lycidas' Joyce recited the whole poem from beginning to end and followed it with 'L'Allegro'.

Joyce's head made Budgen think of an alchemist. His stance suggested 'a tall marshfowl, watchful, preoccupied.' His eyes, a clear strong blue behind thick spectacle lens were uncertain in shape and in moments of suspicion or apprehension Budgen noticed them take on a skyblue glare, an interesting detail, for by then Joyce had already submitted to the first of nine operations and one might have expected his eyes to have lost their lustre. A photograph taken by Gisele Freund (née Bloom) in 1939 reveals a grey opacification of the left cornea.

Budgen recalled how Joyce would take a picture near a window to examine it close up in the daylight 'like a myope reading small print.' He was surprised by Joyce's habit of pencilling notes criss-cross on little writing blocks which he was sometimes subsequently unable to decipher even with his large oblong magnifying glass.

Ezra Pound[20] mentioned to W.B. Yeats in July 1915 that Joyce was subject to 'irido-something or other' and in May 1917 Joyce told Forrest Reid that he was recovering from 'rheumatic iritis complicated with synechia and glaucoma...'[21] To facilitate readers' understanding of technical terms an outline of the anatomy of the eye is provided.

> The human eyeball, a globular structure, has three coats: the outer, visible, dense white *sclera;* the middle, vascular *choroid;* the inner *retina* containing light-sensitive receptors. Anteriorly (i.e. the

19. *Budgen,* 188.
20. *Letters* 2, 354.
21. *Ibid.,* 395.

front) is the transparent cornea.

The choroid, the middle coat, brownish in colour is sometimes called the uveal tract because early anatomists thought it resembled the inside of a purple grape skin (*uva,* a grape) the pupil representing the spot where the stem is pulled out. Anteriorly it thickens to form the *cilary body,* a circular muscular and secretory structure which continues forwards to form the coloured *iris,* possibly the eye's most distinctive feature. The *lens* in its capsule is attached to the cilary body by the suspensory ligament.

The window pane provided by the cornea allows light to enter the eye. The iris, a coloured curtain, alters the size of the pupil which dilates or constricts to control the quantity of light which passes into the eye, traversing the lens and striking the retina.

The space between the cornea and the front of the lens and iris is called the *anterior chamber;* the narrow circular space between the iris in front and the lens and ciliary body is the *posterior chamber.* The chambers contain a watery fluid, the *aqueous humour,* which is secreted by the ciliary body into the posterior chamber and passes forwards between lens and iris to enter the spaces of Fontana (did the poet who wrote 'On the Beach at Fontana' know of these euphonious spaces?) which, communicating with the anterior chamber, are found in the angle of the anterior chamber. Finally the aqueous humour passes through the canal of Schlem which drains it into scleral veins.

The terms *iritis, irido-cyclitis* and *uveitis* denote inflammation of the iris, ciliary body or uveal tract which may cause the iris to adhere to the lens (synechia) at the pupillary margin. Interruption of the circulation of aqueous humour by synechia, or blockage of the canal of Schlem by inflammatory exudate, leads to an abnormally high intraocular pressure which is known as *glaucoma.* An acute rise in pressure causes agony and endangers sight. Opacification of the lens *(cataract)* results in blindness if sufficiently dense.

The vitreous body, an amorphous transparent gel, fills the intraocular space behind the lens. The front of the eye is invested by a delicate, transparent membrane, the *conjunctiva.* Inflammation of the latter, conjunctivitis, is a characteristic feature of Reiter's syndrome; uveitis is less common but when it occurs it is very severe.

Joyce was laid up for some weeks early in 1917 and he referred to this episode when writing to C.P. Curran, a Dublin friend, on March 15: 'I am recovering from a painful — and this time dangerous — illness of the eyes. I am now out of pain and much better and this morning the doctor was very optimistic so that I hope it will not be necessary to operate.'[22] Symptoms of glaucoma recurred in April but he still hoped to avoid surgery for, as he told John Quinn, 'I dislike the idea of cutting out pieces of the iris at intervals.'[23]

His well-wishers included Ezra Pound who felt as competent to advise him on health matters as on literary affairs. Pound mistrusted British doctors, believing they had not yet emerged from the eighteenth century. He evidently also felt uneasy that Joyce should be in the hands of Swiss ophthalmologists and he urged him to consult Dr George Milbry Gould who had treated Lafcadio Hearn.[24] Gould, an American, was a poet, essayist and biographer, the author of *Concerning Lafcadio Hearn.* The snag, of course, was that he was three thousand miles away in Baltimore, Maryland; when Gould eventually replied to Pound's letter his commonsense advice was that Joyce should consult some trustworthy local specialist.

By then he had been examined by Dr Ernst Sidler-Huguenin professor of ophthalmology in the University of Zurich, who told him not to go to the country. 'I must always have a doctor at hand', Joyce explained to Harriet Shaw Weaver, 'glaucoma being very dangerous and my eye "launish" [peevish] like its owner.'[25] The ophthalmologist agreed to postpone surgery but on 24 August 1917, six days after an attack of glaucoma, he performed an iridectomy on the right eye. The operation, Nora Joyce reported to Pound, was 'complicated and difficult' but after three days of 'nervous collapse' the irrepressible patient recovered sufficiently to write limericks in the dark.[26]

He convalesced in Locarno intending to benefit from its kinder climate for several months but Nora was unsettled there and had a nervous breakdown. Uncertain as to what course to take, unwilling to expose himself for the present to Zurich's notorious wind, the *fohn,* and yet anxious to be considerate to his wife, he finally decided that his health must take precedence. They stayed in Locarno until January 1918 and then returned to Zurich.

22. *Ibid.,* 391.
23. *Ibid.,* 396.
24. *Pound/Joyce,* ed. Forrest Read, New York: New Directions, 1967, 85.
25. *Letters* 2, 397.
26. *Ibid.,* 405.

Early that summer ocular symptoms recurred and he apologised in August for the delay in replying to Forrest Reid's letter: 'The fact is I have been in bed for more than two months with an attack of my eyes — the fourth in two years. I really do not know what to say about it.'[27] A poem, 'Bahnhofstrasse' written in 1918 was inspired by ill-health. 'The eyes that mock me sign the way/Whereto I pass at eve of day...' 'Towards the end of the year he felt more optimistic but, as he informed Miss Weaver in February 1919, his eyes remained so 'capricious' that he never knew when they might let him down. 'This time the attack was in my "good" eye [the left] so that the decisive symptoms of iritis never really set in. It has been light but intermittent so that for five weeks I could do little or nothing except lie constantly near a stove like a chimpanzee whom in many things I resemble.'[28] His doctor, influenced by partisanship rather than objectivity, attributed the attacks of iritis to the annoyance caused by his dispute with Henry Carr, an amateur member of 'The English Players' a dramatic company organised by Joyce and Claud Sykes, and to his 'cowardly ill treatment' by officials in the British Consulate but wisely did not hazard an opinion as to how creative turmoil might affect the author of *Ulysses.*

When Joyce settled in Paris in 1920 his literary affairs prospered immediately under the auspices of Sylvia Beach; his health continued to resist the ministrations of a series of doctors. The first of these was a French ophthalmologist, Victor Morax, whom Joyce consulted in May 1922 telling him that the ailment resulted from sleeping rough after a night's drinking in 1910. The iritis improved a little in response to treatment but when there was an exacerbation later in the month Morax, unable to examine Joyce personally, sent his assistant, Dr Pierre Mérigot de Treginy, who called to 9 *rue de l'Université.* The young doctor was amazed at the untidy littered condition of the Joyces' apartment and also so concerned by the author's plight that he believed an operation to be inevitable.[29]

Some days later a fresh emergency caused Joyce's children to summon Sylvia Beach who realised that fear of another

27. *Letters,* 117.
28. *Letters* 2, 437.
29. *Ellmann,* 549.

operation was agitating him just as much as pain. She arranged a consultation with Dr Louis Borsch, an American specialist who practised in the *rue de la Paix.* He agreed that the operation could be postponed.

He was well enough to go to London in August but the journey made him worse and a Dr Henry referred him to Mr Robert Rutson James of Wimpole Street, ophthalmologist to St George's Hospital. They reminded him of Henry and James's drapery store in Dublin which had added a detail to *Ulysses* — 'Henry and James's wax smartsuited freshcheeked models ...' The unwelcome advice that an operation was urgently required sent him back to Paris where Borsch, whom he saw after a delay, was still prepared to temporise. The doctor diagnosed dental sepsis which he believed could be eliminated without provoking an eye attack. He prescribed a correction in the right lens of Joyce's spectacles and a rest in Nice. If dispersal of the nebula did not follow a sphincterectomy should be done.

The weather in Nice, where Joyce arrived on October 17th, was bad and his eyes reacted adversely. Dr Louis Colin used leeches and dionine solution with some advantage. The latter was continued in a weaker solution in Paris by Borsch who planned to operate when this was feasible. He told Joyce that the operation in Zurich during an acute phase had been a mistake and although well done had been spoiled when 'exudation' (emergence of vitreous?) flowed into the incision. 'The question is almost as complicated as Ulysses', Joyce reflected. He was given further food for thought by a doctor who explained that Homer went blind because he lived before iridectomy was available.[30]

The first of the dental operations was done on 4th April 1923 and was followed by a second. An iridectomy and a sphincterectomy on the left eye were performed in two or three stages later in the month.[31] Whatever benefits accrued were negligible as Joyce admitted when writing to Sylvia Beach from Bognor Regis in July: 'I had to visit the oculist twice in London with these — glasses. The improvement of sight is so slow that I have given up thinking about it'.[32] But by then the indefatigable

30. *Letters* 1, 201.
31. *Letters* 3, 76.
32. *Ibid.*, 78.

novelist was writing *Finnegans Wake.*

'In spite of my eye attack', he explained to Miss Weaver,[33] 'I got on with another passage by using a charcoal pencil which broke every three minutes and a large sheet of paper. I have now various large sheets in a handwriting resembling that of the late Napoleon Bonaparte when irritated by reverses.' The *New York World* announced that he was rapidly going blind but he denied the report in a letter to Claud Sykes in June 1923 and referred optimistically to the expected benefits from the last operation. 'I can write and read a fair amount even now.'[34]

Another operation was being contemplated in 1924. Joyce felt dubious of its success and worried in case it should upset Nora's nerves but Borsch performed a second iridectomy on the left eye on June 10 as a safety valve against glaucoma. This was his fourth or fifth eye operation and before the end of the year there was to be another.

Having consulted Borsch again on 15 November 1924 he listened incredulously as the ophthalmologist proposed an operation for cataract. 'Have I cataract as well?' He felt too ill and overcome to ask questions. 'And from time to time I lie back and listen to my hair growing white...' 'These continued operations are dreadful', Joyce told Robert McAlmon[35] but he wrote encouragingly to Miss Weaver on 30 December 1924. 'Since Saturday there is (I am afraid to say it) a small, but definite return of some kind of vision in my eye... I can make out objects dimly even without a lens. Of course I must have one to replace that extracted and another to correct my sight.' He admitted to feeling dreadfully tired and suspected that medication with iodine and scopolamine was responsible.[36]

Borsch postponed a seventh operation because of conjunctivitis and episcleritis in the better (right) eye and prescribed treatment with leeches. He operated on 15 April 1925 intending to perform a capsulotomy on the left eye but was unable to complete it.

33. *Ibid.*, 73.
34. *Ibid.*, 77.
35. *Letters* 1, 223.
36. *Letters* 3, 112.

'I saw Dr Borsch', Joyce reported to Miss Weaver in July.[37] 'He is surprised I cannot see better and is positive I will see. I asked if another operation might be necessary. He said: "I think not".' Borsch's secretary was instructed not to accept a fee. Later in the year Joyce politely declined an invitation from the representatives of a magazine syndicate to write an article on how it felt to be going blind.

Borsch found it necessary to operate again in December 1925 and promised improvement when the blood absorbed. His assistant, Dr Arthur W. Collinson, was less optimistic and by the end of January Joyce was thoroughly depressed, unable to perceive light with the left eye. He was unable to attend *Exile's* first night in London. 'I lie on the couch most of the day, waiting for Ireland's eye this day to do his duty.'[38]

He was fortunate to escape unhurt in a traffic accident in May 1926 and in June submitted to what was to be his final operation at Borsch's clinic in the rue Cherche-Midi which Joyce called Madame de la Vallière's château. Making his way there cautiously on one occasion he found his path blocked by another 'patient', a Boston bulldog with a bandage over the eye Borsch and Collinson had operated on for staphyloma. A more dramatic canine encounter occurred in the following year when, while lying on a beach at Scheveningen, he was attacked by a dog. His glasses were broken and he was badly frightened but when the animal was beaten off he had a friendly chat with its owner as they groped in the sand for his shattered spectacles.[39]

The possible ill-effects of the mistral on his eyes worried him when he visited Avignon in May 1928. Three months later he was laid up with conjunctivitis and episcleritis in Salzburg. He used atropine which reduced his visual acuity but he wrote to Harriet Shaw Weaver in September with the irrepressible good humour characteristic of his letters:

> The complete eclipse of my seeing faculties so kindly predicted by A.M's young friend from Oxford, the ghost of Banquo, I am warding off by dressing in the three colours of successive stages of cecity as the Germans divide them, namely: green

37. *Ibid.,* 121.
38. *Letters* 1, 239.
39. *Ibid.,* 255.

46. *Rue Cherche-Midi, Paris.*

Starr, that is, green blindness, or glaucoma; grey Starr; that is, cataract, and black Starr, this is dissolution of the retina. This therefore forms a nocturnal tri-colour connected by one common colour, green, with Shaun's national flag of peas, rice, egg yolk, the grey of evening balancing the white of something else, the egg probably. So I had a jacket made in Munich of a green stuff I bought in Salzburg and the moment I got back to Paris I bought a pair of black and grey shoes and a grey shirt; and I had a pair of grey trousers and I found a black tie and I advertised for a pair of green braces and Lucia gave me a grey silk handkerchief and the girl found a black sombrero and that completed the picture.[40]

After Louis Borsch's death in 1929 Joyce placed himself under the care of Collinson; he later consulted Dr Edward Hartman and during a visit to England was treated by Professor Euston but then, almost simultaneously, four friends from Zurich — George Borach, Marthe Fleischmann, and the Giedions — urged him to seek help from Professor Alfred Vogt who had succeeded Sidler Huguenin in the chair of ophthalmology at Zurich.[41]

Vogt's practice was enormous and his reputation attracted many foreign notabilities. Joyce consulted him in April 1930 and on May 15 Vogt performed an operation — by his count Joyce's tenth — on the left eye for tertiary cataract but was unable to complete it because of threatened collapse by emergence of the vitreous body. Excessive haemorrhage was avoided but ten days later a brief attack of iritis resulted from the unabsorbed blood.

Vogt used leeches to remove blood from the anterior chamber and when he examined the incision microscopically on June 3 he was pleased to find that unlike what had happened in the previous operations the incision remained open, unaffected by exudate. He also found that Borsch had not managed to remove the back wall of the capsule of the lens which had clouded to form a secondary cataract which obstructed sight.

Vogt expected some improvement, nevertheless, in the left eye and planned to deal with the capsule in September 1930. This

40. *Ibid.*, 269.
41. *Ellmann*, 622.

could be followed at a suitable time by an operation to remove a cataract from the right eye. These interventions, he believed, could ameliorate Joyce's vision considerably; the optic nerve and the periphery of the retina functioned normally and he expected that the macula was also intact.

After an examination lasting an hour, Vogt decided on June 15 not to detain Joyce any longer in Zurich where hotel bills had to be considered. He charged no fee, requesting instead a copy of *Ulysses* signed for his daughter.

On his return to Paris, Joyce attended the Paris Opera where his friend, John Sullivan, was singing in *Guillaume Tell* and during the performance, as a publicity ruse to aid Sullivan, removed his dark glasses and thanked God loudly for having restored his sight. In September he sustained what is nowadays called a 'whiplash injury' when a car ran into the taxi in which he was crossing the Esplanade des Invalides.[42] 'I was flung violently forward [he informed Miss Weaver] and then as violently back but escaped any glass in the eye. I had a big bump on my forehead and a bad pain in my back the doctor who examined me said there was no internal injury.'

It was Vogt's intention to select a time when Joyce's eyes were in a non-glaucomatous condition and to use special instruments which would enable him to give his patient 'a fair measure of clear and practical vision.'[43] Evidently conditions were not suitable in September 1930 which pleased Joyce who hardly felt up to it and may have been relieved further when in November the operation was put off till spring. Vogt told him that the artificial pupil in the left eye would enlarge spontaneously. The ophthalmologist advised him to avoid colds and restated his plan to remove the cataract from the right eye and later to split the post-cataract membrane of the left eye.[44]

Giorgio Joyce's marriage, towards the end of the 1930, led to 'too many celebrations crowded together'. These may have contributed to the deterioration of sight experienced by Joyce in January and certainly left him short of money, unable to

42. *Letters* 1, 294.
43. *Letters* 3, 198.
44. *Ibid.*, 206.

celebrate his birthday with the usual splash.[45] He spent some months in London in 1931 returning to Paris in September. In December he heard that his father was ill in Drumcondra Hospital where John Stanislaus died on December 29.

Throughout the early 1930s, Joyce experienced what Louis Gillet called 'the Passion of the Father' on account of his daughter's mental ill-health. This clarifies what is otherwise difficult to understand — his failure to keep his appointments with Vogt. 'I cannot go to Zurich, of course', he explained to T.S. Eliot on 20 June 1932, 'though Vogt sent me a message to come.'[46]

The unconscionable delay in arranging to see Vogt increased his anxiety over the consultation. On the evening before his eventual departure for Zurich he visited a restaurant with Nora and William Bird and to the annoyance of his wife, who went home alone by taxi, he ordered a bottle of wine which was likely to lead to another.

Professor Vogt's manner was gruff and taciturn but being patient and persistent to a degree he would, as Joyce knew, have expected an equal single-mindedness from those under his care. It is unlikely that he could have understood Joyce's reasons for procrastinating or forgiven them when they finally met in July, particularly when he found deterioration in the eyes. 'He says [Joyce told Stuart Gilbert] I should have left other things aside and come to him before.'[47] The consultation must have been stormy, with Vogt failing to conceal his irritation, even anger, and Joyce was left wondering whether their professional relationship could continue. 'How can I possibly make an engagement with him now even if he does decide to risk the two different operations which he fears he cannot even make?'

Vogt had found the cataract in the right eye denser; there was secondary glaucoma and a new development, partial retinal atrophy. He said bluntly that in the circumstances atropine had been 'pure poison'. He wished to have a further examination before making a decision. Overwhelmed by the ophthalmologist's reaction Joyce wrote him a letter relating the

45. *Ibid.*, 312.
46. *Letters* 1, 320.
47. *Ibid.*, 323.

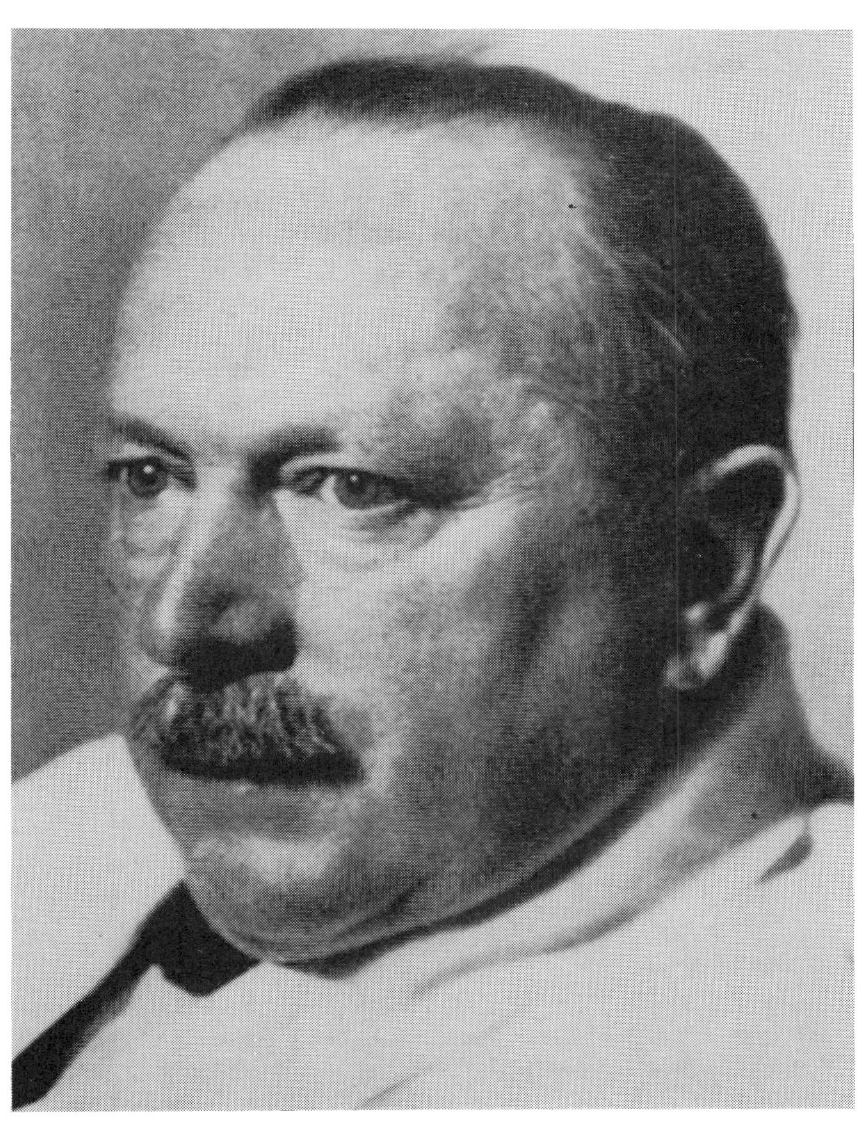

47. Alfred Vogt.

events which had prevented him from coming to Zurich and confided to Budgen that Vogt was the one man in Europe who could help him.

After measuring the ocular tension in September, Vogt decided that the operation should be deferred. He prescribed new glasses and insisted that for the next eighteen months Joyce should make three-monthly visits. He refused to accept other doctors' reports. 'Damn well right too [Joyce told Budgen]. I wish I had met him ten years ago.'[48]

Now reduced to reading with the assistance of a strong magnifying glass, Joyce felt sympathetic when he heard of Eamon de Valera's eye problems and told James Stephens to recommend Vogt, to which advice he added gratuitously that the eye specialists he had consulted in London, 'eight or nine', were quite incompetent.[49] Vogt's gesture in refusing Joyce's fees evoked in the latter a response natural to a writer, the wish to publicise the doctor. His amusing letter, quoted by Ellmann, describes how he had gone,

> ... for supernatural reasons to consult the great oculist VOGT who has already operated on him more than fifty times. Mr. J. contracted his terrible ailment at the early age of 16 on a windy day in Dublin, his home village, when his eyes were suddenly startled by the sight of his life et une autre chose encore que je n'ose pas dire. Mr J. never goes out in Paris except in perambulator wheeled by his Greek and Roman nurse Miss Paval Leopoldovitch [Paul Léon an authority on Benjamin Constant] who reads to him while he sleeps passages from Adolphe Benjamenin's curious poem about love matching entitled Constancy.[50]

A tactless acquaintance, perhaps hoping to moderate Joyce's drinking but with the effect of precipitating a nervous upset, told him early in 1933 that further visits to Zurich were pointless as he had damaged his eyes permanently and Vogt was not likely to operate on him again. Paul Léon had to call in a doctor to calm

48. *Letters* 3, 261.
49. *Ibid.,* 271.
50. *Ellmann,* 658.

him and assure him that he could take wine with his meals. Mrs Léon recalled him drinking Fernet Branca instead of wine to soothe his stomach.

Others in his immediate circle were inclined to discourage further visits to Zurich arguing that he was managing well enough with his present vision and that the expense was unnecessary. Paul Léon, on the other hand, urged him to keep in touch with Vogt and the ophthalmologist examined him in May. The left eye (now the better) had improved a little and could be expected to continue to do so slowly as the pupil opened upwards. The right eye had disimproved, the cataract calcified and vision totally lost.

The feasibility of operating on the right eye either immediately or in September was discussed. Finally it was agreed that Joyce should return for examination in September but the consultation did not take place until April 1934 when operation on the right eye was again postponed in case it should upset the situation in the left eye which had improved a little. A further measurable improvement was noted in the left eye in April 1937.

Mrs Léon noticed that despite his disability Joyce remained conscious of colours and interested to name them and discuss their shades and ranges. One day he said suddenly as they sat in the living room: 'Mrs Léon, are you not wearing a white blouse? I believe I can see something white'. Any manifestation of improvement was discussed at length by Joyce's circle of friends.

In the following January, after months of continuous application to *Work in Progress,* he developed congestion in the left eye — 'the only one really left' he described it to Ezra Pound[51] — and when he visited Vogt reading and writing were forbidden for some weeks. He improved. The projected operations were never done but events validated Vogt's assurance that while Joyce would never see well he would not lose his sight.[52]

Vogt was among those who supported Joyce's wartime application for entry to Switzerland having already received a

51. *Letters* 3, 415.
52. *Ellmann,* 707.

testimony of gratitude in *Finnegans Wake* where he is featured in Ann van Vogt (54.04).

3

Most of Joyce's adult life was dominated by the exigencies of iritis and its complications but he was visited, too, by ill-health's broader assaults. These could be of prostrating severity though generally psychosomatic in nature, a statement that needs to be qualified in the light of the knowledge that duodenal ulceration eventually manifested itself in such a dire manner.

His genetic endowment is not suspect and sheds no light on his genius. The slur of congenital infection has been disposed of in an earlier chapter. His bright infancy passed without record into a boyhood now difficult to separate from Stephen Dedalus's agonised evolution towards adolescence. At Clongowes like others he was bullied a little and beaten with the pandy bat on three occasions — for 'forgetting to bring books to class', for 'wearing boots in the house', and for using vulgar language. He came down with influenza as mentioned earlier, spent some time in the infirmary and was charged eight shillings and sixpence for medical attention. It has not been suggested that he was ever involved in 'smugging' the tentative fondling for which, in *A Portrait,* Simon Noonan, 'Lady' Boyle and five older boys were to be either flogged or expelled but in a letter to his brother Joyce alludes equivocally to homosexuality.[53]

The memory of Joyce retrieved from Clongowes by Kevin Sullivan 'is of a small boy "more delicate than brilliant"...' but may not the impression of frailty have been exaggerated by his extreme youth (six years and seven months) when he entered the school? Sullivan judged his years at Clongowes to have been 'serene and uneventful'[54] He was active in roles appropriate to his age, playing the part of an imp in a play and carrying the incense boat on the altar at benediction. Bruce Bradley, SJ, author of

53. *Letters* 2, 199.
54. Sullivan, K. *Joyce Among the Jesuits.* New York: Columbia University Press, 1958, 14.

James Joyce's Schooldays, cites the evidence of a contemporary who recalled him 'as a blithe and happy boy.'[55]

When the picture of the tiny boy at Clongowes is superimposed on that of the ravaged, middle-aged celebrity, with the image of the aesthete, Stephen Dedalus, sandwiched between, they convey an impression that Joyce was never robust. This is corrected by Stanislaus Joyce's recollection of his brother's athletic prowess in his teens and later. Joyce was a fast runner with a flair for hurdling; he wielded a useful cricket bat and kept Stannie bowling to him for hours; he was fond of swimming, able to beat Gogarty, a swimmer of championship class, over short distances. Stannie described him as 'an indefatigable walker'; hoping to enlist the patronage of an Irish-American millionaire who lived in Celbridge he walked there and back from Cabra in 1903; he cycled from Galway to Oughterard in 1912.

Financially straitened, John Stanislaus Joyce took 'Sunny Jim' away from Clongowes either during or at the end of the Michaelmas term in 1891 by which time the family had moved from Bray to Blackrock. It seems to have been at Leoville, Blackrock, that young Joyce first experienced the wish to write and to have become aware that behind his father's joviality and generosity — 'he always gave him a shilling when he asked for sixpence' — were less commendable qualities. Creativity and the anxiety and poverty imposed by paternal alcoholism would in due course impose significant psychological stress though in what degree it is not possible to say.

Having entered Belvedere College on 6 April 1893 he gained the first of his examination successes, an exhibition in Preparatory Grade, in 1894. A member of the Sodality of the Holy Angels, he was received into the Sodality of the Blessed Virgin Mary in 1895 on the eve of the Feast of the Assumption.[56] He was elected prefect of the sodality shortly after the opening of the academic year in 1896 a position which made him one of the school's leaders. The esteem in which he was held is confirmed by Father William Henry's enquiry as to whether he had a vocation for the priesthood even though the puzzled rector was

55. Bradley, B. *James Joyce's Schooldays.* Dublin: Gill & Macmillan, 1982, 83.
56. Bradley, B. *Ibid.,* 118.

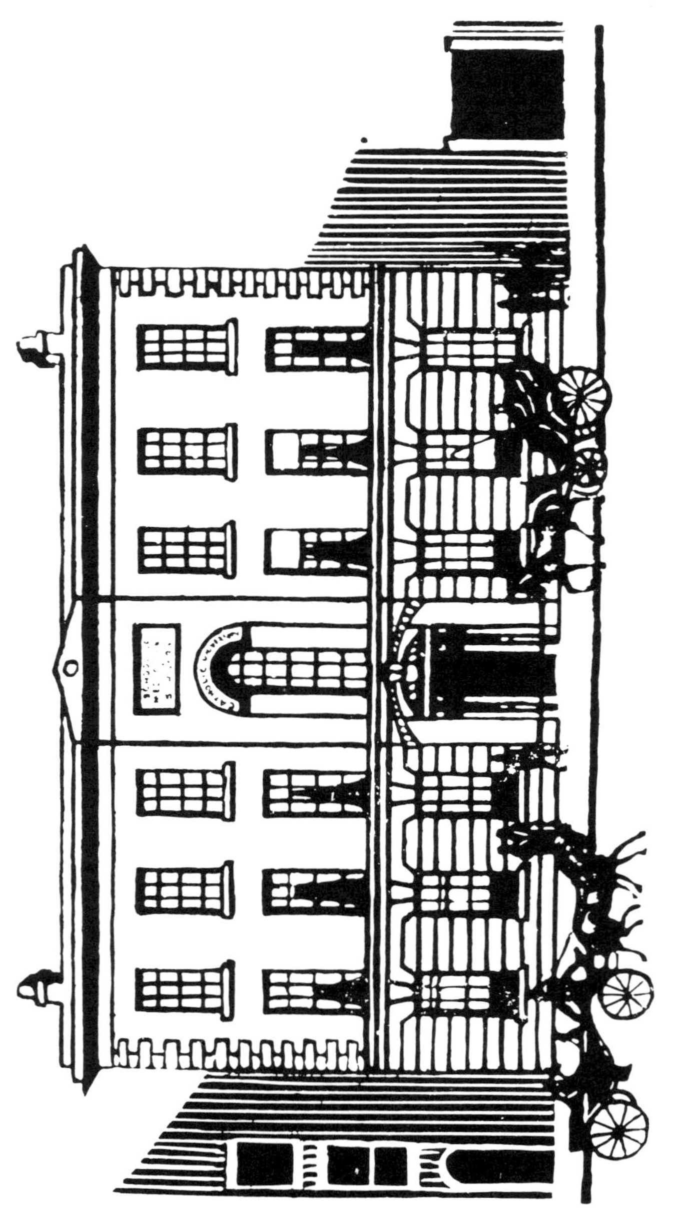

48. *Catholic University Medical School, Cecilia Street.*

simultaneously sufficiently worried about the boy to interrogate Stannie about his brother's behaviour and to issue a vague warning to his parents. The rector's misgivings were confirmed when Joyce and others deliberately ignored the customary catechetical examination not bothering to sit it. His changed attitude is illustrated by deteriorating examination marks, a trend which continued at University College where his intellect never engaged the full range of the curriculum.

Even before taking a mediocre BA degree he toyed with the idea of studying medicine and in March 1902 visited the Catholic University Medical School in Cecilia Street to enquire about registration, accompanied by J.F. Byrne and others.[57] When he told Constantine Curran of his intention when walking on the North Bull Wall in September Curran was surprised but Joyce's name was entered on the Medical School's register on October 2nd. He evidently attended a preliminary course of anatomical lectures (the Michaelmas term did not begin officially until November 2) or engaged in private study for there are 'medical notes' in the Cornell Joyce Collection which consist of thirteen pages listing simple anatomical terms. On 17 October 1902, for instance, the terms he added included *cervix, chiasma, cilia, diaphysis, disastric, diplöe.* Dare one suggest that the optic chiasma, nature's ingenious anatomical arrangement, inspired the frequent occurrence of chiasmus pointed out by Hugh Kenner[58] and others in Joyce's writings?

Failing to establish himself in Cecilia Street, Joyce, to the astonishment of William Archer, decided to enter the École de Médecine in Paris and pay his way by giving English lessons. Archer tried to dissuade him, pointing out that if he managed to get enough teaching to make a living he could not combine it with medical studies. Not in the least put off Joyce tried to enlist Lady Gregory's interest: 'I want to get a degree in medicine, for then I can build up my work securely.'[59]

Leaving Dublin by the night boat on December 1st he obtained a provisional card of admission to the course for 'PCN' (physics, chemistry and natural history) as soon as possible and planned to

57. Byrne, J.F. *Silent Years.* New York: Farrar, Straus and Young, 1953, 76.
58. Kenner, H. *A Golden Eye.* New York: Knopf, 1983, 196.
59. *Letters* 1, 53.

49. Rue de l'école de médecine.

equip himself for the dissecting room by purchasing an apron, sleeves and instruments. Before long, however, he experienced hunger and home sickness to a degree that made him ache to spend Christmas in Dublin. His indulgent parents made this possible but on his return to Paris he spent his time increasingly in the Bibliothèque Nationale and the Bibliothèque Ste Geneviève and forgot about medicine.

Can Richard Brown's claim that Joyce intended to gain 'a knowledge of himself from medicine' be substantiated? It is, indeed, arguable that although doctors observe human nature in all its naked phases their self-knowledge remains largely physiological. Admiration for the healing profession, whether influenced or not by Ibsen, is presumably indicated by Joyce's choice of a doctor as the hero of *A Brilliant Career,* the unpublished play written in 1900. Brown may be correct in suggesting that 'the progressive, free-thinking bourgeois doctors who figure in the Ibsenite drama'[60] determined Joyce's decision to study medicine but the major motivation was probably economic. He had seen acquaintances at the Royal University become affluent in the medical profession. He believed it would provide him with an assured income and allow him, as he explained to Curran, to put enough aside to retire and devote himself to writing.

His failure to persist also was economic. He lacked funds and without money to pay the lecture fees he could not attend a medical school in either Dublin or Paris. A man of Joyce's ability could easily have mastered the chemistry which he described to Harriet Shaw Weaver as the *pons asinorum* which he could not cross. His French was already adequate. Had he reached the stage of clinical studies the instinctive feeling referred to elsewhere to read the face of suffering would have been a great advantage.

Literary creativity ruled Joyce's life; his failure in medicine did not weigh heavily on his mind; his laughter could astonish a café but the privations of this period are relevant to his health record. His precarious budget rarely provided both food and rent. Spells of fasting were inevitable. He learned how to seek his

60. Brown, R. *James Joyce and Sexuality.* Cambridge University Press, 1985, 15.

acquaintances out at lunchtime, a ruse more successful with the French than the Englishmen or Americans. When the arrival of a money order relieved the siege he was inclined to gorge. 'I hope', he wrote to his mother, 'this new system of living won't injure my digestion.'[61] He attributed his attacks of neuralgia to fasting, and feasting led to vomiting.

Pride and obstinacy shielded him from guilt engendered by the knowledge that the occasional comforts made possible by the money orders meant that his parents had sold a carpet or other furnishings. He had cast himself in his personal drama as the victim of circumstances blaming the ignoble authorities in University College for his plight. Nothing, however, shielded him from the revelations of his mother's letters or softened the misery of his home in Cabra. His father had for some time been 'in curious state of mind'; Charlie, his youngest brother, was 'a conundrum', refusing to work and railing against John Stanislaus; the eldest girl, Poppie, dissatisfied with her lot, was unable to buy shoes or even a pair of gloves; May was attending the Eye Hospital.[62] More traumatic still an unexpected telegram: 'Mother dying come home Father.'

Joyce's grief scores the pages of *Ulysses* vibrant, too, with recovered laughter. Stannie's bewilderment is registered in the *Dublin Diary* which depicts squalid scenes in Cabra where his inebriated father upbraided his sodden sons, James and Charlie, for being drunk. Charlie became a habitué of Nighttown and was admitted to the Whitworth Hospital with tuberculous pleurisy.[63]

Fate brought Joyce and Nora Barnacle together in Nassau Street in June 1904 adding to his mind's creative turmoil the turmoil of love, a word he avoided using.

> My home [he explained to her in a letter] was simply a middle-class affair ruined by spendthrift habits which I have inherited. My mother was slowly killed, I think, by my father's ill-treatment, by years of trouble, and by my cynical frankness of conduct. When I looked on her face as she lay in her coffin — a face grey and wasted with cancer — I understood that I was

61. *Letters* 2, 29.
62. *Ibid.*, 33.
63. *Diary*, 43.

looking on the face of a victim and I cursed the system which has made her a victim.[64]

When the couple eloped Joyce's unkind Dublin contemporaries predicted cynically that he would leave Nora on the streets but their unsanctified union (formalised legally in 1931) ripened to form insoluble bonds enduring 'Till Breath us depart'. Unuttered vows sustained them 'in sickness and in health'.

Their first lodging in Pola, a furnished room and kitchen, was unscreened against mosquitos which still tormented them in November, and lacked a stove to lessen December's increasing cold. By then Nora was pregnant. Joyce drank little but smoked heavily. 'One night I had a severe cramp in my stomach...' The first ulcer symptom, perhaps?

As the months passed, despite discouraging editors Joyce worked at his writing; his English lessons were conducted inventively but he sometimes felt like hitting his pupils over their heads and walking out. And when the novelty of continental life wore off he longed for a slice of mutton with turnips and carrots while Nora wanted to see a kettle by an open fire.

Lovers' quarrels were inevitable and becoming increasingly aware of Nora's naivety Joyce began to compare himself to Heine who married an uneducated shopgirl. Having suffered in Pola from the cold Nora wilted in Trieste's summer heat. Her swollen, ungainly body lost its feminine allure and her spirits fell to a degree that caused Joyce's allusive mind to think of Harriet Shelley's death in the Serpentine.

Eventually he poured out his heart to Stannie in a letter lacking the customary hilarity of their correspondence, a letter devoid of irony which claimed that it was only 'Skeffington, and fellows like him, who think that woman is man's equal.' He explained unsympathetically that Nora cried and complained continually, dressed shabbily, was generally helpless and reluctant to cook. She had made no friends and was 'one of those plants which cannot be safely transplanted.' He saw no prospect of happiness for her in Trieste and feared that she was destroying his own

64. *Letters* 2, 48.

natural cheerfulness. He intimated that he was tiring of exile and suggested that if he could put money aside Stannie might join him in renting a cottage outside Dublin. Failing that he invited Stannie to join him in Trieste.[65]

Two weeks later on 27 July 1905, the birth of their son ended this crisis. Joyce informed Stannie that the six-hour labour had been unpleasant for him but had the good grace to add 'it must have been a damn sight worse for Nora.'[66] Then the miracle of parental love welded them into a family unit which, despite later hints to his aunt that a separation was likely, remained as indissoluble as the most piously-entered Roman Catholic marriage. From time to time, of course, the boot was on the other foot and she threatened to leave him. A perceptive biographer has recently shown that Nora was more capable and decisive than earlier accounts would allow.[67]

After a period of indecision which caused his brother 'two days severe gastrical derangement', Stannie decided to accept a post at Trieste's Berlitz School.[68] He had expressed misgivings about 'leaving the children in the lurch' but James pointed out realistically that he could do nothing to help them in Dublin.

Alarmed in the following year by Stannie's revelations from Trieste, Aunt Josephine put family feeling before feminist solidarity. She excused her nephew's drinking, blamed Nora for irritability and a scurrilous tongue and thought it monstrous that she should expect James to cook or mind the baby. She also warned Stannie that the money he sent home was being misused by John Stanislaus.

Joyce moved with his family in July 1906 to Rome — 'the stupidest old whore of a town ever I was in'[69] — where he experienced further hunger and hardship and found difficulty in keeping a roof over their heads. Little wonder that he had nightmares. Some of his money went to the chemist: Giorgio needed medicine for bronchitis, Nora required a tonic and he

65. *Ibid.,* 92.
66. *Ibid.,* 101.
67. Maddox, B. Could Nora Cook? Portrait of the Wife of the Artist. *New York Times Book Review:* 16 June 1985, 28.
68. *Letters* 2, 122.
69. *Ibid.,* 198.

bought rhubarb pills to relieve his own constipation and indigestion.

After the day's work in the bank the frustrated writer gave English lessons for a pittance but with splendid resilience could see humour in his situation. On the anniversary of his 'espousal' he celebrated expansively. 'There is literally no end to our appetites: I don't believe I ever was in better health... I stand fascinated before the windows of grocers' shops.'[70]

Christmas Eve found him with eleven lire in his pocket and evoked a wry reflection: 'Well! (as Mr Pater beautifully says) I have reached the low-water mark in Xmases this 'ere time.'[71] The trio moved in the early weeks of 1907 from one lodging to another; the bustle and trouble upset his stomach and disturbed his nerves. Finally, he decided that because of the higher cost of living in Rome, where he could not write, his long hours of work brought him little more than he had earned in Trieste. From Florence on March 7th he wired to Stannie: 'arrive eight get room.'[72]

Ellmann refers to Joyce's last binge in Rome — he spent an evening drinking with two postmen and another night when drunk in a café was set upon by malefactors who stole his wallet — to Stannie's dismay at the return of his importunate brother, and to Artifoni's refusal to re-employ him, followed by capitulation on realising that as an independent teacher Joyce would attract the better-class pupils away from the Berlitz School.[73]

When Joyce fell ill with polyarthritis in mid-July the cost of his stay in the city hospital was met by the school. He attributed the illness to sleeping rough when drunk but as I have indicated earlier, the cause was more subtle. He had largely recovered by September but the seeds of further tribulations now were sown and meanwhile Nora gave birth to their second child, Lucia.

Cosgrave thought Joyce looked well when they met in Dublin in August 1909. He drank mineral water and told Nora that he felt 'in splendid health again' but Mrs Barnacle noticed his habit

70. *Ibid.*, 172.
71. *Ibid.*, 204.
72. *Ibid.*, 220.
73. *Ellmann,* 250.

of sighing, a common indication of chronic anxiety. 'I have had no trace of rheumatism [he reported to Stannie] in spite of all the rain and think it is the lithia I drink which is curing me.'[74] He arranged for Eva, his stoical sister, to accompany him on his return to Trieste. Her tonsils were removed by Mr Robert Woods, ear-nose-and-throat surgeon to the Richmond Hospital, two days before they set out.

During a second visit to Dublin in October 1909 he had a bout of sciatica. 'Rheumatism seems better [he informed Stannie] but am awfully played out.'[75] He referred, too, in a letter to Nora to a symptom which Ellmann interprets as a minor venereal infection but may have been a recrudescence of urethral discharge which occurs in Reiter's syndrome.[76] This visit culminated in a recurrence of iritis and his eyes were bandaged. Fortunately he had arranged for another sister, Eileen, to join the Trieste branch of the family. 'Had it not been for my sister who travelled with me across Europe I would certainly have ended under the wheels of some train or car.'[77]

Stannie, not surprisingly, had become increasingly impatient with the demands on his time and money but Joyce blandly ignored his brother's irritation and blamed him for the recurring rows. 'Kindly give it up, as I am unwell...'[78]

Nora, taking Lucia with her, went to Ireland in July 1912. Her absence and delay in writing precipitated an acute anxiety state in Joyce: 'I can neither sleep nor think. I have still the pain in my side. Last night I was afraid to lie down. I thought I would die in sleep. I wakened Georgie three times for fear of being alone.'[79] He followed her to Dublin which rather pleased her, increasing her self-esteem. His pleasure in their re-union was diminished when he found his sisters with nothing to eat and his publisher, Maunsell & Company, still obdurate. 'Everything seems to have melted away from me, money, hope and youth.'[80]

74. *Letters* 2, 244.
75. *Ibid.*, 280.
76. *Ibid.*, 259.
77. *Ibid.*, 285.
78. *Ibid.*, 283.
79. *Ibid.*, 297.
80. *Ibid.*, 311.

Nevertheless, 'the rheumatic chamber poet's'[81] general health remained tolerably good and with his unextinguishable optimism where *Dubliners* was concerned he demanded from Grant Richards who finally published it that the royalty of 10 per cent should apply to the first 8000 copies after which he should receive a royalty of 15 per cent. In the event, however, the statement of sales up to 31 December 1914 showed that only 379 copies were sold in the United Kingdom.

Joyce and his family moved to Zurich in June 1915. In the autumn of 1916 he had 'three or four collapses'.[82] He was relieved to be assured that these had a 'nervous' origin and were not, as he had feared, cardiac. If the diagnosis of rheumatic fever were correct he would have had good reason to worry over cardiac complications. Gogarty had warned him in 1907 to get sufficient rest.[83] 'At least 6 months are necessary to ensure safety of the cardiac valves.' He was laid up for a week with fever and tonsillitis in 1917.[84]

From *Dubliners* Joyce earned two shillings and sixpence in three years but he had a change of fortune in Zurich attracting patronage and a civil list pension. By then Nora's nerves were affected and in 1919 Joyce still engaged in the exhausting process of writing *Ulysses* explained to Stannie that he, too, was having treatment for nervous overstrain.

After returning briefly to Trieste the Joyces moved to Paris in July 1920. Before long they were established in reasonable comfort and Joyce remarked on their good fortune to Budgen: 'By the way, is it not extraordinary the way I enter the city barefoot and end up in a luxurious flat?'[85] His introduction to Sylvia Beach which assured the publication of *Ulysses* was another stroke of luck.

By now Joyce and his novel had become a focus of interest and misrepresentation. He was held by some of the more outlandish

81. *Ibid.*, 324.
82. *Letters* 1, 97.
83. Lyons, J.B. *James Joyce and Medicine.* Dublin: Dolmen Press, 1973. 186.
84. *Letters* 1, 103.
85. *Ibid.*, 151.

accounts to be a spy, by others a cocaine addict or a crazy fellow who carried four watches and rarely spoke to anybody except to ask the time. It was rumoured in Dublin that he could no longer write and was dying in New York. A Liverpool man told him he had heard that Joyce owned a chain of Swiss cinemas. The more prosaic truth, of course, was that with obsessional devotion to the task in hand he worked on *Ulysses* daily until the small hours. Eventually he felt like a person who has 'dissolved visibly and possesses scarcely as much "pendibility" as an uninhabited dressing-gown.'[86]

One evening in August 1921 he felt too light-headed to work and accompanied his son to the Alhambra but collapsed during the performance and had to be helped out of the theatre. 'The attack lasted about an hour. I could scarcely breathe and was very pale and weak — and nerves! Still I don't think it was cardiac because my nails remained pink.' He was driven to a night pharmacy and given ether.[87]

After this warning he reduced his work to six hours a day, went for walks and felt better. Excitement mounted as publishing day drew nearer. Nora was nervous, Joyce in a state of 'energetic prostration' and inclined to worry in case the printing house should be burned down or some untoward disaster occur at the last minute.[88]

His irrational fears were unrealised. *Ulysses* was published in 1922 and the earth continued to revolve even though the literary firmament was rent by controversies including a correspondence between Ezra Pound and GBS which the latter closed by writing: 'I take care of the pence because the pounds won't take care of themselves.'[89] Soon Joyce found himself being disturbed increasingly in restaurants by people who asked after some scrutiny 'if I am the great etc etc who wrote the etc etc and requested the pleasure of shaking my hand — an art for which I have very little talent.'[90]

When Nora made no attempt to read *Ulysses* he was offended

86. *Ibid.*, 167.
87. *Ibid.*, 170.
88. *Letters* 3, 57.
89. *Letters* 1, 184.
90. *Ibid.*, 186.

and her decision in April to visit Galway taking the children with her was additionally upsetting. He fainted in Sylvia Beach's bookshop and further 'collapses' occurred in the next few years.

Ezra Pound prevailed upon him in July 1922 to consult a New York endocrinologist, Dr Louis Berman, who was visiting Paris. Dental x-rays were done, treatment prescribed for Joyce's arthritic spine and dental extractions planned. A denture was provided in due course but Joyce told Miss Weaver that it was unsatisfactory. 'The dentist is to make me a new set for nothing as with this one I can neither sing, laugh, shave nor (what is more important to my style of writing) yawn...'[91]

Work in Progress contained references to many illnesses — 'flu, pock, pox and mizzles, grip, gripe, gleet and sprue, caries, rabies, numps and dumps' (209.33) — and references to an almost equal variety of ailments can be extracted from Joyce's letters, a record of unfailing tribulations. He was 'slightly grippé' from time to time and experienced an ague which left him 'shivery-shaky'. There were attacks of tooth-ache, cramps, bronchitis, laryngitis, tracheitis and lumbago. 'My lumbago is gone but I can't sleep at night.' The flu-like illnesses left him tired, weak and listless.[92]

Christmas and New Year 1927-28 were spoiled for him by 'inflammation of intestines' and worry in case a complete nervous breakdown should follow.[93] He explained to Miss Weaver that 'as for my poor brain box why it's falling down all the time and being picked up by different people who just peep inside as they replace it and murmur "So we thought"!'[94] When Dr Thérèse Bertrand Fontaine examined him in October 1928 she found his heart and blood-pressure normal but his nervous resistance low. He was given a course of arsenic injections.

What he called 'miniature fainting fits', lasting seconds, occurred in the early 1930s. He slept poorly and took sleeping tablets in increasing doses. A broken dental plate which he could not afford to have repaired was an annoyance. 'I keep juggling with... [it] in my mouth. This was a novel occupation when I

91. *Letters* 3, 205.
92. *Letters* 3, 205.
93. *Ibid.,* 168.
94. *Ibid.,* 171.

began it in London last August, but I am thoroughly tired of it now...'[95]

He went to Rouen in January 1933 to hear Sullivan sing *Sigurd* and felt ill during the return journey. Two nights later he had auditory and visual hallucinations. Becoming oppressed by alarm in the early morning he went out into the snow to tell Paul Léon that he was in danger. As Dr Fontaine was away Léon called in Dr Debray who diagnosed a toxic-confusional state resulting from sudden omission of the sleeping tablets which Joyce had stopped before setting out for Normandy.

The further suffering which lay ahead in 1933 has been described by Paul Léon in letters to Harriet Shaw Weaver explaining Joyce's need to sell stock to meet expenses incurred by Lucia's illness. During this year Joyce was attended on a number of occasions by either Dr Debray or Dr Fontaine for emotional and abdominal upsets.

A pain at the back of his head in March made him fear meningitis but Dr Debray reassured him. 'He examined the liver and digestive tube and he emphatically says that they are in perfect order...' At this time Joyce was prone to 'states of great irritation and impotent fury' and to episodes of weeping. There was an acute attack of what he called 'colitis' in April. 'You cannot imagine [Léon wrote] how strong these pains can be and how utterly helpless and strengthless they leave him.'[96]

This attack was largely subsided when Dr Fontaine arrived. She found no abnormal signs but was disinclined to accept the diagnosis of colitis, attributing the symptoms to spasms of nervous origin, or as Léon put it, 'to a disequilibrium of the system of the sympathetic nerve with the focus of the dislocation in the epigastric part of his stomach provoking the terrible pains.' She believed absolute and complete calm to be necessary and advised a rest cure.

On his return from Geneva in September, Joyce had another set-back 'with these terrible pains which have poisoned his existence during the last several years' and spent a week in bed. Dr Debray ordered laudanum compresses and attributed the

95. *Letters* 1, 303.
96. *Letters* 3, 276.

50. James Joyce by Pavel Tchetlitchev.

symptoms to nerves. He was critical of some members of Joyce's family and certain over-officious friends 'who put "une interpretation trop facile" on the case, an interpretation which he did not share and which no doctor would agree with after 48 hours examination.'[97]

Whatever the cause of the pain (and with the advantage of hindsight it is impossible to avoid the conclusion that even in 1933 and earlier there was active duodenal ulceration) emotional tension due to financial worry and his daughter's illness was a potent aggravating factor. X-ray examinations were resorted to relatively infrequently in those days and gastroscopy, the most revealing modern investigation in gastric disease, was not then available. Sylvia Beach, possibly one of the 'over-officious friends', summed up the medical profession's limitations: 'I don't believe much in doctors except for setting broken bones and calming acute attacks of maladies. I think that plenty of sleep, food, work and outdoor exercise and perhaps to see one's family as little as possible is the only way to be healthy.'[98] He was laid up again with grippe in March 1938 and complained to Lord Carlow that he was exhausted, 'working literally day and night'.

'Hurray! I have finished this blasted book', he told Paul Ruggiero in November.[99] His daughter-in-law held a banquet in his honour on 2 February 1939 and read the closing pages on the passing out of Anna Livia to an appreciative audience. When the controversial masterpiece appeared in May the *Irish Times* referred to the publication of *Finnegans Wake* by Sean O'Casey a misprint which Joyce attributed to malice rather than inadvertence.

4

Richard Brown's *James Joyce and Sexuality* mentions the relationships of Stephen with Mulligan and with Cranly which 'have sometimes been felt to display a latent or suppressed kind

97. *Ibid.*, 287.
98. Beach, S. Letter to Harriet Shaw Weaver. Ms. 57, 353 British Library, cited by Bonnie K. Scott, *Joyce and Feminism.*
99. *Letters* 1, 403.

of homosexuality.'[100] To those attenuated examples of possible *literary* inversion the fictional paederast in 'Encounter' may be added and Joyce himself drew Budgen's attention[101] to 'an undercurrent of homosexuality in Bloom.' Writing on Oscar Wilde[102] he referred to Wilde's 'unhappy mania (if it may be called that) which later dragged him to his ruin'; elsewhere he pronounced that love was impossible between men because there must not be sexual intercourse and that friendship between men and women was impossible because there must be sexual intercourse.

Joyce's physical sexuality appears to have been exclusively heterosexual. The so-called 'suppressed' letters to Nora (*Selected Letters*), rich fantasies auto-erotic in effect, recalled for him the ardour of their tumultuous love-making. They reveal, too, that with slender titillating fingers* Nora Barnacle took the initiative. He chided her fondly for what he delightedly termed her naughtiness and for so shamelessly setting the pace.[103]

Budgen tells us that sexual love from Joyce's male viewpoint presented 'an irreconcilable conflict between a passion for absolute possession and a categorical imperative of absolute freedom.'[104] Carnal knowledge introduced, as we learn from his letters, the inevitable conflict inherent in the lover's spiritual exaltation of the beloved and the biological need to soil her by copulation. (In one mood he placed her, haloed, on a pedestal of purity; in another he saw her as a shameless Jezebel, half-naked and abandoned.*[105]) His sexual predilections were numerous but the raptures of the honeymoon couple in Trieste and Pola cannot have been unknown to couples in countless bedrooms since first Adam stooped over Eve. Her coital response was cold at first,* as he recalled in a 1909 love-letter which expressed longing to join his body to hers and to feel her yielding limbs melt

*Quotation of Joyce's actual words was forbiddn by the Trustees of the James Joyce Estate.

100. Brown, R. *James Joyce and Sexuality.* Cambridge University Press, 1985, 79.
101. Budgen, 215.
102. *Critical Writings,* 202.
103. *SL,* 182.
104. *Budgen,* 314.
105. *SL,* 166.

beneath him as he kissed her.[106]

Coitus in early antiquity was an acceptable public act with the brevity of the barnyard. Nowadays, potentially an art form, its performance (except for groupies) is private but the secrecy which shrouded it has been dispersed by sex-manuals and novels. The 'Missionary position' adopted by a placid majority seems to have become a staid expedient. The term 'dirty' is outmoded and 'perverse' increasingly difficult to define. It only remains to say that Joyce's letters point to an interest in anality, coprophilia and masochism not generally shared.

At the Frankfurt Symposium (1984) Stephen Joyce deplored the invasion of his grandparents' privacy by *Selected Letters.* Few Joyce scholars, nevertheless, will regret the publication of their 'night words' posted from Dublin in 1909, though some find their ready availability embarrassing, a lapse of good taste. George Steiner argues persuasively that sexual relations should remain a citadel of privacy. 'In that dark and wonder ever-renewed both the fumblings and the light must be our own.'[107]

Is Stannie's assertion[108] that his brother's temperament was 'predominantly sexual' overstated? Joyce's books treated sexual themes with increasing explicitness, and with an unexpected candour disturbing to contemporaries forgetful of the omnipresence of sex in their lives, but a proportional balance between sexual and non-sexual material is constantly maintained.

His thoughts, incidentally, are recognisable, with one exception, as valid representations of male aspiration, curiosity or disgust pondering ill-understood mysteries inseparable from 'pox-fouled wenches and young wives'.[109] As Giacomo Joyce silently regards his Triestine pupil's hands — 'Quiet and cold and pure fingers. Have they never erred'[110] — his thoughts recreate images contained in an earlier love letter. The exception is Molly Bloom's soliloquy which evoked Jung's admiration: 'I suppose the devil's grandmother knows so much about the real psychology of

106. *SL,* 169.
107. Steiner, G. *Language and Silence.* Harmondsworth: Pelican Books, 1969, 100.
108. *Letters* 3, 104.
109. *GJ,* 9.
110. *GJ,* 13.

a woman. I didn't.'[111] Nor, I suspect, did Joyce — the words are the words of Jim but the thoughts are the thoughts of Nora.

To say so is not to burden her with Molly's infidelities. Nora was offended by Joyce's veiled suggestion, while writing *Ulysses,* that she should have an affair. All is grist! His own extra-marital interests have been mentioned in an earlier essay. His mildly amorous feelings for a student in Trieste — 'A pale face surrounded by heavy odorous furs'[112] — were unrequited but inspirational. His iritis influenced a consumate description of the pupils of her eyes dilating and constricting: 'a burning needle prick stings and quivers in the velvet iris.'[113] A more active phase of inflammation determined another impression: 'rancid yellow humour lurking within the softened pulp of the eyes.'[114]

Ellmann calls this an affair 'of eyes rather than of bodies' and proceeds to describe Joyce's encounter in Locarno with Dr Gertrude Kaempffer, 'She was interested in his mind, he indifferent to hers.' Joyce exerted some pressure but his blandishments came to nothing with the serious-minded young doctor.[115]

In the following year Joyce's 'cloacal obsession' was fed by the sight of a young woman in a nearby house pulling the chain in a water closet.[116] When soon afterwards he passed her in the street he noticed that she limped a little but he was attracted, nevertheless, because she reminded him of an unforgettable girl on Merrion Strand. He pursued Marthe Fleishmann with a measure of caution arranging an assignation in Budgen's studio. Ungallantly he reported success in exploring the hottest and the coldest parts of a woman's body.

Was his interest in ladies' lingerie matter for fun or for fetishism? During the Zurich years he carried a pair of doll's panties in his waistcoat pocket until, to his distress, he lost them. But when Budgen reminded him Joyce was sceptical, 'Now', he

111. *Letters* 3, 253.
112. *GJ,* 1.
113. *GJ,* 1.
114. *GJ,* 2.
115. Ellmann, R. *James Joyce,* New and Revised Edition. New York: OUP, 1982, 418.
116. Budgen, F. *Myselves When Young.* London: OUP, 1970, 118.

said, 'I don't care a damn about their bodies. I am only interested in their clothes.'[117] The remark indicates that anxiety, ill-health and overwork had caused a sharp falling off of libido.

By then, in all probability, his active sex life was over. '*Work in Progess* — pfui! — is almost finished. So am I. Since last October I have been working like a mule at it all day long and almost all night long too.' Nora also remained a victim of 'nerves'. She had had an exploratory operation for uterine cancer on 8 November 1928 followed by radium treatment. The diseased womb was removed in February 1929 and fortunately she had no recurrence.

Giorgio Joyce was attempting to establish himself in a singing career but his health, too, gave cause for alarm. He improved following an operation for an overactive thyroid gland. And then Joyce's daughter-in-law became depressed. He sent her flowers on Independence Day 1938 and urged her to cheer up 'and accept these delightful blooms as a present from the garden where the pretties grow.'[118] She recovered her spirits but relapsed seriously in 1939 and was hospitalised in Suresnes. In the following year her brother, Robert Kastor, took her back to a private asylum in Connecticut where she recovered.

Two of Nora's sisters emigrated to the United States. One of them, Delia, returned in ill-health and spent some time as a patient in Ballinasloe mental hospital. Her third sister, Kathleen, who has been described as 'highly strung' was forty-two when she married John Griffin. Before long the surprising news spread that she was 'in the family way' but when this proved to be a phantom pregnancy the Griffins settled in London to escape ridicule. Mrs Griffin eventually died of leukaemia.[119]

Nora Joyce's later lonely years — 'She is white-haired, her face lined and sad'[120] — were to be shadowed by ill-health in the form of rheumatoid arthritis uncontrolled by a new drug, cortisone. She died in Zurich on 10 April 1951.

117. *Budgen,* 319.
118. *Letters* 3, 425.
119. O'Laoi, P. *Nora Barnacle Joyce.* Galway: Kenny, 1982, 113.
120. Edel, L. *James Joyce – the Last Journey.* New York: Gotham Book Mart, 1947, 23.

Stanislaus Joyce became more censorious of his brother's work — 'he referred to 'Circe' as the 'Agony in the Kips' the 'most horrible thing in literature' — as he grew older and escaped from his immediate influence.[121] Hardly was he relieved of the imposition of helping Joyce and his family when confronted by the obligation of assisting his widowed sister, Eileen, whose husband, Frantisek Schaurek, a bank official, had committed suicide.

When the tragedy occurred Eileen was in Paris returned from a visit to Dublin. Refusing to accept the awful news on her arrival in Trieste she insisted on an exhumation to see the evidence with her own eyes. She was then overcome with shock and amnesia lasting several months. On her recovery she returned to Dublin with her three children, Bozena, Nora and Patrick, and worked in the Hospitals Trust. Eileen Schaurek died in 1963.

Stannie married a former student, Nelly Lichtensteiger on 13 August 1928 and they named their son (b. 1943) James. Stannie was prone to kidney stones and pyelitis. He had a heart attack in London in 1954 after an uncomfortable overland journey and died in the following year on Bloomsday.

The youngest brother, Charlie, died in London on 18 January 1941 leaving a large family. Joyce's sisters have also died: Margaret ('Poppy') entered the Order of Mercy and died in her convent in New Zealand in 1964; Eva (d. 1957) was employed by a Dublin solicitor and shared a flat with Florrie who worked in the Hibernian Bank's law department; Mrs May Monaghan (d. 1966) had three children.

Giorgio Joyce and his first wife, his senior by many years, separated and were divorced. Subsequently he married Dr Asta Jahnke-Osterwalder, a Munich ophthalmologist. He died in Konstanz on 12 June 1976.

I have described Lucia's illness more fully elsewhere[122] and Mary Colum[123] and Jane Lidderdale[124] gave details of her

121. *Letters* 3, 58.
122. Lyons, J.B. *James Joyce and Medicine.* Dublin: Dolmen Press, 1973.
123. Colum, M. *Life and the Dream.* London: Macmillan, 1947.
124. Lidderdale J. and Nicholson, M. *Dear Miss Weaver.* London: Faber, 1970.

disturbed behaviour in Paris and London. Her cousin, Bozena Delimata, recalls Lucia's visit to Bray, County Wicklow:

> Lucia was pretty. She had dark, curly, shoulder-length hair and blue eyes with a slight cast, but, like Norma Shearer's, attractive in spite of it. Her way of staring at people, though, was disturbing. She could be serious or gay. Often she sang — in German, French, Italian, or English. One of her favourites was 'You're the Cream in My Coffee'', popular in those days. Sometimes her songs went on from one day to the next without stopping. She had a crush on Samuel Beckett. A letter she received from him began 'You are you because you are you — and only you...'[125]

She liked to lie on the floor before the gasfire wearing only a dressing gown. She was prodigal with the money her father sent her, communicating by telegram and travelling by taxi. Weather permitting she slept on a garden seat. She joined the Kilcroney Country Club but never used it. Instead, she went to the beach after dawn to swim naked in the sea. She tried ineffectually to commit suicide, turning on the gas and taking an overdose of aspirin. Once she lit a turf fire in the middle of a room.

Schizophrenia, formerly called dementia praecox, remains an unexplained mental aberration possibly the response of hereditary neurochemical vulnerability to undetermined environmental factors. Lucia had done a little writing; she tried to be a dancer; she occupied herself with lettrines but to little avail. Joyce and some of his friends tried to promote a career based on these brittle talents but fate or misfortune decreed otherwise, a bitter irony commented on by Bonnie Scott: 'Many gifted women are never let out into the world, as it was then and is now constituted, but this one turned inward and lost what little consciousness and power she had gained.'[126]

Joyce opposed those who counselled shutting her away. When eventually she was admitted to the maison de santé at Ivry he visited her weekly. He refused to accept that she was incurable and was excited in 1937 by the news that the sanity of Vaslav

125. Delimata, B. Reminiscences of a Joyce Niece. *JJQ,* 1981, 19, 45-62.
126. Scott, B.K. *Joyce and Feminism.* Bloomington: Indiana University Press, 1984, 83.

Nijinsky, the great ballet dancer, had been restored at Sanatorium Bellevue, Kreuzlingen.

Nijinsky had insulin shock treatment in the summer of 1937. At about this time, Bleuler, then in retirement visited Kreuzlingen and spoke to Romola Nijinsky in the presence of Dr Stakel. 'My dear Madame', he said, 'many years ago I had the cruel task of informing you that, according to medical knowledge as it was then, your husband was incurably insane. I am happy today to give you hope. This young colleague of mine has discovered a treatment for which I searched in vain for forty years.'

Nijinsky became well enough to leave hospital and live a sheltered existence cared for by his wife. Joyce's indestructible hopes for his daughter, whom he believed to be clairvoyant, remained unfulfilled. After the war she was transferred from Ivry to St. Andrew's Hospital and spent the rest of her life in Northampton or in the hospital's 'ladies house' in North Wales. Harriet Shaw Weaver was appointed her Receiver or guardian by the Court of Protection and was succeeded in this office by Jane Lidderdale who visited her regularly, looking forward to her smile of welcome and impressed by Lucia's sense of fun.[127]

When potent medication became availalble she was less disturbed. Only minimal supervision was required and she was well enough to write letters, to receive more visitors and to go on occasional outings in a hired car. Her later years brought increasing immobility and were spent in the hospital's geriatric wards.

She had a slight stroke in 1982 and died on December 12th, the eve of the feast of Santa Lucia whose protection her father was accustomed to invoke annually. On 13 December 1933, for instance, he wrote: 'Santa Lucia' 33. Her candle is burning quietly in the drawing-room. She has rather a job looking after my occhi!'[128]

127. Lidderdale, J. Lucia Joyce at St. Andrew's. *James Joyce Broadsheet*, 1983, 10, 3.
128. *Letters* 3, 294.

5

Having looked at *Anna Livia Plurabelle* John Stanislaus Joyce said: 'He has gone off his head, I am afraid.'[129] Another early critic said: 'He has determined to write as a lunatic for lunatics.' Such candid expressions of disapproval of *Work in Progress* were common even from those close to Joyce but one is surprised to find a psychiatrist state in a medical journal that *Finnegans Wake* 'must ultimately be diagnosed as psychotic.' Dr N.J.C. Andreasen then proceeds to invalidate her opinion by clearing Joyce himself of the slur of psychosis leaving the reader in a quandry. Can psychotic art exist if the artist is not psychotic? Her unsympathetic article 'James Joyce: A Portrait of the Artist as a Schizoid'[130] illustrates the undesirability of a facile application of demeaning medical terminology primarily intended for a clinical purpose. Every point on which her diagnosis of 'his schizoid character' is based is contestable. She describes as a 'proud loner' a man who all his life needed people about him. Far from being aloof he made friends easily and his apparent selfishness was determined by creative necessity. Joyce offers us in *Dubliners* a perfect picture of a schizoid. Mr Duffy ('A Painful Case') fulfils Dr Andreasen's criteria being 'emotionally detached, aloof, eccentric, intellectual, and self-absorbed.' Joyce's own personality was more complex and more tortured albeit encompassing in some measure traits which might justify the psychiatrist's offensive label.

His contemporaries at University College called him 'the hatter' or 'dreaming Jimmy', responding to an element of eccentricity accentuated by youthful rebelliousness. This changed as he grew older and assumed ultra conservative habits, no longer the bohemian but the respected man-of-letters. His threadbare clothing was replaced by almost dandified attire. His propensity for swearing in a manner that could shock Stannie and Gogarty gave way to a dislike for and avoidance of foul

129. *Letters* 1, 235.
130. Andreasen, N.J.C. James Joyce — A Portrait of the Artist as a Schizoid. *Journal of the American Medical Association,* 1973, 324, 67-71.

utterances. Bawdy songs were permissible as Kay Boyle[131] recalled: 'There were to be times in the thirties when he sang for an entire evening with Giorgio and Laurence Vail, French and Italian ribald drinking songs, and one "naughty" Cockney number that went: "I've a little pink petty from Tommy and a little blue petty from John, but the point that I'm at is that underneath *that,* I haven't got anything on!"'

He was never a recluse. His avoidance of interviewers was self-protection against misrepresentation. He described a cutting from a newspaper to Miss Weaver: 'It is a sensational cablegram saying that I am rapidly going blind and striving desperately to write a letter a cubit high on a huge piece of cardboard measuring ten acres with a piece of carbon worked by a powerful dynamo.'[132] Ill-health increased his diffidence[133] and was among the reasons for refusing many requests to sit to painters and sculptors. He disliked the thought of needless reproduction of his image influenced by recollections most people share of seeing himself reflected from an unusual angle in drapers' mirrors.

He sat to Tuohy, Blanche, John and a few others. He regarded Tuohy's portrait as a failure. Blanche managed to capture the complexion Joyce once described[134] as 'cinnabar and rosbif à l'anglaise'. Their portraits depict a middle-aged man in reasonable health whereas the photographic studies by Gisèle Freund reveal debilitation, premature ageing and considerable physical deterioration.[135]

He discarded some of the friends of his youth and early maturity but remained on terms of undisturbed amity with Curran, J.F. Byrne, Budgen, McAlmon and others. Joyce described himself as 'an escaped continentalized Dubliner inflicted with the incurable levity of youth'[136] but this light-

131. McAlmon, R. and Boyle K. *Being Geniuses Together.* London: Michael Joseph, 1970, 296.
132. *Letters* 1, 202.
133. *Ibid.,* 259.
134. *Letters* 3, 78.
135. Freund, G. and Carleton, V.B. *James Joyce in Paris: His Final Years.* London: Cassell, 1966.
136. *SL,* 345.

heartedness was not always in evidence and to some degree he became the victim of literary gossip which broadcast accounts of his public awkwardness. He did not shine, for instance, at a dinner given by Aldous Huxley. The host served red wine which Joyce disliked. Finding him unconvivial Mrs Huxley made some remark about the flowers on the table. 'I hate flowers', Joyce said resuming his silence. Then there was his only meeting with Proust whose arrival at a party coincided with Joyce's departure. 'Our talk', Joyce told Budgen, 'consisted solely of the word "No". Proust asked me if I knew the duc de so-and-so. I said "No". Our hostess asked Proust if he had read such and such a piece of *Ulysses.* Proust said "No".'[137] An encounter with Harold Nicholson at one of those occasions which Joyce particularly disliked, a publisher's luncheon, left Nicholson unimpressed. Joyce reminded him 'of a slightly bearded spinster'.

Too much has been made of such *bêtises.* Sitting with, say, Frank Budgen in the Pfauen or sipping vervain tea with Louis Gillet in a café at the Invalides he was quite a different person. Budgen met him almost daily in Zurich and found when visiting Paris that Joyce, crowned with success, had adopted an air of established authority which reduced his natural spontaneity. Gillet the French Academician knew six languages and was in a position to appreciate *Work-in-Progress* but as often as not they discussed their children. 'Who could have recognised in this anxious father, tormented by pity for the distress of a daughter, the famous banterer, the cynic and satirical author of *Ulysses?*'[138]

Even with friends he not infrequently lapsed into silence. He was, after all, an observer who expressed himself best with his pen and his warm, amusing letters are eloquent testimony of an ironic mind moved easily to laughter but capable of pity that was not, as Dr Andreasen would have it, exclusively self-pity. Phillipe Soupault referred to him as 'a man who suffers and smiles'.[139]

His letters may be full of his woes but these are described with stoical urbanity and good humour. They may be full of his

137. *Budgen,* 323.
138. Gillet, L. *Claybook for James Joyce.* London and New York: Abelard-Schuman, 1958, 96.
139. Soupault, P. Hommage to Joyce. *Transition,* 1932, 21, 255.

incessant demands but there is ample evidence of this self-centred man's generosity to Curran, Svevo, Sullivan and others.[140] When the early days of dire poverty passed he helped his sisters in Dublin. He paid for Eileen's singing lessons and later joined with Stannie to assist the Schaureks. He was in many ways kin to Mr Micawber, never managing to balance his budget, eternally hoping for something to turn up, congenitally disposed to fritter away the cash in hand.

A much earlier voice than Dr Andreasen's — that of Joseph Collins, a New York neurologist — deals with an earlier book but whereas Andreasen dismissed *Finnegans Wake* as autistic Collins[141] confines specific denigration to 'Bloom's autistic thoughts.'

Collins's critique was ambivalent (if I may venture to resurrect a word recommend for superannuation[142] by Darcy O'Brien); he accepted *Ulysses* as a work of art but resented the novel's desertion of a conventional narrative form; he was unprepared for revelations about Dublin as a place 'sordid, turbulent, disorderly, steeped in alcohol' which would have been duplicated and magnified in the criss-cross streets and avenues of Manhatten which he traversed daily. He experienced 'bewilderment and disgust' and was amazed by Joyce's unexpurgated pages although we learn from Freud's biographer, Ernest Jones, that Collins was 'notorious for his proclivity to indecent jokes.'[143]

Collins objected to Joyce's obscenities and the use of 'words and phrases which the entire world has covenented not to use' but to make his own points he did not hesitate to employ medical terminology as alien to the layman as four letter words in an Edwardian drawing-room. 'It is as impossible to convince Mr Joyce that he is wrong about anything on which he has made up his mind as it is to convince a paranoic of the unreality of his false beliefs...' He applied the ill-adopted metaphor of GPI not to

140. Lyons, J.B. *James Joyce and Medicine.* Dublin: Dolmen Press, 1973, 228.
141. Collins, J. *The Doctor Looks at Literature.* New York: Doran, 1923, 35-60.
142. O'Brien, D. *JJQ,* 1984, 21, 180.
143. Jones, E. *The Life and Work of Sigmund Freud,* abridged edition. Harmondsworth: Pelican Books, 1964, 386.

Dublin but to Austria, 'a country in the last explosive crisis of paretic grandeur.'

Collins recognised a 'master artificer', a genius, and realised the price that many have had to be paid — 'Nature exacts a galling income tax from genius' — but failed to pursue the point. He had met the author in Paris and the latter may have misled him for he errs by saying that Joyce studied medicine 'for two or three years' and gave it up 'even though funds were available for him to continue his studies.'

Macdonald Critchley, discussing psychotic speech, referred to authors who have used 'obscure and reiterative writing as a deliberate art form'; he mentions Joyce without elaborating.[144] Carl G. Jung provided an extended and humourless critique of *Ulysses* which regards Bloom as a 'perverse and impotent sensualist' and describes the novel as a 'ganglionic rope-ladder of visceral thinking', comparing it to a 'tapeworm, rippling, peristaltic, monotonous because of its endless, proglottic proliferation.' Jung was attracted and repelled. 'What pullulating richness — and what boredom! Joyce bores me to tears...'

He appreciated that indignant readers might call *Ulysses* schizophrenic but points out that stereotyped expressions, a characteristic feature of the compositions of the insane, are notably absent.

> It would never occur to me to class *Ulysses* as a product of schizophrenia. Moreover, nothing would be gained by this label, for we wish to know why *Ulysses* exerts such a powerful influence and not whether its author is a high-grade or a low-grade schizophrenic. *Ulysses* is no more a pathological product than modern art as a whole.[145]

Lucia Joyce was Jung's patient but her father never consulted him personally even though his verbal extravagancies and general behaviour had caused some of his acquaintances in

144. Critchley, M. *The Divine Banquet of the Brain.* New York: Raven Press, 1979, 59.
145. Jung, C.G. 'Ulysses': A Monologue. *The Spirit in Man, Art and Literature,* Vol 15. London: Routledge & Kegan Paul 1966, 117.

Zurich, including Mrs McCormick, John D. Rockefeller's daughter to urge him to do so.

> A batch of people in Zurich [Joyce recalled] persuaded themselves that I was gradually going mad and actually endeavoured to induce me to enter a sanatorium where a certain Doctor Jung (the Swiss Tweedledum who is not to be confused with the Viennese Tweedledee, Dr Freud) amuses himself at the expense (in every sense of the word) of ladies and gentlemen who are troubled with bees in their bonnets.[146]

For six weeks after his arrival in Paris in 1920 Joyce neither read, nor wrote nor spoke. He consulted a Dr Schlie whom he referred to as 'a decent sort of fellow — not a psychoanalyst.'[147]

Freud believed that 'the artist is an incipient introvert who is not far from being a neurotic', and from time to time Joyce's nervous upsets were characterstically neurotic. Nevertheless he wrote in *Finnegans Wake:* 'I can psoakoon aloose myself' (522.34) and included a somewhat longer critical comment: 'We grisly old sykos who have done our unsmiling bit of alices when we were yung and easily freudened' (115.21).

Jung said that Joyce and his daughter were two people going to the bottom of a river, one diving, the other falling, a comment which is too picturesque to be the language of medicine where we ask for precise diagnosis and quantification. More relevant, perhaps, the great psychiatrist's definition of the artist as a vehicle and moulder of the unconscious psychic life of mankind: 'This is his office, and it is sometimes so heavy a burden that he is fated to sacrifice happiness and everything else that makes life worth living for the ordinary human being...'[148]

Creativity, for anything that Jung could say, remains an unexplained phenomenon which because of its nature presents an unanswerable riddle. Sir Charles Sherrington, a Nobel-prize winning neurophysiologist who was also a poet, marvelled at the achievements of laboratory investigation but accepted its limitations:

146. *Letters* 1, 166.
147. *Ibid.*, 135.
148. Jung, CG. Psychology and Literature. *The Spirit in Man, Art and Literature,* Vol. 15. London: Routledge & Kegan Paul, 1966, 101.

How camest thou by that strange gift ungiven
to aught else earthly, Eden's fruit forbidden,
to know thyself, as part to glimpse the whole?
And, that within thee, clasping earth and heaven
for comrades of like faring, storm bedridden,
to face, brow-raised, the incognizable goal?[149]

Santiago Ramon y Cajal, a doctor with an artist's eye, falling under 'the bewitchment of the infinitely small' studied the microscopic anatomy of the nervous system. He showed that the basic unit of the nervous system is the neurone, a nerve cell and its fibres; it functions by the emission of nerve impulses — tiny electrical discharges — which flow along to the nerve fibre transmitting its signal (by a chemical process) to the next neurone in series or to an effector organ e.g. muscle or gland. Simple organisms possess relatively few neurones but in the human brain they are as numberless as grains of sand on Sandymount Strand.

The basic brain mechanism is sensori-motor. The terms *afferent* and *efferent* introduced by Dublin-born Robert Bently Todd denote the flow of nerve impulses into and from the brain and spinal cord along the nerve fibres of afferent (sensory) and efferent (motor) neurones respectively. A network of sensory fibres with numerous colaterals leads from the integument and deeper locomotor and visceral structures to ascend in the spinal cord's afferent pathways to the thalamus from where they are relayed to the laminated cortex of the cerebral hemispheres. Olfactory, optic and auditory afferents enter at a higher level and reach the grey matter of the cortex.

The afferent centripetal neurones inform an individual about his/her environment, possibly promoting a centrifugal stream of motor impulses to effect appropriate action. Responses may be banal or extraordinary and presumably the concert pianist's co-ordination of hand, ear and musical memory demands lavish neural connections. It is conceivable that developments in neuro-imaging will eventually adduce evidence for a histological basis for genius and that a minute study of cerebral architectonics and neurochemistry will show that artists possess richer

149. Sherrington, Sir C.S. *The Assaying of Brabantius.* London: OUP, 1936.

endowments of brain-cells in apropriate loci, auditory (musicians), visual (painters and sculptors), or speech centres (writers).

If sensori-motor function is nicely balanced in the average person by complementary afferent/efferent performance what of creative genius? Add to the postulated cellular plethora as an anatomical basis for particular talents disproportionate efferent facility and creativity is understandable. A centrifugal neuronal bias might also indicate a measure of neurophysiological instability, possibly emanating from the temporal lobes of the brain, and accounting for the frequency of emotional and behavioural imbalance among the creative.

A.E. Housman compared creativity to a morbid secretion, 'like the oyster in a pearl' but the combination of affective disturbance and visceral tribulation that he experienced regularly during the composition of his verses points to the participation of the brain's temporal lobes in the creative process.[150] Other examples of travail and torment experienced by composers and writers are described by Anthony Storr: Beethoven felt compelled to rewrite and revise; Chopin might repeat and alter a bar a hundred times; Thackeray sometimes sat for hours at his desk, unable to write and incapable of doing anything else.[151]

Joyce escaped none of the trials which beset writers. He experienced the rigours of creativity ('O, you were excruciated, in honour bound to the cross of your own cruelfiction!' 192.19) augmented by the unparalleled complexity of his books. He suffered the affront of publishers' rebuffs, was assailed by critics and disappointed by slow sales. The inescapable effects on his health of these adverse influences cannot be apportioned.

6

Essays in pathography dwell on matters which biographers ordinarily treat tangentially; it is important to ensure that preoccupation with the morbid does not exclude joy and gladness.

150. Ghiselin, B., ed., *The Creative Process.* New York: Mentor Books, 1964, 91.
151. Storr, A. *The Dynamics of Creation.* Harmondsworth: Pelican Books, 1976, 151.

Even blighting poverty had not altogether barred those manifestations of the human spirit from John Stanislaus Joyce's household. Stephen Dedalus recalled his youngest brother singing *Oft in the Stilly Night.* 'One by one the others took up the air until the full choir of voices was singing.' Stannie, in his maturity, rebuked his brother for the omission of 'serenity or happiness'[152] — the happiness they had experienced — from his descriptions of Dublin. And Joyce himself referred to their better moments in a letter to Alf Bergan: 'We used to have merry evenings in our house, used we not?'[153]

His early struggle for identity resulted in a rich crop of persecutory ideas fertilised by publishers who at first served him so scurvily. Fate finally relented and if by then ill-health and creative effort had undermined his self-confidence they did not prevent his enjoyment of evenings at Les Trianons or Fouquet's where he was welcomed as a celebrity. He was happy, too, in Neuilly with Eugene and Maria Jolas. His fine tenor voice joined Maria's contralto and Giorgio's deep baritone and when they had tired of trios, duets and solos, Paul Léon played Chopin and gypsy music on the piano. The final ritual of these musical evenings was Joyce's high-spirited, high-kicking dance.

He celebrated birthdays and anniversaries indefatigably. On 2 February, 1927, for instance, Joyce's birthday and the fifth anniversary of the publication of *Ulysses* were celebrated at Langer's in the Champs Élyssés by the Joyces and two Irish friends, Valery Larbaud, Mrs Nebbia, Sylvia Beach, Adrienne Monnier, Archibald and Ada MacLeish and Sisley Huddleston. Dr Andreasen's uneven assessment of Joyce finds him 'aloof, cold, detached', but his fondness of birthday parties is stigmatized by her as engaging in 'the pagan ritual of pouring libations down his throat in a local restaurant or pub.'[154]

As the 1930s wore on, Joyce was preoccupied by the demanding gestation of *Finnegans Wake* and harrowed by Lucia's mental illness which increased in severity during the

152. *Letters* 3, 104.
153. *Ibid.,* 333.
154. Andreasen, N.J.C. James Joyce — A Portrait of the Artist as a Schizoid. *Journal of the American Medical Association,* 1973, 224, 69.

51. Hotel des Charmettes, Pornichet, where Lucia was transerred in 1939.

decade. At the outbreak of the second World War the maison de santé at Ivry to which she was committed was transferred to the Hôtel des Charmettes in Pornichet near La Baule. Joyce and Nora visited her there and one evening in a café the soldiers, enchanted by his singing, stood him on a table to lead them in the Marseillaise.[155]

Lucia was still in Pornichet when the Joyces left France. On their arrival in Zurich Joyce was pleased to stay again in the Hotel Pension Delphin believing dolphins to be lucky.[156] These days passed uneventfully and his favourite pastime was to walk with Stephen, his little grandson, to the confluence of the Sihl and Limmat.

The Joyces enjoyed Christmas dinner with the Giedions and after the festive meal Joyce and Giorgio sang at the piano. They joined the Ruggieros on Thursday, January 9th, a wet and snowy evening on which the conversation was of long ago. While they recalled the Joyces' years in Zurich during the first world war they quaffed a *fendant* from Neuchatel unstintingly, enjoying the warmth of the Kronenhalle until the cry of 'Polizeistunde' was sounded. 'Is that your liberty?' asked Joyce objecting to a curfew which thrust them out into frozen, blacked-out streets.

Liberty is for optimists. No curfew is more tyrannical than those imposed by nature as Joyce was to realise when pain woke him before dawn. The rest of the tale has already been told but a detail may have been misrepresented. When Joyce collapsed post-operatively blood donors were summoned; one of them was a soldier from Neuchatel a point which according to John and Vera Russell[157] was noticed as a favourable portent by Mrs Giedion-Welcker rather than by the patient who just then, in Dr Löffler's version, was 'apart' far beyond comment. And ahead lay January the thirteenth.

The news of Joyce's death reached Dublin in a brief Associated Press report at 4 a.m. on January 13. Headlines for early editions were already set up — FIREBOMBS ON LONDON, BRITISH CUT ROAD FROM TOBRUK — but in the *Irish Independent's*

155. *Ellmann,* 740.
156. Giedion, A. letter to J.B.L. 16 January 1985.
157. Russell, J. and V. Death in Zurich. *The Sunday Times,* 17 January 1965, 50.

office a young reporter, Harry Kennedy, was asked to prepare an obituary notice. In less than 20 minutes, writing almost wholly from memory, he had written half a column about James Joyce incorporating a richness of detail that surprised his colleagues.

The autopsy spared the head. A sculptor, Paul Speck, took a casting in which Louis Gillet saw defiance. 'This was not the look of someone vanquished... It was the NO! of the unsubdued, the refusal of a rebellious angel.'[158] Under a bitter sky on February 15th Joyce's mortal remains were laid in the Fluntern Cemetery's grave number 1449. And now: 'His works are a garden in which some of us may play. All that we can claim to know is merely a small bit of that garden.'[159]

52. Joyce's grave.

158. Gillet, L. *Claybook for James Joyce.* London and New York: Abelard-Schuman, 1958, 81.
159. Nolan, B. in *A Bash in the Tunnel,* ed. John Ryan. Brighton: Clifton Books, 1970, 20.

53. Nora's grave.

INDEX

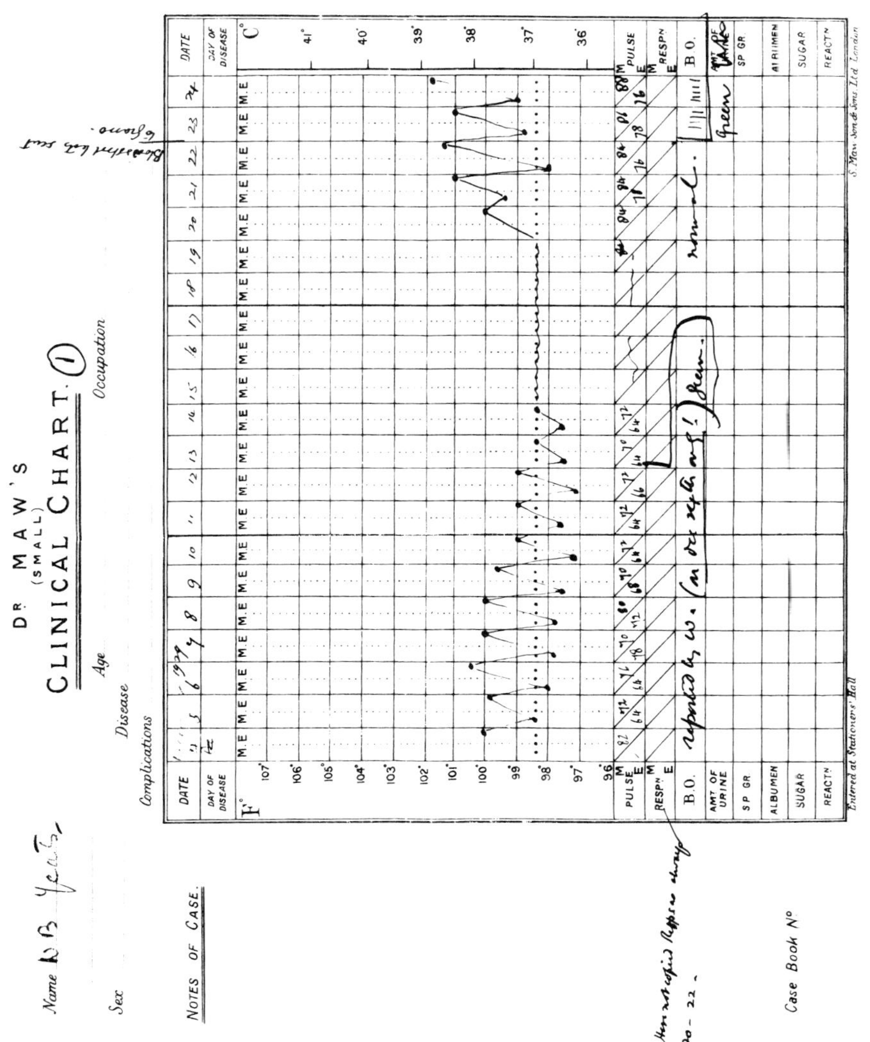

DR. MAW'S
(SMALL)
CLINICAL CHART
Name
Sex
Age
Disease
Complications
Occupation
NOTES OF CASE.
Case Book No
DATE
DAY OF DISEASE
F°
C°
PULSE
RESPN
B.O.
AMT OF URINE
SP GR
ALBUMEN
SUGAR
REACTN
Entered at Stationers' Hall
S. Maw Son & Sons Ltd London

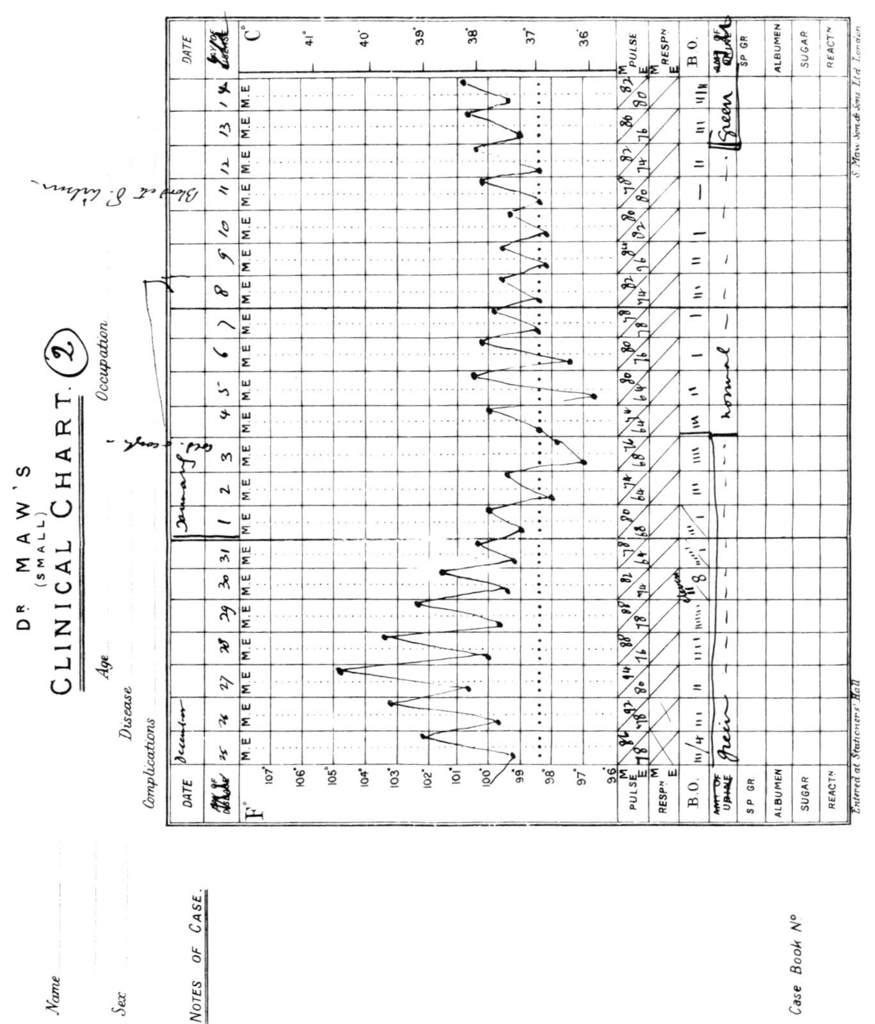
DR. MAW'S
(SMALL)
CLINICAL CHART
Name
Sex
Age
Disease
Complications
Occupation
NOTES OF CASE.
Case Book No
Entered at Stationers' Hall
S. Maw Son & Sons Ltd London

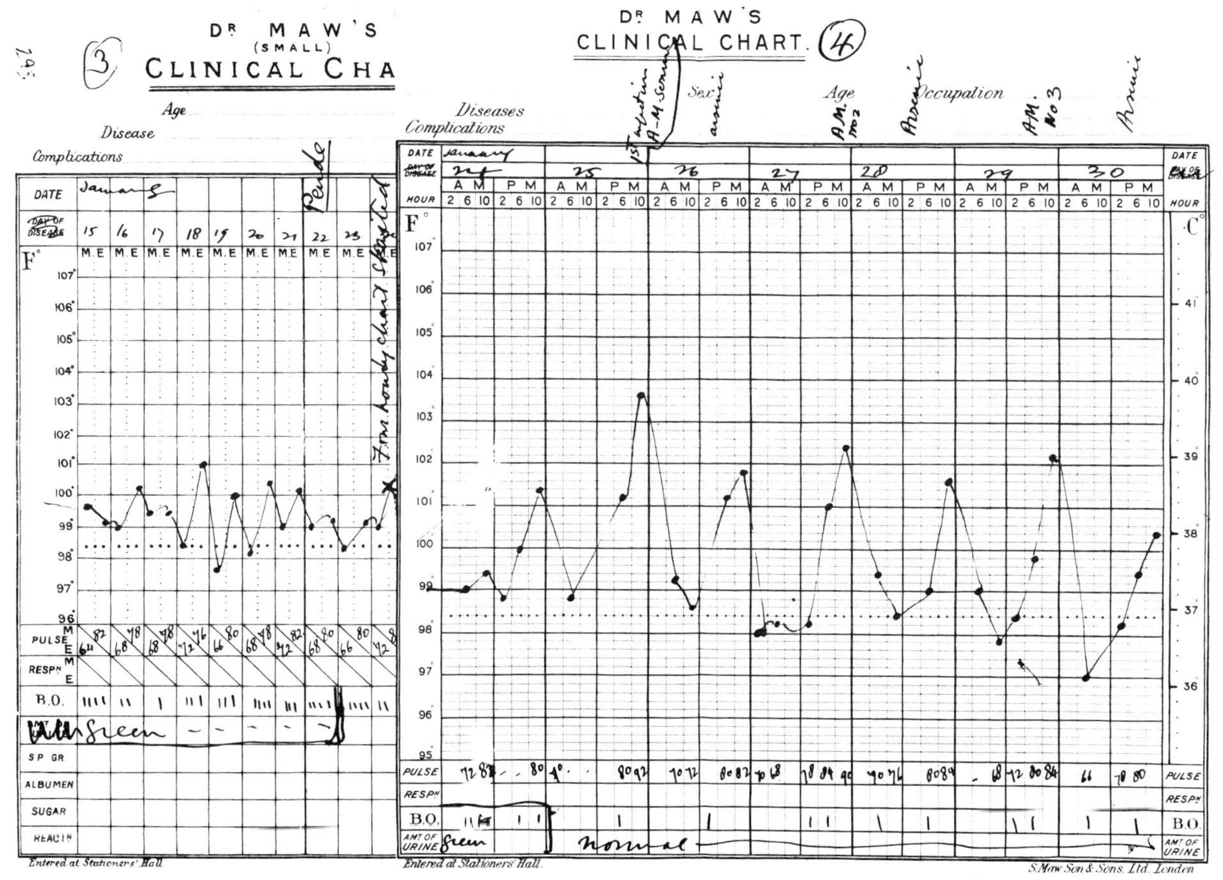
DR. MAW'S (SMALL) CLINICAL CHA
Age
Disease
Complications
Entered at Stationers' Hall
DR. MAW'S CLINICAL CHART
Sex
Age
Occupation
Diseases
Complications
Entered at Stationers' Hall
S. Maw Son & Sons Ltd. London

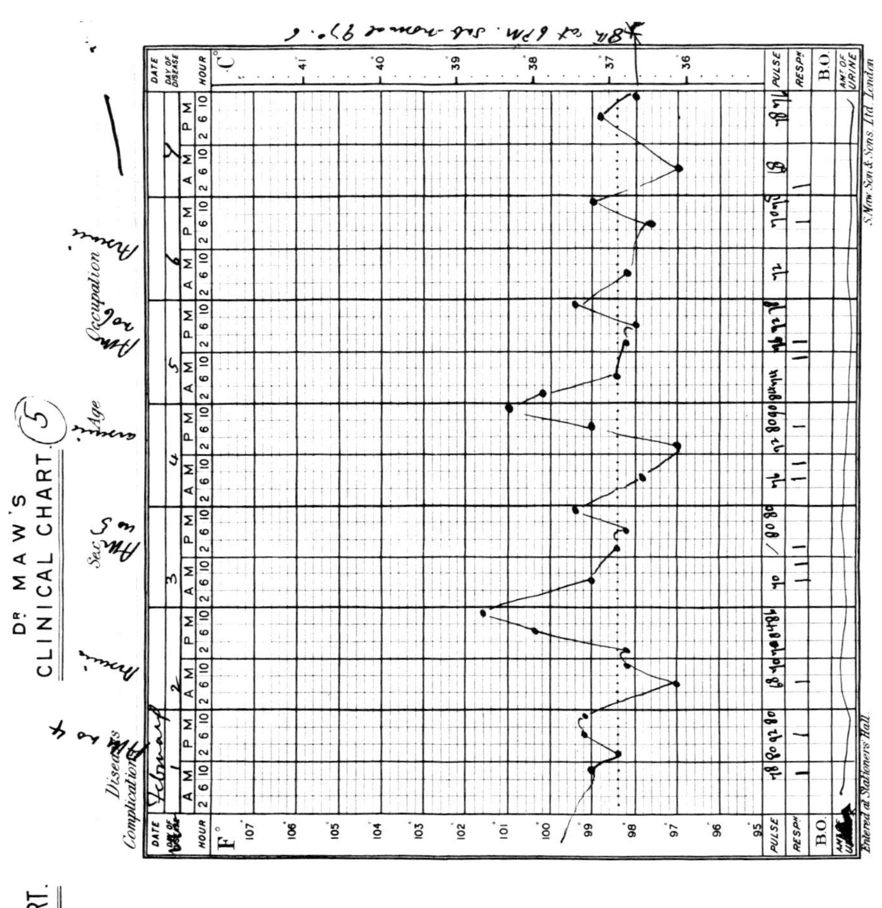
4 HOUR CHART.
Name
Notes of Case.
Dr. MAW'S
CLINICAL CHART.
Disease
Complications
Sex
Age
Occupation
PULSE
RESPN
B.O.
AMT. OF URINE
Entered at Stationers' Hall.
S. Maw Son & Sons Ltd. London

GEORGES BORACH

21, Bellerive

Zurich

Télégr.: ECKERTCO - ZURICH

3

Si je puis vous être utile, disposez de moi.

Acceptez les meilleurs